The Moonlit Rose of Isfahan

Jamila Mikhail

Keep Your Good Heart
Ottawa, Canada

Copyright © 2026 Jamila Mikhail

ISBN-13: 9781775308959 (paperback)

All rights reserved. No part of this publication may be reproduced, distributed, or transmitted in any form or by any means, including photocopying, recording, or other electronic or mechanical methods, without the prior written permission of the author, except in the case of brief quotations embodied in critical reviews and certain other non-commercial uses permitted by copyright law. Write to keepyourgoodheart@arcticmail.com or visit www.jamilamikhail.com for inquiries and requests.

The poetry of Jalal ad-Din Rumi (1207-1273) and Hafez (c. 1315-1390) quoted in this work represents either the author's own English translations from the original Persian texts, or translations from public domain sources published prior to 1928. No copyrighted translations have been used.

The historical events depicted in this novel are based on the Iran-Iraq War (1980-1988). While the narrative is inspired by real events, all characters are fictional, and any resemblance to actual persons is coincidental.

First edition, 2026.

Cover by Jamila Mikhail

All illustrations and vector images on the cover and interior are available under a CC0 1.0 Universal Public Domain Dedication license <https://creativecommons.org/publicdomain/zero/1.0/>. Used with permission.

To Meagan, my sister in everything but blood,
and Luis, my ride or die homie

Table of Contents

Acknowledgements...i
Chapter One...1
Chapter Two...13
Chapter Three...27
Chapter Four..41
Chapter Five..51
Chapter Six...59
Chapter Seven..65
Chapter Eight...91
Chapter Nine..101
Chapter Ten...113
Chapter Eleven..123
Chapter Twelve..135
Chapter Thirteen..143
Chapter Fourteen...153
Chapter Fifteen...165
Chapter Sixteen...185
Chapter Seventeen..195
Chapter Eighteen..203
Chapter Nineteen...211
Chapter Twenty...217
Chapter Twenty-One...227
Chapter Twenty-Two...239
Chapter Twenty-Three...245
Chapter Twenty-Four..253
Chapter Twenty-Five...265
Chapter Twenty-Six..273
Chapter Twenty-Seven...281
Chapter Twenty-Eight...295
Chapter Twenty-Nine..311
Chapter Thirty..319
Chapter Thirty-One..329
Chapter Thirty-Two..337
Chapter Thirty-Three..347
Chapter Thirty-Four...363
Chapter Thirty-Five..379
Afterword..395
Reader's Guide 397
Glossary of Terms..399
About the Author...405

Acknowledgments

First and foremost, I owe my gratitude to God for the gift of storytelling and the perseverance to see it through. I must also thank my mom and my three cats Squeaker, Carling and Radwan for moral support (Radwan especially for not deleting my work the times he walked across my keyboard). The biggest thanks go to my homies Meagan and Luis, whose encouragement kept this story alive when I needed it most. Thanks to my friends Christy, Obaida and Shadowhawk as well, for your friendship that sustains me beyond the page. You've also read some pretty terrible early versions of what only became publishable books years later. Thank you to my former professors Navid and Shamim at the University of Ottawa, who taught me far more than the syllabus—thank you for opening a window into Iran, your homeland, which breathed life into Isfahan's streets and the hearts of these characters. Lastly, thank you Claude for your valuable insight, feedback and assistance in helping to shape this story. I would not have had a complete story without your help.

Chapter One

Isfahan, 1988

The Isfahan sun dipped low, painting the sky in hues of saffron and rose, casting long shadows across the whitewashed walls of Reza and Zahra Azad's modest home. In the courtyard, Zahra knelt beside her rosebush, her slender fingers trembling as they snipped a wilted petal. The scent of roses mingled with her jasmine perfume, a fragrance she'd chosen that morning with deliberate care, hoping it would stir memories of their stolen honeymoon nights in Shiraz—nights that felt like they belonged to another lifetime, another world before war fractured everything.

Her long, dark hair, freed from the modest headscarf she wore in public, spilled over her shoulders, catching the fading light like silk. The green dress she'd sewn herself—sitting up late by lamplight, her fingers working the needle with anxious precision—clung softly to her curves, its hem brushing her ankles. She'd made it specifically for today, knowing he would notice, hoping he would still find her beautiful. But beneath the careful preparation, her heart thundered with uncertainty.

Eight years. Eight years of war, of Reza's letters—ink smudged with trench dirt, stained with what she tried not to imagine was blood—clutched to her chest in the lonely dark. Eight years of sleeping alone in the bed they'd shared for only three weeks. Eight years of tending this garden, growing food for strangers at the mosque, waiting, hoping, praying he would return whole. And now, today, the radio inside had crackled with news of the ceasefire, and his last letter, tucked in her pocket, anchored her to this moment: *"My moonlit rose, I dream of your touch under these cursed stars. Wait for me."*

She'd read that letter until the paper frayed at the folds, her fingers tracing his poetic words—a soldier's heart wrapped in a poet's soul, still writing verse even from the frontlines. But doubt gnawed at her like a persistent ache. Her body, untouched since their three-week marriage in 1980, felt like a stranger's—softened by time, curves fuller where there had once been girlish angles. She was twenty when he left. Now she was twenty-eight, a woman shaped by years of solitude, of learning to be strong alone. Would he still recognize her? Would he still want her?

A sound made her freeze: the metallic creak of the courtyard gate, its familiar groan echoing in the still evening air. Her breath caught. For a moment she couldn't move, couldn't turn, afraid that if she looked it would be a neighbour, a messenger, anyone but him. Her hands gripped the pruning shears so tightly her knuckles whitened.

She turned.

And there he was.

Reza stood framed against the twilight, his military coat hanging loose on shoulders that seemed narrower than she remembered, the fabric worn and faded from years of war. His olive skin was weathered, darkened by the desert sun, and his face—oh, his face—was both familiar and utterly changed. The beard was new, neatly trimmed but flecked with premature grey that caught the evening light. More grey threaded through his hair at the temples, silver against black. A white *chafiyeh* was draped around his neck, incongruous against the domestic peace of their garden.

But his eyes. Those deep-set, soulful brown eyes that had first captured her heart during their chaperoned courtship—those were the same, even if they now held shadows she'd never seen before. Ghosts lived behind those eyes. She could see them, lingering in the depths, even as his gaze found her and held.

He looked heroic in his uniform, like the commander she'd seen in photographs, but also achingly human—thinner, worn, carrying the weight of eight years in every line of his body. A canvas bag slipped

The Moonlit Rose of Isfahan

from his shoulder, thudding to the ground unnoticed. Shirin, their tabby cat—the one Hossein had given them as a wedding gift, joking they were "practice children"—darted from beneath the rosebush to wind around his boots, purring loudly. But Reza's gaze never left Zahra.

"Zahra," he whispered, his voice a soft baritone, raw with emotion, like a prayer he'd held too long in his chest. "My moonlit rose."

He took a step forward, then stopped, as if afraid she might dissolve like a desert mirage if he moved too quickly. His hands—scarred, calloused, one bearing a jagged knife wound that began at his wrist and disappeared under his sleeve—hovered midair, uncertain. She could see him cataloging her changes just as she cataloged his: the way her body had filled out, the woman's curves where girlish thinness had been, the way she held herself with a quiet strength she hadn't possessed at twenty.

The weight of his absence hung between them like something physical, tangible: years of trenches, of letters that could never say enough, of his brother Hossein's death five years ago in 1983—a loss they'd grieved separately, oceans of grief apart. Years of comrades lost, of nights when he must have clung to thoughts of her to survive, just as she'd clung to thoughts of him.

Zahra's initial shyness gripped her, rooting her feet to the earth as surely as if she'd grown roots like her rosebushes. Her cheeks warmed, old habits of modesty rising up despite the fact that this was her husband, *her* Reza. But then longing broke through—a tide too strong to contain, too powerful to resist. The last eight years had taught her many things, and one of them was that hesitation could cost you everything.

She dropped the pruning shears, not caring where they fell. She crossed the courtyard in a rush, her bare feet quick against the warm stones, her dress whispering against her skin, and threw her arms around him with an intensity that surprised them both.

Her face pressed into his chest, inhaling deeply—the scent of him beneath layers of dust, sweat, and war. Beneath it all, he still smelled like *Reza*. Her Reza. Unchanged in the ways that mattered most.

"Reza," she murmured against his coat, her voice trembling,

muffled by fabric and emotion. "You're home. You're really home."

Tears slipped down her cheeks—hot, unbidden, unstoppable. But a laugh bubbled up too, shaky and bright, breaking through the tears. Joy and relief and disbelief all tangled together. Her fingers dug into the rough fabric of his coat, holding tight, as if he might disappear if she loosened her grip even slightly. She could feel the solid warmth of his body beneath the uniform, leaner than before but real, alive, *here*.

He exhaled—a sound of relief and surrender, a breath he seemed to have been holding for eight years—and wrapped his arms around her. Tentative at first, as if relearning her shape, the feel of her in his embrace. Then tighter, more certain. His scarred hands settled on her waist, their roughness catching on the soft cotton of her dress, and she felt him shiver at the contact.

"My moonlit rose," he said, his voice cracking. "I thought—" He stopped, swallowed hard. "I thought I'd never see you again. There were so many times..."

He pulled back just enough to look at her, his eyes tracing her face with the desperate attention of a man memorizing something precious. Her almond-coloured eyes, now bright with tears. Her full lips, trembling with emotion. The curve of her cheek, the line of her jaw. His gaze traveled lower, taking in the way her dress hugged her hips, her breasts, and she felt simultaneously exposed and desired—and also afraid.

"You're more beautiful than I dreamed," he said softly, his words carrying the careful cadence of a poet, each syllable weighted with longing. "And I dreamed of you every night, Zahra. Every single night."

But she saw the flicker of doubt that crossed his face even as he spoke, saw the way he angled his scarred forearm slightly away, unconsciously trying to hide the worst of the damage. His jaw tightened almost imperceptibly.

"I'm not the same, Zahra," he admitted, his voice dropping low, almost a confession. "The war... it marked me. Inside and out."

Her heart ached at his vulnerability, at the careful way he was preparing her for disappointment. She reached for his hand—the scarred one he'd tried to hide—and her fingers traced the rough ridges of old burns, the jagged line of the knife wound. She brought his hand to her lips and kissed it softly, tenderly, her lips warm against his damaged skin.

"Nor am I the same," she whispered, her voice barely audible, her shyness making her tremble even as she forced herself to meet his eyes. "But you're mine, Reza. Every scar, every piece of you. You're mine, and I'm yours."

Her lips lingered on his knuckles, pressing gentle kisses to each scarred finger. His breath hitched, and she saw something kindle in his eyes—a spark of hope, of desire, of the old Reza she remembered.

He cupped her face with both hands, his thumbs grazing her cheeks, tracing the curve of her jaw with a tenderness that made her breath catch. "And you're mine," he said, a playful glint breaking through the shadows in his eyes. "My rose, still blooming even in this weary world."

He leaned closer, his breath warm against her lips, and kissed her. Slowly. Tenderly. As if savouring the taste of her after years of starvation. Her lips parted, welcoming him, and the kiss deepened. A quiet hunger stirred—eight years of longing compressed into this single moment. Her hands slid up his chest, feeling new ridges of scar tissue beneath his shirt, but also the steady, strong beat of his heart. *Alive. Home. Hers.*

His fingers tangled in her hair, tugging gently, and she gasped—a soft sound swallowed by his mouth. Her body pressed closer instinctively, her breasts brushing against his chest, and she felt heat pooling low in her belly, a sensation almost forgotten, now suddenly overwhelming.

He pulled back, resting his forehead against hers, their breaths mingling in the space between them. "Zahra," he murmured, his voice rough, low. "I dreamed of this. Of you. Every night in those cursed trenches. Your face was what kept me alive."

His hand slid down her back, coming to rest at the curve of her spine, his touch both reverent and possessive. She could feel the weight of his desire mirrored by her own, but her shyness made her hesitate. Her body, so long untouched, felt both alive and uncertain under his hands.

A polite cough interrupted them—gentle, discreet, but

Jamila Mikhail

unmistakable. They turned to find Mrs. Heydari standing at the gate, her husband lingering a respectful distance behind. She held a steaming dish of *ghormeh sabzi*, its rich aroma drifting across the courtyard, and her smile was warm but carefully tactful.

"Welcome home, Commander Azad," she said, her voice kind. "We've been praying for your safe return. The whole neighbourhood has." She placed the dish on the courtyard step, steam rising from it. "You'll both need your strength. I won't keep you."

Mr. Heydari nodded solemnly, hand over his heart in the traditional gesture of respect. "Welcome home, brother. God is merciful."

Zahra flushed, stepping back slightly from Reza's embrace, suddenly aware of how they must look—clinging to each other like teenagers, tears on her cheeks, his hand still possessive on her waist. But Reza's hand caught hers, grounding her, his fingers lacing through hers.

"Thank you," Reza said, his voice rough with emotion. "Your kindness—all these years—Zahra has told me in her letters..."

Mrs. Heydari waved away his thanks with a gentle smile. "We look after our own. Rest now. Both of you." She retreated with her husband, leaving them alone once more.

Zahra laughed—a shy, melodic sound that made Reza's face soften. He grinned, and for just a moment she glimpsed the boyish playfulness she'd fallen for during their courtship, the lightness that war had tried to steal from him.

"Come," she said softly, tugging his hand. "Come inside. Come home."

Inside, the house enveloped them in familiar warmth, but Reza stood in the doorway for a long moment, just looking. His eyes traveled over every detail as if seeing it for the first time: the low wooden table where they'd shared meals during those three brief weeks of marriage, the embroidered cushions Zahra's father had given them as a wedding gift, the oil lamp she'd lit countless evenings while reading his letters. Everything was exactly as he remembered, preserved like a shrine to the life they'd barely begun.

"It's strange," he said quietly, his voice thick. "I've imagined this

The Moonlit Rose of Isfahan

room so many times. Thousands of times. And now I'm here, and it's real, but it almost doesn't feel real. Does that make sense?"

"Yes," Zahra whispered, because she understood. She'd lived in this house for eight years, but it had never quite felt like home without him in it. It had been more like a carefully maintained memory, waiting for his return to become real again.

The scent of saffron rice lingered from the meal she'd prepared earlier, hopeful and uncertain. Simin, their grey cat—Hossein's other gift, the companion to Shirin—leapt onto the table with elegant grace, regarding them with lazy curiosity before settling into a loaf shape, purring.

Reza kicked off his boots slowly, methodically, his eyes never leaving Zahra as she moved to light another lamp. The warm glow softened the room further, casting gentle shadows. He watched the way lamplight caught in her hair, the graceful efficiency of her movements—eight years of living alone had made her even more capable, more self-sufficient. She'd grown without him.

"Would you like to eat?" she asked, gesturing toward the kitchen. "There's rice, and Mrs. Heydari's *ghormeh sabzi*, and I made—"

"Later," he said softly, crossing to her. His hand found hers again, that same desperate need for contact. "First... Zahra, I need..."

He trailed off, uncertain how to voice what he needed. To be clean. To wash away eight years of war. To feel human again, instead of like a weapon that had been used and used until nearly broken. She understood without him having to finish. "Let me draw you a bath," she said, her voice trembling with shy resolve. "Let me care for you."

He looked at her, hesitation flickering in his eyes. His hand moved unconsciously to touch the scarred forearm beneath his sleeve. "Zahra... I'm not sure you want to see—"

"I do," she interrupted, gentle but firm. Her cheeks warmed with boldness, but she held his gaze. "I want to see all of you. I want to know what you've endured. I want to care for you, Reza. Please."

His eyes softened, though doubt still lingered at their edges. He nodded slowly, and her heart surged—with love, yes, but also with her own quiet fear. Her body felt foreign after eight years alone, her curves fuller than the girl he'd married. What if he found her changed in ways that disappointed him?

But she pushed the doubt away. They would discover each other again. Together.

In the small bathroom, Zahra filled the copper basin with warm water, her movements practiced from years of this same routine—though always before, she'd been washing alone, thinking of him. She poured rosewater from a glass vial, its sweet, floral scent curling through the steam and filling the small space with perfume and memory. She added sandalwood soap, its earthy aroma blending with the roses.

The air grew heavy, intimate. Lamplight glinted off the blue tiles, casting everything in a golden haze. She laid out a soft towel, her hands trembling with anticipation—and fear. In moments, she would see him, *all* of him, marked by war in ways his letters could never fully convey.

Reza entered quietly, and she turned to find him with his shirt unbuttoned, revealing a chest now covered with dark hair—leaner but stronger than their wedding night, all boyish softness burned away by war and survival. He paused when he saw her watching, vulnerable, almost boyish despite everything.

"Zahra," he began, voice low and raw. "My scars... they're not just on my arms." He swallowed hard. "There's one on my stomach. From shrapnel. It goes..." He gestured downward, unable to say it. "Lower. It's ugly."

Tears pricked her eyes, her heart clenching—not from disgust, never that, but from a fierce ache to erase his pain, to cradle every wounded part of him. She stepped closer, her fingers grazing his chest, feeling the warmth of his skin, the coarse texture of his chest hair, the slight ridges of other, smaller scars.

"Nothing about you could ever be ugly to me," she whispered, her voice breaking with emotion. "You're my Reza. My heart. My home. Every scar is part of you, and I love every part."

Her words, soft but fierce, made his breath catch. He nodded slowly, then began removing the rest of his clothes with hesitant movements, each piece revealing more damage: burns on his hands, the bullet graze on his leg, chemical burns on his thighs from gas exposure. And then—the large, jagged scar running down his stomach, an angry line of raised tissue that extended past his navel, disappearing into the dark hair at his groin.

He looked away, jaw tight, shame written in every line of his posture. "The blast that killed Hossein," he said quietly. "Same one that marked me. I should have died too. Sometimes I think..." He stopped, shaking his head.

"No," Zahra said firmly, kneeling by the basin and guiding him to sit on the low wooden stool. "Don't think that. You survived for a reason. You survived to come home. To me."

The warm water lapped at his feet, rose-scented steam rising around them. She dipped a cloth, her touch infinitely gentle as she began washing his shoulders, tracing the knife wound on his forearm with tender fingers. Her touch lingered on each scar as if rewriting his pain with love, as if her gentleness could somehow reach back through time and ease the moment each wound was made.

"You're still my home," she murmured, echoing words he'd whispered on their wedding night, her voice a soothing balm in the steamy quiet.

The cloth glided over his chest, the sandalwood soap blending with his scent, and she felt his tension gradually ease. His eyes fluttered closed as her fingers brushed his skin, stirring memories of their first touches—nervous, eager, full of discovery. How young they'd been. How innocent.

She moved lower, washing his thighs with trembling hands, her breath catching as she neared the shrapnel scar. Tears welled in her eyes again—not from revulsion but from the fierce desire to absorb his pain, to love every wounded part of him until he could see himself through her eyes.

"May I?" she asked softly, her voice barely audible above the soft lap of water. Her eyes sought his, asking permission.

He nodded, his breath uneven, vulnerable in a way he'd never been even on their wedding night. She touched the scar gently, reverently, her fingers tracing its path from his stomach downward. The skin was rough, raised, still pink in places where healing had been difficult. To her, it was beautiful—not the scar itself, but what it represented. His survival. His strength. His journey home to her.

"You're beautiful," she said, meeting his eyes. Her shyness was melting into something deeper—adoration, desire, fierce protective love. "Every part of you."

Then, with a courage that surprised them both, she leaned forward and pressed her lips to the scar. Softly. Tenderly. A gentle kiss at his stomach, then another, following the path of the wound downward—her way of loving every part of him, of showing him that nothing could make her turn away.

He gasped, his hand gripping the edge of the stool. "Zahra—"

She looked up, her eyes meeting his, and spoke softly, words rising from the poetry they'd shared in letters, inspired by all those verses from Rumi they'd quoted to each other across the years: "In your eyes, I learn what it means to be whole. Through your touch, I remember what it means to be loved."

The words hung between them—a vow, a promise, a bridge across eight years of separation.

"I love you," she whispered against his skin, her voice trembling with the weight of it—eight years of love preserved and deepened by distance. "I love every part of you, Reza. Every scar, every wound, every piece. I love you."

His hand caught hers, pulling her up, water dripping between them, soaking her dress. The wet fabric clung to her body, outlining her curves—her fuller breasts, her hips—in the lamplight, and she saw his eyes darken with desire even through the emotion.

"Zahra, my rose," he murmured, his voice thick with gratitude and longing. "You make me feel whole again. You make me feel like maybe I can learn to be a man again, not just a soldier."

He stood, pulling her close despite the water, despite everything. "I love you too," he said fiercely. "I never stopped loving you. Not for a single moment in eight years."

Their lips met—slow and deep, tasting of rosewater and tears and promise. His hands settled on her hips, tentative but hungry, feeling the soft give of her body through the damp dress. The bath had become a ritual of healing, their touches a language of rediscovery, and now, clean and loved and real, they were ready to begin again.

The Moonlit Rose of Isfahan

They moved slowly into the main room, Reza wrapped in a towel, Zahra's dress still damp and clinging. The embroidered quilts on their bed beckoned in the lamplight—soft, inviting, waiting eight years for this moment.

He pulled her close again, his lips brushing her ear. "Tonight," he whispered, his voice thick with promise and tenderness, "we start again. Slowly, my love. We have all the time in the world now."

His fingers traced her arm, raising goosebumps, and she leaned into him, her shyness transforming into anticipation. They had weathered eight years apart. They had survived war and separation and grief. And now, finally, they could begin to rebuild—not just their life together, but themselves.

In the sanctuary of their home, in the soft lamplight, with the scent of roses and sandalwood still lingering in the air, Reza and Zahra Azad prepared to rediscover each other. Scar by scar. Touch by touch. Word by word.

Together.

Chapter Two

Isfahan, 1988

They moved through the house slowly, as if any sudden movement might shatter the fragile magic of the moment. Reza, wrapped in the soft towel, felt the fabric's gentleness against his war-hardened skin—such a stark contrast to the rough canvas and coarse wool that had been his only comfort for eight years. Zahra's dress still clung to her curves, damp and clinging from the bath, outlining the fullness of her breasts, the soft roundness of her hips. She was aware of his eyes on her, tracing every line, and the awareness made her breath catch.

She took his hand—scarred, calloused, the knife wound still raised and rough under her fingers—and led him through their modest home. Past the low wooden table where they'd once shared meals during those three precious weeks. Past the embroidered cushions that had been her father's wedding gift. Each step felt weighted with significance, as if they were walking toward something sacred.

The bedroom awaited them like a sanctuary. The oil lamp cast its golden glow over the embroidered quilts on their bed—quilts she'd repaired countless times over the years, keeping them perfect for his return. The woven Persian rug softened the tiled floor beneath their feet. In the corner, Shirin and Simin were curled together on a cushion, two small bodies forming one purring mass, as if they too understood the sacredness of this reunion.

The scent of saffron from her earlier cooking mingled with the jasmine of her perfume and the lingering rosewater from the bath, wrapping the room in warmth. Outside, the Isfahan night was still, the ceasefire's fragile peace allowing stars to shine unmarred by gunfire or explosions. But inside, the air was thick with something else entirely—with unspoken emotion, with eight years of longing, with the weight of everything they'd endured to reach this moment.

Zahra guided him to the bed, her hand trembling slightly in his. The towel slipped from his body, and he stood before her—lean, scarred, bearing the marks of survival etched into his flesh. The knife wound on his forearm. The bullet graze on his leg. The burns on his hands from chemical exposure. And that large, jagged shrapnel scar running down his stomach, disappearing into the dark hair below his navel—the scar from the blast that had stolen Hossein from them both.

She sat beside him on the bed, the damp fabric of her dress brushing against his bare thigh, and reached out to touch his face. Her fingers traced the coarse texture of his beard—grey-flecked now, no longer the smooth jaw of the young man who'd left—feeling the lines etched by war's toll. His eyes fluttered closed, and she watched his shoulders ease, the tension draining from his body under her gentle touch.

"My Reza," she murmured, her voice trembling with love and lingering shyness. Her touch was gentle as she caressed his jaw, his cheekbones, the space where laugh lines had once been but were now replaced with deeper furrows of worry and loss.

For the first time in eight years, he felt truly safe. His heart—scarred deeper than his skin by the loss of Hossein, by the faces of comrades who'd died beside him in gas-choked trenches—found solace in her tenderness. The weight of survival began to lift, allowing him to breathe again. To feel again. To want again.

His hand found her thigh, his scarred fingers resting lightly on the damp fabric, feeling the warmth of her skin beneath. "Zahra, my rose," he whispered, his voice soft, carrying echoes of the poet he'd once been—the poet he hoped he could be again.

His touch was tentative at first, reverent, tracing the curve of her thigh. Fuller now than on their wedding night. Everything about her was fuller—more womanly, shaped by eight years of solitude and survival. They were different people. Her heart, once open and unguarded, now carried the quiet strength of endurance. His, once playful and hopeful, bore wounds of guilt and survivor's remorse. Yet in this moment, their touches were a bridge, rebuilding what war had tried to destroy.

The atmosphere thickened with unspoken desire, yet underneath ran a current of nervousness—almost like their first time. Zahra's fingers lingered on his beard, her thumbs brushing his lips, and he kissed them softly, his breath warm against her skin. She shivered, her body remembering what eight years had tried to make her forget.

Reza sensed her hesitation and leaned closer, his eyes searching hers. "Let me see you, Zahra," he said gently, his voice thick with need but patient. "Let me see the woman you've become."

His hands moved to her dress, slowly working the buttons with deliberate care, as if unwrapping something precious and fragile. Each button revealed more of her skin—glowing in the lamplight, soft and warm. The fabric fell away from her shoulders, and she instinctively crossed her arms over her chest, her cheeks flushing with an old shyness that eight years alone hadn't erased.

"You're beautiful," Reza said, his voice thick with sincerity, his eyes tracing her with reverence. "More beautiful now, my love. You're not a girl anymore, Zahra. You're a woman. My woman."

His words melted her doubt. She laughed—a shy, melodic sound—and let her arms fall to her sides, allowing him to see her. Her fuller breasts, the soft curve of her stomach, the roundness of her hips. He reached out, his fingers brushing her collarbone, then lower, his touch gentle and worshipful. Different from his memory, but hers. Still hers. Always hers.

Her breath hitched as desire sparked—familiar yet new, like rediscovering fire after years in the cold. Their lips met, tender and slow, tasting of rosewater and longing and eight years of separation. His tongue brushed hers softly, exploratory, relearning the taste of her. His hands roamed her body with careful reverence—stroking her sides, her hips, her thighs—each touch gentle and deliberate.

And then, as his fingers traced the curve of her hip, something shifted. A memory rose unbidden, powerful and sweet—flooding through him with such clarity it was as if he'd been transported through time.

Shiraz, 1980

The Shiraz guesthouse had been a cocoon of warmth, its walls aglow with flickering oil lamps casting dancing shadows over the woven Persian rug. It was mere hours into their marriage, and the world outside hadn't yet begun to tremble with war's first rumblings, but inside, time had stopped for them—a sanctuary of their own making.

Zahra, twenty years old and impossibly beautiful, had sat on the edge of the bed. Her white chador lay discarded, replaced by a cream-coloured dress that clung to her slender curves, its neckline modest yet revealing the soft swell of her breasts. Her long, dark hair—unpinned for the first time before him—had spilled like a midnight cascade over her shoulders, and her almond-coloured eyes had sparkled with nervous excitement, a shy smile tugging at her lips.

He had been twenty-four, standing by the window with his suit jacket tossed aside, his lean frame taut with anticipation and uncertainty. His jaw had been clean-shaven then, smooth beneath her touch, and his brown eyes had glowed with love and a touch of boyish fear. They had waited for this moment, bound by faith and tradition, their touches until then limited to fleeting hand-holds and stolen kisses when their chaperones looked away.

"Zahra, my moonlit rose," he had whispered, his voice a trembling melody, his poet's heart laid bare and betraying his inexperience. He had knelt before her, his hands hovering over hers, then gently brushing her fingers, sending shivers through her like a breeze over a rose garden. "I want this to be perfect for you."

The warmth of his touch—the texture of his fingertips grazing her knuckles—had ignited something in her, spreading heat through her chest, down her spine, settling low in her belly.

The Moonlit Rose of Isfahan

Her cheeks had flushed, her shyness melting into a giggle. "I don't know what I'm doing, Reza," she had confessed, her voice soft, her fingers playfully twisting the hem of her dress. "But I want you. Only you."

Her boldness had made her blush deeper, and his eyes had lit up with a playful glint. He had leaned in, his lips brushing hers—soft and tentative at first, then deepening into something more urgent. They had tasted the rosewater sharbat they'd sipped at dinner. Her hands had found his shoulders, pulling him closer, and they'd tumbled onto the bed together, the mattress creaking beneath them as they laughed, their nerves dissolving into joy.

Their clothes had fallen away in a clumsy, giggling flurry. His fingers had fumbled with her dress buttons, his breath hitching as he revealed her skin—soft, untouched, glowing like moonlight in the lamplight. Her hands had shaken as she tugged at his shirt, exposing the smooth olive skin of his chest, her fingertips tracing the muscles there, feeling his heart race beneath.

"Is this... right?" she had asked, laughing as a button snagged, and he had grinned, his playful side emerging. "Let's find out, my love," he had teased, kissing her neck, his lips warm and ticklish, drawing a surprised squeal from her.

When they were finally bare before each other, their exploration had been a dance of reverence and playfulness. His hands had traced her body with wonder, discovering what made her gasp, what made her arch toward him. She had explored him in turn—tentative touches that grew bolder as his responses encouraged her.

"My rose blooms here," he had murmured with boyish delight, his teasing touch making her squirm and giggle, her shyness giving way to delight. "Reza!" she had protested, laughing, her hands swatting his playfully, but her body had responded to his attention with unmistakable desire.

Their first joining had been a nervous, sacred leap into the unknown. His eyes had locked on hers, seeking permission, his breath uneven. "Zahra," he had whispered, his voice thick with emotion, wrapping the moment in poetry as only he could. "I want to... insert my love into you."

The phrase had been so earnest, so vulnerably poetic, so utterly Reza that it had made her heart overflow. She had nodded, her breath shallow, her heart pounding with trust.

As he had entered her—slowly, carefully—she had felt a sharp sting, then a fullness that was both strange and profound, like a secret shared between their souls. Her nails had dug into his back, her gasps mingling with his groans, their bodies fumbling into a rhythm that was awkward but earnest. The pain had faded into something else—pleasure, yes, but more than that. A closeness so intense it had felt like their hearts beat as one.

"You're my home," he had murmured against her ear, his voice breaking as they moved together, sweaty and breathless, their laughter punctuating each misstep, each moment of awkward adjustment.

Afterward, they had lain tangled together, her head on his chest, his heartbeat a steady drum beneath her ear. He had reached for a damp cloth, his touch gentle as he cleaned her, his fingers reverent and careful, lingering with tenderness. "My rose must shine," he had teased, his smile boyish, and she had blushed, swatting his arm, their laughter sealing the memory.

They had promised each other countless nights to perfect their dance, to learn each other's bodies fully, to grow together in intimacy and love.

❀ ❀ ❀

But the war had stolen that promise, leaving only three weeks of perfect memories to sustain them through eight years of separation. The memory released him gently, and he found himself back in their bedroom, his hand still resting on Zahra's hip—but everything was different now. They were different now.

His eyes met hers, and he saw that she understood. Perhaps she'd been remembering too. That first night in Shiraz. Their fumbling innocence. The laughter and nervousness and overwhelming joy. How young they'd been. How untouched by the world's cruelty.

"We're not those people anymore," he said softly, his thumb tracing circles on her hip.

"No," Zahra agreed, her hand coming up to touch his face, feeling the grey in his beard, the lines around his eyes. "We're not. But Reza—" Her voice caught with emotion. "I love who we've become. I love the man you are now, even with all the pain you carry. Especially because of it."

His eyes shimmered with unshed tears. "And I love you, Zahra. The woman who survived eight years alone. The woman who kept our home, who kept hope alive when I had none. You're so much stronger than that girl I married."

"Then let's begin again," she whispered. "Not as we were, but as we are now."

He kissed her then—deeply, hungrily—and this time there was no fumbling uncertainty. This time they knew what they wanted, even if their bodies needed to relearn how to express it.

His lips traveled from her mouth to her jaw, to her neck, tasting the salt of her skin mixed with jasmine perfume. She arched into him, her hands sliding up his back, feeling the raised lines of scars—so many more than that smooth skin from their wedding night. Each one she touched, she loved. Each one was proof he'd survived, proof he'd come back to her.

"Your body is still my garden," he murmured against her skin, his voice rough with desire, echoing that playful line from their wedding night but with a depth of meaning it hadn't held before. "Where love blooms eternal, even after the longest winter."

He kissed his way down—her collarbone, the valley between her breasts, her stomach. Each kiss was soft, reverent, worshipful. When he reached her thighs, he paused, looking up at her, seeking permission.

She nodded, her breath already shallow with anticipation.

His beard—coarse and grey-flecked now, so different from the smooth jaw of their wedding night—brushed against her inner thighs, the sensation both familiarly exciting and entirely new. When his mouth found her centre, she gasped, her fingers tangling in his hair. His touch was devoted, unhurried—as if he had all the time in the world to love her this way, to relearn what brought her pleasure, to give her this gift of focused attention.

Her body responded with a rush of warmth and need. She'd almost forgotten what this felt like—to be desired, to be cherished, to be the centre of someone's devoted care. Her hips lifted slightly, instinctively seeking more, and he gave it to her willingly, his hands gripping her thighs gently, holding her steady as he continued.

"Reza," she breathed, her voice trembling. "I want—I want to—"

She tugged at his shoulders, pulling him up, and he came willingly, understanding without words. She wanted to give back. To love him as he'd loved her. To show him that his scars didn't diminish him in her eyes.

She guided him to lie back against the embroidered quilts, and for a moment she just looked at him—really looked. His lean body, harder and more defined than it had been. The scars that mapped his survival: burns on his hands and thighs, the knife wound on his arm, the bullet graze on his leg. And that large shrapnel scar running down his stomach, disappearing into dark hair.

She traced it with her fingers first—from his stomach downward—then followed the path with her lips. Soft kisses along the raised, damaged skin. She heard his breath catch, felt his body tense beneath her touch.

"Zahra, you don't have to—"

"I want to," she whispered against his skin. "I want to love every part of you."

She kissed her way lower, following the trail of dark hair, wanting to show him through her touch that nothing about him could ever repel her, that she found beauty in every scarred inch of him. Her lips brushed against him, and she heard him groan—a sound of such raw pleasure and vulnerability that it emboldened her. She continued, learning as she went, guided by his responses—the way his breath hitched, the way his hand came to rest gently in her hair, not directing but simply connecting.

It wasn't about experience. It was about love. About showing him, without words, that every part of him was precious to her. That war hadn't made him less desirable—if anything, his survival, his strength, his gentleness despite everything he'd endured made her love him more fiercely than she'd thought possible.

After a few moments, his hand tightened gently in her hair.

"Zahra," he said, his voice rough and urgent. "I need—I want—"

She understood. She moved up his body, kissing her way back to his mouth, and he rolled them over so she was beneath him, cradled in the quilts. Their eyes met, and in that gaze was everything—eight years of separation, the memory of their wedding night, the reality of who they'd become, and the promise of who they might yet be.

"Are you ready?" he asked softly, his hand cupping her face with infinite tenderness.

"I've been ready for eight years," she whispered back.

He positioned himself above her, his scarred hands steadying her hips, and began to enter her slowly. So slowly. Giving her body time to adjust, to remember, to welcome him home.

She gasped as she felt him—her body needing a moment to remember how to accommodate him after so long. Eight years. It had been eight years since she'd felt this, and beneath the newness was something more powerful: the rightness of it. The completion. The sense of him filling not just her body but the empty spaces in her heart.

"Breathe," he murmured against her ear, holding still, giving her time. "I'm here. I'm not going anywhere."

She breathed, and as she did, her body softened, opened, accepted. She wrapped her legs around his hips, her arms around his back, pulling him closer, deeper. Wanting not just his body but everything—his grief, his ghosts, his scars, his survival. All of it.

"Yes," she breathed. "Reza, yes."

He began to move—slowly at first, carefully, giving her time to adjust to the rhythm. One arm wrapped around her back, holding her close, while his free hand cradled her face. Their eyes stayed locked on each other, unable to look away, unwilling to miss a single moment of this reunion.

"You're my home," he whispered, echoing that line he'd told her so many times over eight years, and their lips met in a kiss that was both tender and hungry—tongues entwining as their bodies found their rhythm together.

Their bodies were different now—his scarred and leaner, hers fuller and softer—but their love was unchanged. Constant. Enduring. A thread that war couldn't sever, that distance couldn't fray, that eight years of separation had only strengthened.

Zahra's hands roamed his back, feeling the ridges of scars, her legs tightening around him, urging him deeper. What had begun as adjustment transformed into pleasure—not just physical pleasure, though that was building like a tide, but emotional pleasure. The pleasure of being reunited, of being whole again, of being loved so completely.

"I dreamed of this," Reza breathed against her neck, his hips moving in a steady rhythm now. "Every night in those trenches. Your face. Your touch. The thought of coming home to you was what kept me alive when everything else told me to give up."

"I'm here," she gasped, her voice breaking with emotion even as pleasure built within her. "I'm here, and I'm yours, and you're mine, and we're together. Finally together."

Their movements grew less careful, more urgent, driven by eight years of pent-up longing. The awkwardness of their wedding night was gone—they were no longer fumbling newlyweds trying to figure out how bodies fit together. But there was still something beautifully imperfect about it, because they were learning each other anew. Learning how pleasure had changed for her. Learning where his scars made him sensitive. Learning how to move together after so long apart.

Reza's hand slid between them, finding where they were joined, moving in gentle circles as he continued within her. The combined sensations made Zahra cry out—a sound of pure pleasure that she immediately tried to muffle against his shoulder, shy even now.

"Don't hide," he murmured, his voice rough. "Let me hear you. I've dreamed of hearing you for eight years."

So she didn't hide. She let herself make sound—gasps and moans and his name repeated like a prayer. She let herself feel without restraint, without shame, without holding anything back. Because this was Reza. Her Reza. Her husband. Her home.

The pleasure built like a wave—higher and higher, carrying them both. She could feel him everywhere: filling her, surrounding her, loving her. His breath hot against her neck, his heart pounding against her chest, his scarred hands holding her like she was the most precious thing in the world.

"Zahra," he gasped, his movements becoming less controlled. "I—I can't—"

"Don't hold back," she whispered fiercely, her fingers digging into his shoulders. "Give me everything. All of you."

The wave crested. She felt it break within her first—pleasure radiating out from her core in pulsing waves that made her entire body respond to him. She cried out his name, her vision blurring with tears and sensation and overwhelming emotion.

Moments later, he followed—his rhythm faltering as he buried himself deep within her, his body shuddering, a groan torn from his throat that sounded almost like a sob. She held him through it, her arms and legs wrapped around him, keeping him close, feeling the warmth of their joining—a physical manifestation of their reunion, of coming home.

For a long moment, neither of them moved. They simply held each other, breathing hard, hearts pounding, bodies still joined. The oil lamp flickered, casting dancing shadows on the walls. Outside, the night remained still and quiet. Inside, everything had changed.

They were no longer two people trying to bridge eight years of separation. They were one again. United. Home.

Eventually, reluctantly, Reza moved—slowly withdrawing from her, mindful of her sensitivity. Zahra's breath hitched at the loss of him, her body tender but satisfied, a pleasant ache settling where he'd been.

He reached for a cloth that had been warming by the lamp, and with the same tender care he'd shown on their wedding night, he cleaned her gently. This time there was no giggling shyness—just quiet intimacy, his touch reverent and loving. When he was done, he pressed a soft kiss to her stomach, then looked up at her with eyes that shimmered with emotion.

"Thank you," he whispered.

"For what?" she asked, her hand coming down to stroke his hair.

"For waiting. For loving me still. For seeing past the scars to the man underneath. For making me feel human again instead of just a weapon that survived."

Tears slipped down her cheeks. "Reza, you never stopped being human. Not to me. Never to me."

Jamila Mikhail

He climbed back up beside her, pulling her into his arms, and she nestled against his chest with her head on his shoulder. He drew the embroidered quilts over them both—a cocoon of warmth and safety. She traced the scars in his flesh idly—the knife wounds, the shrapnel marks, each one a story she wanted to hear eventually, but not tonight. Tonight was for healing and reconnecting, not for anything else.

His arm wrapped around her, his hand stroking her hair where it spilled across the pillow. The scent of sandalwood soap from the bath still lingered, mingling with the musk of their lovemaking, with rosewater and jasmine. The cats—Shirin and Simin—had emerged from their corner to curl up at the foot of the bed, their purring adding a soft rhythm to the quiet.

"I dreamed of this," Reza said softly, his voice thick with emotion. "Holding you like this. Feeling you breathe beside me. The trenches stole so much from me—my brother, my comrades, pieces of my soul I'll never get back. But they couldn't steal this. They couldn't steal us."

Zahra's hand found his, their fingers interlacing. "I waited for you," she said, her voice quiet but steady. "Every night, I read your letters. Your poetry. The verses you sent me kept me alive, Reza. They reminded me that somewhere out there, you were still the man I married. Still the poet with the gentle heart."

She paused, her own memories rising—the loneliness, the rationed food, the air raid drills, the nights she'd lain in this bed wondering if he was cold, if he was hurt, if he was even still alive. "We're here now," she continued, her voice strengthening. "Together. And that's what matters."

He kissed her forehead, his lips lingering there, grounding them both in this moment. They talked softly as the night deepened—about small things at first, tentative steps toward normalcy. Her rose garden, which had kept blooming despite the war. His hope to maybe teach again someday, to write poetry not just in secret letters but openly, joyfully. The possibility of children in the future, when they'd had time to heal, to rebuild.

Their voices grew quieter, softer, the conversation drifting like the lamplight's glow. Zahra felt Reza's body begin to relax against hers, the tension that had been coiled in his muscles for eight years finally beginning to unwind.

"I think I'll sleep well tonight," he murmured, his voice surprised, almost wondering. "For the first time in years, I think I'll actually sleep."

"Then sleep, my love," Zahra whispered, continuing to stroke his hair. "I'm here. I'll keep you safe."

He nestled closer, his head settling more comfortably on her chest, her heartbeat a lullaby beneath his ear. His breathing began to deepen, to slow, to even out into the rhythm of sleep. Zahra held him, believing—hoping—that perhaps the war's ghosts might finally let him rest.

For a while, it seemed her hope would be realized. His body was heavy and relaxed against hers, his breathing deep and steady. The room was peaceful, warm, safe. Outside, the stars continued to shine, unmarred by the violence that had filled the night sky for eight years.

But then, gradually, something changed.

His breathing shifted—becoming shorter, more rapid. His body tensed against hers, muscles coiling tight beneath scarred skin. His hand, which had been resting gently on her hip, clenched into a fist, gripping the quilt with sudden intensity.

"Reza?" Zahra whispered, her hand pausing in his hair.

He didn't respond. His eyes were closed, still lost in sleep, but his face had changed. The peace that had settled over his features was dissolving, replaced by something darker. His jaw clenched. A furrow appeared between his brows. His lips moved, forming soundless words.

Then, so quietly she almost didn't hear it, a single word escaped his lips:

"Hossein."

Zahra's heart sank, because she understood. The war had followed him home after all. It lived in his sleep, in his dreams, waiting to drag him back to the trenches, back to the moment his brother died, back to all the horrors he couldn't leave behind.

She held him tighter, her own eyes filling with tears, and whispered prayers into the darkness—prayers that love would be enough, that home would be enough, that she would be enough to help him fight the ghosts that haunted him.

But as his body began to tremble against hers, as his breathing grew more ragged, as another name—then another, then another—fell from his lips like prayers for the dead, she knew the battle for his peace had only just begun.

Chapter Three

Isfahan, 1988

Zahra looked at Shirin and Simin lay curled together at the foot of the bed, two small bodies forming one purring mass. They seemed blissfully unaware of whatever turmoil was brewing inside Reza. His body tensed further. Muscles coiling tight beneath scarred skin. His hand, which had been resting gently on her hip, suddenly clenched—fingers digging into the quilt, gripping with desperate strength.

"Reza?" Zahra whispered, lifting her head, her hand moving to his face.

He didn't respond. His eyes remained closed, but his face had transformed. The peace that had settled over his features was dissolving like morning mist burned away by harsh sun. His jaw clenched. A furrow appeared between his brows, deep and pained. His lips moved, forming soundless words.

Zahra didn't know if she should wake him up or pray that the nightmare would pass. Would be return to peaceful sleep? It didn't seem likely. Reza's chest rose and fell beneath her cheek with increasing urgency, as if he were running, or struggling, or drowning in air that wouldn't quite fill his lungs.

Then his whole body jerked—a violent spasm that made her gasp. A strangled sound escaped his throat. Not quite a scream. Not quite a word. Something raw and animal and afraid.

And Zahra knew: the nightmare had found him and wasn't about to let him go that easily.

The smell hits first.

Sulphur. Blood. The chemical sweetness of mustard gas—so thick he can taste it on his tongue, feel it burning down his throat even through the mask that never quite fits, never quite seals. The stench of rotting flesh, of death left too long in the heat. Copper and iron and something worse, something that makes his stomach heave.

He's in the trench. No—he's running toward the trench. No—he's already there, has always been there, will always be there. Time doesn't work right. Everything happens at once and in the wrong order.

Hossein's voice cuts through the chaos: "Reza, stay low!"

But when Reza turns, his brother isn't beside him—he's across the trench, impossibly far away, and also right there, hand on his shoulder, close enough to feel the warmth of him.

The ground beneath him isn't ground at all. It's liquid, viscous, pulling at his boots. He looks down and it's blood. It's all blood. Ankle-deep, knee-deep, rising. The crimson is so bright it hurts to look at, unnatural, wrong.

Artillery screams overhead. The sound is too loud, splits his skull open, makes his teeth ache. He tries to cover his ears but his hands won't move, or they're already covering them, or they're holding his rifle, or they're reaching for Hossein—

Hossein.

His brother is reading Hafez, sitting calmly in the trench as shells explode around them, his voice clear and beautiful, reciting poetry as if they're back in Isfahan under the stars. But there's blood on the pages. Blood on his hands. Blood spreading across his uniform in a dark stain that grows and grows and—

The explosion.

It happens ten times, a hundred times, forever. The air rips apart. The sound is the end of the world. Dirt and blood and shrapnel—angry metal bees that scream as they fly, that bite through flesh like it's nothing, that burn and tear and—

Reza is running through the mud toward Hossein but his legs won't work right, too slow, like moving through water. He can see his brother falling, stumbling, the wound opening in his side, and Reza is screaming but no sound comes out, or maybe too much sound, maybe he's been screaming forever—

Hossein's eyes. Wide. Fierce. Kind. Exactly the same as always except they're dimming, the light going out like a candle flame being slowly smothered—

The Moonlit Rose of Isfahan

"*Live, Reza.*" The words are blood-flecked, bubbling from lips that are already too pale. "*For her. For Zahra. For Leyla.*"

Reza's hands are on Hossein's chest, pressing down, trying to stop the blood but there's so much of it, hot and slick and it keeps coming, soaking into the mud, into the earth, taking Hossein with it. His brother's hand grips his—strong, then weak, then barely there at all—

"No," Reza begs, the word tearing out of him. "Brother, stay with me. Please. Please."

But Hossein is already gone. Or not gone—still there, still looking at him, mouth moving to form words Reza can't hear over the artillery, over the screaming, over his own sobs—

And then Reza sees himself from above, from outside his own body—a strange, impossible perspective. He's kneeling in the mud beside his brother's body, but he's also floating, watching it happen, unable to stop it, unable to change anything—

The shrapnel.

White-hot agony explodes through his body—his thigh, his stomach, lower, tearing through the most vulnerable parts of him with surgical cruelty. The pain is beyond pain, beyond anything that should be possible to feel and remain conscious. It's fire and ice and knives and—

He can feel the metal inside him, foreign and wrong, burning as if the shrapnel itself is still hot from the explosion. It's tearing him apart from the inside. He looks down and sees blood spreading across his uniform, pooling between his legs, and the shame is almost worse than the pain—

But he can't leave Hossein. Can't let go. His hand is still on his brother's chest, feeling for a heartbeat that isn't there, that was never there, that stopped before Reza even reached him—

Time fractures again. Amir is dying, clutching his chest, blood bubbling through his fingers. But it's not Amir—it's another comrade, then another, then all of them at once, a chorus of the dead calling his name: "*Commander. Commander. Why didn't you save us? Why did you live when we died?*"

Hossein's letters to Leyla are scattered in the mud, ink running, words dissolving into illegibility. Reza tries to gather them but they disintegrate in his hands, turn to ash, to blood, to nothing—

The explosion happens again. And again. An endless loop. Hossein falling. Blood spreading. Pain tearing through Reza's body. The smell of sulphur and death. His brother's eyes dimming. "*Live, Reza. Live.*" But how can he live when everyone *else is dead? How can he live when Hossein isn't there to show him how?*

Someone is dragging him away. He fights them, screaming, reaching for Hossein's body, but the hands are too strong, pulling him through the blood-mud, through the corpses, away from his brother, away from—

"Hossein!"

The scream tore from Reza's throat as he jolted awake—violent, sudden, his body arching off the bed. His eyes flew open, wild and unseeing, still trapped between the nightmare and reality. Sweat soaked his skin, his hair, the sheets beneath him. His breath came in ragged, desperate gasps, as if he'd been drowning and just broke the surface.

For a moment—terrible, disorienting—he didn't know where he was. The trench walls seemed to close in around him. The stench of sulphur and blood clogged his nostrils. Hossein's blood was still warm on his hands, sticky between his fingers—

"Reza!" Zahra's voice cut through the chaos, urgent but gentle. "Reza, my love, you're here. You're home."

Her hands found his face, cradling it, grounding him. Her touch was warm, real, solid—so different from the phantom sensations of the nightmare. He blinked, his vision slowly clearing, and saw her face above him in the lamplight. Her almond-coloured eyes were wide with concern, bright with unshed tears, but her voice remained steady, anchoring.

"Zahra," he choked out, her name a desperate anchor, his only lifeline to reality. His hands flew up to grip her shoulders with frantic strength, pulling her close, needing to feel her solidity, her warmth, proof that this was real and the nightmare was not.

But his body was still in the trench. His senses wouldn't release their hold on the horror. The acrid stench of sulphur still burned his throat. The metallic taste of blood coated his tongue. The roar of artillery still echoed in his ears, making Zahra's words sound distant and muffled.

And the pain—oh God, the phantom pain in his stomach and groin pulsed with cruel intensity, as real as the moment the shrapnel had torn through him. He could feel it burning, tearing, the white-hot agony that had marked him forever.

Hossein's voice echoed in his mind, blood-flecked and fading: *"Live, Reza. For her. For Zahra."*

The dam broke.

Years of held-back grief came pouring out in wrenching sobs that shook his entire frame. Tears spilled over, hot and unstoppable, as the stoic mask he'd worn for years finally crumbled. He buried his face in Zahra's neck, his arms wrapping around her with desperate strength, clinging to her as if she alone kept him from being dragged back into the nightmare's grip.

Each sob tore through him like something physical, releasing years of buried pain—Hossein's death, the loss of comrades like Amir, the shrapnel's burn that had nearly claimed him, the weight of command, the faces of men he couldn't save, but especially the civilians caught in the crossfire. All of it poured out in that dark bedroom, witnessed only by his wife and the cats who'd been Hossein's gift.

"It was so real," he rasped between sobs, his voice raw and broken. "Zahra, it was so real. I was there again. The blood... his blood on my hands... I couldn't save him. I couldn't—"

His words dissolved into another wave of anguish. His whole body trembled against hers, the careful control he'd maintained for so long completely shattered.

Zahra's heart clenched with a pain that was both fierce and tender. This was her Reza—the gentle poet who'd tickled her on their wedding night, who'd written verses about roses and moonlight, who'd always been so careful with his words and his touch. War had reshaped him, carved wounds into his soul deeper than any shrapnel scar, and now he was breaking apart in her arms.

For a moment, she felt overwhelmed. Eight years she'd endured—solitude, rationed food, air raid drills, the constant fear that he wouldn't come home. She'd thought she was prepared for anything, but his letters, poetic and hopeful, hadn't prepared her for this: a husband whose strength was crumbling, whose pain ran so deep she couldn't see the bottom of it.

Her shyness rose up, that old familiar uncertainty. Was she enough? Could her love truly reach him across this chasm of trauma? Could she heal wounds this deep?

But then she felt the dampness of his tears against her neck, heard the raw vulnerability in his sobs, and something fiercer than doubt surged through her. Love. Pure, unwavering, fierce enough to burn away hesitation.

He had survived eight years of hell to return to her. The least she could do was hold him through this.

"You're safe, my love," she whispered, her voice trembling but resolute, her lips brushing his forehead. "You're with me. You're home."

Her hands stroked his back, feeling the ridges of scars beneath her fingers—each one a story of survival, each one proof that he'd made it back to her. She traced them gently, lovingly, as if her touch could somehow reach back through time and ease the moment each wound was made.

"I'm here," she murmured, repeating it like a prayer, each word poured from her heart. "The war can't take you from me. Not anymore. You're here, Reza. You're here with me."

She rocked him gently, the way one might soothe a child, her touch a lifeline pulling him back from the trenches, from the blood and death and unbearable loss. Her own tears slipped down her cheeks—grief for his suffering, for all he'd endured, for the brother he'd lost and the comrades whose names he cried out in his sleep.

"You survived," she whispered against his hair. "For Hossein. For me. You survived, my love, and you're here now. That's what matters. You're here."

She felt his pain when he managed to speak about it—the phantom agony of the shrapnel wound especially—and understood without words what he needed. Gently, carefully, she loosened her embrace enough to slide one hand down between them. Her fingers found the raised line of the scar on his stomach, tracing it with reverent tenderness, following its path downward.

Her shyness flickered, but love overwhelmed it. This was her husband. Every part of him was hers to love, to cherish, to heal if she could. Her hand moved lower still, cradling him gently, her warm touch a stark contrast to the phantom sensation of tearing metal. She held him with infinite tenderness, as if her love could seep through the scarred skin, could replace the memory of pain with the reality of gentle comfort.

The Moonlit Rose of Isfahan

"I'm here," she murmured again, her lips near his ear. "Feel me, Reza. Not the war. Not the pain. Me. I'm real. This is real."

His breath hitched, a shuddering gasp that wasn't quite a sob. His hands covered hers where she held him, his fingers trembling, and she felt the moment the phantom pain began to ease—replaced, slowly, by the warmth of her touch, the safety of her presence.

"Zahra," he choked out, his voice breaking on her name. "You... you make it bearable."

Gratitude flooded through him, so intense it was almost painful. She wasn't repulsed by his vulnerability, by his breaking, by the ugliness of his scars and his trauma. She was here, holding him, loving him, grounding him in reality with her gentle touch.

"My body remembers," he whispered, the admission shameful and necessary. "The shrapnel... I can still feel it. Like it's happening again."

"I know," Zahra whispered back, pressing her cheek to his, her tears mingling with his. "But you're not there, my love. You're here. And I will hold you through every memory, every nightmare, every moment. I will be here."

She continued to hold him—one hand cradling the most wounded parts of him, the other stroking his hair—as his sobs gradually quieted. Not stopping, not yet, but softening. The trembling in his body began to ease, though his grip on her remained tight, desperate.

"You're allowed to feel this," she said, her voice steady now, a beacon in his darkness. "You're allowed to grieve, to hurt, to break. I'll hold you through all of it, always."

She kissed his temple, his forehead, his tear-stained cheeks. Then, remembering the poetry they'd shared in letters, the verses that had sustained them both, she whispered words that rose from her own heart: "In your wound, I see your strength."

It wasn't Rumi, wasn't Hafez this time. It was hers. Born from her love for him, from the poetry they'd both learned to speak through their years of letters and longing.

"You survived, Reza," she continued, her eyes locking on his in the lamplight. "Every scar is proof of that. You came back to me. You lived, just as Hossein asked you to. And I love every part of you—every wound, every scar, every broken piece. You're my Reza. My home. My heart."

Her words wove through him like a thread of healing, echoing their wartime letters, reminding him of their love's endurance. His trembling eased further. His sobs softened to quiet tears, then to shuddering breaths, then to something almost like calm. She began to hum—a Persian lullaby her mother had sung to her as a child, its melody soft and ancient and soothing. The notes wrapped around them like a blanket, filling the quiet spaces between his breaths.

"I love you so much, my moonlit rose," Reza murmured finally, his voice faint but sincere, gratitude overwhelming the shame. "I'm sorry... for breaking like this."

"Don't be," she whispered fiercely, kissing him again. "Don't ever apologize for feeling. I would rather have you here, broken and real, than perfect and lost. I'll hold you through every nightmare, my love. I promise."

She guided him to lie back down, pulling the quilts over them both, enveloping them in warmth. She drew him close, his head settling on her chest, her heartbeat steady beneath his ear—a rhythm to ground him, to remind him where he was. Her fingers stroked his hair, his beard, grounding him in the present moment.

Her legs entwined with his. Her arms held him secure. And slowly, gradually, she felt his body relax against hers. The tension drained from his muscles. His breathing deepened, synchronized with the gentle rise and fall of her chest.

"Sleep," she whispered, continuing her lullaby. "I'm here. You're safe."

And this time, when sleep came for him, it came peacefully. No trenches. No blood. No screaming. Just her heartbeat, her warmth, her love surrounding him like a shield.

The room settled into quiet. The oil lamp's glow softened to a gentle flicker. The scent of jasmine and sandalwood lingered, mixing with the salt of tears. And Reza Azad, survivor of eight years of war, slept in his wife's arms—truly at peace for the first time since 1980.

But Zahra lay awake.

Her eyes fixed on the ceiling, where shadows danced in the lamp's fading light. Her heart, so full of love, churned with a storm of emotions she hadn't expected—couldn't have prepared for.

The man in her arms was almost a stranger now. Not in the ways that mattered—his gentleness, his devotion, his poet's soul. Those remained. But eight years of war had reshaped him in ways her imagination hadn't captured, ways his letters couldn't convey.

His lean frame, scarred and weathered. His soul, fractured by losses she could only begin to imagine. The nightmare's intensity—the way he'd clung to her as if she were his only lifeline to sanity—revealed a depth of trauma she hadn't fully grasped. His letters had been poetic and hopeful for their eventual reunion, sustaining her through lonely nights. But they hadn't prepared her for this: a husband whose heart carried wounds deeper than the shrapnel scars she'd kissed.

Who was this Reza? This man haunted by Hossein's death, by the trenches' horrors, by the ghosts of comrades whose names he cried out in his sleep? Could she truly reach him? Could she heal him?

Her thoughts spiralled, doubt creeping in despite the fierce love in her heart. She'd endured eight years of solitude—rationed food, air raid drills, the constant fear of his death. She'd grown strong out of necessity. But Reza's pain was a chasm, vast and dark, and she felt small against it.

Her shyness resurfaced, that old uncertainty. Was she truly strong enough for this? Could her nurturing soul hold up under the weight of his trauma?

She traced his shoulder gently, feeling the ridges of scars beneath her fingertips. Her heart ached for the boyish poet who'd made her laugh on their wedding night, who'd been so earnest and tender and fumbling. That boy was buried now, beneath war's weight, and she mourned for what they'd lost even as she held tight to what remained.

But beneath the doubt, something fiercer burned: determination. Love. An unwavering resolve to be his home, as he was hers. She had waited eight years for him. She would not fail him now. She wouldn't let her insecurities claim her as another casualty of war.

"In your wound, I see your strength," she whispered to him. And she meant it. His scars were proof of survival. His breaking was proof he was still human, still capable of feeling, still *alive* in all the ways that mattered.

Her own tears slipped down her cheeks, silent in the darkness. Tears for his pain. Tears for the years they'd lost. Tears for the difficult road ahead. But also tears of gratitude—because he was here, breathing steadily against her, warm and real and hers.

She pressed her cheek to his hair, inhaling his scent—still him, beneath the war and trauma and fear. Still her Reza.

Exhaustion crept over her gradually, her body sinking deeper into the quilts. Eight years of sleeping alone, with only Shirin and Simin for warmth. Eight years of cold nights and colder fear. But now his solid presence beside her was a comfort beyond words.

Her curves molded against his lean frame. Her legs remained entwined with his. The soreness between her thighs was a sweet reminder of their lovemaking earlier—unfamiliar after so long, but cherished. He had filled her again, body and heart, and that thought brought a small smile to her lips despite her tears.

She would be enough. She had to be. They would heal each other, slowly, day by day, night by night. She would hold him through every nightmare until the ghosts finally released their grip. And he would hold her through her own fears and doubts.

Together. They would do this together.

The lullaby's echo faded from her lips as sleep finally claimed her too, her heart finding comfort in the rhythm of his breathing, the safety of their shared bed, the promise of tomorrow.

Morning light filtered through the curtains—soft, golden, gentle. It stirred Reza awake slowly, coaxing him back to consciousness with warmth rather than violence.

For a moment, he lay perfectly still, afraid to move, afraid to open his eyes. But then he felt it: Zahra's warmth against him. Her dark hair spilling across the pillow. The soft rise and fall of her breathing. The reality of her presence.

Relief flooded through him like water breaking through a dam. He was home. Not in a trench. Not bleeding or grieving on some godforsaken battlefield. Home. In their bed. With Zahra sleeping peacefully beside him.

He opened his eyes carefully and turned his head to look at her. Her face was peaceful in sleep, though he could see faint shadows under her eyes—evidence of a night spent awake, watching over him. Guilt twisted in his chest. Their first full night together in eight years, and he'd spent half of it breaking apart, sobbing like a child, needing her to hold him together.

Shame crept in, familiar and heavy. Shame for his nightmare's intensity. For breaking down in her arms. For the scars on his body that made him feel less than whole. For turning what should have been a joyous reunion into something marked by trauma and tears.

But beneath the shame, something else grew: gratitude. Deep, overwhelming gratitude for this woman who'd held him through his darkest moment. Who'd touched his most wounded places with tenderness instead of revulsion. Who'd whispered poetry and promises while he fell apart.

He studied her face, memorizing it in the morning light. She'd changed—her features more mature, her body fuller and more womanly. Eight years had shaped her just as they'd shaped him, though in different ways. She'd grown strong in his absence, resilient and capable. He could see it in the set of her jaw, in the quiet confidence that had allowed her to hold him last night without flinching.

She was beautiful. More beautiful than his memories, than his dreams, than any poem he could write. As if sensing his gaze, Zahra stirred. Her eyes fluttered open, focusing on him, and a sleepy smile curved her lips—warm, genuine, without a trace of the pity or disgust he'd feared.

"Reza," she whispered, her voice soft and warm like honey.

Her heart swelled with gratitude—a silent prayer of thanks that he was here, alive, whole in the ways that truly mattered despite the scars and trauma. The soreness between her legs pulsed gently, a tender ache that felt both unfamiliar and sweet. His love, satisfying and profound, had filled her last night, rekindling a bond eight years hadn't broken.

She reached for his hand, her fingers finding his, tracing the scars on his knuckles with gentle reverence.

"I love you," Reza said, his voice thick with emotion. His free hand came up to cup her cheek. "I'm sorry... for last night. For—"

"No." Zahra shook her head, her eyes fierce despite the softness of her smile. "Don't apologize. Not for that. Never for that."

She shifted closer, pressing her forehead against his. "You're here, my love. You're alive. You came back to me. That's enough. That's everything."

"But I broke—"

"You felt," she corrected gently but firmly. "You grieved. You let me see your pain instead of hiding it. Do you know how precious that is? How much trust that takes?"

Her thumb brushed across his cheekbone, wiping away the ghost of last night's tears. "I would rather have you here, close and hurting, than perfect but distant. I would rather hold you through a thousand nightmares than spend one more night alone wondering if you're alive."

His eyes glistened with fresh tears, but these were different—not born of anguish but of overwhelming emotion, of being seen and loved despite everything.

"How did I deserve you?" he whispered.

"You don't have to deserve love, Reza. You just have to accept it." She kissed him softly, tenderly. "And I will give it to you every day, through every nightmare, through every moment of doubt and pain. I'm not going anywhere. I've waited for you for too long to walk away now."

They lay together as morning light strengthened, warming the room, chasing away the last shadows of night. The quilts were soft around them. The scent of jasmine and sandalwood still lingered faintly in the air. In their corner, Shirin and Simin began to stir, stretching and yawning.

"What do we do now?" Reza asked quietly. It was a bigger question than it seemed—encompassing not just today, but all the days to come. How did they rebuild a life after eight years apart? How did he learn to live with the ghosts that haunted him?

Zahra was quiet for a moment, considering. Then she said simply: "We start with today. With this moment. We get up, we eat breakfast, we live. And tomorrow we do it again. And the day after that. One day at a time, my love. Together."

He nodded against her forehead. It seemed impossible and utterly simple at the same time. One day at a time. Together.

"Will you..." He hesitated, vulnerability in his voice. "Will you tell me if it becomes too much? If I become too much?"

"You could never be too much," Zahra said fiercely. "But yes. I promise. We'll be honest with each other. About everything. No more hiding, no more pretending. Just truth, even when it's hard."

"Just truth," he echoed. "Even when it's hard."

She smiled and kissed him again—a seal on the promise, a vow for the future. "Come," she said softly. "Let's face today together."

And as they rose from the bed, wrapped in morning light and quiet hope, Reza felt something he hadn't felt in eight years: the possibility of peace. Not today, perhaps, not even tomorrow maybe, but the nightmares would return—he knew that. The ghosts wouldn't release their grip so easily.

But with Zahra beside him, with her love as his anchor and her strength as his shield, perhaps—just perhaps—he could learn to live again.

One day at a time.

Together.

Chapter Four

Khuzestan, 1980

The air tasted of diesel and death. Reza crouched in a shallow ditch near Khorramshahr, his heart a war drum pounding against his ribs, and tried to remember how to breathe. The autumn sun beat down with merciless intensity, baking the cracked earth of Khuzestan until heat shimmers rose like ghosts from the ground. In the distance, the Arvandrud River—broad and brown and indifferent—glinted beneath the smoke-choked sky, its waters mocking the parched soldiers who dreamed of its coolness.

His uniform was stiff and new, the fabric coarse against skin still soft from civilian life. It chafed at his neck, his wrists, the small of his back where sweat pooled and ran in rivulets down his spine. The rifle in his hands—a Soviet-made Kalashnikov that still smelled of factory grease—was heavy in a way that basic training never prepared him for. Not the physical weight, though his arms already ached from holding it. The other weight. The weight of knowing what it was meant to do.

Ten weeks ago—no, eleven now, maybe twelve, the days blurred together—he had been in Zahra's arms. Their honeymoon bed in Shiraz had been warm with laughter and clumsy love, her jasmine scent filling his lungs as he whispered poetry against her skin. Three weeks of marriage, sweet and fumbling and theirs, before the draft notice came. Then forty-five days of basic training at a camp outside Tehran, where they'd run him ragged under the sun and taught him to strip a

Jamila Mikhail

rifle blindfolded and drilled into him the mechanics of killing.

But nothing—nothing—had prepared him for this.

The training had been mechanical. Targets painted on wooden boards. Shouts and drills and the careful choreography of combat practiced on dusty fields where no one shot back. They'd taught him how to aim, how to reload, how to move in formation. What they hadn't taught him—what couldn't be taught—was this: the way his hands shook when artillery screamed overhead. The way his stomach lurched when the ground heaved beneath him. The way his poet's heart, trained to find beauty in the curve of a rose petal, recoiled from the stark brutality of men trying to kill him.

Hatred burned in his chest—sharp and hot and new. Saddam Hussein. The name tasted like ash in his mouth. That bastard's invasion had stolen everything: his honeymoon with Zahra, their quiet mornings in the garden, the poetry he'd been writing for her. Iraq's president had sent his tanks rolling across the border barely weeks ago, a lightning strike of greed and ambition, and now Reza crouched in this ditch with a rifle in his hands instead of a pen.

The tyrant had betrayed decades of neighbourly peace, turned brothers into soldiers, families into grieving widows. For what? Land? Oil? Pride? Whatever Saddam's reasons, they'd ripped Reza from Zahra's arms after only three weeks of marriage. Reza had never been interested in politics but he knew this: he hated Saddam, and he wasn't going to let Iran go down without a fight.

The ground shook. Iraqi artillery roared somewhere beyond the smoke, and shells exploded in the distance, sending plumes of dirt skyward like the earth itself was bleeding. Reza's unit—a ragtag mix of conscripts like him and volunteers who'd signed up with fire in their eyes—huddled in the ditch, their faces pale beneath layers of dust and sweat, eyes wide with the kind of fear that stripped away pretence.

Hossein was beside him.

His older brother, strong-jawed and steady-handed, checked his rifle with the kind of calm that seemed impossible in this chaos. The same hands that once turned the pages of Hafez under Isfahan's stars now gripped a weapon with practiced ease. Hossein had volunteered—insisted on it, actually, when Reza's draft notice came. *"I'm not letting you*

The Moonlit Rose of Isfahan

face this alone," he'd said, and their mother had wept but hadn't argued. Brothers. Always brothers, even here in hell.

"Stay sharp, Reza," Hossein said, his voice calm but tight, like a rope stretched taut but not yet snapping. His eyes—fierce and kind and exactly like their father's—met Reza's for a moment, and in that glance passed everything they couldn't say aloud. Stay alive. Stay human. We'll get through this.

"Remember training," Hossein added quietly, his hand finding Reza's shoulder. "Stay low, watch my back. I'll watch yours. We're in this together."

The words hit Reza harder than he expected. His throat tightened. They'd said the same thing a hundred times during those gruelling forty-five days of drills near Tehran—crawling under barbed wire together, taking turns spotting each other at the rifle range, sharing canteen water on the long marches. Hossein had refused to let him struggle alone then, just as he refused now.

Reza swallowed hard, finding his voice. "Together," he echoed, meeting his brother's eyes. "I've got your back too, brother. Like always. I'll be right there beside you." The vow settled in his chest, solid and real. It wasn't one-sided—this brotherhood, this bond. They'd defend each other. They'd survive this nightmare together or not at all.

Hossein's mouth quirked in something that might have been a smile if they weren't in hell. He pulled a small dented flask from his pack, unscrewed it, and took a sip before passing it to Reza. Tea—lukewarm and bitter, but the cardamom scent was a ghost of home. Isfahan afternoons. Their mother's kitchen. The courtyard where he and Hossein had read poetry as boys, where Hossein had teased him mercilessly about finding love before him as adults.

"For Iran," Hossein murmured as Reza drank. "For our families. For everyone and everything that bastard Saddam is trying to destroy."

"For Zahra," Reza added quietly, the tea warming his throat. "And for Leyla." He'd seen the letters Hossein tucked into his pocket—careful, private, from the girl who'd captured his brother's eye just before deployment. Another stolen future, another reason to hate the man who'd started this war.

Hossein's jaw tightened at the mention of her name, but he nodded.

"We'll make it home to them. The poet will win his rose again, brother." The old tease from their courtship days—but now it carried weight, a promise wrapped in memory.

Reza nodded, his throat too dry despite the tea. He reached into his breast pocket—carefully, as if sudden movement might shatter something fragile—and touched the folded letter there. Zahra's first, written in her delicate script, the paper already soft from how many times he'd read it. He didn't need to unfold it to remember the words.

My beloved,

The garden misses you. The roses you planted before you left are blooming now, white and red and pink, and I tend them each morning thinking of your hands in the soil beside me. Shirin and Simin ask for you—well, they don't ask with words, but they sleep on your pillow and wait by the door at sunset as if they expect you to walk through it.

I pressed a rose petal between these pages for you. Can you smell it? I hope you can. I hope it reminds you of home, of our courtyard in the evening when the air turns cool and the jasmine opens. I hope it reminds you that I am here, waiting, loving you across whatever distance separates us.

Come home to me, my love. Come home to your rose.

Always yours,

Zahra

The dried rose petal had crumbled the first week, reduced to crimson dust in the corner of the envelope, but the scent lingered—faint and sweet and hers. He clung to that memory like a lifeline: Zahra in their garden, her hair loose and catching the evening light, her smile shy and warm as she handed him the letter before he left for training. *"So you won't forget me,"* she'd said, and he'd kissed her temple, tasting salt from her tears.

As if he could ever forget.

A sergeant—grizzled, his face weathered like old leather, voice hoarse from shouting over artillery—appeared above the ditch. "Move! To the ridge!" He didn't wait to see if they followed. Officers didn't stay exposed for long.

Reza's body moved before his mind caught up. Muscle memory from training kicked in—up, rifle raised, feet scrambling for purchase in the loose soil. His boots slipped, sent him stumbling, and Hossein's

The Moonlit Rose of Isfahan

hand caught his elbow, steadied him. Around them, the unit moved like a startled flock of birds, all frantic motion and barely-controlled panic.

The air was alive with sound, overwhelming and all-consuming sound. Gunfire cracked like whips snapping. Mortars thudded with bass notes that he felt in his chest cavity. Men shouted in Farsi and Arabic, their voices swallowed almost instantly by the din. Somewhere close—too close—an Iraqi tank rumbled, its treads grinding earth and stone, its barrel swivelling with mechanical precision.

They sprinted toward a low ridge, the ground pockmarked with craters like the surface of the moon. Debris littered the battlefield in a grotesque still life: shattered rifles twisted into abstract sculptures, torn uniforms that still held the shape of the men who wore them, a bicycle—absurdly intact, absurdly normal—lying on its side, wheels still spinning slowly in the wind.

And then Reza saw the body.

An Iranian soldier. Young—younger than Reza, maybe nineteen or twenty, with a wispy attempt at a moustache and eyes that stared at nothing, at everything, at the smoke-choked sky with an expression caught somewhere between surprise and resignation. Blood pooled beneath him, seeping into the thirsty earth, already attracting flies that buzzed in lazy circles.

Reza's stomach lurched. Bile rose, hot and acidic, burning the back of his throat. His feet stutter-stepped, momentum carrying him forward even as his mind screamed to stop, to look away, to not see this. But he couldn't not see it. The boy's hands were still clutching his rifle. His wedding ring—gold, simple—caught the light. Someone's husband. Someone's son.

"Don't look, brother." Hossein's voice cut through the roar, his hand firm on Reza's arm, pulling him forward, pulling him away. "Keep moving. You can't help him now."

But the image seared itself into Reza's mind with the permanence of a photograph. The flies. The wedding ring. The eyes that would never close. He stumbled forward, his breath coming in short gasps that had nothing to do with the running. In training, the targets had been paper. Clean. Impersonal. They'd taught him to shoot at silhouettes, not at men who wore wedding rings and looked up at the sky as they died.

More of Saddam's handiwork. More blood on that tyrant's hands. Reza's rage flared hot and desperate—this boy had probably been a poet too, or a farmer, or a shopkeeper. Someone with dreams. Someone who'd never wanted to die in the dirt of Khuzestan because an ambitious dictator decided to invade.

They reached the ridge and threw themselves behind a crumbling mud wall. Bullets snapped overhead, pinging off the earth with vicious little sounds like angry insects. Reza pressed himself flat, his cheek against the sun-baked mud, and tried to remember what he was supposed to do. *Aim. Breathe. Squeeze, don't pull. Aim. Breathe. Squeeze.*

His hands shook as he raised the rifle. The metal was hot against his palms, slick with his sweat. Through the smoke—thick and acrid, burning his eyes until tears streamed down his face—he could make out shapes. Iraqi soldiers, advancing in a loose line, their own rifles raised. Shadows in the haze. Not men. Not fathers or brothers or husbands. Just shadows. Just targets.

"Steady," Hossein breathed beside him, his own rifle up and ready. "Like we practiced. Breathe."

Reza aimed. His training took over, muscle memory guiding his movements. Sight picture. Breathing steady despite the fear. Finger on the trigger.

He fired.

The recoil jarred his shoulder, harder than he remembered, and the acrid smell of gunpowder—sharper, more chemical than anything he'd known before—burned his nose, his throat. Through the smoke, a shadow fell. Crumpled. Became something other than a shadow, became a person who had been standing and now wasn't.

Reza froze.

His breath caught. Time did something strange—stretched like taffy, became elastic and wrong. Had he—? Was that—? The question lodged in his throat, too huge to swallow. *Did I just kill someone?*

"Reza!" Hossein's shout snapped him back. "Stay with me! Focus!"

Reza blinked, sucked in air that tasted of cordite and dust. His brother's face swam into focus—intent, fierce, alive. Hossein was firing, working his rifle with mechanical precision, and Reza forced his own hands to move, to reload, to aim again. Don't think. Don't feel. Just survive. Get home to Zahra. Keep Hossein alive.

The ridge became a slaughterhouse. That was the only word for it. Men fell—Iranian, Iraqi, it didn't matter, they all fell the same way, all bled the same red, all screamed with the same agony. Bodies crumpled in the dust. Some didn't move again. Some did, writhing, reaching for help that didn't come.

Reza fired again. And again. Not thinking now, just surviving. Each shot was another moment alive. Each shot was one step closer to Zahra. He didn't look at where his bullets landed. Couldn't. Wouldn't. If he looked, if he saw, he'd fall apart completely, and he couldn't afford that. Not here. Not now.

Hossein dragged him to a new position—a shallow trench, their backs pressed against earth that still held the warmth of the day's heat. They huddled there, breathing hard, the air thick with cordite and gas and fear.

"We'll make it," Hossein said, his voice fierce, trying to convince them both. "We'll make it, brother."

"Together," Reza gasped, the word torn from somewhere deep. His hands found his brother's arm, gripped hard. "You hear me, Hossein? We're getting out of this together. Both of us. I'm not losing you."

Hossein's eyes met his, and for just a moment, beneath the dirt and sweat and fear, Reza saw his brother—really saw him. Not the steady soldier, but the boy who'd defended him from bullies in Isfahan's alleys. Who'd laughed when Zahra chose the poet over him as a suitor. Who'd read Hafez with him under the stars and teased him about love and stood beside him through everything.

"Both of us," Hossein agreed roughly. His hand found Reza's, squeezed once. Hard. A promise.

But Reza saw fear in his brother's eyes. Fear that mirrored his own. This wasn't like the stories. This wasn't heroic or noble or any of the things the recruiting posters promised. This was just survival. Raw and ugly and desperate.

An Iraqi tank's roar grew closer. The shell tore through the mud wall they'd sheltered behind moments ago, sending chunks of earth

Jamila Mikhail

skyward. If they'd stayed there—if Hossein hadn't pulled him away—

Reza's mind flashed to Zahra's face. Her shy smile on their wedding night. Her body beneath his in Shiraz, soft and warm and trusting. The way she'd looked up at him afterward, her eyes bright with tears and joy and something that might have been wonder.

He closed his eyes for just a moment—just one breath—and let himself remember. The scent of jasmine in their room. The sound of her laughter. The feel of her fingers threading through his hair.

Then he opened them and returned to this hell.

Words surfaced in his mind—Rumi's words, from the worn copy of the Masnavi he'd studied in better days, in Isfahan's quiet evenings when poetry felt relevant and beautiful and true: "Till the cloud weeps, how should the garden smile? Till the babe cries, how should the milk begin to flow?"

The verses had seemed abstract then, contemplative exercises in spiritual metaphor. Here, now, with blood on his hands and cordite burning his throat, they took on brutal clarity. He must weep now—they all must, the whole nation bleeding in the desert—so that someday, somehow, their garden might smile again. So that Zahra's roses might bloom in peace. So that Saddam's invasion would be repelled and Iran could heal.

But where was the milk? Where was the relief the babe's cry was supposed to summon? He saw only more death. More screaming. An endless cascade of suffering with no end in sight.

Still, he whispered the words anyway. A prayer. A plea. A reminder that somewhere, beyond this smoke and chaos, beauty still existed. Poetry still existed. Zahra still existed, tending their garden, pressing rose petals into letters, waiting for him to come home.

He had to survive this. For her. For the life they'd barely begun. For the poetry still unwritten and the children not yet born and the mornings they hadn't yet shared over tea in their courtyard.

The battle stretched on. Hours that felt like days. The sun tracked across the sky with maddening slowness, and still the shooting didn't stop. Reza's body ached—his leg throbbed where a bullet grazed it, his hands were blistered from the rifle's heat, his lungs burned from the gas he couldn't fully keep out. But he was alive. Against all odds, impossibly, he was still alive.

Hossein's presence beside him was the only anchor to sanity. His brother's steady hand. His quiet encouragement when Reza's hands shook too badly to reload. The way he shared his water when Reza's canteen ran dry. Their bond—forged in childhood, tested now in fire—was the thread that kept Reza from unraveling completely.

As dusk finally fell, the fighting slowed. The Iraqis retreated under Iranian counter-fire, pulling back across the cratered landscape, leaving the ridge—this anonymous piece of earth that meant nothing and everything—in Iranian hands.

But the cost.

The ridge was a graveyard now. Bodies lay where they fell, Iranian and Iraqi alike, all distinctions erased by death. The young soldier with the wedding ring was still there, still staring at the sky. Others had joined him. Too many others.

Reza collapsed in the trench, his chest heaving, his mind numb but alive—frantically, desperately alive—with images he'd never unsee. The smell of blood and cordite and burnt flesh clung to his uniform, to his skin, seeped into his pores until he wondered if he'd ever be clean again.

His hands shook as he reached for Zahra's letter. The paper was smudged with dirt now, stained with his sweat, one corner darkened with what might be blood. But her words were still there, still legible in the fading light: *Come home to me, my love. Come home to your rose.*

He pressed the letter to his lips. The paper tasted of dust and salt and desperation. He closed his eyes and pictured her: in their garden, her hair catching the evening light, her hands gentle as she tended the roses they'd planted together. The image was so vivid it hurt. So beautiful it ached.

"I'll come home," he whispered into the gathering darkness, making a vow to her, to himself, to whatever God might be listening. "I swear it, Zahra. I'll come home to you."

Even if he had to crawl. Even if it took eight years. Even if the man who returned was changed beyond recognition, scarred in body and soul. Even if it meant fighting through every one of Saddam Hussein's battalions and walking back to Isfahan over the tyrant's broken ambitions.

He'd survive this. He had to. Because she was waiting.

Beside him, Hossein exhaled slowly. His hand found Reza's shoulder, squeezed once. "Both of us, brother," he murmured, echoing their earlier promise. "We're going home. Both of us."

"Both of us," Reza agreed, his voice raw but certain.

No words after that. None needed. They were both alive. For now, that was enough.

The stars began to emerge overhead, indifferent and eternal, the same stars that shone over Isfahan, over Zahra in their courtyard, over the life that felt impossibly far away. Reza tilted his head back and searched for the moon—her moon, the one he called her by—and found it rising in the east, pale and luminous against the darkening sky.

He held onto that. The moon. The stars. The letter pressed against his heart. Zahra's love like a light in the darkness. Hossein's solid presence beside him, another anchor to keep him from drifting into the void.

And somehow—despite everything, despite the horror and the death and the blood on his hands—he found a shred of hope.

Tomorrow would be worse. He knew that. Tomorrow they'd move out, chase the retreating Iraqis, and the killing would start all over again. This was just the beginning of a war that would devour years of his life. Saddam's war. Saddam's greed. A war that shouldn't exist but did, grinding up young men like grain between millstones.

But tonight, under these stars, with Hossein beside him and Zahra's letter over his heart, Reza Azad allowed himself to breathe.

One breath at a time.

Until he could come home to his rose.

Chapter Five

Isfahan, 1988

The morning sun filtered through the kitchen's thin curtains, casting a golden glow over the modest Isfahan home. The scent of fresh *lavash* bread, still warm from Zahra's baking, mingled with the earthy aroma of brewed tea and the sweet tang of date syrup, filling the air with a comfort Reza hadn't known in eight years.

He sat at the low wooden table, his scarred hands resting awkwardly on its surface, his civilian clothes—a loose cotton shirt and trousers Zahra had laid out—feeling foreign against his skin. The fabric was soft, unlike the stiff military uniform he'd worn in the trenches, but its unfamiliarity made him restless.

He tugged at the shirt's hem, strangely longing for the familiar weight of his soldier's garb, though he knew that desire was a crutch he'd need to leave behind. Shirin, the tabby cat, leapt onto the table, brushing against his arm, her purrs a stark contrast to the chaos he'd faced in Khuzestan. The surreal normalcy of this moment—breakfast, cats, his wife—felt like a dream he might wake from.

Zahra stood by the stove, stirring a pot of *aush*, its herbs scenting the air. She'd changed from yesterday's green dress into a simple cream-coloured tunic and loose trousers—comfortable house clothes that made her look softer, more at ease. Her long, dark hair was pinned up, a few strands escaping to frame her face. After eight years alone, with only Shirin and Simin to warm her bed, having Reza here still felt strange, almost like hosting a guest she was still learning to know again.

Yet the sight of him—his strong jaw now framed by that dark beard flecked with gray, his soulful brown eyes catching the sunlight—made her heart swell. He was no longer the clean-shaven boy of twenty-four who'd tickled her on their wedding night. War had matured him, his face refined, handsome in its ruggedness, etched with lines of survival.

Reza took in the kitchen, its changes a quiet shock. The walls, once mostly bare, now held shelves with clay jars of spices and dried roses from Zahra's garden. A small radio, silent now, sat in the corner—a relic of wartime broadcasts. The table bore new scratches, marks of Zahra's solitary meals, and the absence of his presence ached in his chest. He sipped the tea, its warmth spreading through him, a far cry from the bitter army rations he'd choked down in trenches near Ahvaz. The taste of Zahra's cooking—the *aush* soft and chewy, flavourful and rich with herbs—was a revelation, stirring memories of their brief honeymoon in Shiraz, when they'd shared sweets and laughter.

Simin, the grey cat, padded over, nuzzling his knee, and he scratched her ears, a smile tugging at his lips. "These two kept you company," he said, his baritone soft, almost reverent. "I'm jealous of their time with you."

Zahra laughed, a shy, melodic sound, setting more food on the table. "They're spoiled now," she teased, sitting across from him, her eyes meeting his, sparkling in the sunlight. "But they're happy you're home." Her words carried weight—home, a word they'd both clung to through his letters, her replies filled with poetry and love. She watched him eat, his movements tentative, as if relearning the act of savouring food. The normalcy felt surreal to her too, after years of cooking for one, her heart hardened by solitude, air raid drills, and the fear of losing him. Yet his presence, solid and real, warmed her more than the morning sun.

They ate slowly, the clink of spoons and the cats' meows filling the quiet. Conversation began haltingly, their shyness a remnant of their first full day together, the awkwardness of strangers relearning each other.

"The garden's grown," Reza said, glancing toward the courtyard, where Zahra's roses bloomed despite the war. "You made beauty in all this."

His voice held admiration, and she blushed, her fingers tracing the edge of her teacup. "I had to," she said softly. "It kept me close to you." Her words stirred him, and he reached for her hand, his rough fingers intertwining with hers, the touch dissolving their awkwardness. They talked, voices softening, affection replacing hesitation. Reza shared fragments of his hopes—to perhaps eventually teach again, to write poetry not just in letters but for everyone to hear. Zahra spoke of her embroidery, her books, the small joys that sustained her through the lonely years.

"I reread your letters," she admitted, her cheeks flushing. "Every night, your words... they were my light."

Reza's eyes softened, his thumb stroking her hand. He again noticed the faint shadows under her eyes from last night's comforting, and gratitude mixed with shame—for his nightmare, his shrapnel scar, the way their reunion had been shadowed by trauma.

Zahra's gaze lingered on his face, the sunlight illuminating his beard, its premature grey flecks a badge of survival. "You're more handsome now," she said, her voice shy but earnest. "The war... it shaped you, but you're still my Reza."

Her words eased his shame, and he leaned across the table, kissing her forehead, his lips lingering. The cats circled, Shirin nudging Zahra's leg, and they laughed, the sound bright, a step toward normalcy.

Reza broke a piece of *lavash*, spreading date syrup on it, his movements deliberate, echoing their first meal together after their wedding. "Like old times," he said, his voice soft, a smile tugging at his lips as he offered the bread to Zahra, holding it to her mouth.

Her cheeks flushed, her shyness resurfacing, but she leaned forward, taking a bite, her lips brushing his fingers, sending a spark through them both. The sweetness of the syrup mingled with the bread's warmth, and she laughed. "You always knew how to make me smile," she said, her eyes meeting his, the memory of their honeymoon—giggling over shared sweets, their clumsy love—warming her heart.

He fed her another piece, his fingers lingering near her lips, the act intimate, a bridge to their past. "I'm trying to remember how," he admitted, his voice tinged with vulnerability, his hand fidgeting with his shirt again, the cotton feeling wrong, too light.

Zahra reached across the table, her hand resting on his, stilling his restless fingers. "You look handsome in these," she said, her tone gentle but flirtatious, a playful glint in her eyes. "But... I must admit, you were dashing in your uniform too."

Her words, bold for her shy nature, made him laugh, a soft, surprised sound, easing the tension in his shoulders. "My rose, teasing me already?" he said, his poet's heart stirring, grateful for her patience as he navigated this unfamiliar life.

They finished eating, the table scattered with crumbs, the tea cooling in their cups. Together, they cleared the dishes, moving to the sink in a quiet dance, their shoulders brushing as they washed the plates. The warm water and soap's scent grounded them, a simple act that felt profound after years apart. Reza scrubbed a plate, his hands clumsy, unused to such domestic tasks, while Zahra dried, her movements sure but gentle.

"What comes next?" he wondered out loud again, his voice low, worry creeping in. The war's end left a void—would he teach again, write poetry, rebuild a life in a country scarred like him? The uncertainty gnawed, his fingers tightening on the plate.

Zahra set her towel down, turning to him, her eyes soft but resolute. "We have time, Reza," she said, her hand touching his arm, feeling the scars beneath his sleeve. "The country is healing, like us. We'll figure it out together, day by day."

Her words, a soothing balm, echoed her comforting after his nightmare, her love a steady anchor. He nodded, his worry easing, and leaned down to kiss her forehead, his lips lingering, the gesture sealing their shared hope.

They moved to the living room, where Reza's canvas bag sat untouched from his arrival. Zahra knelt beside it, her fingers brushing the worn fabric, and looked up at him. "Let's unpack," she said, her voice gentle, sensing his need to reclaim this space.

He joined her, his hands hesitant as they opened the bag, revealing folded clothes, a battered notebook of his poetry, and a bundle of

The Moonlit Rose of Isfahan

letters—her letters, creased and smudged from countless readings in the trenches. Zahra's breath caught, her fingers trembling as she lifted them, their paper worn but precious.

"You kept them," she whispered, her eyes shimmering with tears.

"Every one," Reza said, his voice thick, his hand covering hers.

She unfolded one carefully, and a faded rose petal fell out—brittle, fragmented, but still faintly pink. Her heart clenched. She'd pressed flowers into so many of her letters, hoping their scent would reach him, that a piece of their garden could travel to the frontlines. "I thought... I hoped you could still smell the roses," she said, her voice breaking.

"I could," he whispered, picking up the petal with reverence. "Even when it crumbled to dust, I could still smell it. It reminded me of home. Of you."

They stood, moving to a shelf where Zahra's letters from him rested, tied with a ribbon. Beside them sat other bundles—letters from Hossein, sent to her before his death in 1983, checking on her welfare, always calling her *sister*. Letters from Reza's parents, offering comfort during the war years. A few from her own mother and brother Farhad, though those were less frequent. They placed Reza's letters beside them, a quiet ritual, their shared history a bridge across the war's divide.

"Hossein wrote to you too," Reza said, his voice soft, a flicker of grief in his eyes as he touched one of the letters.

"He loved us both so much," Zahra said, her heart aching for the brother-in-law she'd lost. "He always asked if I needed anything, if the house was holding up. He worried about me like I was his own sister."

Reza's jaw tightened, and she saw the shadow pass over his face—the guilt of surviving when Hossein hadn't. She squeezed his hand.

"He'd be glad you're home," she said firmly. "He'd want you here, living."

The cats circled, Shirin nuzzling Reza's leg, Simin leaping onto the shelf, eyeing the letters curiously. Reza and Zahra laughed, the sound bright, dissolving the weight of grief for a moment.

The late morning sun filtered through the living room's lattice shutters, casting intricate patterns across the woven Persian rug. The air was soft with the scent of roses from the courtyard garden, mingling with the faint earthiness of tea lingering from breakfast. The letters on the shelf stood as a quiet testament to their years apart, and the weight of those words—inked promises of love, grief for Hossein, hopes for a future—pressed heavily on them both.

Reza pulled Zahra into a sudden, tight embrace, his scarred arms wrapping around her. She melted into him, her tunic soft against his cotton shirt, her cheek pressed to his chest, feeling the steady thud of his heart. His beard tickled her forehead, and she inhaled his scent—sandalwood from last night's bath and the warmth of his skin. The embrace was fierce, almost desperate, as if they could anchor each other against the tide of emotions swelling within.

"Zahra, my moonlit rose," Reza whispered, his voice trembling, his hands tightening on her back, fingers tracing the curve of her spine. His heart churned with the joy of being home, shadowed by the weight of eight years—trenches, blood, Hossein's fading voice, the shrapnel scars in his flesh.

Zahra's arms encircled him, her touch gentle but firm, her own heart heavy with the realization of how war had reshaped him. "Reza," she murmured, her voice breaking, "you're here now."

Her words were a vow, echoing her comforting whispers from the night before, when she'd cradled his scarred flesh to ease his pain. Seeking solace, Reza pulled back slightly, his eyes searching the room, landing on Zahra's ever-growing collection of books lining a wooden shelf—novels, histories, poetry, her passion since girlhood. He reached for a worn volume of Hafez, its cover familiar, the same one he'd carried when they first met in 1979.

"Let me read to you," he said, his voice soft but urgent, as if poetry could mend the fractures of their separation.

Zahra nodded, her smile shy but warm, and led him to a cushioned divan by the window, where sunlight spilled over them like a blessing. They curled together, her head resting on his shoulder, his arm around her, a light quilt draped over their laps. Shirin leapt up, nuzzling Reza's knee, while Simin sprawled nearby, her gray fur catching the light.

Reza opened the book, his scarred fingers trembling as he turned to a familiar page—not Hafez this time, but his own words, scrawled in the margins years ago during their courtship. His voice, rich with the

The Moonlit Rose of Isfahan

cadence of a poet, filled the room as he read his own verse: *"The rose blooms for love, not for duty."*

His voice grew stronger as he continued, reciting another line he'd written to her in a letter from the trenches this time, words that had sustained him through the darkest nights: *"Your love reminds me how to be whole again."*

Zahra's breath caught, her heart swelling with memory—the jasmine he'd given her under the mulberry tree, his boyish smile, Hossein's brotherly tease. Tears welled in her eyes, the weight of eight years crashing over her: the lonely nights with only her cats, the air raid drills, her father's death in 1983, his last wish for her happiness fulfilled now in Reza's return. She pressed closer, her hand resting on his chest, feeling his heartbeat, her fingers brushing his beard.

Reza's voice faltered, his own tears rising. "I wrote that in a trench," he said, his voice raw. "Thinking of you, of us. Hoping I'd live to say it to your face."

The memory of 1980—his first battle, the blood and chaos, Hossein's steady presence—flooded him, and the years apart felt like a chasm. He'd longed for this moment, this quiet with Zahra, yet the reality of their changed lives—his scars, her resilience—hit hard.

Zahra lifted her head, her almond eyes meeting his, shimmering with love and sorrow. "I kept your letters, your poems," she whispered, her voice trembling. "They were my light when you were gone."

Her words echoed their courtship, when she'd read novels to him, her voice shy but clear, and the pain of their separation tightened her chest.

They clung to each other, the divan a sanctuary, the Hafez book resting on Reza's lap, its pages a bridge to their past. His own words—not Rumi's, not Hafez's, but his—had carried them through the war. And now, here in the light, they were enough.

"We're home," Zahra said softly, her voice a vow, her eyes locked on his.

Reza kissed her forehead, his lips lingering, the gesture a promise to rebuild what war had stolen. The cats purred, the sunlight warmed, and the letters on the shelf stood sentinel, a testament to their enduring love. Emotions ran high, joy and grief intertwined, but their embrace held a promise: they would face the weight of those years together, moment by tender moment.

One day at a time.

Chapter Six

Isfahan, 1979

The late afternoon sun bathed Isfahan in amber and gold, its light filtering through the lattice shutters of the Azad family home, casting intricate patterns on the woven Persian rug. It was late fall, and the air outside had turned crisp, carrying the scent of wood smoke from evening fires and the last jasmine blooms clinging stubbornly to courtyard vines. Inside, the warmth of brewing tea and the earthy sweetness of rosewater filled the air, a comfort against the chill that crept through the streets as evening approached.

Zahra, only nineteen, stood nervously in the living room, her hands smoothing the modest blue dress that clung to her slender frame, her long dark hair tucked beneath a delicate scarf. Her eyes flickered with shy anticipation, her heart fluttering under the weight of her father's hopes.

Since her high school graduation, her father, a kind but ailing man, had been seeking suitors, determined to see his only daughter married to a good man before his illness worsened. Today, he'd brought her to meet Hossein, a respected twenty-six-year-old teacher whose family's reputation for piety and warmth made them a suitable match in his eyes.

The room buzzed with quiet formality, the scent of rosewater from a tray of sweets mingling with the earthy aroma of brewing tea. Ahmed, Zahra's father sat on a cushioned bench, his face pale but proud, exchanging pleasantries with Hossein's parents Salar and Fatemeh, their voices low and warm.

Hossein, tall and strong jawed, entered with a polite smile, his clean-shaven face and neat suit exuding the quiet confidence of a dedicated teacher. He greeted Zahra respectfully, his dark eyes kind but distant, as if sensing her youth. She returned his greeting, her voice soft, her cheeks flushing under his gaze, but her heart remained steady, unstirred. He was honourable, yes, but not hers.

Then Reza stepped into the room, and the world shifted.

At twenty-four, he was leaner than his older brother, his brown eyes soulful, a poet's heart shining through his boyish features. His clean-shaven face, younger than his years, carried a quiet intensity, and his simple shirt and trousers, slightly rumpled, hinted at a man more at home with books than formalities. He carried a small volume—not Hafez this time, but Saadi—his fingers brushing its worn cover, a gesture that caught Zahra's eye.

Their gazes met, and her breath caught. A spark, sudden and undeniable, warmed her chest, spreading like wildfire. His eyes held hers, soft yet piercing, as if he saw her, truly saw her, beyond the shy girl in the blue dress. She knew, in that moment, he was the one she wanted to get to know better. Not Hossein.

"Zahra, this is Reza, my brother," Hossein said, his voice warm, a smile playing on his lips as he noticed her reaction.

Reza bowed slightly, his smile shy but genuine, and offered a quiet *"Salaam."* Her reply was barely audible, her shyness making her hands tremble, but she couldn't look away. Her father, sensing the shift, raised an eyebrow but said nothing, his frail hand resting on his cane, his eyes flickering with hope for her happiness.

The families sat together, the low table set with tea, pistachio nougat, and rosewater-soaked *zulbia*. Zahra's mother poured tea, the clink of glass cups punctuating the conversation about family ties and shared values. Hossein, gracious and composed, spoke of his teaching and his upcoming scholarly projects, his tone respectful but detached when addressing Zahra. She nodded politely, her thoughts drifting to Reza, who sat quietly, his fingers tracing the Saadi book, his eyes stealing glances at her. When their gazes met again, he smiled—a small,

The Moonlit Rose of Isfahan

playful curve that made her heart skip, almost as if forecasting the joy she'd later know in their marital bed.

As the women retreated to the kitchen to prepare more sweets, Zahra lingered near the doorway, catching Reza's voice as he opened his book to show Hossein something. She glimpsed his handwriting in the margins, cramped but careful, and heard him recite softly: "Love is a flame that burns the soul gently." The words felt meant for her, his own creation rather than Saadi's, and she blushed, her fingers twisting her scarf. Hossein laughed, clapping Reza's shoulder. "Poetry again, brother? Save it for your own bride." His tone was teasing but kind, and Zahra sensed his approval, a brotherly warmth that saw her as too young for him, more like a sister he'd never had.

Later, in the courtyard where the last jasmine vines climbed the walls despite the autumn chill, Reza approached her, a single rose from the garden in his hand. The air was cool, their breath visible in small clouds, but the warmth between them was undeniable.

"For you," he said, his voice low, his eyes searching hers.

She took it, her fingers brushing his, the contact sending a shiver through her—whether from the temperature outside or his touch, she couldn't say. "Thank you," she whispered, her shyness battling her longing to know him. "Do you... read Saadi often?" she asked, bold for her.

His smile widened, boyish and warm. "Every day," he said. "His stories teach me about love. But sometimes—" He paused, glancing down at the book in his pocket. "Sometimes I write my own words in the margins. Things he didn't say, but I wish he had."

Her heart raced, the spark between them undeniable, a promise of the love they'd build.

Hossein watched from a distance, his smile supportive, his eyes reflecting a brotherly affection for Zahra. "She's like a sister already," he told Reza later, when the families parted, his blessing sealing their path.

Over the following weeks, as fall deepened into early winter, their courtship unfolded in chaperoned visits—tea in courtyards wrapped in quilts against the cold, walks by the Zayandeh River with Zahra's mother nearby and fallen leaves crunching underfoot, her father's approving nods from his sickbed. The city transformed around them: the domes of Isfahan caught the pale winter sun, the air smelled of wood smoke and cinnamon from street vendors' carts, and the first frost painted the garden walls in silver.

Reza shared poems he'd written, his voice trembling as he read to her under a bare mulberry tree, its branches stark against the grey sky: "Your eyes, my rose, hold the stars I'll follow home." Zahra, emboldened, read him passages from her novels, her voice soft but clear, her love for stories matching his for poetry. Their hands brushed over shared books, their glances lingered, each touch electric despite the winter chill, their smitten hearts weaving a bond. Zahra dreamed of a home with Reza, cats purring by a fire, roses blooming come spring, while he envisioned her as his muse, his partner in a life of love and verse.

He'd recently graduated from an engineering program, his intellectual brilliance earning him a teaching position thanks to Hossein's academic contacts. But his true passion was poetry—Hafez, Rumi, Saadi, and now his own words scribbled in margins—whose verses wove love and longing into his heart. Now, with a job secured, he dreamed of building a life not of complex equations, but of simple devotion, of being a husband to the girl whose almond eyes had captivated him. The rose he'd given Zahra at their first meeting was pressed between the pages of her own book, a dried promise she carried everywhere.

One evening in late winter, as the sun set early, painting the courtyard in hues of violet and rose, frost glittering on the stones, Reza offered her a sprig of jasmine—winter jasmine, stubborn and brave in the cold—his fingers lingering on hers.

"Will you build this life with me?" he asked, his voice raw, his eyes searching hers.

Zahra's heart soared, her shyness giving way to certainty. "Yes," she whispered, her smile radiant despite the cold, and Hossein, nearby, clapped Reza's shoulder, his grin wide. "She's family now," he said, his brotherly affection sealing their union.

Zahra's father Ahmed, frail but joyful, blessed their engagement from his sickbed, his last wish fulfilled. He would live to see them wed the following summer in Shiraz, unaware that just weeks after the wedding, war would loom on the horizon, ready to tear Reza from her side. But on this winter evening, with frost sparkling in the courtyard and jasmine brave against the cold, their love was a flame beginning to burn—gentle, as Reza's poetry promised, but strong enough to weather whatever storms lay ahead.

Chapter Seven
Isfahan, 1988

The mid-morning sun softened in Reza and Zahra's Isfahan home, its golden light filtering through the living room's lattice shutters, casting intricate shadows across the woven Persian rug. The air carried the faint scent of roses from the courtyard garden, mingling with the earthy warmth of tea from their breakfast, where Reza had fed Zahra pieces of lavash bread with date syrup, his fingers lingering near her lips—a sweetness that echoed their honeymoon mornings in Shiraz.

On the shelf across the room, the wartime letters stood as quiet sentinels—Zahra's to Reza with their pressed rose petals, his to her stained with trench dirt, and Hossein's before his death in 1983, calling her "sister" and checking on her welfare, as well as those from friends and extended family. They'd placed them there together just that morning, after unpacking Reza's worn canvas bag, each bundle tied with ribbon, a testament to love preserved across eight years of separation.

Reza and Zahra curled together on the cushioned divan by the window, quilts draped over their laps despite the warmth of the day. Shirin sprawled in a patch of sunlight on the rug, her tabby fur glowing amber, while Simin nuzzled Reza's knee, purring with the contentment only cats seem to possess. The Hafez volume lay open on Reza's lap, his scarred fingers resting on a page they both knew well—the poem

Jamila Mikhail

from their 1979 courtship under the mulberry tree.

Zahra's head rested on Reza's shoulder, her fuller curves pressed against his lean, scarred frame, her cream-coloured tunic soft against his cotton shirt. The weight of their separation—the trenches of his first battle in Khuzestan, her lonely nights tending their garden, Hossein's loss that still ached like an open wound—hung in the air between them. But his voice reading poetry that morning, and her gentle responses, had begun to weave something lighter, more comfortable. A bridge across the chasm.

"Your turn, my rose," Reza said, his baritone soft and playful, a smile tugging at his lips.

His grey-flecked beard caught the sunlight, and his soulful brown eyes—those eyes that had first captured her heart nine years ago—held a glint of mischief. He offered her the Hafez book, his scarred fingers brushing hers, the contact sparking that familiar warmth that had never dimmed, not even across oceans of time and distance.

Zahra blushed, her shyness resurfacing as it always did under his gaze, but she took the book, her almond-shaped eyes sparkling with love and a hint of playfulness. "Only if you promise to actually listen," she teased, her voice melodic, echoing those chaperoned afternoons under the mulberry tree when she'd been nineteen and so nervous her hands had trembled.

She flipped through the pages, her fingers tracing the worn edges, until she found what she was looking for—not Hafez's words this time, but Reza's own poetry, written in his careful script in the margins. The handwriting was cramped but deliberate, each letter formed with the precision of a man who understood that words were sacred things, vessels for the soul.

"This one," she said softly, her finger resting on the page. "The one you wrote during our courtship. Do you remember?"

Reza's breath caught. He remembered. Of course he remembered. He'd written it under that mulberry tree after she'd read him passages from her novels, her voice soft but clear, and he'd been so overcome with feeling that the words had simply poured out of him.

"Read it to me," he whispered, his voice suddenly thick with emotion. "I want to hear it in your voice."

The Moonlit Rose of Isfahan

Zahra's cheeks flushed deeper, but she began to read, her voice trembling at first, then growing steadier with each word: *"In your eyes, I find the sky where my heart soars, A poet's soul reflected in almond depths. The mulberry tree shelters our whispered vows, And jasmine blooms where your footsteps fall."*

The words hung in the air between them, heavy with memory. Reza's hand tightened on hers, his thumb tracing circles on her palm. Tears pricked his eyes—not the anguished tears of last night's nightmare, but something gentler. The bittersweet ache of remembering who they'd been before war fractured everything.

"I was so nervous that first day we met," Zahra said softly, closing the book but keeping her finger on the page. "Your brother Hossein was there, chaperoning, and he kept smiling at us like he knew something we didn't. Like he could see our future."

"He did know, Reza said, his voice rough. "He told me afterward that you were the one for me. That you'd looked at me the way our mother looks at my father." His jaw tightened at the mention of his brother, but Zahra's hand squeezed his, grounding him before the grief could pull him under.

"Another one," she said gently, turning the pages. "This one. 'The rose blooms for love, not for duty.' You wrote this one later, didn't you? After we were engaged?"

Reza nodded. "In the winter. We were in the courtyard, and you were shivering even though you wore that thick shawl. The last jasmine was blooming despite the frost, and you said it was stubborn. Brave. And I thought—" His voice broke slightly. "I thought that's what love is. Not duty. Not obligation. Just... blooming because that's what it's meant to do."

Zahra's eyes shimmered with unshed tears. She set the book aside and cupped his face, her palms warm against his beard. "Read me yours," she said. "The one about home. I need to hear it. After everything..."

He understood without her having to finish. After everything—the war, the nightmares, the way he'd broken in her arms last night—she needed the reminder that they were still *them*. Still Reza and Zahra, the poet and his rose.

He picked up the book again, finding another margin note, this one written in darker ink, the letters slightly larger. "I wrote this one in the trenches," he admitted. "After I got your letter with the rose petal. The one that crumbled to dust but still smelled like home."

His voice was barely above a whisper as he read: *"Your love is my home, Not walls of clay or stone, But the shelter of your heartbeat, The sanctuary of your touch. In trenches dark with blood and smoke, Your words are light, Your letters are my compass north, Your love is my home."*

Zahra made a sound—half laugh, half sob—and buried her face against his shoulder. Her body shook, and for a moment Reza feared he'd brought back last night's pain, but then he heard it: laughter. She was laughing even as she cried, her joy and grief so tangled they'd become inseparable.

"I kept every letter," she said against his shirt, her voice muffled. "Every single one. Even the ones where the ink ran from rain or... or worse. I'd read them until the paper fell apart, and then I'd read them again. Your poetry kept me alive, Reza. When I thought I couldn't bear one more night alone, one more air raid siren, one more day not knowing if you were—" She broke off, unable to finish.

"I'm here," he said, the words an echo of her comforting whispers from the night before. "I'm here, my rose. I came home to you."

They sat in silence for a long moment, holding each other as sunlight shifted across the room. Simin leaped onto the divan, purring loudly, and Zahra laughed again—this time pure joy—as the cat settled between them, demanding attention.

"Hossein would have liked this," Reza said quietly, scratching Simin's ears. "Us, here, reading poetry with the cats he gave us. He always said they were practice children." A smile tugged at his lips despite the ache in his chest. "He was so pleased with himself when he brought them to our wedding. Do you remember?"

"He said 'If you can keep these two alive, you'll be ready for actual babies,'" Zahra recalled, her own smile widening. "And I was so mortified because my mother was right there and she gave him such a look."

Reza's laugh was genuine this time, not weighted with grief. "And then Shirin immediately scratched you, and Hossein tried to convince you it was a sign of affection."

"It was not a sign of affection," Zahra said, mock-seriously. "It was a sign that I needed to learn how to hold cats properly." She paused, her expression softening. "He wrote to me about them, you know. During the war. Asked if they were behaving. Told me to give them extra food from him."

Reza's throat tightened. "He loved you like a sister. From the moment he decided you were too young for him but perfect for me."

"I'm glad he did," Zahra whispered. "Decide I was perfect for you, I mean. Even if..." She trailed off, but Reza understood. Even if it meant losing Hossein. Even if the price of their love had been higher than either of them could have imagined.

They traded the book back and forth after that, taking turns reading—Hafez's actual words now, not just Reza's additions. The poems wove around them like a blanket, softening the edges of their grief. Zahra read about gardens and nightingales, her voice steadier now, while Reza read about wine and beloved friends, his poet's heart finding solace in the familiar rhythms.

The hours slipped into early afternoon, the sun climbing higher, the room growing warmer. Shirin stretched in her sunbeam and padded over to join Simin on the divan, and soon both cats were purring loudly, a gentle soundtrack to the poetry.

Zahra glanced toward the window, toward the courtyard beyond where her roses grew. "Do you feel up to seeing the garden?" she asked, her voice gentle, remembering how fragile he'd seemed last night, how the nightmare had left him shaking and gasping for air.

Reza hesitated, his fingers fidgeting with the hem of his cotton shirt. The civilian clothes still felt wrong—too soft, too light, too *peaceful* after eight years of rough military uniforms. And the thought of going outside, of being exposed beyond these walls...

The sanctuary of their home—Zahra's books lining the shelves, her embroidered cushions, her dried roses in clay jars, the letters tied with ribbon—felt safer. Here, he could pretend the war was just a nightmare. Here, he could almost believe he was just a man in love with his wife, not a soldier learning to be human again.

"Not yet," he said softly, his voice apologetic. "I want to stay here. With you. With all this." He gestured vaguely around the room, encompassing the life she'd built during his absence, the home she'd maintained despite everything. "Is that... is that alright?"

Zahra's smile was warm, patient, understanding in a way that made his chest ache with love. She kissed his cheek, her lips lingering against his beard. "Then we'll stay," she said simply, as if there was no other answer she could have given. "The roses will still be there tomorrow. And the day after. We have time, my love."

We have time. The words settled something in Reza's chest, easing a tightness he hadn't fully acknowledged. They had time. Days. Weeks. Years, perhaps, if they were blessed. Time to relearn how to live. Time to heal. Time to be more than the ghosts that haunted him.

"Thank you," he whispered against her hair, breathing in her jasmine scent—the same perfume she'd worn on their wedding night, chosen deliberately to stir his memories. "For being patient with me."

"Always," Zahra promised, and kissed him again—on the forehead this time, gentle and reverent. "One day at a time, remember? We decided that yesterday."

He could manage that. With her beside him, he could manage anything.

As the afternoon light began to soften, stretching shadows across the living room floor, Zahra's stomach gave a quiet rumble. Reza heard it—his poet's attention to detail missing nothing—and laughed, the sound bright and unexpected even to himself.

"Hungry, my rose?" he teased, his eyes crinkling at the corners.

Zahra blushed, swatting his arm playfully. "We did miss lunch," she pointed out, her voice carrying that mix of shyness and boldness he'd always loved. "I was too content to move."

"Then let's remedy that," Reza said, setting the Hafez book aside with care, as if it were a precious thing. Which, he supposed, it was— filled with his youthful scribblings, the poetry of his heart before war tried to silence it. "What shall we make?"

Zahra stood, stretching, and the movement drew his eyes to the curve of her waist, the fullness of her hips beneath the cream tunic.

The Moonlit Rose of Isfahan

Eight years had changed her body in ways that stirred something warm and primal in him—she was no longer the slender girl of twenty he'd married, but a woman of twenty-eight, shaped by time and survival into something even more beautiful.

"*Khoresht-e bademjan,*" she said decisively, heading toward the kitchen. "With *tahdig*. Proper *tahdig*, not the rushed kind. The kind that takes patience."

Reza followed her, the cats trailing hopefully behind, their noses already lifted toward the promise of food. The kitchen still felt surreal to him—the clay jars of spices on the shelves that Zahra had organized, the worn wooden cutting board, the copper pots hanging from hooks. In the trenches, he'd dreamed of this. Of standing in a kitchen with his wife, chopping vegetables, talking about nothing important.

But now that he was here, his hands felt clumsy. Wrong. As if they didn't quite remember how to do simple, domestic things. His fingers, so used to gripping a rifle, to digging trenches, to pressing against wounds trying to stop the bleeding, fumbled with the eggplant Zahra handed him.

"Here," she said gently, moving to stand beside him at the low counter. Her hand covered his, guiding the knife. "Like this. You've forgotten, haven't you? How to do the simple things?"

He nodded, not trusting his voice. There was no judgment in her tone, only understanding. Only love.

"It'll come back," she promised, her hand still warm over his. "Your body and your mind both need time to remember peace."

Together they prepared the meal. Zahra showed him how to cut the eggplant into even pieces, how to salt them to draw out the bitterness. She set him to chopping herbs—fresh basil, mint, parsley from her garden—while she browned the lamb in the pot, the sizzling meat filling the kitchen with rich, savoury aroma.

"This reminds me of how I used to cook for the displaced families," Zahra said as she stirred, her voice thoughtful. "By the mosque. During the war. It helped, having something useful to do. Feeding people who'd lost their homes." She glanced at him. "I thought about you every time. Wondered if you were eating well. If you were warm. If you were..."

"Alive," Reza finished quietly. He set down the knife and moved behind her, wrapping his arms around her waist, resting his chin on her shoulder. "I thought about you too. Imagined you here, in this kitchen. Tending the garden. Reading your books. Living."

They stood like that for a moment, just breathing together, the lamb crackling in the pot, the scent of cooking meat and fresh herbs surrounding them. Zahra leaned back into his embrace, her body fitting against his as if eight years had never separated them.

"The herbs are going to burn if you don't finish chopping them," she said finally, but there was laughter in her voice.

Reza kissed her neck—just once, quick and playful—before returning to his task. "Slave driver," he teased, and she laughed, the sound bright and unguarded.

They fell into a rhythm after that, moving around each other in the small kitchen with increasing ease. Zahra added the eggplant to the pot with the lamb, along with dried limes that she pierced with a fork, releasing their tart perfume into the air. Tomatoes and onions followed, and then she covered it all to simmer, turning her attention to the rice.

"Watch," she told Reza, and he did, fascinated by the precise way she prepared the *tahdig*—the crispy rice that would form at the bottom of the pot. She heated oil and butter until it shimmered, then carefully layered the par-boiled rice, creating the foundation for that perfect golden crust. "This part takes patience," she said, adjusting the heat just so. "Too hot and it burns. Too cool and it never crisps."

"Like love," Reza said without thinking, and Zahra turned to look at him, her eyes soft.

"Yes," she agreed. "Like love. It takes patience. The right conditions. Careful tending."

As the rice steamed and the *khoresht* simmered, they worked together to clean up—washing cutting boards, wiping counters, moving in companionable silence. Reza found himself smiling at nothing in particular, just the simple domesticity of it all. His hands still felt clumsy, but less so. His body was beginning to remember.

When the food was nearly ready, Zahra retrieved the bottle of rosewater from the shelf—the same one she'd used in their bath last night—and drizzled a small amount over the rice before covering it again. "My grandmother's trick," she explained. "Makes the house smell like a garden."

And it did. The kitchen filled with the *scent* of roses layered over lamb and lime, herbs and butter, the *tahdig* beginning to crisp at the bottom of the pot. Reza's mouth watered. In the trenches, they'd eaten whatever they could get—often nothing more than stale bread and weak tea. The idea of a proper meal, prepared with care and love, felt almost decadent.

They set the low table in the living room together, spreading a cloth and arranging cushions. Zahra brought out the *khoresht* in a clay serving bowl, the eggplant tender and glossy in its fragrant sauce, and Reza watched with something like reverence as she inverted the pot of *tahdig* onto a platter, revealing the perfect golden crust.

"You've mastered it," he said, genuinely impressed.

"I had eight years to practice," Zahra replied, but there was no bitterness in her voice. Just simple truth.

They sat across from each other at first, but quickly abandoned that formality—Reza shifting to sit beside her instead, their shoulders touching, their knees brushing. Shirin and Simin appeared immediately, circling the table with hopeful mews, and Zahra laughed, breaking off a small piece of lamb for each cat.

"Spoiled," Reza accused, but he was smiling.

"Hossein would have done the same," Zahra said softly, and Reza nodded, the ache of his brother's absence present but bearable. Yes. Hossein would have spoiled these cats rotten.

They ate slowly, savouring each bite. Zahra broke off pieces of *tahdig* and fed them to Reza, her fingers lingering near his lips in a way that made his pulse quicken. He returned the favour with bites of eggplant soaked in the rich sauce, watching the way her eyes closed in appreciation.

"Good?" she asked, her smile knowing.

"Perfect," he said, and he wasn't just talking about the food.

They talked as they ate—small things at first. Zahra told him about the neighbours, about how Mr. Heydari had repaired the roof of the house after a bad storm. Reza told her about the other soldiers, the ones who'd survived, the letters he'd sent to their families of those who didn't. Not Amir. Not Hossein. He couldn't talk about them yet, not without the grief swallowing him whole. But the others. The ones whose deaths had been quick. Merciful, if such a thing existed in war.

As the meal wound down, their touches grew bolder. Zahra's hand rested on Reza's thigh, her fingers tracing idle patterns through the cotton of his trousers. His hand found the small of her back, thumb rubbing small circles that made her breath hitch slightly.

"Bath?" Zahra suggested, her voice soft but carrying a note of invitation that made Reza's pulse quicken.

He nodded, not trusting himself to speak. The memory of last night's bath—her hands on his scars, her acceptance of every wounded part of him—rose vivid and warm. But there was something different in her eyes now. A spark. A playfulness mixed with desire.

Together, they cleared the table, leaving the cats to fight over the last scraps of lamb. And as evening light began to paint the room in shades of amber and gold, they moved toward the small bathroom, toward the copper basin and the waiting rosewater, toward the next step in their rediscovery of each other.

The oil lamp cast its golden glow over the small bathroom's blue tiles, the flame steady and warm. Zahra filled the copper basin with water, testing the temperature with her fingertips until it was just right—hot enough to relax, but not scalding. Steam began to rise, curling through the air, and she added rosewater from the glass vial, its sweet floral scent immediately filling the small space.

Reza stood in the doorway, watching her with an intensity that made her aware of every movement—the way her tunic shifted as she reached for the sandalwood soap, the curve of her neck as she bent over the basin, the strands of hair that had escaped her pins to frame her face.

"Come," she said softly, turning to him with a shy smile. Even after last night, after years of marriage, there was still something about his gaze that made her blush. Something about being desired by him that felt new each time.

He stepped into the room, closing the door behind him. The space was intimate, small enough that they had to move carefully around each other. Zahra's hands went to his shirt, fingers working the buttons with deliberate slowness. This felt different than last night. Less urgent. Less intense. More playful.

"You're still too thin," she murmured as the shirt fell away, her fingers tracing the visible outline of his ribs. "We need to feed you properly. Build your strength back."

Reza caught her hand, bringing it to his lips. "Are you saying my wife doesn't think I'm handsome anymore?" His tone was light, teasing, but she heard the vulnerability beneath it—the fear that war had made him less in her eyes.

"I think," Zahra said, her free hand cupping his bearded cheek, "that you're the most handsome man I've ever seen. Scars and all. Especially the scars." She stood on her toes to kiss him, soft and sweet. "They're proof you came back to me."

His arms went around her waist, pulling her close, and the kiss deepened. His beard scratched pleasantly against her skin as his mouth moved over hers, and she made a soft sound of appreciation that seemed to embolden him. His hands slid down her back, tracing the curve of her spine, coming to rest at her hips.

When they broke apart, both breathing slightly harder, Zahra stepped back to remove her tunic, her movements slow and deliberate. She watched his eyes darken as more skin was revealed—her fuller breasts, her soft stomach, the curve of her hips. She'd been self-conscious about her body's changes at first, worried he'd find her less attractive. But the way he looked at her now, with such raw hunger tempered by tenderness, dispelled any doubt.

"Beautiful," Reza breathed, and she believed him.

She helped him with his trousers, careful around the shrapnel scar that extended down all the way to his groin—that angry line of raised tissue that still caused him phantom pain. Her fingers traced it gently, reverently, and she felt him shiver under her touch.

"Does it hurt?" she asked, concern creasing her brow.

"Not when you touch it," he said honestly. "When you touch it, it just feels like... like you're loving that part of me too. The broken part."

Her eyes stung with sudden tears, but she blinked them away. "There are no broken parts," she said fiercely. "Only parts that survived. Only parts that brought you home."

Naked now, they stepped into the basin together, the warm water rising to their calves, then their thighs as they sank down. It was a tight fit—the basin meant for one, or perhaps two people willing to sit very close—and their bodies pressed together in the warmth. Reza's back against the copper, Zahra nestled between his legs, her back to his chest.

For a moment, they simply sat, adjusting to the heat, to the intimacy of skin against skin. The water lapped gently around them, and the scent of rosewater and sandalwood wrapped them in a cocoon of peace. Simin appeared in the doorway, surveyed the scene with typical feline disdain for water, and padded away again.

Zahra reached for the cloth, dipping it in the water and bringing it to Reza's shoulder. She washed him slowly, reverently—his shoulders, his arms, down to his hands. Each burn mark from chemical exposure, each callus from gripping a rifle, each cut that had healed rough and uneven—she washed them all with the same tender care.

"Your turn," Reza murmured, taking the cloth from her. His hands were less practiced, but what they lacked in grace they made up for in devotion. He washed her back, his touch firm but gentle, and she felt the tension of the day—hell, of eight years—begin to drain away.

His hands ventured lower, tracing the curve of her spine down to the small of her back, and she arched slightly, a soft sound escaping her lips. Encouraged, he let his hands drift to her waist, her hips, fingers splaying across her stomach.

"Reza," she said, half protest, half invitation, as his hands moved higher to cup her breasts. The soap made his palms slick, and the sensation of him touching her like this—unhurried, exploratory—sent heat pooling low in her belly.

"Too much?" he asked against her ear, his breath warm. But his hands didn't stop their gentle kneading, thumbs brushing over her nipples in a way that made her gasp.

"No," she managed, her head falling back against his shoulder. "Not too much. Just... it's been so long. My body is remembering."

She could feel him against her back—his arousal evident, warm and firm—and knowing that she affected him this way, that even after everything he still desired her, made her own desire flare brighter.

She turned in the basin, water sloshing slightly, until she faced him. The movement brought them even closer, their chests pressed together, and she saw his eyes widen at her boldness. Taking the soap, she lathered her hands and began to wash his chest, her fingers tracing the scars there—the knife wound, the smaller marks from shrapnel. Her hands drifted lower, following the line of dark hair down his stomach, and when her soapy fingers wrapped around him, he sucked in a sharp breath.

"Zahra—" Her name was half prayer, half warning.

"Shh," she said, her movements gentle but deliberate. "Let me. You're always taking care of everyone, you've always been this way. Let me take care of you."

She stroked him slowly, carefully, mindful of the scar tissue nearby. His hips shifted, seeking more contact, and she obliged, her grip firm enough to give pleasure without causing pain. His hands found her thighs, sliding upward, and when his fingers slipped between her legs, finding her already slick with more than just bathwater, she moaned softly.

They touched each other like that in the cooling water—a slow, sensual exploration that was both familiar and new. Their kisses grew deeper, tongues tangling, breaths mingling. The lamp flame flickered, casting dancing shadows on the tiled walls.

"Bed," Reza finally managed, his voice rough with need. "I want you in our bed, my rose. Properly."

Zahra nodded, reluctantly releasing him. They helped each other from the basin, water streaming off their bodies, and grabbed towels to dry off with quick, impatient movements. The air felt cool against their heated skin.

Reza wrapped his towel around his waist, and Zahra did the same with hers, tucking it above her breasts. But before they could leave the bathroom, he pulled her close again, kissing her deeply, his hands tangling in her wet hair.

"I love you," he said against her lips. "Every day in those trenches, I dreamed of this. Of you. Of coming home and making love to my wife without fear that it might be the last time."

"It won't be the last time," Zahra promised, her hands framing his face. "We have so many nights ahead of us, my love. So many mornings. God willing, so many years to rediscover each other."

Hand in hand, still damp and flushed, they made their way to the bedroom, where their marital bed awaited and the evening light painted everything in shades of amber and gold.

The bedroom welcomed them with familiar warmth—the embroidered quilts Zahra had maintained so carefully, the woven Persian rug soft beneath their feet, the oil lamp already lit and casting its gentle glow. Shirin and Simin had claimed their usual spot at the foot of the bed, curled together in a purring mass, but they barely glanced up at the arrival of their humans.

Reza and Zahra climbed into bed, the quilts cool against their still-damp skin. For a moment they simply lay facing each other, not touching yet, just looking—really looking—at each other in the lamplight.

"How are you feeling?" Zahra asked softly, her hand reaching out to trace the line of his beard. "After everything today. The poetry, the cooking, the bath. Is it... too much? Too fast?"

It was a question she'd learned to ask after last night's nightmare, after watching him break apart in her arms. She'd realized then that she couldn't assume—couldn't take for granted that just because he was home, he was *fine*. That healing would be a long, winding road with setbacks and detours, not a straight line from broken to whole.

Reza caught her hand, pressing his lips to her palm. "It's not too much," he said, his voice low and sincere. "It's... overwhelming sometimes. Being here. Being *home* after so long of surviving. But it's a good overwhelming. Does that make sense?"

"Yes," Zahra said, because it did. She felt it too—the strangeness of having him here after eight years of absence. The way her heart would suddenly seize with joy just at the sight of him reading across the room. The way she kept touching him, needing the confirmation that he was real, solid, *here*.

"And you?" Reza asked, his thumb stroking the inside of her wrist. "How are you feeling, my rose? Your body... after last night, I know you were sore. Are you—" He paused, suddenly shy despite the intimacy they'd just shared in the bath. "Are you comfortable? Do you

The Moonlit Rose of Isfahan

need more time before we..."

"I'm tender," Zahra admitted, her cheeks flushing. "But not in pain. And I want this, Reza. I want you. I've dreamed of this for so long—having you home, being able to touch you, to love you properly without fear or separation. I've had to wait long enough, I don't want to wait anymore."

She shifted closer, closing the small distance between them, and rested her hand on his chest, feeling the steady beat of his heart beneath her palm. "But I need you to tell me," she continued, her voice dropping to a whisper. "If something triggers you. If a touch or a memory becomes too much. Promise me you'll tell me?"

Reza's eyes shimmered with emotion. "I promise," he said. "And you promise the same? If I'm too rough, too eager, if something hurts—"

"I promise," Zahra interrupted, leaning in to kiss him softly. "We'll take care of each other. That's what we do."

They kissed again, longer this time, and Reza felt something loosen in his chest—a knot of anxiety he hadn't fully acknowledged until it began to unravel. They would be all right. They would stumble, surely, but they would face it together. One day at a time. He held on to that belief.

"There's something else," he said, pulling back slightly. His hand moved down to rest on his stomach, near the large shrapnel scar. "This position we're about to try... woman-on-top, like in Shiraz. It's not... I mean, I can see the scar more clearly. You can see it more clearly. And I worry—"

"Stop," Zahra said gently but firmly, her hand covering his. "I've seen your scars. I've kissed your scars. I've held you through the phantom pain. There is nothing about your body that could ever make me turn away." Her eyes met his, fierce with conviction. "You're beautiful to me, Reza. Every part of you. Especially the parts that survived."

His throat worked as he swallowed hard. "I don't know what I did to deserve you."

"You loved me," Zahra said simply. "You came home to me. That's enough. That's everything. That's all I've ever asked for."

She paused, then added with a shy smile, "Besides, I'm the one who should be nervous. My body has changed so much. I'm not the girl you married. I'm... softer now. Fuller. What if—"

"What if I love every new curve?" Reza interrupted, his hand sliding down to her hip, squeezing gently. "What if I think you're even more beautiful now than you were then? What if the thought of you on top of me, your breasts above me, your hair falling around us like a curtain—what if that's all I've been able to think about since you mentioned it?"

Zahra laughed, swatting his chest playfully even as her cheeks flamed. "You're still a poet, even when you're being scandalous."

"Especially when I'm being scandalous," Reza countered with a grin. "Poets are experts at beautiful sin."

They kissed again, and this time the hesitation was gone, replaced by mutual desire and trust. Zahra's hands moved to untuck Reza's towel, letting it fall away, while he did the same for hers. Naked now beneath the quilts, they pressed together, skin against skin, warmth against warmth.

"Ready?" Zahra asked, a hint of self-consciousness creeping into her voice despite her earlier boldness.

"Ready," Reza confirmed, lying back against the pillows, his eyes never leaving hers. "Show me, my rose. Show me how strong you've become. Show me the woman who survived eight years and kept our home alive. Show me my Zahra."

And with a shy smile that slowly transformed into something bolder, more confident, Zahra moved to straddle him, ready to rediscover the intimacy they'd first explored in Shiraz, in the early days of their marriage when the world was simpler and war hadn't yet scarred either of them.

Zahra moved slowly, carefully, as she straddled Reza's hips, the embroidered quilts falling away from her body. The lamplight painted her skin in shades of gold and amber, catching in her dark hair that spilled over her shoulders in still-damp waves. She was acutely aware of her body—the way her fuller breasts swayed slightly with the movement, the soft curve of her stomach, the width of her hips—all the changes that eight years had wrought.

The Moonlit Rose of Isfahan

But when she looked down at Reza, at the way the soulful brown eyes she'd always adored had darkened with desire, at the way his scarred hands reached up to steady her hips with such tenderness, all her insecurity melted away. He was looking at her like she was the most beautiful thing he'd ever seen. Like she was poetry made flesh.

"Zahra," he breathed, his voice rough with want. His hands slid up from her hips to her waist, thumbs tracing idle patterns on her skin. "My moonlit rose."

She leaned down to kiss him, her hair creating a curtain around their faces, and his hands moved to cup her breasts. The touch was gentle at first, almost hesitant, as if he were afraid of being too bold. But when she made a soft sound of encouragement against his mouth, his touch grew more confident, more sure.

The weight of her breasts in his palms felt different than he remembered—fuller, heavier, more womanly. Everything about her felt different, and yet fundamentally, perfectly *Zahra*. His thumbs found her nipples, already hardened, and he circled them gently, drawing a gasp from her that broke their kiss.

"Is this—" he started to ask, but she cut him off with another kiss, her hands framing his bearded face.

"Perfect," she whispered against his lips. "You're perfect. This is perfect."

She reached between them, her hand wrapping around him, and his breath caught at the contact. She stroked him once, twice, feeling him pulse in her grip, warm and firm and ready. Then she positioned herself above him, the tip of him just barely pressing against her entrance.

For a moment, they simply looked at each other, breathing in sync, hearts racing in tandem. This was it—the moment of joining, of becoming one again after so long apart. The weight of eight years hung between them, but also the promise of all the years ahead.

"I love you," Zahra whispered, and slowly, carefully, she began to lower herself onto him.

The sensation was intense—the stretch, the fullness, the slight sting as her body adjusted to accommodate him. She was still tender from their lovemaking the night before, and she had to move slowly.

Reza's hands tightened on her hips, his breath coming in short gasps as her warmth enveloped him. "Slow," he managed, his voice strained. "Take your time, my rose. We have all night."

She nodded, pausing when she'd taken about half of him, giving her body time to adjust. Her hands braced on his chest, feeling his heart racing beneath her palms, feeling the ridges of scars, his chest hair he didn't have when they'd gotten married—all testaments to survival, to coming home, to love that endured even through hell.

"Do you remember?" she asked softly, a small smile playing at her lips despite the intensity of the moment. "The first time we tried this? In Shiraz?"

Reza's eyes crinkled at the corners, a smile breaking through the desire. "How could I forget?"

Shiraz, 1980

The guesthouse bedroom had been warm despite the autumn evening, the oil lamp casting dancing shadows on the walls. They'd been married for perhaps a week—maybe two—and were still learning each other's bodies with the fumbling eagerness of youth.

"Like this?" Zahra had asked, her voice trembling with nervousness as she straddled Reza for the first time. At twenty, she was slender as a reed, her breasts small but pert, her hips narrow. Her long hair fell around them both, and she was so nervous she was shaking.

Reza, twenty-four and no more experienced than his bride, had reached up to steady her. "I think so?" he'd said, making it a question, and they'd both laughed—nervous, giddy laughter that eased some of the tension.

"The book said—" Zahra had started, referring to the marriage guide her mother had slipped her before the wedding, her cheeks flaming.

"Forget the book," Reza had interrupted gently, his hands sliding up to cup her face. "Let's just... try. Together. If it doesn't work, we'll laugh about it."

She'd nodded, taking a breath, and began to lower herself onto him.

The sensation had been overwhelming—different from the missionary position they'd grown accustomed to. Deeper. More intense. The sensation had made them both gasp.

"Oh," Zahra had breathed, her eyes wide. "Oh, this is—"

"Different," Reza had finished, his hands moving to her hips, his own eyes glazed with sensation. "Very different."

She'd tried to move, lifting herself slightly and sinking back down, but her movements were clumsy, uncertain. Her thighs had begun to shake with the effort, unused to this particular exertion. And then she'd looked down at herself—at the way her breasts bounced with even her small movements—and had immediately tried to cover herself with her hands, mortified.

"No," Reza had said, catching her wrists gently. "Don't hide, my rose. You're beautiful. Let me see you."

"But they're—" she'd protested, her face burning. "They're moving so much, and I look—"

"You look like my wife," Reza had said firmly, sitting up to kiss her, his hands replacing hers on her breasts. "You look like the woman I love. You look like you're mine."

His touch had been tentative but affectionate, cupping her breasts, his thumbs brushing her nipples in a way that made her gasp and forget her embarrassment. And when she'd started to move again—still clumsily, still uncertain—his hands had guided her, showing her the rhythm, encouraging her.

"There," he'd murmured, his voice thick. "Like that, Zahra. Just like that."

They'd made love that way for a few minutes before Zahra's trembling legs had given out and they'd collapsed together, laughing and gasping and tangled in the sheets. It had been awkward and imperfect and utterly beautiful.

Afterward, as they lay curled together, Reza had traced patterns on her stomach and whispered poetry: "Your body is a garden where love blooms eternal." And she'd blushed and swatted him, but she'd glowed with the compliment, feeling cherished despite their fumbling.

"We'll get better at it," he'd promised, kissing her temple. "We have all the time in the world to practice."

❊ ❊ ❊

"We were so young," Zahra said now, continuing her slow descent onto Reza until she was fully seated. "So nervous. So... innocent."

"We still didn't know what war was," Reza agreed, his voice rough, his hands sliding up her sides to cup her breasts—fuller now, heavier, changed by time. "Didn't know what eight years apart would do to us."

"Are we still innocent?" Zahra asked, beginning to move slowly, carefully, finding her rhythm. The sensation was overwhelming—pleasure tinged with that sweet ache of tenderness, fullness that bordered on too much but was somehow exactly right.

"No," Reza said honestly, his hands kneading her breasts gently, his thumbs teasing her nipples in a way that made her movements falter. "But we're still *us*. Still Reza and Zahra. Still learning each other. Rediscovering each other."

She leaned down to kiss him, her hair falling around them again in that curtain of intimacy, and he met her mouth eagerly, his tongue tangling with hers as she continued to move above him. One of his hands left her breast to guide her hip, helping her find the angle that made them both gasp with pleasure.

"That's it," he murmured against her lips. "You're so beautiful like this. So strong. My Zahra who survived eight years. My Zahra who kept our home alive. My Zahra who loved me even when I was a world away in the trenches."

His words, paired with the steady rhythm of their bodies, with the friction and the way he filled her so completely, made tears spring to Zahra's eyes even as pleasure built low in her belly. "I never stopped loving you," she gasped, sitting up straighter now, her hands braced on his chest as she moved with more confidence. "Not for one moment. Not even when I was afraid you were dead."

Reza's hands slid down to grip her hips, guiding her movements, and he began to lift his own hips in counterpoint, meeting her rhythm. The angle change made them both moan with exquisite pleasure.

"Your breasts," Reza managed, his eyes fixed on them, watching the way they bounced with each movement, the way her nipples had tightened into hard peaks. "Zahra, you're so—"

She felt the familiar flush of embarrassment—the same shy modesty that had overtaken her in Shiraz when she'd tried to cover herself—but she fought it down. This was her husband. The man who'd survived hell to come home to her. The man who looked at her scars and changes with nothing but love.

"Touch them," she said boldly, and his hands obeyed immediately, cupping her breasts, kneading them with that same affectionate gentleness from their youth, but tempered now with the confidence of a man who knew his wife's body, who still remembered what pleased her.

"Reza," she gasped, her movements becoming less controlled, more urgent. "I'm—I can't—"

"Yes you can," he said, his voice firm despite being breathless. "Let go, my rose. I've got you. I'll always have you."

His hands left her breasts to grip her hips again, and he took over the rhythm, lifting his hips to meet hers, thrusting up into her with deep, measured strokes that made her see stars. Zahra felt herself spiral toward the edge, her breath coming in short gasps.

"Reza," she managed, his name a prayer, a plea, a promise. "Reza, I—"

"I'm here," he said, his own control beginning to fray. "I'm right here with you, Zahra. My moonlit rose. My home. My heart."

The words pushed her over. She came with a cry, her body clenching around him in rhythmic waves, pleasure crashing over her in pulsing cascades that made her vision blur. She felt him follow moments later—his grip on her hips tightening almost to the point of pain, his back arching off the bed as he buried himself deep and found his own release.

For a long moment, neither of them moved. Zahra collapsed forward onto his chest, their hearts racing against each other, their breathing harsh and uneven. She felt only satisfaction. Completion.

"Zahra," Reza breathed, his arms wrapping around her, holding her close. "My God, Zahra."

She laughed—a small, breathless sound—and kissed his shoulder, his neck, his beard-roughened jaw. "We've gotten better at it," she said, referencing his long-ago promise. "We definitely needed the practice."

He laughed too, the sound rumbling through his chest beneath her ear. "Eight years of dreaming about this," he said. "Eight years of imagining your body above mine, your hair falling around us, the feeling of coming home to you. And somehow the reality is even better than the fantasy."

Zahra lifted her head to look at him, her heart so full it ached. "Even with my changes? Even with—"

"*Especially* with your changes," Reza interrupted, his hand coming up to trace her face. "You're not a girl anymore, Zahra. You're a woman. Strong and capable and so beautiful it makes my heart hurt. I love every curve, every change, every sign of the years you lived without me. Because you survived. You kept going. You waited for me."

Tears slipped down her cheeks—happy tears, overwhelmed tears—and he caught them with his thumbs. "I love you," she whispered. "I love you so much I don't have words for it. And I'm a reader. I should have words."

"Then let me give you words," Reza said, his poet's heart rising to the surface. "Let me give you the poem I've been writing in my head since I came home."

And there, in the lamplight, with her still joined to him, their bodies cooling in the evening air, Reza recited: "Eight years apart could not diminish The flame that burns between us still. Your body, changed by time and solitude, Is the map of your survival, and I trace it with reverence. Your love, constant as the stars above Isfahan, Guided me through trenches dark with death, Through nights when I forgot my own name, But never yours. You are my moonlit rose, Blooming in the garden of my heart, And I am home, Finally, eternally, Home."

By the time he finished, they were both crying—soft tears that spoke of joy and grief intertwined, of love that had endured the unsurvivable, of coming home to each other across a distance measured not in miles but in scars and nightmares and years stolen by war.

Zahra kissed him then—long and slow and deep—pouring into it everything she couldn't say aloud. And when she finally rolled off him, reaching for the warm cloth by the lamp that had become their ritual, she cleaned them both with tender care.

They settled under the quilts afterward, her head on his chest, his arm around her shoulders, their legs tangled together. The cats had long since fled the disruption, but Zahra could hear them in the living room, probably curled together on the divan where she and Reza had read poetry that morning.

"That was better than Shiraz," Zahra said sleepily, her fingers tracing idle patterns on his chest. "Much better."

"Mm," Reza agreed, his own eyes heavy with satisfaction and exhaustion. "Though Shiraz had its charm. We were so eager. So fumbling."

"We giggled so much," Zahra remembered, smiling against his skin. "I thought we'd never figure it out."

"But we did," Reza said, pressing a kiss to the top of her head. "Just like we'll figure out everything else. Day by day. Night by night."

"Together," Zahra added, the word both promise and benediction.

"Together," Reza echoed.

Sleep came gently this time, not as the ambush it had been the night before. There were no sudden jolts into nightmare, no screams for Hossein, no phantom pain from shrapnel wounds long healed. Just the slow, natural descent into dreams, wrapped in warmth and love and the feeling of being home.

Zahra felt Reza's breathing even out first, his chest rising and falling in the steady rhythm of deep sleep. His arm remained draped over her waist, his hand splayed across her stomach, and even in sleep he held her as if she were precious. As if she were the thing that anchored him to this world.

She stayed awake a bit longer, savouring this moment—the weight of him beside her, the sound of his breathing, the way the lamplight flickered across his peaceful face. No furrows of pain creased his brow. No tension pulled at the corners of his mouth. He looked, for the first time since coming home, truly at peace.

Tomorrow would bring its own challenges, she knew. The nightmares wouldn't disappear after just one good night. The war's scars—physical and mental—wouldn't heal overnight. Reza would still struggle with civilian clothes, with loud noises, with the simple act of living without constant vigilance. And she would still wake sometimes in the night, reaching for him in fear that he'd disappeared, that his return had been nothing but a cruel dream.

But they had tonight. And tomorrow night. And all the nights that followed. They had poetry and cats and rose gardens. They had Hossein's letters and the memory of his blessing. They had each other.

Outside, the Isfahan night was quiet, the ceasefire holding. The stars—the same stars that had watched over Reza in the trenches, that had witnessed Zahra's lonely vigil—shone down with indifferent beauty. The moon, Reza's moonlit rose, cast its gentle light through the bedroom curtains, painting silver stripes across the quilts.

Eventually, Shirin and Simin padded back into the room, having decided the humans were finally settled. They leaped onto the bed—Shirin at the foot as always, Simin curling into the space between Zahra's legs—and began their nightly purring before falling asleep too, a sound that spoke of contentment and simple feline satisfaction.

Zahra finally let her own eyes close, her hand covering Reza's where it rested on her stomach. She could still feel the pleasant ache between her legs, the tenderness that spoke of their lovemaking. Her breasts were sensitive where Reza had touched them, her lips slightly swollen from his kisses. Her body was a map of their reunion, and she cherished every sensation.

"I love you," she whispered into the darkness, not sure if he could hear her in sleep, not caring if he couldn't. The words needed to be said anyway. "Thank you for coming home to me. Thank you for surviving. Thank you for loving me through everything."

In sleep, Reza's arm tightened around her waist, drawing her closer against his chest. And if it was simply an unconscious movement, some primal need to hold onto warmth and safety, it was enough. More than enough.

The lamp flame guttered and went out, leaving only moonlight to illuminate the bedroom. The scent of rosewater still lingered in the air, mixing with the sandalwood from their bath, the musk of their lovemaking, and the faint jasmine of Zahra's perfume. The embroidered quilts rose and fell with their synchronized breathing.

And in that quiet room, in that Isfahan home that had waited eight years for this moment, Reza and Zahra slept—truly, peacefully, deeply—in each other's arms.

Tomorrow they would wake to sunlight and cats demanding breakfast and the start of another day in their rebuilding of a life together. There would be more poetry to read, more meals to share, more scars to kiss, more nightmares to survive, more love to give and receive.

But tonight, they simply slept.

Together.

Home.

Finally.

Chapter Eight

Southern Front, 1982

The night air on the southern front hung thick and foul, carrying the stench of death that no man could ever forget—gunpowder, smoke, unwashed bodies packed too close in trenches that had become mass graves for the living. The world could shatter at literally any moment with the distant thud of artillery or the whistle of an incoming shell. The trench itself was a jagged wound carved into the earth in Khuzestan, its walls slick with mud from recent rains, crumbling under their own weight, the sandbags rotting and split, spilling their guts like the men who'd fallen here days before.

Reza, now twenty-six, slumped against the trench wall, his uniform stiff with dried sweat and caked mud, the fabric chafing against skin that had long ago lost its softness from civilian life. His rifle—a Kalashnikov that had jammed twice in yesterday's skirmish—leaned beside him, its metal cold against his thigh. His lean frame, once boyish and graceful when he'd married Zahra nearly two years ago, had grown gaunt from hunger and the endless grind of patrols. Meals were irregular: sometimes stale bread and weak tea, sometimes nothing but the gnawing emptiness that made his stomach clench and his hands shake.

The war's toll was etched deep. His cheeks, once full, had hollowed, his jawline sharp beneath stubbled skin he hadn't had time to shave in days. His brown eyes, those eyes Zahra had fallen in love with in

Isfahan's courtyards, were now shadowed with exhaustion and something darker—the weight of things seen that could never be unseen. The faces of the dead haunted him: young soldiers, boys really, their bodies twisted in the mud, their wedding rings catching the light, their mothers' names on their lips as they died. He'd watched comrades fall, their blood soaking into the thirsty earth, and each time a part of him died with them.

His hands trembled slightly as he clutched Zahra's latest letter, the paper worn soft from countless readings, the ink smudged where his tears had fallen. Her words were his lifeline, the only thing tethering him to the man he'd been—the poet, the dreamer, the gentle husband who'd whispered verses against her skin. She wrote of the garden they'd planted together, of roses blooming despite her loneliness, of the cats Hossein had given them curled together on their bed. She pressed flowers into the pages—jasmine, lavender, roses—and even when they crumbled to dust, their scent lingered, a ghost of home that made his chest ache with longing.

Hossein, now twenty-nine, sat close beside him, his broad shoulders hunched against the cold, his strong jaw hidden beneath several days' growth of stubble. His eyes, bloodshot from smoke and sleepless nights, still held that stubborn spark of life—the same determined glint that had made him volunteer for this hell the moment Reza's draft notice arrived. *"I'm not letting you face this alone,"* he'd said, gripping Reza's shoulders, his voice fierce with brotherly love. *"You'll need someone to watch your back."* And so Hossein had left everything behind: his teaching position, his careful plans for a future he'd been building brick by patient brick, but what he'd left most painfully was Leyla.

They'd met briefly before the war, at a gathering of teachers in Isfahan. Leyla taught literature at a girls' school, her passion for poetry matching Hossein's own love of words. They'd spoken for perhaps an hour, maybe two, standing beneath a pergola heavy with wisteria, discussing Persian poetry while the evening light turned golden. She'd quoted a verse, her voice soft but clear, and when she'd looked up at him, her dark eyes bright with intelligence and warmth, something in Hossein's chest had shifted. He'd asked permission to write to her. She'd said yes, her cheeks flushing pink.

The Moonlit Rose of Isfahan

That should have been the beginning of their courtship. In normal times, he would have visited her family, brought gifts, sat in formal living rooms drinking tea while their parents assessed his character and prospects. There would have been chaperoned walks, shared books, the slow dance of getting to know each other under the watchful eyes of tradition. They would have married within a year, perhaps two. He'd imagined it all—their wedding, her in white, his hands shaking as he placed the ring on her finger.

But then came September 1980, Iraq's invasion, and Reza's draft notice. And Hossein had made his choice without hesitation: his little brother needed him. Everything else—career, home, the future he'd dreamed of with Leyla—all of it went on hold. *"I'll come back,"* he'd told her when he'd visited to explain, his heart breaking at the tears in her eyes. *"Wait for me. We'll have our courtship when this madness ends. I promise."*

She'd waited. And she'd written.

Her letters came regularly, each one a small miracle that made it through the chaos of war. She wrote about her students, about books she was reading, about the garden behind her family's home where a jasmine tree bloomed. She quoted poetry—sometimes classical verses from Hafez, sometimes her own words, tentative and beautiful. She wrote about the stars she watched at night, wondering if he could see them too from wherever he was. She wrote about dreams of a life after the war, of quiet evenings and shared books and growing old together.

And through those letters, Hossein had fallen completely, irrevocably in love.

The brief meeting before the war had sparked interest, attraction, possibility. But these letters—raw and honest in ways formal courtship never allowed—had revealed her soul. He knew her now: her fears and hopes, her sharp humour and gentle kindness, the way she saw beauty in small things—a bird's song, sunlight through leaves, the smell of rain. He knew she cried at sad poetry and laughed at terrible puns. He knew she worried about her aging grandfather and doted on her younger sisters.

He knew she dreamed of having a fountain in the courtyard, a large herb garden, of teaching her own children to read, of being loved. He loved her. God, he loved her. And he ached with the fear that he might not survive to marry her, that all these promises and plans might end with his blood soaking into the soil.

Now, in this wretched trench with death an ever-present shadow, Hossein pulled a battered metal flask from his pack and passed it to Reza. The tea inside was lukewarm, bitter and gritty with the dregs that hadn't settled, but it was something. A faint echo of their mother's brewing back in Isfahan—that perfect balance of bergamot and sugar that she'd mastered over decades of practice.

"Drink, little brother," Hossein said, his voice hoarse from shouting orders during yesterday's artillery barrage, but still warm, still carrying that familiar note of protective affection. A flicker of mischief broke through the weariness in his eyes, that spark that had never quite died despite everything they'd endured.

Reza took the flask, their fingers brushing in the exchange—a touch that carried the weight of brotherhood, of shared childhood memories. Hossein teaching him to climb the mulberry tree in their courtyard, shielding him from neighbourhood bullies, teasing him mercilessly during his courtship when Zahra had chosen the younger brother, the poet, over the practical teacher.

The tea burned Reza's throat going down, the heat a fleeting warmth against the bone-deep cold of the night. He handed it back, and their shoulders pressed together in the cramped trench, a silent vow of brotherhood. Whatever horror tomorrow brought—artillery, chemical gas, hand-to-hand combat with Iraqi soldiers who were just as frightened and far from home as they were—they'd face it together.

Twenty meters down the trench, a soldier coughed wetly, the sound thick with fluid that might be infection or worse—the lingering effects of the mustard gas that had rolled over their position three days ago. The masks never fit properly, never sealed completely, and the gas found every gap. Reza's own throat still burned when he breathed too deeply, his eyes still watered and stung. Men had died from it, their lungs melting, drowning in their own fluids while comrades could only watch helplessly.

Hossein leaned closer, his breath visible in the cold air, scanning the darkness beyond the trench for eavesdroppers or, worse, Iraqi scouts. The night was never truly quiet—distant artillery rumbled like thunder,

The Moonlit Rose of Isfahan

flares occasionally painted the sky in sickly yellow, revealing the cratered no-man's-land between the lines, the bodies still lying where they'd fallen because retrieval meant certain death.

"Reza," Hossein whispered, his voice softening, vulnerability cracking through his usual stoic facade—the strong older brother who'd always had answers, always knew what to do. "I've got something to tell you."

Reza turned, concern etching lines into his young face that made him look older than his years. "What is it, brother?" His baritone was low, careful not to carry beyond their small space.

Hossein paused, a tired smile tugging at his cracked lips, his hand gripping Reza's shoulder tightly, as if anchoring them both against the war's unrelenting current. "I've fallen in love," he confessed, the words a fragile light in the trench's oppressive gloom. "Completely, hopelessly in love."

Reza's eyes widened, surprise cutting through his exhaustion. For a moment, the war receded—the stench, the cold, the constant fear—replaced by something achingly normal. His brother, talking about love. "Leyla?" he asked, though he already knew. Hossein had mentioned his growing feelings for her in passing before they'd deployed, describing how they grew briefly, carefully, as if the words themselves might jinx the fragile possibility.

"Leyla," Hossein confirmed, his voice thick with emotion, his eyes glistening in the dim light of a hidden lantern. "I may have only met her three times before all this started—just one proper evening when you really think about it. We'd talked for maybe two hours. But Reza, her letters... they're poetry. She writes about the stars, her garden, her students. She tells me about the jasmine tree in her family's yard that reminds her of me—stubborn, she says, still blooming despite everything trying to kill it." He pulled a crumpled letter from his chest pocket, his fingers tracing the delicate script as if touching something sacred.

"She dreams about us having a life together after this," Hossein continued, his voice dropping to barely a whisper, as if speaking too loudly might shatter the dream. "A home, children, growing old side by side. She wants to plant a garden together—jasmine and roses, just like you and Zahra have. Simple things. Normal things. Things that feel impossible from here."

Reza's heart swelled, joy and sorrow intertwining. Joy for his brother finding love, sorrow for the timing of it all—this beautiful thing blooming in the shadow of death. "Hossein... love," he said, his voice cracking with emotion, pulling his brother into a fierce, trembling hug, their foreheads touching in the lantern's faint glow. The moment was raw, tender, their bond a sanctuary against the war's brutality. "Tell me about her. Tell me everything."

Hossein pulled back slightly, his eyes twinkling with mischief despite the tears threatening to fall, the old teasing brotherly dynamic surfacing like a life raft. "But you'll have to school me, little brother," he said, his tone playful, poking Reza's chest with one finger. "You're the expert—you snagged Zahra and married first. What's the secret to pleasing a woman? Does Zahra write about your... other poetic talents?" He waggled his eyebrows suggestively, and despite everything—the horror, the death, the uncertainty—Reza found himself laughing.

The sound felt foreign, almost wrong in this place, but also necessary. A rebellion against death, a declaration that they were still human, still capable of joy. "You, asking me?" Reza retorted, warmth flooding his chest, the teasing as familiar as breathing. "The big brother who taught me everything—now begging lessons from the poet? I bet Leyla's already charmed by your terrible jokes. Remember how you tried to impress Zahra's family by quoting Saadi, but you mixed up the verses and made it sound like the poet was describing a donkey?"

Hossein laughed louder, the sound rich and full, ruffling Reza's hair like he used to when they were boys racing through Isfahan's streets, chasing dreams and sunlight. "Oh, she likes my jokes," he insisted, though his grin admitted the truth. He pulled another letter from his pocket—he carried them all, Reza realized, every single one, as if they were talismans against bullets and bombs. "She wrote about that jasmine tree, said it reminds her of me because it keeps blooming even when frost threatens. I told her I'd plant one with her someday. A whole garden of them. We'd sit beneath their branches and read together, and I'd finally get all those Saadi verses right."

The Moonlit Rose of Isfahan

His voice softened, the teasing fading into something deeper—longing, hope, fear. His fingers traced Leyla's handwriting with such tenderness that Reza's throat tightened. This wasn't just infatuation or passing fancy. This was the real thing, as deep and true as what he felt for Zahra. His brother had found his rose, his moonlit garden, and fate had been cruel enough to dangle it before him while keeping them apart.

"You'll learn with her, Hossein," Reza said softly, his hand on his brother's arm, feeling the solid warmth of him, alive and whole for this moment. "Like Zahra and I did in 1980. It's not about secrets or techniques. It's about love. About being present with each other, vulnerable, willing to fumble and laugh about it together." He thought of his own wedding night, the nervous sweetness of it, how Zahra had trembled in his arms and he'd whispered poetry because he didn't know what else to do. How they'd learned each other slowly, tenderly, and the awkwardness had become a cherished part of their story.

Hossein nodded, his eyes glistening, pulling Reza close again, their shoulders pressed together in the cramped trench, two brothers against the world. "If I make it back," he said, his voice firm but trembling with the weight of 'if,' that terrible word that haunted every soldier's thoughts, "I'll marry her. We'll have a proper courtship, chaperoned visits with her family, the whole traditional dance. And then a wedding—nothing grand, just family and friends, Zahra singing, you reciting Hafez to make us all cry. I'll take her home, plant that jasmine garden, teach alongside her, grow old watching the roses bloom."

The words hung in the air, a vow against the war's uncertainty, as fragile and defiant as hope itself. Reza gripped his brother's hand, both of them aware of what went unspoken—the bodies they'd seen, the friends they'd lost, the randomness of death that picked men like flowers, showing no mercy to the good or brave or loved.

"You'll make it back," Reza said, needing to believe it, needing his brother to believe it. "We both will. You'll marry Leyla, and I'll recite the most beautiful verses. Zahra and I will give you terrible advice about married life, and you'll pretend to listen while doing exactly what you want anyway."

Hossein smiled, but his eyes held a shadow—the knowledge that promises made in trenches were as fragile as morning mist. Still, they clung to it, this vision of a future where they both survived, where love won and families were whole and gardens bloomed.

A flare burst overhead, painting the night in harsh yellow light, and both brothers instinctively ducked, hands reaching for their rifles. The moment of peace shattered, replaced by the war's constant vigilance. The flare drifted down slowly, illuminating the nightmare landscape—cratered earth, twisted metal, the bloated bodies of men and animals rotting in the cold. Then darkness returned, heavier than before.

Down the trench, someone whimpered—a new recruit, barely eighteen, crying for his mother in the dark. The sound cut through Reza like a knife. They were all someone's son, someone's brother, someone's beloved. Adib, killed three weeks ago, had carried a photo of his young son, a child he'd never see grow up. Mahmoud, lost to a sniper last month, had been engaged to marry in the spring. The war consumed them all, grinding lives into mud and memory.

"I'm afraid," Hossein admitted quietly, the confession raw. The older brother, the protector, allowing himself to be vulnerable. "Afraid I won't make it back to her. Afraid she'll wait for nothing. Afraid all these letters and dreams will end with my name on a list of the dead."

Reza's chest tightened, his own fears mirroring his brother's. "Me too," he whispered. "Every day, I'm afraid. Afraid of dying here, afraid of dying slowly from gas or infection, afraid of what this place is doing to my soul. Afraid Zahra will spend her life as a widow, tending a garden for a ghost." His hand tightened on Zahra's letter, the paper soft and precious. "But we can't live in that fear. We hold onto what we love, let it be our anchor. That's all we can do."

As the night deepened, the temperature dropped further, cold seeping through their uniforms despite the wool and layers. Artillery echoes grew closer—the Iraqis were active tonight, probing defences, reminding everyone that the ceasefire was temporary, breakable, meaningless. The trench's dampness chilled their bones, and exhaustion pulled at them like gravity.

Reza settled against the wall, his rifle close, his body aching from the day's labor—digging latrines, reinforcing sandbags, the endless maintenance of survival. His eyes grew heavy despite the cold, despite

The Moonlit Rose of Isfahan

the fear, despite everything. Sleep was a cruel thing in the trenches, coming in fitful snatches, never deep, always haunted.

In the haze between wakefulness and dreams, his thoughts turned to Zahra—they always did. He imagined her beside him, her slender body tucked under his arm, her petite frame pressed against him for warmth. Her dark hair spilling over the pillow, smelling of rosewater and jasmine, that scent that had been hers since their courtship. Her soft breath on his neck, her hand in his, their fingers intertwined. The quilts of their bed in Isfahan, heavy and warm, wrapping them in safety.

The vision was vivid, almost real enough to touch—her skin warm against his, her heartbeat steady, the gentle rise and fall of her breathing. He could almost smell the jasmine, almost feel her fingers tracing the lines of his face. It was his sanctuary, this imagined moment, his escape from the horror. Every soldier had one—some vision of home, of love, of the life they'd return to if they survived.

Beside him, Hossein's breathing had evened out, the steady rhythm of sleep. Even in rest, his brother's hand remained close to his rifle, his body tensed for the alarm that could come at any moment. But for now, for these few precious hours, there was peace—or at least the illusion of it.

Reza's heart ached with longing, with love, with the terrible knowledge that tomorrow could bring anything. That one or both of them might not survive to see their loves again, might not feel their wives' arms around them, might not plant those gardens they dreamed about.

But tonight, they had this: brotherhood, shared dreams, the warmth of tea and the comfort of not being alone. Tonight, love was still possible, still worth fighting for. Tonight, somewhere in Isfahan, Zahra and Leyla tended their gardens and wrote their letters and waited with the fierce patience of women who loved men at war.

And in this wretched trench, as stars dimmed behind the haze of smoke and Reza drifted into uneasy slumber, he held onto one truth: love was worth surviving for. Love was the light they carried through the darkness. Love was the garden they would return to, if fate allowed, if mercy existed, if their promises meant anything in a world that seemed bent on destroying everything beautiful.

Tomorrow would bring what it brought. But tonight, two brothers slept side by side, dreaming of jasmine gardens and the women they loved, their hope a small and stubborn flame against the vast and indifferent night.

Chapter Nine

Isfahan, 1988

The morning sun spilled through the thin curtains of the bedroom, casting a golden glow over the embroidered quilts tangled around their bodies. The air was soft with rosewater from the previous night's bath, mingling with the warm, musky scent of sleep and skin. Shirin and Simin dozed on the rug nearby. Reza and Zahra lay entwined, bodies pressed together, her dark hair spilling over the pillow like ink, his grey-flecked beard tickling her shoulder.

They had made love slowly the night before, rediscovering each other with tender patience, and now in the soft morning light, they found themselves stirring again with gentle desire. Reza shifted closer behind her, his arm wrapping around her waist, pulling her against him. The intimacy was unhurried, sweet—his body curving around hers like a protective shell, her back against his chest, their breathing falling into sync.

"My rose," he murmured against her neck, his voice still rough with sleep, his lips brushing the curve where her shoulder met her throat. His hand traced lazy patterns on her hip, a tender claim, and she sighed softly, pressing back into him. There was no rush, no urgency—just the quiet pleasure of being together, of feeling whole after so many years apart.

"I love you," she whispered, her voice thick with emotion and lingering drowsiness. Her hand found his where it rested on her stomach, their fingers intertwining. The moment stretched, golden and perfect, a small sanctuary carved from the morning light. They stayed like that for long minutes, bodies pressed close, hearts beating in rhythm, the world outside their bedroom door forgotten.

Eventually, they stirred, reluctant to leave the warmth of their bed but drawn by the promise of a new day together. Reza pressed a kiss to her temple before pulling away gently, and Zahra turned to face him, her eyes still heavy-lidded with contentment. They smiled at each other—private, knowing smiles that spoke of shared intimacy and deepening reconnection.

After washing and dressing, Reza chose his old military uniform—the khaki fabric worn but familiar, its weight grounding him in a way civilian clothes still couldn't manage. The uniform hugged his frame, the medals on his chest catching the morning light, a reminder of battles fought and survived. Zahra watched him button it, her eyes warm with affection, finding him handsome in the uniform despite—or perhaps because of—what it represented.

They moved to the kitchen together, where the air was fragrant with fresh lavash bread, brewing tea, and the lingering aroma of last night's *khoresht-e bademjan*. As they prepared breakfast—crispy *tahdig*, yogurt, and dates—Zahra's gaze kept drifting to Reza in his uniform. There was something about the way he carried himself in it, the military bearing softened by domestic tasks, that stirred something playful in her.

She leaned close, her fingers brushing the medals on his chest, her voice dropping to a teasing whisper. "You know, Commander," she said, her cheeks flushing even as mischief danced in her eyes, "next time, I think I'd like to be with the commander, not just my husband. Someone dashing and commanding in uniform—and maybe even a little dangerous."

Reza's eyes widened in surprise before a slow grin spread across his face. He straightened, squaring his shoulders with exaggerated military bearing, his voice dropping to a mock-authoritative tone. "Oh, the commander is a dangerous man, my lady," he said, pulling her close by the waist, his eyes twinkling. "He might sweep you off your feet before you can protest."

Zahra giggled, swatting his chest playfully, her blush deepening. "I'd like to see him try," she quipped, her eyes sparkling with challenge. "But I warn you, Commander, I'm not so easily swept."

Reza puffed out his chest theatrically, his medals clinking. "Challenge accepted, my rose," he said with a wink. "But beware—the commander's orders are irresistible." He stole a quick kiss, their lips brushing with playful affection, and Zahra laughed, bright and musical, pushing him away with gentle hands even as her fingers lingered on his arms.

Their teasing wove a lighthearted intimacy through the morning, the weight of their years apart easing in the warmth of playful banter. "You're trouble in that uniform," Zahra said, stirring yogurt with a coy smile. "Good trouble," Reza countered, his tone warm. "The kind that keeps you blushing." Their laughter filled the kitchen, the *tahdig's* crisp aroma grounding their joy, a stark contrast to the bitter tea and mud of trenches Reza had endured.

After breakfast, Zahra took Reza's hand, her fingers warm and sure around his scarred ones. "Come with me," she said softly, leading him toward the back door. "There's something I want to show you." His heart quickened—this would be his first real step outside since his return, free from the war's shadow.

The courtyard garden greeted them like a living embrace. The afternoon sun bathed everything in golden light, filtering through jasmine vines and casting dappled shadows over crimson and white roses. The air was heady with floral scents—jasmine's sweetness, lavender's calming musk, the crisp bite of mint—all mingling with the faint earthiness of soil warmed by sun. Reza paused at the threshold, mesmerized, his hand tightening on Zahra's.

"You made this," he breathed, his voice thick with awe. His eyes traced the neat rows of herbs, the climbing jasmine, the roses blooming in defiant beauty, the mulberry tree casting dappled shade where they'd once courted as young lovers. "It's... alive. Like you."

The sensation of soft grass beneath his boots felt surreal after years of mud and stone. The absence of gunfire, the gentle rustle of leaves instead of artillery's roar—it overwhelmed him. This was the world he'd been fighting to return to, the world Zahra had preserved in his absence. Shirin and Simin had followed them outside, Simin chasing a butterfly while Shirin sprawled in a patch of sunlight beneath the tree.

Zahra smiled, her shyness giving way to quiet pride. Her dress swayed as she knelt beside a particularly vibrant rose, her fingers brushing its petals with practiced gentleness. "I tended it for us," she said, echoing the dreams they'd shared during their courtship. "Every day, every season, I kept it alive."

Reza knelt beside her, his uniform brushing the grass, and picked a rose—crimson and perfect, its petals soft as silk. He offered it to her as he had all those years ago, when they were young and the world felt full of promise. "You made this a sanctuary," he said, his baritone soft, his soulful brown eyes meeting her almond ones. "Will you... let me tell you about it?" Zahra asked, her voice melodic but tinged with memory. "About what it meant to me, those years you were gone?"

Reza nodded, his hand squeezing hers, the rose he'd picked now tucked into her hair. They sat on a woven mat under the mulberry tree, the air cool in the shade, and Zahra's voice softened as she pulled them both into her wartime memories.

Isfahan, 1982

The sky hung grey over Isfahan, the distant wail of air raid sirens a sound Zahra had learned to live with. She was twenty-two, her slender frame clad in a simple dress, her hands streaked with dirt from planting. The war's shadow pressed heavy on everything—rationed water, food scarcity, the constant low hum of anxiety that never quite left her chest. But here, in her courtyard garden, she found something that still felt like hers.

The roses were barely surviving, their blooms fragile but defiant. Every day, she knelt in the soil, her fingers trembling as she watered the roots, whispering words from poetry—not Hafez's words, but Reza's own verse that he'd written in the margins of books during their courtship: *"The rose blooms for love, not for duty."* The garden was her rebellion against despair, her promise to Reza that she would keep their home alive until he returned.

Inside the family home, her father's illness worsened, his cough echoing through rooms that felt too empty without the pre-war optimism for the future. The city strained under the war's weight—neighbours disappeared, bombs shook the night, grief became as common as bread. Yet Zahra found strength in the garden, its soil grounding her when everything else felt uncertain.

She planted herbs—mint for refreshing tea when water was scarce, basil to flavour meagre meals, lavender for sachets that she shared with neighbours. Small acts of defiance against the war's hunger. The tulips she buried like secrets in the earth, their bulbs symbols of renewal, pushing through cold winter to bloom in spring. Much like her hope for Reza's return. The jasmine vines climbed the courtyard walls, their white flowers a beacon of purity and persistence, twining around obstacles just as she learned to navigate the war's hardships.

Gardening calmed her. The repetitive motions—pruning, weeding, planting—became a meditation that stilled her racing mind. The earth's cool texture under her fingers soothed her anxiety. As she tended the lavender, its calming scent filling her lungs, she found moments of peace. Her thoughts drifted to her books stacked inside, to Shirin and Simin sitting in the window, to the life she'd dreamed of during their courtship.

She had almost everything she'd wanted from those 1979 dreams—a quiet life surrounded by books, cats curling at her feet, plants blooming under her care. The garden was her world, calming her soul amid chaos, each petal a whisper of normalcy. But it felt incomplete, a beautiful picture with the most important element missing: Reza himself. His poetry, his touch, his gentle presence—she craved them like plants crave sunlight.

Sometimes she slipped away to volunteer at a community centre, sewing uniforms for soldiers or distributing rationed goods. Her hands stayed steady despite the fear, and it felt like a way to stay connected to Reza's fight, to contribute something tangible. But always, she returned to the garden. It became her sanctuary, its roses a mirror of her own resilience, their thorns a reminder that beauty could survive pain.

One night, after a bombing left the city trembling and her ears ringing, she buried one of Reza's letters in the soil beneath a lavender bush. It was a ritual, irrational perhaps, but it felt like magic—keeping him safe by binding his words to the earth. "Come back to me," she whispered to the plants, her tears watering the soil. The garden became her silent vow to survive for him, its growth a calming rhythm in the storm of war.

Zahra's voice trailed off, her eyes glistening with unshed tears, the memory raw even softened by Reza's presence. He reached up, his scarred thumb gentle as it brushed away a tear that had escaped down her cheek. His own throat felt tight, his heart swelling with love and grief for the strength she'd carried alone.

"You kept us alive here," he said, his voice thick with emotion, gesturing to the garden blooming around them. "All this beauty—it's a testament to your hope. To your refusal to let the war take everything." He paused, overwhelmed by the contrast between this sanctuary and the trenches he'd endured. The soft grass beneath them, the sweet scent of lavender, the complete absence of gunfire—it felt almost unreal. "I didn't know how much you carried," he added, his eyes tracing her face, matured but radiant, like the roses she'd tended through seasons of uncertainty.

Zahra leaned into him, her head resting on his shoulder, her hand entwined with his. "It was for us," she said, her voice steady now. "Every rose, every herb—it was so we'd have this moment. So we'd have a home to return to."

They spent the afternoon moving slowly through the garden, their companionship a quiet joy. Reza touched the plants with wondering fingers, marvelling at textures that felt alien after years of mud and metal—velvety rose petals, crisp mint leaves, the soothing softness of lavender buds. They sat under the mulberry tree and shared tea from a thermos Zahra had brought out, its earthy warmth reminding Reza of the tea Hossein had shared with him in those trenches countless times, though this was sweeter, gentler, carrying no bitter edge of fear.

Zahra pointed out her favourite rose, its crimson petals bold and unapologetic, and Reza laughed softly—the sound still felt new in his throat, as if his body were relearning how to express joy. His uniform's weight felt lighter in her presence, the medals on his chest less like burdens and more like memories he could finally set down.

But as he breathed in the garden's peace, his thoughts began to turn inward, vulnerability surfacing like roots breaking through soil.

"Zahra," he said, his voice hesitant, his fingers tightening on hers as if to steady himself against the current of uncertainty. "I can't stop thinking about what comes next. Teaching again, like before the war—it feels so foreign. I'd barely started after graduation, and then I was sent off. How do I go back to that? Everything's different now."

His eyes dropped to the grass, the weight of change pressing on him like the war's lingering shadow. The garden's serenity contrasted sharply with his inner turmoil. The blooms reminded him of life's persistence, yet his heart ached with the voids left behind—comrades lost, years stolen, the man he'd been before transformed into someone he barely recognized.

Zahra shifted closer, her hand tracing the scars on his fingers, grounding him as she had after his nightmare days ago. She listened quietly, her own losses echoing his—her father's death after his long illness, occurring shortly before Hossein's death in 1983. Her father's last wish had been to see her married, fulfilled when she'd wed Reza in 1980.

Reza's voice trembled as he continued, vulnerability laid bare. "I no longer have Hossein," he said, the name reopening a wound that might never fully heal. Tears pricked his eyes. "He was my guide—teaching for years, always knowing what to do. I looked up to him for everything. Our immediate family was just us two brothers. He never got the chance to marry, to build that life he dreamed of."

The memory of their many trench nights flooded back—Hossein's hand on his shoulder, the tea they'd shared, the vulnerability they'd allowed themselves in that brief moment of peace. Hossein talking about Leyla, about the jasmine garden they'd plant together, about the wedding that would never happen.

"He was writing love letters to that woman he'd met briefly before deployment," Reza said, his breath catching. "Dreaming of her, planning a future. But he never made it back."

He wiped his eyes with the back of his hand, the gesture rough. "He'd have known how to navigate this—returning to teaching, rebuilding a life. And from the days you chose me over him during our courtship, he became like a brother to you too. He treated you as the little sister he never had."

Zahra nodded, her throat tight with shared grief. She remembered Hossein's brotherly affection—his teasing during their first meeting in 1979, the way he'd watched them with fond amusement as their courtship unfolded, his letters during the war filled with protective concern. "He indeed was family to me too," she whispered, her fingers squeezing Reza's. "And now... we're what's left."

Reza's gaze met hers, the shared grief creating a deeper bond between them. "My parents," he said, his voice cracking, "they're older now, frail. They fled to Shiraz to live with relatives since both of us were on the frontlines. I haven't seen them since before everything began. And your family—" He paused, knowing this territory was painful for her too.

"Scattered," Zahra finished softly. "Father gone, my half-brother Farhad in Tehran. He was so much older, married with his own life when I was still a child. We were never close—he was like a distant uncle more than a brother." Her eyes glistened with the memories surfacing. "And Mother... she remarried after Father's death. To a Lebanese man. She moved to Damascus where his family had fled Lebanon's own war."

Reza's eyes widened slightly—this detail was new to him, revealed in a letter he must have missed or perhaps she'd been too hesitant to share during the war. "Damascus?" he asked gently.

Zahra nodded, her tone tinged with sadness. "She has two stepchildren there now. I've never met them. She writes, but it's not the same. In many ways, Reza, it feels like we only have each other left. A few cousins and relatives nearby who survived the war's brutality, but not the family we once had."

She paused, her gaze drifting to the roses—symbols of the

resilience she'd clung to through those lonely years. "Our families suffered tremendous losses. Bombs, illness, separation. The war redrew our world, took people and scattered the rest. But we're here, Reza. We have this garden, this home." Her voice strengthened slightly. "I refused to leave it, even when Mother begged me to join her in Syria. The memories of you here, in this space—they kept me rooted."

Reza pulled her closer, his arm wrapping around her shoulders, the garden's scents enveloping them like a balm. "You're right," he murmured, his voice thick. "It's just us now, in so many ways. Hossein never had a family of his own—those letters he wrote to Leyla, all those dreams... he deserved that chance." Fresh tears slipped down his cheeks. "And your mother's new life in Lebanon, with stepchildren I pray one day we get to know. It's like the war took a knife to our family tree and cut away so many branches."

The vulnerability in his voice exposed his deepest fears—the future felt like a haze without the anchors of family, without Hossein's guidance, without the certainty of who he was supposed to become. "How do we build from this?" he asked, almost pleading. "Teaching was Hossein's path, his guidance. Without him, without our parents close... it feels impossible. I feel lost coming back here and everything being different."

Zahra cupped his face in her hands, her thumbs brushing away his tears with infinite tenderness. Her love was fierce and steady, an anchor in his storm. "We build anew, together, my love," she said, her voice carrying the weight of a vow. It echoed the comfort she'd offered after his nightmare, the same fierce determination to face whatever came. "The garden taught me that—things grow in their own time, from what's left behind."

She gestured to the blooms surrounding them, to the life she'd coaxed from soil during the darkest years. "You'll teach again if you want to, or you'll find something new. Our cousins nearby, they'll be part of our life too. And Hossein..." Her voice softened. "He's with us in spirit, in those letters we keep on the shelf, in every memory we carry. We honour him by living, by loving, by refusing to let the war's darkness consume the light we still have."

Her words, inspired by the tulips' renewal and lavender's calm, wove a thread of hope through his despair. Her resilience became a light for his darkness. "Things grow in their own time," she repeated softly. "We don't have to know everything right now. One day at a time, remember?"

Reza nodded, his throat too tight for words. He pulled her into a tight embrace, the garden's peace enveloping them both. The losses were profound—Hossein, their scattered families, the years stolen by war—but their love ran deeper still. It was a root that had survived drought and storm, and it would sustain them through whatever came next.

They lingered under the mulberry tree as the afternoon light began its slow descent toward evening. Reza's head rested on Zahra's shoulder now, their positions reversed, and he let himself simply feel—the softness of grass, the warmth of sun-dappled shade, the floral scents that seemed to promise that beauty could still exist in a world marked by so much loss.

The call to prayer drifted through the garden from a nearby mosque, the muezzin's voice carrying across Isfahan's rooftops. "It's time for prayer my love," she said softly, squeezing Reza's hand before she got up. He nodded but didn't get up. He touched the plants again, letting his fingers trail over their many textures. Each texture was a small miracle to him, a reminder that his hands could touch gentle things again, that they didn't have to grip rifles or dig trenches or cradle dying brothers.

He'd prayed sporadically in the trenches, desperate bargains with God when shells screamed overhead, frantic pleas when comrades fell. But since returning, the words felt hollow in his mouth, the movements mechanical. How did one pray after seeing what he'd seen? How did one bow before God when so many prayers had gone unanswered?

When she finished and returned to sit with him, he pulled her close again. "I used to pray with you," he said quietly. "Before."

"I know," she said, her hand resting over his. "When you're ready, we'll pray again my love. No rush."

"Does it still bring you peace?" Reza asked, his voice tentative. "After everything?"

The Moonlit Rose of Isfahan

"Some days more than others. During the war, it was complicated—I was angry sometimes, had doubts. But yes, it still brings me peace. It always has." She paused, her eyes meeting his with gentle understanding. "You don't have to have it figured out yet, Reza. Faith isn't something you lose all at once or find all at once. It ebbs and flows, like the seasons in this garden."

Reza's throat tightened. He brought her hand to his lips, kissing her knuckles. "I used to pray diligently every morning before the war," he confessed. "Now I... I don't know what to say to God anymore."

"Then don't say anything," Zahra whispered. "Just be. The words will come when they're ready." Zahra poured more tea from the thermos, the earthy warmth spreading through him, grounding him in this moment.

"Your love is my home," Reza whispered, speaking the words of his own poetry—the verse he'd held on to for years and years, when home felt impossibly far away. Now, surrounded by the garden Zahra had nurtured, he understood what those words truly meant. Home wasn't just a place. It was this: her hand in his, her resilience teaching him how to hope again, their shared grief and shared joy intertwining like the jasmine vines on the courtyard walls. "I'll pray with you again someday, my rose."

Zahra smiled, her shyness fading in the afternoon's golden light, her heart full. She leaned her head against his, and they sat in comfortable silence, watching Simin pounce on a fallen leaf while Shirin stretched luxuriously in a patch of sun. Their laughter rang out when Simin tumbled spectacularly, the sound bright and unguarded.

The garden wrapped them in its peace, and for the first time since his return, Reza felt something shift inside him. The war's echoes were still there—they might always be there—but they were growing quieter, softened by this sanctuary Zahra had built. Their love was blooming anew in this space she'd tended, and though the future remained uncertain, they would face it together. That would be enough.

Chapter Ten

Shiraz, 1980

The morning sun bathed Shiraz in golden light, the air warm and fragrant with jasmine and orange blossoms drifting from the garden where Reza and Zahra's wedding would unfold. It was August now, and the garden—verdant and alive—stood as a sanctuary of joy, its cypress trees rising tall against the cloudless sky, their leaves rustling softly in the gentle breeze. The rose beds were in full bloom, their petals—crimson, pink, and white—scattered across the tiled paths like nature's confetti, while fountains bubbled with cool water, misting the air with a refreshing sweetness that mingled with the scent of fresh mint from nearby herb beds.

In a room overlooking the garden, Zahra stood before a mirror, her slender frame draped in a white dress embroidered with delicate gold thread that caught the morning light. She was radiant, her dark hair pinned underneath a bridal chador with jasmine flowers, her almond eyes wide with nervous excitement. Her hands trembled as she adjusted her lace veil, the weight of wanting everything to be perfect pressing against her chest.

She could hear the hum of activity from below—relatives arranging platters of sweets, the scent of freshly baked *noon-e sangak* mingling with the garden's fragrance. Her mother Maryam stood beside her, adjusting the veil with gentle hands, her eyes glistening with tears of joy and pride.

Jamila Mikhail

"What if I trip walking out?" Zahra whispered, her voice trembling slightly, her cheeks flushed with shyness and anticipation. "What if the words don't come?"

Her mother smiled, brushing away a tear as she cupped Zahra's face in her weathered hands. "You're radiant, my dear. Reza sees only you. He always has." She pressed a kiss to Zahra's forehead, her voice thick with emotion. "Your father is so proud, even from his sickbed. He wanted to be here to walk you through the garden, but his blessing is with you."

Zahra nodded, her heart racing as she pictured the ceremony ahead—the *sofreh aghd* spread beneath the ancient trees, its mirror and candles waiting to reflect their union. She wanted this day to be everything they had dreamed of during their courtship, a memory to carry forward into whatever life would bring them.

In another room, Reza fidgeted with his dark suit, the crisp fabric foreign compared to the casual clothes of his teaching days. His frame was tense, his soulful brown eyes darting to the mirror as he smoothed his clean-shaven face for what felt like the hundredth time. His hands lingered on the small poetry volume in his pocket—his own writings, bound in leather—a gift he planned to give Zahra after the ceremony. The verses inside were for her, only her, words born from their courtship beneath the stars.

"What if I stumble over the vows?" he muttered to himself, his baritone voice shaky with nerves. "What if my voice cracks?" The fear of imperfection gnawed at him. He wanted this day to be flawless for Zahra, the woman whose shy smile had captured his heart the first time he'd laid eyes on her.

A knock interrupted his thoughts, and Hossein, commanding yet warm, stepped into the room with a grin. His strong jaw was framed by a neatly trimmed beard now, his hazel eyes crinkling with mischief and brotherly affection. Dressed in a beige tunic and trousers, he carried himself with the easy confidence of a beloved teacher, a man who could draw laughter from any room.

"You look like you're facing an execution, little brother," Hossein teased, clapping Reza's shoulder with a firm, reassuring grip. "Relax. She loves you. That's all that matters." His voice softened. "And if you stumble, I'll make a worse fool of myself to distract everyone. It's my duty as best man."

Reza managed a shaky laugh, some of the tension easing from his shoulders. "You've already done enough by introducing us. I don't know what I'd do without you, brother."

Hossein's eyes gleamed with warmth. "You'd probably still be reading poetry to an empty courtyard, waiting for the muse to appear." He ruffled Reza's hair affectionately, the gesture so familiar from their childhood it made Reza smile despite his nerves. "Come on. Your bride is waiting."

The garden had been transformed into a vision of beauty for the ceremony. About fifty guests—family and close friends—gathered under a canopy of white linen strung with lanterns that would glow softly as evening fell. The *sofreh aghd* was spread on a silk cloth beneath the trees, its items meticulously arranged according to tradition: a mirror to reflect the couple's faces, symbolizing brightness in their future; two candelabras flickering with flames of hope; rose petals scattered for love and passion; a bowl of honey for sweetness; crystallized sugar cones for prosperity; coins for wealth; decorated eggs for fertility; and a copy of poetry—not Hafez or Rumi this time, but Reza's own verses, handwritten and bound, a testament to their unique love story.

The tables were laden with Persian delicacies that filled the air with mouthwatering aromas: saffron rice studded with barberries, its golden hue gleaming in the sunlight; *kofte tabrizi*, meatballs fragrant with herbs and spices; *fesenjan*, the rich walnut-pomegranate stew that was a staple of celebration; and platters of fresh fruits, glistening *gaz*, and delicate pastries dripping with rosewater syrup. Guests dressed in their finest—women in flowing dresses and colourful patterned scarves, men in crisp tunics or suits—mingled and laughed, their Farsi chatter creating a warm buzz of anticipation.

The air was alive with music as a *santur's* plucked notes wove through the gathering, accompanied by the gentle rhythm of a *daf* drum and the melodic strains of a *setar*. Children chased each other around the fountain, their giggles like birdsong, while the older aunties gossiped about matches made and futures predicted, dabbing at their eyes with embroidered handkerchiefs.

Reza stood at the *sofreh*, his suit crisp despite the warmth, his heart pounding a rhythm that seemed to sync with the distant music.

And then Zahra appeared, escorted by her cousin since her father could not make the journey from his sickbed. The moment she stepped into view, time seemed to slow. Her ivory dress shimmered in the sunlight, the gold embroidery catching every ray, and her veil—delicate lace that cascaded like a waterfall—swayed gently with each step. Her eyes found his across the garden, and the world narrowed to just them. All the nerves, all the fear of imperfection, melted away. There was only her—his moonlit rose—radiant and breathtaking.

She walked toward him slowly, each step deliberate, her heart visible in the trembling of her hands clutching a small bouquet of roses from their courtship garden. When she reached the *sofreh* and stood across from him, separated only by the mirror that reflected their faces side by side, she smiled—shy but certain—and he knew he would remember this moment for the rest of his life.

The officiant, an elderly mullah with a kind face and a voice weathered by years of blessing unions, began the ceremony. "In the name of God, the Most Gracious, the Most Merciful," he intoned, his words carrying across the garden with gentle authority. He spoke of love as a sacred trust, of marriage as a partnership blessed by faith, of two souls choosing to walk together through life's joys and sorrows.

Zahra's mother and aunts held a white cloth above the couple, and with practiced grace, they rubbed two sugar cones together, showering sweetness over Reza and Zahra's heads—crystallized blessings that caught the light as they fell. The guests watched in reverent silence, broken only by the occasional sniffle from a moved relative or the rustle of fabric as someone leaned forward for a better view.

When the time came for vows, Reza's voice steadied, his eyes locked on Zahra's. He spoke from his heart, his poet's soul laid bare: "Zahra, my moonlit rose, in your eyes I have found my home, in your love I have found my purpose. You are the garden where my heart blooms, the poem I will spend my life writing. With you, every moment is sacred."

The Moonlit Rose of Isfahan

His words, born from months of writing and rewriting verses for her, flowed perfectly. A tear slipped down Zahra's cheek, catching the sunlight like a diamond.

Zahra responded, her voice soft but clear, trembling with emotion but steady in conviction: "Reza, my beloved, your love is the sky that shelters me, boundless and true. In your words I have found beauty, in your heart I have found my forever. I choose you, today and always."

The crowd erupted in soft applause and murmurs of approval. Hossein, standing beside Reza as witness and brother, whispered just loud enough for them to hear, "Don't faint now, poet. You've got the hard part ahead—being married to someone who reads your terrible drafts."

Despite the solemnity of the moment, Reza couldn't suppress a chuckle, and even Zahra's lips quirked into a smile. The levity was perfect, easing the last vestiges of tension.

The officiant smiled knowingly and gestured to the honey bowl. "Now, taste the sweetness of your union."

Reza dipped his finger into the honey, its golden thickness clinging to his skin, and offered it to Zahra. She leaned forward, her veil brushing against his hand as she closed her lips around his finger, tasting the sweetness and holding his gaze with an intimacy that made his breath catch. Then it was her turn. She dipped her own finger, the honey warm and fragrant, and brought it to his lips. He took it slowly, savouring not just the taste but the significance—the beginning of a life shared, sweet and full of promise.

The mirror before them reflected their smiles, the candles' flames burning steady and bright, the rose petals vibrant at their feet. It was a moment frozen in perfection, a tableau of love witnessed by those who mattered most.

Hossein stepped forward then, his presence commanding attention even in a crowd. He cleared his throat dramatically, drawing chuckles from the guests who knew his penchant for theatrics. From his pocket, he pulled a small, worn volume of Rumi knowing exactly which verses his little brother and his bride—now his little sister—adored.

"For my brother and his bride," he announced, his baritone voice carrying across the garden, "I offer a blessing in verse." He recited at length poems about roses blooming in gardens of love, about souls intertwining like vines, about the endurance of true connection. His delivery was flawless, moving several aunties to tears and earning nods of approval from the elder guests.

But as he closed the volume and tucked it away, his expression shifted to one of playful mischief. He raised his glass of *sharbat-e sekke*—the rosewater-lemon drink sparkling in his hand—and adopted a mock-serious tone.

"Now," Hossein declared, his eyes dancing with humour as he gestured grandly to the assembled crowd, "I have one very important demand for this marriage. A condition, if you will."

Reza groaned good-naturedly, while Zahra covered her mouth with her hand, trying not to laugh. The guests leaned in, anticipation rippling through the crowd.

"If you have a son—and I know you will, with all this poetry and passion flying about—" Hossein paused for dramatic effect, stroking his beard theatrically, "—you must name him Hossein. It's only fair, really. The world needs more handsome, brilliant, humble men like me to carry on the family name!"

The garden erupted in laughter, guests clapping and calling out their agreement or mock protests. One uncle shouted, "He's got a point!" while an auntie swatted her husband playfully, giggling behind her hand.

Zahra's eyes widened, her laughter bubbling up as she shook her head, the veil fluttering with the movement. "Oh, Hossein, you're impossible!" she said, her voice bright with amusement. "A son named Hossein would have to live up to your ego—poor child!"

Reza pulled Zahra closer, his arm sliding around her waist, and grinned at his brother. "If we name a son Hossein, he'll need your charm and none of your terrible jokes, brother. We want him to have friends."

Hossein clutched his chest in feigned offence, his *sharbat* nearly sloshing out of the glass. "Terrible jokes? These are masterpieces! You'll thank me when your son's reciting them at his own wedding someday."

The crowd roared with laughter and approval, the joy contagious.

The Moonlit Rose of Isfahan

Even the children stopped their games to watch, sensing something special in the exchange between the brothers and the bride.

Zahra leaned into Reza, her head resting briefly on his shoulder, the scent of her jasmine perfume mingling with the other flowery fragrances air. She whispered, her voice teasing but tender, "He's right, you know. A little Hossein would be sweet. As long as he has your heart and my patience."

Reza's heart swelled, his hand tightening on hers, the thought of a future child—a son who might carry his brother's name—stirring a warmth that spread through his chest. "As long as he has your eyes, my rose," he murmured, pressing a kiss to her forehead. The gesture drew soft gasps and approving murmurs from the watching guests.

Hossein raised his glass higher, his voice softening but still carrying that infectious playfulness. "To Reza and Zahra," he toasted, his hazel eyes glistening with genuine pride and love, "and to the little Hosseins who'll run through gardens like this someday, carrying forward the best of all of us."

The guests cheered, glasses clinking, the lanterns beginning to glow as the sun dipped lower in the sky. Rose petals caught the breeze and danced through the air like blessings, settling on the *sofreh* and in Zahra's hair. The moment was perfect—a snapshot of love, laughter, and hope, untouched by any shadow of what might come.

As evening descended and the feast began in earnest, the garden transformed once more. The lanterns cast a warm, golden glow over the tables where guests helped themselves to heaping plates of jewelled rice, tender kebabs, and aromatic stews. The *santur's* notes grew livelier, joined now by the rhythmic clapping of guests encouraging dancers to the centre of the garden.

Reza and Zahra sat together at the place of honour, their hands entwined beneath the table, stealing glances at each other between bites of food they barely tasted. The nerves had been replaced by a radiant joy that seemed to emanate from them both, drawing smiles from everyone who looked their way.

"Dance with me," Reza whispered to Zahra as the music swelled, a traditional melody that spoke of celebration and new beginnings.

Jamila Mikhail

She looked at him with wide eyes, her shyness returning for a moment. "Here? In front of everyone?"

"Especially in front of everyone," he said, standing and offering his hand with a gallant bow that made her giggle. "Let them see how beautiful you are. Let them witness how lucky I am."

She took his hand, and he led her to the space beneath the mulberry tree where they had exchanged their vows. The guests formed a circle around them, clapping in rhythm with the music, voices rising in encouragement and joy. Reza and Zahra moved together—tentative at first, their steps shy and careful—but as the music carried them, they found their rhythm. His hand at her waist, her palm pressed against his, they swayed and turned, their eyes never leaving each other's faces.

The world faded away again. There was only the music, the warmth of his touch, the smile on her lips, the way his eyes reflected the lantern light. They were no longer nervous bride and groom but partners in a dance that would last a lifetime—sometimes graceful, sometimes stumbling, but always together.

When the song ended, the crowd erupted in applause and cheers. Hossein led a chorus of well-wishers calling for another dance, but Reza and Zahra, breathless and laughing, begged for mercy and returned to their seats, their faces flushed with happiness and exertion.

As the night deepened and the celebration continued around them—children falling asleep in their mothers' laps, uncles trading stories over tea, aunties pressing sweets into the newlyweds' hands with blessings whispered in Farsi—Reza leaned close to Zahra and whispered, "This is just the beginning, my rose. Our story starts here."

Zahra's eyes shimmered with tears of joy as she rested her head against his shoulder. "Then let it be a long one," she whispered back. "Full of gardens and poetry and days like this."

"Always," he promised, pressing a kiss to her temple. "Always."

And in that moment, beneath the stars of Shiraz, surrounded by the people who loved them most, with the scent of roses and jasmine hanging in the warm August air, Reza and Zahra believed it with every fibre of their beings. Their future stretched before them, bright and full of promise—a blank page waiting for the poetry of their shared life to be written.

The Moonlit Rose of Isfahan

The ceremony was everything they had dreamed of and more—beautiful, intimate, perfect. A celebration of love in its purest form, a foundation strong enough to weather whatever storms might come. And though they could not know what the years ahead would bring, on this night, they had each other. And that was more than enough.

Chapter Eleven

Ahvaz, 1983

The air was thick with the acrid stench of sulphur and blood, the sky choked with smoke as artillery screamed overhead, shaking the muddy trench where Reza crouched. The ground was slick, a mix of dirt and crimson, the remnants of men he knew—friends, comrades, their bodies twisted in the chaos. The southern front near Ahvaz had become a meat grinder of human wave assaults and Iraqi gas attacks, the war's brutality unrelenting.

Reza, his lean frame pressed against the trench wall, his uniform soaked with sweat and mud, gripped his rifle, his heart pounding like a drum of dread. The human wave order had come—waves of Iranian soldiers charging into the enemy lines, their lives fodder for the advance.

"Stay low!" Hossein shouted, his voice cutting through the din, his face streaked with mud, eyes fierce but kind, the same eyes that had read Hafez with Reza under Isfahan's stars. Hossein was beside him, his strong jaw set, his hand on Reza's shoulder, a protective anchor as always.

The brothers shared a glance, a flicker of hope amid the carnage, Hossein's letters to Leyla tucked in his pocket, Reza's to Zahra in his. The air burned with mustard gas, its sickly sweet smell clawing at Reza's throat through his ill-fitting mask, his lungs aching, eyes watering.

A scream pierced the din. Amir—jovial Amir with his gap-toothed

Jamila Mikhail

smile and perpetual optimism, who'd joined their unit three months ago from Mashhad, who carried a worn photo of his newborn daughter in his breast pocket, who'd shared his mother's lavash bread with them just yesterday, laughing about how she'd somehow smuggled it to the front—clutched his chest, blood bubbling through his fingers as he collapsed. His eyes, those dark eyes that had sparkled with comedic stories about his wife's terrible cooking and his father's carpet shop, went wide with shock. The photo slipped from his pocket, landing face-up in the mud, the infant's face already spattered with her father's blood.

Reza lunged, dragging Amir to cover, his hands slipping in the blood, the ground quaking under another shell. "Hold on!" Reza yelled, his voice raw, pressing desperately against the wound, but Amir's eyes glazed, his body going limp in Reza's arms, the life draining out like water through cupped hands. The last thing Amir saw was the smoke-choked sky above, not the stars over Mashhad, not his daughter's face. Just smoke and fire.

Reza barely had time to lower Amir's body before the world exploded.

The blast erupted—a massive explosion from an Iraqi mortar, the air ripping apart, shrapnel whining like angry bees, the ground heaving in a roar that deafened. Dirt rained down, the trench wall collapsing in a cascade of mud. The force of it threw Reza backward, and in the same instant, he saw Hossein stumble, a jagged wound tearing through his side, blood soaking his uniform, pooling in the sludge.

White-hot agony exploded through Reza's own body—his stomach, tearing downward toward his groin, shrapnel slicing through flesh with surgical cruelty. He screamed, the sound raw and animal, his hand instinctively going to his stomach where blood was already spreading across his uniform, warm and slick. But the pain was nothing compared to what he saw before him.

"Hossein!" Reza screamed, the sound lost in the chaos, crawling through the mire toward his brother, the ground slick under his knees, the air heavy with death. His own wound burned and throbbed, but he barely felt it. All that mattered was reaching Hossein.

His brother's hand grabbed his, weak but desperate, eyes wide with pain and love. "Live, Reza," Hossein gasped, blood flecking his lips, his voice fading like a dying ember. "For her. For Zahra. For Leyla."

Reza clutched him, his hands slippery with blood—his own, Hossein's, Amir's, all of it mixing together in the mud—shaking Hossein's shoulder, the world blurring with tears and gas. "No, brother, stay with me!" he begged, his voice breaking, the memories flooding—childhood games in Isfahan's alleys, Hossein defending him from bullies, teaching him to ride a bike, his steady hands on the seat. The night Hossein had teased him about Zahra during their courtship, that brotherly grin. The night in the trench when they'd shared weak tea and Hossein had confessed his love for Leyla, his voice soft with longing. "You were supposed to make it back," Reza choked. "You were supposed to marry her."

Hossein's eyes dimmed, the light fading like a candle in the wind. His grip on Reza's hand slackened. His last breath came as a whisper, barely audible over the roar of artillery: "For Zahra… for Leyla."

Reza leaned close, his forehead pressing against his brother's, his voice a desperate whisper. "I won't leave you. I won't—" But even as he spoke, he felt the stillness in Hossein's chest, the absence of breath, the terrible quiet where his brother's heartbeat should be.

"Brother," he whispered, his voice breaking. "My brother." He tried to speak the words that might bring him back, tried to find the poetry they'd shared under Isfahan's stars, but all that came was grief, raw and unfiltered. "You can't be gone. You can't—"

The pain in his own body suddenly flared, demanding attention. His stomach was on fire, blood pooling between his legs, and the dizziness hit him like a wave. He looked down, seeing the extent of the damage—the shrapnel had torn through his uniform, leaving a gruesome-looking wound that ran from his stomach downward, blood spreading dark and fast across the fabric.

The trench filled with shouts, the wave order echoing: "Advance!" Men charged past, their feet churning the mud, gunfire cracking, bodies falling like wheat under a scythe. Reza's world narrowed to pain and loss, his hand still on Hossein's chest, feeling the stillness, tears streaming down his dirt-caked face.

Comrades dragged him, their voices distant through the roar of pain: "He's hit! Get him to the rear!" The pain was blinding, his stomach and groin a fire of torn flesh, blood soaking his uniform. He clung to Hossein's jacket, refusing to let go, but they pulled him away, their hands rough with urgency. "No!" he screamed. "Not without him! Not without my brother!"

But the hands were strong, insistent, and the trench receded, Hossein's body left in the mud. The last thing Reza saw was his brother's face, peaceful despite everything, the mud spattering his cheeks, his eyes closed as if in sleep. Amir's photo lay beside him, father and daughter together in death. Then there was only the blur of movement, the jarring bump of the stretcher, artillery thundering, his mind screaming Hossein's name again and again and again.

The journey to the infirmary was a haze. The ground jolted beneath the stretcher, each bump sending waves of nausea through him. His thoughts fractured between grief and survival, between the brother he'd lost and the wife waiting for him at home. The pain pulsed, his stomach and groin a raw agony, each step sparking fire through his body. He tried to hold onto consciousness, but the edges of his vision darkened, and all he could see was Hossein's eyes dimming, that final breath, the terrible stillness.

The infirmary tent loomed, canvas flapping in the night wind like weary lungs struggling to breathe. The air inside was a choking cocktail—sharp antiseptic battling the coppery reek of blood, the sour tang of sweat-soaked bandages, the underlying rot of infected wounds, and the damp, moldy smell of wet earth seeping through the canvas. Lanterns swung from rusted poles, their flickering flames casting long, grotesque shadows that danced across the crowded space, illuminating the rows of cots jammed together like forgotten graves.

Each cot held a broken soldier—some writhing in fevered agony, their groans a low, guttural symphony; others silent, faces pale and vacant, staring at the ceiling with eyes hollowed by shock or the dull glaze of morphine. The floor was a chaotic mess: discarded bandages clumped in crimson piles, empty syringes glinting under the light, puddles of muddy water reflecting the lanterns' glow, and scattered personal items—a tattered photo, a crumpled letter, a broken rosary—

reminders of lives interrupted.

A young medic with hollow eyes shouted orders to an assistant, "More gauze—this one's bleeding out!" Another medic, an older woman with her scarf tied tight, knelt by a cot, whispering prayers as she cleaned a soldier's mangled leg, the man's screams muffled by a rag between his teeth. The sounds were a cacophony of groans, ragged breaths, and the occasional cry for mother or God. Death hung in the air, patient and inevitable.

Medics swarmed Reza, their hands rough but efficient, stripping his uniform, cleaning the wounds with stinging alcohol. One medic, a grizzled man with wire-rimmed glasses, examined the shrapnel wound that ran from Reza's stomach down toward his groin, probing gently. "Lucky," he muttered. "Looks worse than it is. Tore through flesh but missed the important parts. Not deep. You'll heal." He began stitching, his needle working methodically. "You'll be back on your feet sooner rather than later."

But Reza barely heard him. *Lucky*. The word was a mockery. How could he be lucky when Hossein was dead? When Amir would never see his daughter grow up?

"You'll live," the medic said again, tying off the last stitch, the needle's prick a minor torment compared to his heart's ache. The morphine began to dull the pain to a distant roar, but it couldn't touch the agony in his chest.

He lay on a cot in the corner, his body numb from painkillers, his wounds treated—gruesome-looking gashes from the shrapnel, jagged and raw, the flesh torn but not deep enough to threaten life, just as the medic had said. The stitches pulled tight, a burning itch under the bandages. His tattered uniform lay in a blood-soaked heap beside the cot, his rifle propped against the tent pole, a useless sentinel.

He stared at the canvas ceiling, the lantern light dancing like mocking ghosts, tears streaming silently down his dirt-streaked face. Hossein was gone. The words repeated in his mind, a mantra of disbelief. Gone. Killed right in front of him. His brother's last gasp echoing endlessly: "Live, Reza. For her. For Zahra. For Leyla."

The vulnerability crashed over him like a wave. Hossein—his guide, his protector, the big brother who'd ruffled his hair, teased him, defended him, taught him—had been ripped away in an instant, his body left in the mud, his letters to Leyla unfinished, his life cut short before he could marry, before he could live. Without Hossein's affection, his steady hand, his teasing laugh, the world felt empty. The war's horrors magnified in the absence of his brother's strength.

"Why him?" Reza whispered to no one, his voice breaking. "Why not me?" The fear was a constant companion, a clawing terror that he'd been so close to death, the shrapnel tearing through his body a breath away from ending him, leaving Zahra a widow. The vulnerability was crushing, his heart exposed, raw, the grief a storm that battered him relentlessly.

He'd been so close. The same blast that killed Hossein had torn through him. If the shrapnel had gone a few inches deeper, if it had struck a different angle, he would be lying in the mud beside his brother right now. Zahra would receive a letter, not her husband. She would be alone, widowed before she'd even truly had time to be a wife.

And Amir. God, Amir. That gap-toothed smile, those stories about his wife's terrible cooking, the pride in his voice when he'd shown them his daughter's photo just three days ago. "She has my nose," he'd said, grinning. "Poor thing." They'd all laughed. And now Amir would never hold her, never teach her to walk, never see her grow up. The photo was still in the mud, spattered with blood.

How many more? How many more friends would he lose? How many more faces would haunt his dreams?

Around him, the tent's chaos amplified his isolation. A man on the next cot mumbled incoherently, his jaw half-missing, blood seeping through bandages. Another writhed, clutching a gut wound, his cries sharp and animalistic. A soldier nearby lost his battle with a severed artery, his death rattle cutting through the air like a knife. The flap of canvas sounded like a funeral shroud.

Reza curled on the cot, his hands clutching the thin blanket, grief and fear intertwining. He felt utterly alone, adrift in a sea of strangers. The vulnerability laid him bare. But somewhere in the depths, beneath the crushing weight of loss, a spark remained—Zahra's love, Hossein's last words. He clung to it, even as the infirmary's hell threatened to swallow him whole.

The Moonlit Rose of Isfahan

The first day passed in a blur of morphine and fitful sleep. Every time he closed his eyes, he saw Hossein's face. Saw Amir collapsing. Saw the photo in the mud. Heard the blast, felt the shrapnel tearing through him, watched his brother die again and again and again.

The second day, he lay awake, staring at nothing. His body was a map of recovery and ache. The shrapnel wounds on his stomach, thigh and groin, gruesome but not life-threatening, had been cleaned, dressed, and bandaged, the flesh puckered and red under the gauze, pulsing with a dull throb that flared with every movement. The morphine dulled the pain to a distant hum, but his leg was stiff, his groin a sensitive fire that made even shifting position a grimace. His body was damp from sweat and the tent's humidity.

Medics came and went, changing his bandages, checking his wounds. "No signs of infection," they said. "Lucky man." But he didn't feel lucky. He felt hollow, carved out, empty.

How was he supposed to go on without Hossein? His brother had been his compass, his north star. When Reza was seven and terrified of the dark, Hossein had slept on the floor beside his bed. When Reza was twenty-three and nervous about proposing to Zahra, Hossein had straightened his collar and said, *"She's already yours, brother. She's been yours since the moment she saw you."*

Every important moment of Reza's life, Hossein had been there. And now he wouldn't be. Reza would go home to Zahra—if he survived—and Hossein wouldn't be there to celebrate. He would have children—God willing—and Hossein wouldn't be there to meet them, to be the uncle who taught them to ride bikes and shared stories and read them stories.

The thought was unbearable.

Fear surged through him—what if he died too, leaving Zahra alone, her letters unanswered? The war's toll felt infinite, his near-death a haunting ghost, the shrapnel's burn in his flesh a reminder of how fragile life was, how close he'd come to never holding her again. He could still die. Infection. Another attack. A stray shell. The war wasn't over. He wasn't safe yet.

The tent's canvas walls sagged under relentless rain, water dripping in rhythmic plops onto the muddied floor. The smell of damp earth mingled with antiseptic and blood. Around him, men groaned and wept and died. The war ground on, indifferent to individual grief.

On the third day, a comrade approached. Navid, a lanky soldier with a scarred face from a previous skirmish, his uniform patched and dirty. He carried a small bundle wrapped in oilcloth, his steps hesitant, his eyes downcast as he knelt beside Reza's cot.

"Reza," he said, his voice rough with emotion, placing the bundle on the blanket. "They recovered some of Hossein's things. Thought you should have them."

Reza's breath caught, his hands shaking as he unwrapped it, the oilcloth crinkling under his fingers. Inside: Hossein's notebook, a few letters, and an unfinished one to Leyla, the paper creased and mud-stained, Hossein's familiar script stopping mid-sentence. A pocket watch from their father, its face cracked, ticked faintly. And a small Hafez volume, the one Hossein had carried for luck, its pages worn from reading.

Reza's heart broke anew. A fresh wave of sobs wracked his body, the stitches pulling painfully as his chest heaved. He clutched the letter to Leyla, his fingers tracing the words, Hossein's handwriting a ghost of his voice: *"My Leyla, the stars here are dim, but your light guides me. I dream of our jasmine tree, of holding you..."*

It cut off, the ink trailing as if Hossein had been interrupted by the blast. Tears blurred Reza's vision, the paper absorbing them like blood. The grief was a physical ache, sharper than his wounds. "He never finished," Reza choked, his voice breaking.

The emotional weight crushed him. He imagined the reverse—Hossein surviving, writing to Zahra about Reza's death, breaking the news with his steady hand. The thought twisted like a knife. "Dear Zahra," Reza whispered, imagining Hossein's words, "Reza was brave. He loved you to the end." The idea shattered him, sobs shaking his body, the cot creaking.

Childhood memories flooded: Hossein teaching him to ride a bike in Isfahan's alleys, his big hands steady on the seat, laughing as Reza wobbled. "You've got it, little brother!" Summers by the Zayandeh River, Hossein sharing stories of heroes, inspiring Reza's poetry. The night Hossein had defended him from bullies, his fists bruised but his grin triumphant: "No one touches my brother." Their laughter when Zahra had chosen Reza, Hossein's tease, "You're the lucky one, poet." The trench night when Hossein had confessed his love for Leyla, their embrace in the cold.

Each memory was a dagger, beautiful and devastating. Reza clutched the blanket like it was Hossein's hand, the grief mixing with love, stripping him bare.

And Amir. He kept seeing Amir's face too. That moment when his eyes had gone wide, the shock and fear and realization all at once. Amir had been so young, only twenty-two. His daughter would grow up without ever knowing him. She'd see photos of her father, and that would be all she had. A frozen moment. A gap-toothed smile she'd never see in person.

Reza had tried to save him. Had pressed his hands against the wound, had felt the blood pumping hot between his fingers, had watched the light go out in those dark eyes. And he'd failed. Just like he'd failed Hossein, unable to stop the bleeding, unable to keep him alive.

How many more would die? How many more letters would go unfinished, photos spattered with blood, dreams cut short before they could bloom?

He decided then, through the pain, to finish the letter to Leyla. His hands trembled as he found a pencil in the bundle, the wood splintered, the point blunt. The act was excruciating, each word a wound reopened, but it was the only gift he could give his brother now—the only way to honour Hossein's love. He wrote, his script shaky, tears dropping on the paper, smudging the ink.

Leyla,

This is Reza, Hossein's brother. I wish I were writing to you with better news, but my heart is broken, and I know yours will be too when you read this. Hossein spoke of you constantly. In the trenches, when everything was dark and terrible, your name was a light on his lips. He dreamed of your jasmine tree, of the life you would build together. He carried your letters next to his heart. He loved you deeply, completely, with every part of himself.

Jamila Mikhail

He was killed in combat three days ago. He died bravely, as he lived, protecting others. His last thoughts were of you, and of my wife, Zahra. He told me to live—for you, for her. He wanted us to carry his love forward into the world. I am so sorry. I would give anything to change what happened, to bring him back to you. He deserved the life he dreamed of with you. He deserved to see the jasmine tree bloom. He deserved to grow old and read poetry in your garden. When I return to Isfahan, if you will allow it, I would like to visit you. To share his stories with you, to tell you about the brother who was my whole world. Until then, know that he loved you. He loved you so much.

With deepest sorrow,
Reza

He sealed the letter with trembling hands, handing it to Navid with a whispered "Send it." The act felt sacred, a final gift to his brother, a way to ensure Hossein's love didn't die with him in the mud.

Navid took the letter carefully, as if it were made of glass. "I'm sorry about Hossein," he said quietly. "He was a good man. One of the best."

Reza could only nod, his throat too tight for words.

The days continued to blur. The morphine doses decreased as his wounds healed. The pain became more bearable, though the grief did not. He watched men arrive and depart—some walking, some carried, some covered with sheets. The war churned on, indifferent.

At night, when the tent was quieter, when the moans and cries had faded to occasional whimpers, Reza lay awake and endlessly wondered how he was supposed to exist in a world without Hossein. How was he supposed to go back to Isfahan and walk past Hossein's empty house? How was he supposed to face their parents and tell them their eldest son was gone? How was he supposed to teach again, to write poetry, to laugh, to live, when half of himself had been left in the mud near Ahvaz?

But Hossein's words kept echoing: *"Live, Reza. Live."*

It wasn't a suggestion. It was a command. An act of love. Hossein's final gift to him—permission, obligation, desperate plea—to survive.

A medic returned another day, adjusting Reza's bandages, the antiseptic's sting a fleeting distraction. "You'll be back to light duty before you know it," he said. "Wounds aren't deep and are healing clean. You were lucky."

The Moonlit Rose of Isfahan

There was that word again. *Lucky.*

The tent's cacophony continued—a soldier's death rattle, a medic's curse, the flap of canvas like a heartbeat. Reza lay back, the vulnerability lingering, fear and grief a storm that threatened to drown him.

But Hossein's memory was a light in the darkness. His brother's final words echoed: "Live, Reza. For her. For Zahra. For Leyla." It was a command, a plea, a gift. Reza closed his eyes, clutching Hossein's Hafez volume to his chest, and made a vow.

He would survive. He would endure. He would carry his brother's love forward into the world. He would live—for Zahra, for Leyla, for the jasmine trees that would bloom long after this war was forgotten. He would live because Hossein had asked him to, because his brother's sacrifice demanded it, because love—even in the midst of this hell—was worth holding onto.

He would live for Amir's daughter, who would never know her father. For all the men who wouldn't make it home. For every unfinished letter, every dream cut short, every love left waiting.

The infirmary's hell would be his crucible. His wounds would be scars on body and soul. But he would survive. For her. For them.

For Hossein.

He had to.

That night, as the tent quieted to occasional groans and the lamp's flame dimmed, Reza's lips moved in prayer for the first time since the blast. Not the formal prayers of his youth—those words felt too clean for the filth of this moment—but something raw, desperate.

"Ya Allah," he whispered into the darkness, his voice barely audible. "Why him? Why Hossein and not me?" The questions felt blasphemous, but they poured out anyway. "He was better than me. Stronger. He had Leyla waiting. I don't understand Your mercy."

His hand found the small Quran in his belongings—the one Ahmed had gifted him before deployment. Reza opened it with trembling fingers, the script swimming in his tears. He couldn't read it properly in this state, couldn't focus, but holding it felt like holding on to a piece of Hossein somehow.

"Keep him safe," Reza prayed, though his brother was already gone.

"Let him be in peace. Let Leyla find peace. Let me...let me be worthy of surviving when he didn't."

The prayer brought no answers, no comfort. But it was all he had.

Chapter Twelve

Isfahan, 1988

The mid-afternoon sun bathed the courtyard garden in a warm glow, its light filtering through the jasmine vines that climbed the stone walls, casting intricate shadows over the vibrant beds of crimson roses, white tulips, and lavender. The air was rich with layered scents—jasmine's heady sweetness, lavender's calming musk, mint's crisp bite, and the faint earthiness of freshly turned soil— blending with the lingering musk of Reza's khaki military uniform, still worn from the morning's breakfast, its medals glinting softly.

Reza and Zahra sat close together under the mulberry tree, its broad leaves offering cool shade that reminded them of their courtship. Their hands were entwined, fingers interlaced, her dress brushing the soft grass, his boots resting gently on the earth. Shirin and Simin lounged nearby—Simin batting lazily at a fallen leaf, Shirin sprawled in a sunbeam, her purrs a gentle hum in the quiet of the ceasefire.

Reza's scarred hand traced Zahra's palm, his soulful brown eyes meeting her almond ones, shimmering with love and a trace of the grief they had shared earlier. The garden—Zahra's creation through eight years of war—was a living testament to her resilience. Roses for hope, tulips for renewal, lavender for calm. Its serenity was a balm to Reza's heart, still raw from Hossein's death and the toll of the war that had just recently ended.

Their earlier conversation about the scattered remnants of their families had deepened their bond—Hossein's absence, their parents in Shiraz, Zahra's mother in Syria, her distant half-brother in Tehran. Now they held each other, Reza's arms wrapped around her frame, her head resting against his chest, the steady thump of his heartbeat mingling with the garden's soft sounds: the rustle of leaves in the breeze, the distant chirp of a sparrow, the faint trickle of water from a small clay fountain Zahra had crafted during the war.

Zahra pulled back slightly, her hand still in his, her eyes bright with a tender memory. "Reza," she said, her voice melodic, tinged with a shy reverence, "before we go inside, there's something I want to show you."

She rose, guiding him gently to his feet, her dress swaying as she led him to a corner of the garden where a sturdy lavender bush thrived, its purple buds vibrant against the dark soil. Reza followed, his boots sinking slightly into the soft earth, the sensation foreign after years of hard-packed trenches, his heart stirring with curiosity and love.

Zahra knelt beside the lavender, her fingers brushing the leaves, releasing a fresh wave of fragrance. She looked up at him, her expression a mix of devotion and wistfulness. "This is where I buried one of your letters," she said softly, her voice steady but thick with emotion. "In 1982, after a bombing shook the city. It was a ritual, to keep you safe. I buried it here, under this lavender, and I still remember every word."

Reza's breath caught, his eyes widening as he knelt beside her, his scarred hand resting on the soil, the cool, crumbly texture grounding him. The memory of his wartime letters—most often scribbled in the dim light of trenches, poured out to Zahra between patrols—flooded him. Each one had been a lifeline to her, to home.

"You... remember it?" he asked, his baritone trembling, a tear pricking his eye as he imagined her alone, tending this garden, clinging to his words.

Zahra nodded, her smile shy but radiant, and she began to recite the letter from memory, her voice clear, carrying the weight of those war-torn years:

"My dearest Zahra, my rose," she began, her tone soft but deliberate, as if the words were etched in her soul. "The nights here are cold, the stars dim through the smoke, but you are my light, my warmth. I carry you in every breath, every beat of my heart. The war tries to break us, but it cannot touch what we have. I wrote this for you, my love: 'In the desert of my days, you are the oasis, your laughter the water that saves me. Your eyes, twin stars, guide me through the dark, and I vow to return to you, to bloom where your love grows.' I dream of our garden, of holding you under the mulberry tree, of a life where war is only a memory. Yours forever, Reza."

Her voice trembled on the final words, the poem's cadence echoing their courtship in 1979, when Reza had first recited Hafez to her, and their wedding less than a year later, when he had vowed to be her home. Tears streamed down Reza's face, his chest heaving with sobs, the vulnerability raw, the garden blurring through his grief and love. The letter, buried under the lavender, had been her act of faith, a prayer for his survival, and hearing it now, spoken from her memory, broke his heart anew.

"Zahra," he choked, pulling her into his arms, their bodies pressed close, her warmth a contrast to the cold of his memories—comrades' deaths, the shrapnel's bite, the infirmary's own hell. "You kept me alive," he whispered, his voice breaking, his tears soaking her hair. "Every word... you carried me through."

Zahra held him tightly, her own eyes glistening, her hands stroking his back, feeling the tension in his scarred frame. "I had to," she murmured, her voice thick with love. "Your words, your love—they were my strength, just as this garden was. I memorized every letter, but this one... it was my heart's anchor." She pressed her forehead to his, their breaths mingling, the lavender's scent wrapping them like a vow.

They lingered there, kneeling by the lavender bush, Reza's hand on the soil where his letter lay buried, Zahra's fingers entwined with his. The sun dipped lower, painting the garden in hues of amber and rose, the mulberry tree's shade deepening. Simin batted at a butterfly, Shirin stretched in the sunbeam, and their soft laughter broke through Reza's tears, a fragile joy.

"Your love is my home," Reza whispered, his poetry a vow, his voice steadier now, his eyes locked on hers.

Zahra smiled, her shyness fading, her heart full. "And you are mine," she replied, her voice a promise, sealing their bond in the garden's peace.

As the late afternoon sun faded into soft twilight, they made their way inside. The air grew cooler, and Reza retreated to the bathroom while Zahra moved to the kitchen to prepare their evening meal.

The bathroom was a sanctuary, its quiet broken only by the soft splash of water as Reza settled into the copper basin filled with rosewater-scented water. Steam curled upward like whispered prayers. The tiled walls, adorned with intricate blue and white patterns, reflected the dim light of a single oil lamp, its flame flickering, casting shadows that danced across the room. His military uniform lay folded on a wooden stool, medals gleaming—a reminder of battles, victories, survival, but also the incredible price paid.

Reza dipped a cloth into the warm water and ran it over his arms, his fingers tracing the jagged scars from shrapnel. Each mark was a story of survival—the blasts that had killed his comrades, the shrapnel that had torn his flesh in multiple areas, the mustard gas that had burned his lungs. He paused, his hand trembling, the cloth dripping, as he thought how any fragment could have pierced his heart, how a single infection could have ended him in the infirmary's chaos.

Yet God had spared him. A miracle he felt in his bones. His heart surged with a vow to devote every waking moment to Zahra, his anchor, his home.

His tears fell, mixing with the bathwater, the rosewater's fragrance mingling with the salt of his grief and gratitude. Eight years married—since their radiant wedding in Shiraz—yet they had never properly celebrated an anniversary. The war had stolen those moments, scattering their families, leaving Hossein's love letters to Leyla unfinished, their parents frail in Shiraz, Zahra's mother in Syria.

"I'll make it up to you, my rose," he whispered, his baritone thick, the vow a prayer to honour her love, to build a life free of war's shadow.

In the kitchen, Zahra moved with quiet grace, her dress swaying as she stirred a pot of *fesenjan*. The rich aroma of pomegranate and walnut filled the air, mingling with the earthy scent of brewing tea and the warm crust of fresh *noon-e sangak* cooling on the counter. The kitchen

The Moonlit Rose of Isfahan

was small but alive, its tiled walls gleaming under the glow of a hanging lamp, a wooden table set for two—a rarity after eight years of cooking for one.

Shirin and Simin curled near the stove, their eyes quietly following Zahra's movements. She chopped herbs—mint, parsley, basil—from her garden, the knife's rhythm steady, her hands practiced but adjusting to the new weight of preparing meals for two. Her heart was full, a quiet happiness blooming like the roses she had tended through the war.

She hummed a melody from their wedding day, the *setar's* notes echoing in her mind, and smiled, still marvelling at finally being able to enjoy the garden with her husband—reciting Reza's letter, his tears, their embrace under the mulberry tree. This was what she had wanted, what she had waited for through air raids, her father's illness, Hossein's death, the loneliness of war.

She glanced at the table, set with plates and a small vase of lavender from the garden, and felt a pang of joy tempered by the memory of those lost years. Cooking for two felt foreign, the portions larger, but it was a happiness she clung to, each stir of the pot a promise of their future.

Reza rose from the bath, dried himself with a soft towel, and dressed in loose cotton clothes, the fabric cool against his skin. The absence of the uniform's weight was a relief. His heart, still raw, pulsed with love, the vow to Zahra burning bright.

In the kitchen, Zahra turned as he entered, her eyes meeting his, her smile shy but radiant. "It's almost ready," she said, her voice melodic, gesturing to the *fesenjan*.

Reza stepped close, his hand brushing hers, the scent of her herbs and his rosewater mingling. "Your love is my home," he whispered, his poem a vow, and she leaned into him, their foreheads touching, the kitchen's warmth wrapping them in peace.

The twilight deepened as they sat at the table, the kitchen aglow with the warm flicker of the hanging lamp. Its light reflected off the blue and white tiled walls, casting a soft sheen on the wooden table set for two. The small vase of lavender stood at the centre—the same lavender from the garden where Zahra had buried Reza's 1982 letter—its calming scent a reminder of their afternoon embrace.

They began the meal, their hands brushing as they tore pieces of *sangak*, dipping them into the *fesenjan*. The sauce's richness coated their fingers, its flavour a burst of memory—Zahra's wartime meals, shared with neighbours, and their wedding feast. The act of eating together felt new, a rediscovery after eight years apart.

Zahra's almond eyes met Reza's, her smile shy but radiant. She took a sip of tea, its warmth spreading through her, and spoke, her voice thoughtful. "Reza, I've been thinking," she said, her fingers tracing the edge of her glass, the steam curling upward. "If you decide to return to teaching, I might... I might attend university myself."

Reza paused, a piece of *sangak* halfway to his mouth, his eyes widening with surprise and pride. "University?" he asked, his baritone soft, a smile tugging at his lips.

Zahra nodded, her cheeks flushing, her gaze drifting to the lavender vase. "I never cared much for school," she admitted, her tone reflective. "Father's books—Hafez, Rumi, his old botany texts—were always enough for me. I loved learning from them, from the garden, not classrooms. But having you back, seeing how brilliant you are, how you light up talking about ideas even through your doubts... it inspires me. I want to learn more, maybe study literature or even horticulture, to understand the plants I've tended all these years."

Her voice grew steadier, her dream taking shape, inspired by Reza's intellect, his poetry, the letters she had memorized through the war.

Reza's heart swelled. He reached across the table, his scarred hand covering hers, the texture of her skin soft against his calloused fingers. "Zahra, my rose," he said, his voice thick with emotion, "I'm so proud of you. Whatever you choose—university, the garden, anything—I'll support you. You're brilliant, too, you know. The way you kept this home, this garden, through rationing and shortages because of the war... it's a kind of wisdom no classroom can teach."

His words echoed their courtship, when her shy intelligence had captivated him, and their tender moment in the garden. He squeezed her hand, his eyes glistening, the *fesenjan's* aroma grounding their shared joy.

The Moonlit Rose of Isfahan

But the mention of teaching stirred a bittersweet ache in Reza's chest, his smile faltering. He set down his tea, the glass warm against his palm, and his gaze drifted to the lavender, thoughts of Hossein surfacing like a tide.

"Teaching again... it's hard to imagine without Hossein," he said, his voice quieter, the vulnerability raw. "He was the teacher, the one who knew how to command a room, guide students. I always lived in his shadow, and I liked it there—safe, following his lead."

He paused, his fingers tracing a scar on his wrist, a remnant of the shrapnel that had nearly taken him. The memory of Hossein's death in the trench flooded back—his brother's blood, his last words.

"Now he's gone, and I... I don't know if I can step into that role without him. Maybe it's time to find my own path."

Zahra leaned forward, her hand tightening on his, her eyes steady with love. "Reza, you're not in his shadow anymore," she said, her voice firm but gentle. "You never were, not to me. You're a poet, a dreamer, and you have so much to give."

She paused, her thumb brushing his scar. "What if you used your engineering degree? The country needs rebuilding—roads, bridges, homes. You could help repair what the war broke, make something lasting."

Her words sparked a flicker of hope, her belief in him a light through his grief.

Reza nodded, his throat tight, the idea taking root like the lavender in their garden. "Repairing the country," he murmured, his voice steadier. "It feels... right. Something real, something Hossein would've been proud of."

He lifted her hand, pressing a kiss to her knuckles, the gesture tender, their eyes locked. The *fesenjan's* richness, the tea's earthy comfort, the lavender's calm—they grounded this moment, a shared meal that felt like a new beginning, a promise to build a future together despite the war's scars.

They continued eating, their laughter soft as Simin leaped onto the table, swiping at a stray piece of *sangak*. Zahra gently shooed her down, and Reza whispered again, "Your love is my home."

Zahra smiled, her heart full, the table a testament to their resilience, their love a steady root in the uncertain soil of tomorrow.

Chapter Thirteen

Isfahan, 1988

The twilight deepened into early evening, the kitchen now quiet after their shared meal. The air was still rich with the lingering aromas of *fesenjan's* pomegranate-walnut tang, the earthy warmth of tea, and the faint musk of lavender from the small vase on the wooden table. The hanging lamp cast a soft glow across the blue and white tiled walls, its light glinting off the now-empty plates and the cooling samovar.

Shirin and Simin sprawled near the stove, stomachs full, their purrs a gentle undercurrent to the faint clink of dishes as Reza cleared the table, his movements deliberate but tender, his cotton tunic and pants soft against his skin, a feeling that was both still strange and comforting. The act of cleaning together—scraping remnants of food, washing plates in the small sink with soap—felt grounding, a domestic peace he had never quite known before.

His heart, warmed by Zahra's earlier talk of university and her belief in his engineering path, pulsed with love. Her recitation of his letter in the garden remained vivid in his mind, fuelling his desire to create something special tonight. He had a lot to make up for, and he didn't want to waste even a single moment.

In the bathroom, Zahra bathed, the air thick with steam and the soothing scent of sandalwood. The copper basin reflected the flicker of an oil lamp. The tiled walls, patterned with intricate swirls, gleamed softly, the sound of water splashing gently as she moved, her fuller curves relaxed in the warmth.

She hummed a melody from their wedding, her voice soft, the notes mingling with the drip of the faucet and the occasional rustle of her dress, draped over a stool as the wind picked up. Her thoughts lingered on Reza—his pride in her university dreams, his bittersweet reflection on teaching, his kiss on her knuckles at the table. How she had missed those tender kisses! Such simple acts of affection, yet they carried so much weight.

The bath was a rare moment of solitude since Reza's arrival—she'd missed him so much she didn't want to leave him alone even for a moment—her hands gliding over her skin with the soapy cloth, the water caressing her body, soothing the faint ache still lingering from the morning.

She felt a tingle of anticipation, her skin flushing not just from the heat but from the memory of Reza's touch, his playful *commander* tease at breakfast, and the way his eyes lit up when he looked at her. She lingered a bit longer, savouring the warmth, her heart full with the joy of their reunited life, the promise of a future together at last.

Reza finished in the kitchen, drying his hands on a cloth, the scent of soap clinging to his fingers. He glanced at the lavender vase—a reminder of Zahra's wartime ritual—and a spark of inspiration ignited.

He moved quietly to the bedroom, the hallway dimly lit, the air carrying a faint jasmine scent from the garden. The bedroom was intimate, its woven Persian rug soft underfoot, the walls adorned with embroidered hangings, the wooden bed draped in quilts of deep blue and gold.

Reza set to work, his heart racing with anticipation, wanting to surprise Zahra with a romantic ambiance. He lit two small oil lamps, their flames casting a warm, flickering glow across the room, shadows dancing on the walls like lovers in an embrace. He scattered rose petals from the garden across the bed, their crimson hue vivid against the quilts, their fragrance filling the air with a heady sweetness.

From a drawer, he retrieved a vial of rosewater, sprinkling a few

The Moonlit Rose of Isfahan

drops on the pillows, the scent a tender echo of their bath-time rituals. He arranged a small tray on the bedside table with dates and a glass of sharbat, the pomegranate drink's ruby colour glinting in the lamplight.

Then, with a playful grin, Reza slipped on his khaki military uniform jacket—the one Zahra had teased him about that morning, calling him *Commander*. The fabric was worn but familiar, its medals glinting faintly, a way to rekindle the lighthearted intimacy of their earlier banter.

He adjusted the collar, his hands smoothing the fabric, his reflection in a small mirror showing a man both rugged and tender, his soulful brown eyes sparkling with mischief and love. He stood by the bed, the room now a haven of warmth and fragrance, his heart beating with anticipation for her return.

Zahra emerged from the bath, her skin glowing with a soft sheen from the rosewater, wrapped in a light robe that clung slightly to her damp curves, her dark hair loose and cascading over her shoulders in waves that caught the light. The steam followed her like a veil, the scent of sandalwood soap mingling with her natural fragrance.

She stepped into the bedroom, her eyes widening at the sight—the scattered rose petals, the flickering lamps creating a romantic haze, the tray of dates and sharbat, and Reza in his uniform jacket, his grin boyish yet commanding, the medals glinting like stars.

Her breath caught, a flush creeping up her cheeks, her shyness mingling with delight.

"Oh, Reza," she whispered, her voice melodic, a smile blooming on her lips. "What's all this?"

Reza stepped forward, his posture straightening in mock formality, embracing the "commander" role with a playful glint in his eyes.

"My lady," he said, his baritone low and commanding, but laced with tenderness, "the Commander has prepared the quarters for your pleasure." He extended a hand, his fingers open, inviting. "I command you to surrender to romance."

Zahra laughed, her shyness giving way to joy, her cheeks flushing deeper as she placed her hand in his, feeling the warmth of his palm, the callouses a reminder of his strength.

"Oh, Commander," she teased back, her tone flirtatious, her eyes sparkling, "have you come to sweep me away? Or are you just a poet in a commander's uniform?"

Reza pulled her close, his arms wrapping around her waist, the uniform jacket a firm contrast to the softness of her robe.

"Guilty as charged, my rose," he admitted, his voice husky, his lips brushing her ear. "But I have eight years of loving you to make up for. Eight years of nights I should have been holding you, pleasuring you, worshipping you." His words were fervent, sincere. "Tonight is just the beginning."

He led her to the bed, his hands gentle on her hips, the rose petals crunching softly under their feet, releasing more fragrance into the air. They sank onto the quilts, the fabric cool and inviting, the petals sticking to their skin.

Zahra's robe fell open slightly, revealing the curve of her breast, and Reza's eyes darkened with desire, but he kept the pace slow, his fingers tracing her arm, sparking goosebumps.

Their lips met in a slow, tender kiss, the passion building as tongues brushed, tasting the sweetness of dates from the tray and the lingering rosewater on their skin. Reza's hands slid under her robe, caressing her curves, his fingers gliding over her breasts, circling her nipples with a gentle pressure that drew a soft gasp from her.

The sensation sent a tingle through Zahra, her body responding with a warm flush, her shyness adorable as she blushed, her thighs pressing together in anticipation.

"Commander," she murmured against his lips, her voice breathy, "your orders indeed are... irresistible."

Reza grinned, his role-play deepening, his voice commanding but loving. "Then surrender, my lady," he said, his hands exploring her, parting her thighs gently, his fingers teasing her, finding her ready, the touch sparking a pulsing warmth in her core.

As they undressed, the robe slipping from her shoulders, the jacket shed with a playful toss, their bodies pressed close, skin against skin. The scars on Reza's chest were a map Zahra traced with reverent fingers, her touch healing.

Reza began to recite his own poetry, his voice a low rumble as his hands caressed her:

"In the garden of your body, I am the wanderer returned," he whispered, his fingers finding her sweet spots, pleasuring her with a rhythm that matched his words. "Every petal of your skin, a verse I've dreamed to write. In the desert years, I thirsted for your rain, and now I drink deep, my beloved, my oasis of light."

The words washed over her, sparking waves of pleasure through her body, her moans soft, her body arching into him. He continued, his lips brushing her neck, his hand fondling her breast:

"Let our love be the country we rebuild," he murmured. "Let each touch lay foundation, each kiss raise walls of home. In your arms, the war dissolves to ash, and I am born again, no longer scattered bones but flesh made whole in your embrace."

Zahra revelled in it, her shyness melting into adoration, her hands exploring his hardness, stroking with affectionate pressure, sparking a throbbing heat in him.

"Poet or commander?" she teased breathlessly, her fingers lingering on his scars, her eyes sparkling.

Reza laughed, his role-play unwavering, his voice commanding as he rolled her beneath him. "The Commander demands your pleasure," he said, his lips trailing down her body, kissing her breasts, the sensation sending electric tingles through her, her body flushing with heat.

He parted her legs, his fingers dipping into her entrance, the slick warmth drawing a gasp, her hips lifting to meet him.

"Surrender to me," he commanded playfully, his eyes dark with desire.

She giggled, her voice breathy. "Yes, Commander... but I know the poet's heart beats beneath."

Their lovemaking deepened, Reza entering her gently, his thrusts slow and commanding, her body welcoming him with a warm embrace, the friction sparking pleasure for both.

He whispered more of his poetry, his voice rhythmic with their movements:

"Beyond the smoke and blood and grief, there blooms a field of jasmine white. Meet me there, my rose, where scars become the ground for flowers, where loss transforms to love, where every broken piece of me finds home in you tonight."

The words heightened the sensuality, his hands on her skin, fondling with affectionate pressure, her moans mingling with his verses. Zahra's hands clutched his back, her nails grazing his scars, the sensation a sweet ache for him, their bodies moving in unison, her warmth enveloping him, sparking a building heat in his core.

They kissed passionately, tongues entwining, the taste of rosewater and tea lingering, their breaths mingling as pleasure crested. Zahra's shyness gave way to revelling in his "command," her giggles turning to moans, her body arching, the waves of warmth crashing through her.

Reza's role-play softened into pure love, his thrusts deepening, the friction a delicious fire for both. Their climax came in a shared burst of sensation—her pulsing warmth, his throbbing release.

They collapsed, breathless, tangled in quilts, rose petals clinging to their sweat-glistened skin. Laughter bubbled as they held each other, foreheads pressed together.

"I love you," Zahra whispered, her voice teasing yet sincere, her eyes shimmering with emotion. "My Commander. My poet."

Reza chuckled, kissing her softly, his heart full. "I love you, my moonlit rose. Always yours."

The bedroom glowed softly in the late evening, the two oil lamps casting a warm, flickering light that danced across the walls. The room felt like a cocoon, intimate and sacred, the quiet broken only by the soft rustle of quilts, the distant chirp of crickets, and the gentle purrs of Shirin and Simin, now curled at the foot of the bed—their own nightly ritual—their fur catching the lamplight. Reza and Zahra lay entwined, their bodies warm, her head resting on his scarred chest, his arm draped over her, their breaths slowing as they basked in the afterglow.

Zahra's fingers traced lazy circles on Reza's skin, her touch featherlight, her almond eyes shimmering with love and mischief as she lifted her head to meet his soulful gaze, now heavy with the onset of sleep. The quilts cocooned them, the rose petals clinging to their skin.

She smiled, her shyness giving way to playful affection, her voice melodic and teasing. "My Commander," she murmured, her lips brushing his jaw, the stubble rough against her softness, "you're good at more than just the battlefield."

The Moonlit Rose of Isfahan

Her tone was light but suggestive, her eyes sparkling, her hand sliding down his chest, lingering on a scar. "You're gaining ground in mapping and exploring my body, aren't you?"

She giggled, her cheeks flushing.

Reza chuckled, a low, sleepy rumble, his hand squeezing her hip, the warmth of her skin grounding him. "My rose," he said, his baritone thick with affection and fatigue, "this Commander's only mission is to conquer your heart."

Zahra's expression softened, becoming more serious even as playfulness lingered in her eyes. She propped herself up on one elbow, her hair falling over her shoulder, rose petals caught in the dark strands.

"Reza," she said, her voice quieter now, more vulnerable. "I need to confess something. I hadn't realized... the true depth of my body's longing for you. All those years, I thought I was managing, that I was strong enough to wait. And I was—I did wait."

She paused, her fingers tracing the line of his collarbone. "But now that you're here, now that I can touch you again... I can't keep my hands off you. It's like my body is trying to make up for every night I slept alone, every morning I woke reaching for you and finding only emptiness."

Her cheeks flushed deeper, her characteristic shyness warring with her honesty. "Eight years of hunger I didn't even know I was carrying. And now..." She smiled, a little embarrassed but radiant. "Now I understand what it means to starve and then feast."

Reza's eyes glistened, his heart swelling with love and a touch of regret for those lost years. He pulled her closer, kissing her forehead tenderly. "My rose, you never have to apologize for wanting me. I'm yours—every moment, every touch, every breath. We'll make up for all of it, together, because I must admit that I am also hungry beyond what food can satisfy."

His eyes caught sight of his military *chafiyeh*, the white scarf folded neatly on a nearby chair where he'd left it earlier. A playful glint sparked in his eyes.

"Speaking of new missions," he said, reaching for the *chafiyeh* with a grin, "this old battlefield companion needs a new purpose."

Before Zahra could respond, he draped the soft fabric around her shoulders, then playfully wrapped it around her like a cocoon, pulling her close until she was bundled against him, laughing.

"There," he said with mock seriousness, his Commander voice returning. "Now you're captured. The *chafiyeh* that once shielded me from sun and sand now has a far better use—keeping you close to me."

Zahra giggled, her voice muffled slightly by the fabric. "Oh no, I've been captured by the Commander! What will he do with his prisoner?"

"Keep her," Reza murmured, his voice softening as he kissed the top of her head through the *chafiyeh*. "Forever."

He began unwrapping her slowly, the fabric sliding away to reveal her face, her neck, her shoulders, each revelation punctuated with a kiss. "This scarf saw me through the worst of it," he whispered. "Now it gets to see the best—you, here, in my arms."

Zahra's eyes shimmered with emotion as he finished unwrapping her, the *chafiyeh* now draped loosely around them both like a shared embrace.

His eyes began to flutter, the exertion of the day pulling him toward sleep. He pulled her closer, their legs tangling, the quilts soft and warm, the rosewater scent on her skin a soothing balm. Zahra sensed his drowsiness, her heart swelling with tenderness. She shifted to sit up slightly, loosely draping her robe over her shoulders.

"Rest, my love," she whispered, her hands moving to his back, her fingers beginning a gentle massage, kneading the tense muscles along his spine, the texture of his scars now familiar under her touch.

Reza sighed, his body melting under her ministrations. Zahra traced his skin delicately, her touch reverent, feeling the at times rough, puckered texture. Her heart ached, not because the scars were ugly—she found them beautiful, a part of Reza, a testament to his resilience—but because of the pain he never fully voiced, the grief she knew he silently carried.

She prayed silently, her lips moving with soft murmurs. "Let my touch erase his pain," she whispered. "Let him feel only love. Let these scars be places where light enters, where healing grows. Let him know peace."

Her fingers lingered on a scar near his shoulder, no doubt shrapnel from one of the endless artillery blasts he'd endured on the frontlines.

The Moonlit Rose of Isfahan

She imagined smoothing away the hurt, her love a balm for wounds deeper than skin.

"You are whole," she breathed, barely audible. "You are loved. You are home."

She continued for a while, her massage steady and loving, the room's quiet enveloping them—the lamps' soft flicker, the crickets' song, the cats' purrs.

Reza's breathing slowed, deepening into the rhythm of sleep, his face peaceful in a way it rarely was—no tension at his temples, no tightness at his jaw, the war's weight lifted entirely in this sanctuary they'd created together.

She watched him, her eyes glistening, her heart full of gratitude for his survival, their reunion, the life they were rebuilding.

She lay beside him, her arm draping him, her body curling against his, the quilts wrapping them in warmth. The rose petals clung to her hair, their scent a reminder of their lovemaking, and she fell asleep, her breath syncing with his, the night a gentle embrace.

Reza woke early, the first light of dawn filtering through the window, painting the room in hues of pink and gold, the lamps now extinguished, the air cool and fresh with morning dew and jasmine.

He lay still for a moment, Zahra's arm over him, her face serene in sleep, her dark hair splayed across the pillow, a rose petal caught in the strands. His heart swelled, the peace of his sleep—a rarity, unmarred by nightmares—grounding him in gratitude.

He wanted to keep loving her, to surprise her with a gesture as tender as her massage the night before. He slipped from the bed, careful not to wake her, the quilts rustling softly, and padded to the kitchen, his cotton tunic and pants quiet against his skin.

The kitchen was still, the lavender vase catching the dawn light, the scent of last night's *fesenjan* faint but lingering. Reza set to work, preparing Zahra's favourite breakfast—*kaleh pache*, a hearty soup of lamb's head and hooves, a dish her father had also loved, and had in fact taught her.

The rich aroma filled the air as he simmered it with garlic and herbs from the garden. He added a plate of fresh *barbari* bread, its crust golden and crisp, and a bowl of *mast-o-khiar*, yogurt mixed with cucumber and mint, its cool freshness a balance to the soup's warmth.

He brewed tea, the samovar humming, and set the table with care, placing a single white tulip from the garden beside her plate, its petals a nod to renewal, their shared hope.

Zahra stirred as the scents wafted into the bedroom, her eyes fluttering open, a smile spreading as she saw Reza's empty side of the bed, knowing he was up to something loving.

She rose, wrapping her robe around her, the rose petal falling to the floor, and stepped into the kitchen, her heart full at the sight of Reza, his scarred hands arranging the breakfast, his eyes bright with love.

"My Commander," she teased softly, her voice warm, leaning against the doorway. "You're full of surprises, this time commanding my stomach with deliciousness!"

Reza turned, his grin boyish, pulling her into a gentle embrace, the tulip's scent mingling with the breakfast's warmth. "For you, my rose," he said, kissing her forehead. "Always."

They sat at the table, the dawn light streaming through the window, the kitchen cozy with the aroma of *kaleh pache*. Reza tore a piece of *barbari*, dipping it into the soup. Zahra sipped her tea, the glass warm in her hands, and glanced at him, her eyes sparkling with affection.

"Reza," she said, her tone practical but playful, "we're low on supplies. Would you come with me to the market today? We need more meat, rice... maybe some saffron for next time."

She smiled, her fingers brushing the tulip, the act of planning their day together a novelty after so long apart.

Reza nodded, his heart lifting at the simple joy of her request, a reminder of their new life. "Of course, my love," he said, his baritone warm, reaching for her hand. "The market with you sounds perfect. Maybe we'll also find some of those dates you love."

He winked, recalling the tray from the night before, and she laughed, her shyness fading.

"As long as my Commander doesn't try to command the vendors," she teased, her eyes twinkling.

The breakfast was a shared promise, their love a steady root in the dawn's light.

Chapter Fourteen

Isfahan, 1983

The Behzadi home in Isfahan stood silent under a leaden sky, the rain pattering against the tiled roof like insistent fingers tapping for entry. The house, Zahra's childhood home where she had grown up, was a modest single-story structure with whitewashed walls tinged beige from years of dust storms, its wooden window frames painted a faded turquoise—traditional protection against the evil eye. A small courtyard garden, now sodden and drooping under the downpour, held a struggling pomegranate tree her father had planted when she was born, its branches bare in the late autumn chill.

The arched doorway, carved with geometric patterns worn smooth by decades of hands, led into a dim interior where narrow corridors connected small, square rooms with low ceilings, their plaster cracked in places, revealing the clay brick beneath. The floors were covered in mismatched Persian rugs, their once-vibrant reds and blues now muted by time and foot traffic, their patterns telling stories of bazaars and weddings and births. The house felt heavier than usual that day, its corridors echoing with the muffled sounds of sorrow.

The air inside was thick and stagnant, carrying the sharp, medicinal scent of herbal tonics and camphor from the sickroom, mingled with the underlying mustiness of old rugs and the faint, comforting aroma of saffron tea brewing in the kitchen—a futile attempt to ward off the

Jamila Mikhail

chill of impending loss. The rain drummed steadily on the windows, a relentless rhythm that mirrored the laboured breathing of Zahra's father, lying on his bed in the dimly lit room at the end of the hall.

Zahra sat by her father's bedside, her slender frame perched on a wooden stool with a frayed cushion, her simple grey dress clinging slightly to her skin from the humidity, her long dark hair pinned back in a loose bun, a few strands escaping to frame her face. Her eyes, usually shimmering with quiet intelligence, were now red-rimmed and swollen from hours of watching, her hands clasped tightly around her father's frail one, feeling the cool, papery skin and the faint pulse beneath.

The room was small and cluttered with the remnants of a life winding down—a low wooden bed with faded quilts embroidered in intricate patterns of vines and flowers, a reminder of her mother's skilled hands; a small table crowded with medicine bottles, their glass labels smudged from frequent use, and a brass lamp casting a yellowish glow that fought the gloom filtering through the curtained window.

The walls, painted a soft cream years ago, were adorned with a framed photo of the family—Zahra as a child, her father strong and smiling, her mother beside him, and her half-brother standing awkwardly at the edge, his expression distant even then. The floor was covered in a worn Persian rug, its colours muted by time, muffling the creak of the stool as Zahra shifted, her heart aching with every ragged breath her father Ahmed took.

He was sixty-three but looked a decade older from the long illness that had ravaged him—cancer, the doctors said, though they could do little in wartime—lay propped on pillows, his once-robust frame now skeletal. He had been a handsome man in his youth, with warm brown eyes that crinkled at the corners when he smiled, a strong nose that gave his face character, and thick black hair he'd worn neatly combed.

Now his skin was sallow and stretched tight over sharp bones, his hair completely white and wispy against the pillow, his once-powerful hands—hands that had taught her to read, to tend roses, to find beauty in literature—reduced to fragile talons, the knuckles swollen with age and illness. His breathing was shallow, a wheezing rattle that filled the room like a broken accordion, each inhale a struggle, each exhale a sigh of resignation.

His eyes, clouded with pain but still holding that spark of love that had defined him as a father, flickered open occasionally, focusing on Zahra with a mix of devotion and regret. He had always doted on her, his only daughter, believing girls deserved special care and attention—extra sweets, stories at bedtime, encouragement to dream beyond tradition's constraints. Where other fathers might have dismissed a daughter's education, he had filled her childhood with his library, teaching her Hafez by candlelight, nurturing her love of gardens and poetry, treating her as precious as any son.

His hand weakly squeezed hers. "My daughter," he whispered, his voice a faint rasp, barely audible over the rain's patter. "You... married well. Reza... good man." The words were a balm and a wound, recalling the 1979 introduction to Hossein and Reza, her father's wish fulfilled before the war stole so much. Zahra nodded, tears slipping down her cheeks, dripping onto their joined hands, the salt mingling with the camphor's sting on her skin. "Rest, *Baba,*" she said, her voice trembling, smoothing his thin hair with her free hand, the strands brittle under her fingers.

As the hours stretched, the room grew darker, the lamp's flame sputtering on its wick, the rain intensifying into a downpour that hammered the roof like a mournful drum. Ahmed Behzadi's breaths grew shallower, his chest rising less with each laboured inhale, his hand slackening in hers. He mustered a final surge of strength, his eyes locking on Zahra's, his voice a whisper of wisdom and encouragement.

"Zahra, my jewel," he rasped, each word an effort. "Life is like the garden you love—storms come, petals fall, but the roots endure. Keep tending your heart, my girl. Love Reza fiercely, build a family, read your books, let the world see your light. Girls like you deserve the stars—don't let the darkness take that. I go in peace, knowing you're strong."

His words, laced with the love he'd always shown his only daughter, hung in the air, a final gift. Zahra sobbed, nodding. "I will, *Baba.* I love you." His eyes fluttered closed, a faint smile on his lips, and with a final, peaceful sigh, he passed, the room suddenly silent except for the rain's patter, the lamp's light dimming as if in sympathy.

Zahra collapsed forward, her forehead on the bed, her sobs

wrenching, her body shaking as grief poured out, the quilts absorbing her tears. Her mother Maryam, in the doorway, rushed to her, her arms wrapping around, but Zahra pulled away gently, needing solitude. "I need... a moment," she whispered, her voice broken, and her mother nodded, tears streaming, leading Farhad, her half-brother, out of the room.

Farhad, in his late thirties, stood tall but slightly stooped, as if perpetually uncomfortable in his own skin. He had inherited their father's strong nose and dark colouring, but where their father had been warm and demonstrative, Farhad was withdrawn, his face etched with a permanent expression of detachment. His eyes, a darker brown than Zahra's, rarely made direct contact, always seeming to look past or through people rather than at them. His black hair was cropped short, practical rather than stylish, already showing threads of grey at the temples, and his thin beard was trimmed close to his jaw.

He wore a simple dark shirt and trousers, his posture stiff as he hovered awkwardly in the doorway, clearly feeling the weight of obligation but unable to express the grief that surely lived beneath his distant exterior. He was the child of their father's first marriage, and Zahra's mother—his stepmother—had never quite won his affection. He had always remained distant, never quite connecting with their father's second family, already married with his own life by the time Zahra was a toddler. Now his face showed sorrow, but it was muted, as if filtered through years of practiced emotional distance.

Zahra stumbled to the adjoining dark room, a small storage space with stacked books and old rugs, the air musty and cool, dust motes floating in the faint light from the door crack. She sank to the floor, her back against the wall, the rough stone cold through her dress, her knees drawn up, her arms wrapped around them, rocking slightly as sobs racked her body.

Her father had been her whole world—the man who doted on her, believing girls deserved special care, indulging her with extra time in his library, teaching her to read Hafez by candlelight, encouraging her garden dreams despite tradition's constraints. He'd been her protector, her guide, much like Hossein had been to Reza. Now he was gone, the loss a void that swallowed her, the room's darkness mirroring the emptiness in her heart. The musty smell of old books reminded her of his study, the faint creak of the house settling like his cough, the rain's drum on the roof an echo of his laboured breaths.

She wept, her tears hot on her cheeks, her longing for Reza more powerful than ever—her husband, away on the frontlines, his letters her only connection. "Reza," she whispered, her voice choked. "I need you." Without her father, and with Reza gone, she felt utterly alone, the war's shadow lengthening, her heart fracturing under the weight of loss.

In the darkness of the storage room, Zahra's sobs gradually quieted into ragged breathing. She wiped her face with shaking hands and, almost without thinking, turned to face Mecca. Her body remembered the movements even when her mind was fractured with grief.

She didn't perform full salat—couldn't, not in this state—but she whispered Al-Fatiha, the opening prayer, her father's favourite. *"Bismillah ar-Rahman ar-Rahim..."* The familiar Arabic was a lifeline, each word a small stone to step across the river of grief. "Guide him, *Ya Allah*. Grant him peace. He was a good father. He loved Your gardens, Your poetry, Your creation."

The prayer didn't ease the pain, but it gave her something to hold onto—a ritual as old as grief itself.

The Persian mourning rituals began that night, the house transforming into a space of grief. Neighbours and relatives arrived, their footsteps soft on the rugs, bringing trays of *halva* and dates, the sweet scents cutting through the heaviness. The body was washed with rosewater by the men, including Farhad, his hands steady but his expression somber, the ritual a solemn cleansing. The water, scented with rose petals gathered from the courtyard garden, was poured reverently as prayers were murmured in Arabic, the liquid a purification for the soul's journey to the afterlife.

Women, including Zahra and her mother, prepared the house according to custom. Mirrors throughout the home were draped with black cloth to avoid vanity in grief, to prevent the soul from being trapped by its reflection, and to keep the focus on mourning rather than worldly concerns. Candles were lit in every room, their flames flickering like stars in the darkened spaces, their wax melting slowly, the scent of beeswax blending with frankincense burned in small brass censers. The *azan* called from the mosque, a mournful melody that echoed through the streets of Isfahan, signalling the time for the *janazah*—the funeral prayer that would be offered the next day.

Zahra participated numbly, her hands folding black scarves for the women who would attend, the fabric soft but heavy in her lap, her mind on her father's final words, his encouragement to keep tending her heart. That night, the family kept vigil, sitting in the main room on cushions arranged in a circle, reciting verses from the Quran in soft, rhythmic tones—Surah Yasin, the heart of the Quran, read for the deceased to ease their passage. The samovar hissed in the corner, tea poured and passed in small glass cups, its warmth a small comfort against the chill of loss.

The funeral the next day was held after the *zuhr* prayer, the midday time when the sun stood highest—tradition dictated that burials should happen swiftly, preferably before sunset on the day of death or the day after. The body, cleansed and wrapped in a simple white *kafan*—a seamless shroud symbolizing equality before God, for all returned to earth the same—was carried on a wooden bier by male relatives and neighbours, including Farhad, who walked with his jaw set, his grief locked behind his stoic expression.

The procession moved through Isfahan's narrow streets toward the cemetery, a blur of black-clad mourners under a grey sky. The rain had stopped, as if in respect, but the earth remained soft and muddy underfoot, the air heavy with the scent of wet stone and distant cooking fires. Men walked ahead, women followed behind, their black chadors pulled close, faces tear-streaked. Zahra walked with her mother and the other women, her steps mechanical, her heart hollowed out.

At the cemetery, the grave had been dug the night before—a simple rectangular plot oriented so the deceased would lie on his right side facing Mecca, as was required. The imam led the *janazah* prayer, the funeral salat performed standing in rows, with no bowing or prostration, the prayers offered silently in each person's heart for God to forgive the deceased and grant him peace. The communal prayer was brief but profound, each whispered *Allahu Akbar* a collective sending-off.

The body was lowered carefully into the grave, placed directly on the earth without a casket, as was custom, positioned on the right side to face the *Qiblah*. The men began covering the body with wooden planks to protect it, then filled the grave with earth, each shovelful a soft thud that echoed through the cemetery.

Mourners took turns tossing handfuls of soil, the dirt clumping in their palms, the gesture both final and communal. Zahra stepped forward when it was time for the women, her hand trembling as she released the earth, watching it scatter across the shroud. The finality of it broke her anew, tears streaming silently down her face.

The imam concluded with a *du'a*, a prayer asking God to grant mercy and forgiveness, his voice rising and falling like a wave over the gathering. Fresh flowers—white and yellow chrysanthemums—were placed on the now-covered grave, and someone sprinkled rosewater over the mound, its fragrance mingling with the smell of fresh soil and frankincense from the censer carried by an elderly woman.

Back at the house, the *aza*—the mourning gathering—began in earnest. The main room and courtyard were filled with neighbours, relatives, and community members who came to offer condolences and support. Women gathered in one space, men in another, as was customary. The Quran was recited continuously, the rhythmic verses a soothing drone that filled the house, verses about paradise and mercy and God's infinite compassion washing over the mourners like a balm.

Plates of dates and *halva* were passed around—the sweetness a symbolic reminder that even in death, there is sweetness in God's plan. Guests also brought *noon-e berenji* and *shirini* to share, acts of charity for the deceased's soul. The women wailed softly, their cries a cathartic release, Zahra joining them, her voice raw, the room's air thick with smoke from the samovar and the weight of shared grief. Her mother sat in the centre, receiving visitors who clasped her hands and murmured condolences and words of comfort.

Farhad stayed for several days, his presence awkward but dutiful. He helped with arrangements—organizing the food donations, ensuring guests were received properly, coordinating with the mosque for the upcoming memorial services. Despite his emotional distance, he fulfilled his obligations as a son, his letters from Tehran over the years now made real in this shared mourning. He spoke little, but his actions showed a commitment to honouring their father, even if his grief remained locked inside.

The mourning rituals continued according to tradition. On the third day after burial, the *sé roozé*—a gathering was held with more Quran recitations and prayers, neighbours sharing memories of her father's kindness, his generosity, his love of poetry and gardens. They spoke of how he had helped families during hard times, how he always had a kind word, how he treated his daughter with unusual respect and encouragement in an age when many fathers did not.

On the seventh day, the *haft roozé* brought another wave of visitors, more food, more prayers. The house never quite emptied during this time—there was always someone sitting with them, ensuring the family was not alone in their grief. Zahra moved through these days in a fog, accepting embraces, receiving prayers, responding automatically to condolences while her heart remained fractured.

The fortieth day—the *chehelom*—loomed ahead as a milestone, a major memorial when the community would gather again to honour the deceased and mark the completion of the intense mourning period. Until then, Zahra and her mother would continue to receive visitors, to pray, to light candles and burn incense, to keep their father's memory alive through ritual and remembrance.

Weeks passed in this rhythm of mourning, the house quieter now as the initial rush of visitors slowed. Zahra tended the garden when she could, her hands in the soil a therapy even in the autumn chill, the roses still blooming despite the cold, their petals a symbol of life enduring. The pomegranate tree her father had planted stood bare but resilient, its branches reaching toward the grey sky like prayers.

Her mother, grieving deeply, had begun to speak of practical matters—the house, the future, the reality of life continuing even as they mourned. But Zahra clung to this space, her father's memory in every room, in every book on his shelves, in the courtyard garden he had taught her to tend as a girl.

The Moonlit Rose of Isfahan

Then, one crisp morning when Zahra had returned to the home she shared with Reza, the post arrived with a knock at the. The mail carrier's voice was muffled as he called through the wood. Zahra opened it, her hands trembling as she took the bundle—two letters among the bills and notices, their familiar handwriting making her heart skip.

One from Hossein, his script bold and confident, the other from Reza, his handwriting neat but hurried. She clutched them to her chest for a moment, feeling the precious connection to the frontlines, to her husband, to the brother-in-law who had become family. Then she moved to the kitchen, sitting at the low wooden table where she usually wrote her own letters. The lamp's light illuminated the papers as she opened Hossein's letter first, his familiar warmth radiating from the page even before she read a word.

Little sister Zahra,

The days here near Ahvaz are heavy, the air thick with death and destruction. The earth trembles with each shell, the sky weeps smoke, and the cries of the wounded pierce the heart. I've seen things no man should—homes reduced to rubble, families torn apart, young lives snuffed out like candles. Yet, amidst this hell, I trust in God's mercy to guide us. I pray daily that Reza and I will return to you, to the garden in Isfahan where your roses bloom, their scent a memory that keeps me sane when Reza carries the dried flowers you send him.

Today, I saw the poet do something that stirred my soul. A little girl, an orphan of this cruel war, was among the civilians fleeing. She was terrified, alone, her eyes wide with fear. Reza knelt beside her, his gentle hands braiding her hair to calm her, his voice soft as he promised her safety until she could be taken to a camp. It was a small act, but it spoke of his heart, Zahra. He will be a wonderful father someday, a man who builds a home filled with love, just as you nurture your garden with care.

If God wills that only one of us returns, I pray it is Reza. He deserves to build a life with you, to hold you under Isfahan's stars, to recite Rumi by your side. My heart is full knowing you two have each other, your love a light that outshines this darkness.

Little sister—and you are my sister, the one I never had but always wanted—I love you dearly. Your kindness, your fierce loyalty to my brother, your quiet strength, all inspire me. Watching Reza love you with such devotion has taught me what real love looks like. It gives me hope that I might build something as beautiful with Leyla when this war ends. Tell Reza to write more poems—I need something to laugh at in the trenches, and his romantic verses about your eyes and roses always make me smile.

Keep tending your garden, Zahra, and know that my prayers are with you both. When we return—God willing—we will plant that jasmine tree with Leyla, and the four of us will sit in your garden drinking tea and laughing about these dark days as if they were only a bad dream.

With all my love,

Hossein

She smiled through tears, his affection warming her even as her heart ached. His words—calling her little sister, speaking of Leyla and future jasmine trees, his brotherly teasing about Reza's poetry—were so alive, so full of optimism and love. The letter was dated weeks ago, just after her father's death, before whatever hell had unfolded since.

She pressed the letter to her chest for a moment, grateful for his love, for the way he had embraced her as family. Then, with trembling hands, she reached for Reza's letter.

Her heart skipped as she unfolded it, the paper crinkling under her fingers, the ink slightly smudged—perhaps from mud, perhaps from tears. His words started tender, his love pouring out, familiar phrases that echoed the letters she had memorized during their separation:

My beloved Zahra, my rose—In the desert of my days, you are the oasis...

But then the words shifted, and the news hit like a mortar blast:

I must tell you the worst—Hossein is gone, killed in an assault near Ahvaz. He was brave to the end, his last words of you and Leyla. He shielded me, Zahra... the shrapnel that hit me could have been fatal, but he saved me. I am wounded but alive. I will heal. But Hossein—my brother, my north star—is gone, and I am broken...

The room spun, the lamp's light blurring through sudden tears. The kitchen's warmth turned cold, the lavender's scent from the courtyard garden choking rather than comforting. Zahra's sobs erupted, raw and wrenching, her hands clutching the letter as if she could crush the terrible news, make it untrue through sheer force of will.

The grief was a double blow—her father, dead just weeks ago, his body barely cold in the ground, and now Hossein. Her brother-in-law, her family, the one who treated her like the sister he never had, his teasing warmth, his protective love, his dreams of planting jasmine trees—gone. The soul-crushing pain was visceral, a knife twisting in her chest, her breaths coming in gasps.

She looked at Hossein's letter again, still on the table, his words about returning home, about laughing in the garden, about jasmine trees and hope. All of it cut short. All of it impossible now. His unfinished dreams with Leyla, mentioned so tenderly in both letters, would never be realized. His love letters forever incomplete.

Her mother, who had been visiting, rushed in from the courtyard, her face paling at Zahra's cries, and wrapped her arms around her daughter. The embrace was a fragile hold against the wave of loss. Zahra clung to her, her body shaking, the kitchen chair creaking under her weight, the samovar's hum a mocking normalcy in the background. "Hossein... gone," she choked, the words tasting like ash. The rain started again outside, pattering on the windows like fate's cruel laughter. The grief was all-consuming, the house feeling even emptier than it had since Reza's departure. The war's cruelty invaded every corner of their lives, stealing beloved men with ruthless efficiency.

As her sobs subsided to ragged breaths, Zahra pulled back from her mother's embrace, her eyes wide with a new terror, her voice dropping to a whisper of dread. "Mother, what if it had been Reza?" She gripped the letter tighter, her knuckles white. "He was there—shrapnel hit him too. He says he'll heal, but... what if he's next? How could I live without both Father and Reza? The war takes everything—Hossein gone, Father gone. If Reza..."

Her voice broke, the fear a vice on her heart. The kitchen's lamp cast long shadows across the table, across the letters—one full of hope and life, the other bearing news of death. Her mother held her, whispering comforts, murmuring prayers, but the doubt lingered like smoke.

The war's shadow lengthened across everything. Zahra sat there, caught between grief for the father and brother-in-law she had lost, and terror for the husband who remained in danger. Her longing for Reza burned like a desperate flame in the darkness, the need to see him, to touch him, to know he was truly alive becoming almost unbearable.

She looked down at Hossein's letter again, his words about being her brother, about loving her like a sister, about being inspired by Reza's devotion to her. Tears fell onto the paper, blurring the ink. She would carry these words with her always, would honour his memory by tending the garden he had praised, by loving Reza with the fierceness Hossein had admired.

But for now, she could only weep—for her father, for Hossein, for Leyla's shattered dreams, for the jasmine tree that would never be planted, for all the futures the war had stolen. The rain drummed on, relentless, washing Isfahan in grey, and Zahra sat at her father's table, surrounded by loss, clinging to the fragile hope that Reza would survive to come home to her.

Chapter Fifteen
Isfahan, 1988

The mid-morning sun was bright over the bustling market streets—a labyrinth of narrow alleys lined with stalls overflowing with vibrant wares. The ceasefire held fragilely after years of war, and Reza and Zahra walked toward the bazaar, their fingers interlaced, her green dress swaying gently against her legs, his cotton tunic and pants soft against his skin.

The air was alive with a cacophony of scents layered thick enough to taste: roasted cumin's sharp, almost burning bite from a spice stall where copper bowls overflowed with crimson paprika and golden turmeric; the syrupy sweetness of fresh dates, their sticky skins glistening in woven baskets; the earthy, musty aroma of burlap sacks brimming with rice, the grains catching sunlight like tiny pearls; the sharp, vinegary tang of pickled turnips in cloudy brine, their pale pink hue visible through glass jars; and the faint, gritty musk of dust kicked up by countless feet—sandalled, booted, bare—scuffing across uneven cobblestones worn smooth by decades of traffic.

Voices wove a frenetic tapestry: vendors bellowing prices in hoarse, competing shouts—"Fresh pomegranates! Best in Isfahan!"—their voices cracking from hours of hawking; children laughing in high, piercing peals as they wove between legs like nimble sparrows; women bargaining in rapid, staccato Farsi, their hands gesturing emphatically over eggplants and onions, gold bracelets clinking at their wrists; the rhythmic clatter of wooden carts rolling over cobblestones, wheels squeaking protest; and the occasional plaintive bleat of a tethered goat, its rope straining against a wooden post, its golden eyes blinking slowly in the heat.

The streets were overcrowded, Isfahan having swelled as a haven for refugees fleeing the Iran-Iraq War's frontlines—families displaced, their homes reduced to rubble, now scraping by in this city. They were everywhere: a mother with hollow cheeks holding a listless infant, her threadbare black chador patched at the hem; an old man with a grey beard selling tarnished copper bangles from a tattered cloth spread on the ground, his fingers gnarled with arthritis; a teenage boy with one leg missing, balanced on crude wooden crutches, his eyes too old for his years as he begged with an upturned cap; women with worn shawls huddled in doorways, their faces etched with exhaustion and the particular haunted look of those who had seen too much.

Their presence was a silent testament to the war's reach—displacement made visible in patched clothes, in the way they moved with the careful economy of those who had learned to make every rial stretch, in the resilience that burned behind eyes that had witnessed homes crumbling under bombardment.

For Zahra, the market was a familiar ritual, her almond eyes scanning the stalls with practiced ease, her woven basket swinging lightly from the crook of her arm as she navigated the throng, her steps sure on the uneven cobblestones. She had been coming here for years, even during the war's darkest days—bartering for rationed rice with precious coupons, picking herbs for her garden when vegetables were scarce, sharing tea from her flask with vendors who had become like family over cups poured in quiet corners between customer rushes.

The chaos was comforting in its predictability, the bustle a reminder of life persisting despite everything. She glanced at Reza, her smile shy but radiant, squeezing his hand with gentle reassurance, sensing his tension in the way his fingers tightened around hers, his knuckles going pale, his palm growing damp with nervous sweat despite the morning's relative coolness.

For Reza, the market was a sensory assault that hit him like a physical blow, overwhelming after eight years on the frontlines where silence meant danger and crowds were rare. The press of bodies—merchants shouting with faces red from exertion, refugees with tattered bags shuffling past with downcast eyes, children darting underfoot like startled rabbits—closed in around him, making his chest tighten. The noise was a roar that built and built: the clang of metal pots being stacked, the rapid-fire bargaining in Farsi that sounded almost like arguing, the scrape of wooden crates being dragged across stone, the sudden sharp cry of a vendor hawking pistachios, a baby's wail cutting through it all.

Each sound seemed to echo and multiply, bouncing off the narrow alley walls, creating an overwhelming cacophony that resonated with too many battles, too many trench nights with Hossein where they'd huddled together listening for the whistle of incoming shells, too many moments of chaos before the shrapnel blast that had killed his only brother.

The scents—cumin mixing with sweat, overripe fruit fermenting in the heat islands cast from buildings, the tang of human bodies pressed close—mixed with unbidden memories of gunpowder's acrid bite and blood's metallic sweetness. His soulful brown eyes darted constantly, never settling, always scanning for threats that weren't there, his scarred hand gripping Zahra's like a lifeline, his fingers intertwined with hers so tightly he worried he might be hurting her.

His heart raced in his chest, a trapped bird beating against his ribs, his breath shallow and quick despite his efforts to control it. The cobblestones under his boots were uneven, some cracked, others missing entirely, the sensation of unsteady footing reminding him viscerally of muddy trenches where every step could mean sliding into contaminated water or tripping over something—or someone—best left unseen.

He tried to focus on Zahra, on her presence grounding him—the rosemary scent of her headscarf when she leaned close, the warmth of her hand, the gentle sway of her green dress—but the crowd's clamour kept intruding: a vendor's bell clanging insistently to attract customers, its tinny ring making him flinch; a child's sudden cry of delight that sounded too much like a scream; the rapid-fire Farsi shouts that sparked flashes of comrades' voices calling warnings he hadn't heeded in time, Hossein's last words echoing: *"Live, Reza."*

They paused at a rice stall where burlap sacks were stacked waist-high, their tops folded back to display the contents: long-grain basmati that gleamed like ivory, shorter varieties with a slight translucence, wild rice mixed with white creating patterns like river stones. The vendor, a wiry man with a grey beard streaked with white and weathered skin like tanned leather, wore a white skullcap and a vest with deep pockets for his money. His hands, stained permanently with grain dust in the creases, moved with practiced efficiency as he piled fragrant basmati into a cloth sack using a dented metal scoop, its nutty scent rising in a cloud that mingled with the ambient dust hanging in the slanted morning light.

Zahra bargained lightly, her voice melodic even in negotiation, her Farsi flowing smoothly as she gestured at the rice, testing a few grains between her fingers to check for quality—no weevils, no excessive dust—while the vendor protested the price was already fair, his hands spread wide in exaggerated dismay before finally relenting with a gap-toothed grin, securing her a price that made her smile with satisfaction.

Reza stood close behind her, his gaze flickering to a nearby vegetable stall where wooden crates overflowed with produce: vibrant parsley and mint that looked almost obscenely green and alive, their leaves still beaded with water drops from morning washing; deep red tomatoes with their tops still attached, the vines' earthy smell cutting through the other scents; purple onions with papery skin that rustled when touched; and eggplants so glossy and dark they looked lacquered.

The colours were a stark contrast to the war's monochrome horrors—the brown mud of trenches, the grey smoke, the red blood that looked black in dim light. Here everything was saturated, almost painfully vivid: the oranges in their pyramids, the yellow lemons, the crimson pomegranates split open to reveal their jewel-like seeds. It should have been beautiful. It was beautiful. But it also made his head spin with the sheer intensity of it all.

Zahra selected dates next, moving to a stall where they were displayed in shallow wicker baskets lined with parchment paper, their glossy brown skins sticky with natural sugars that caught the light. The vendor—a woman with hennaed hair peeking from beneath her

The Moonlit Rose of Isfahan

headscarf and warm, brown eyes crinkled at the corners from years of smiling—tossed in a few extra with a wink and a knowing look. "For your poet husband," she said, her voice rich with affection, having heard the neighbourhood gossip about Reza's return.

Zahra laughed, the sound like wind chimes, glancing at Reza who forced a smile, his heart still pounding despite his best efforts, the market's vibrancy both beautiful and dizzying, his mind struggling to reconcile this overwhelming life with the trenches' desolation.

As they turned a corner into a slightly wider street where the alleys opened up, Reza froze mid-step, his breath catching audibly in his throat, his entire body going rigid. His eyes fixed on something ahead: a bombed-out building, a rare scar in Isfahan from an Iraqi airstrike years ago that the city hadn't yet rebuilt or demolished, one of the few scars from Iraqi attacks that had mostly spared Isfahan.

Its skeletal remains loomed like a ghost of the frontlines—crumbling brick walls with rebar exposed like broken bones, the metal rusted a deep orange-brown; collapsed floors creating a tumbled pile of concrete chunks and shattered wooden beams; window frames hanging askew with jagged glass teeth still clinging to the edges, reflecting the sun in sharp, painful glints; blackened scorch marks climbing up what remained of the façade like smoke frozen in stone; and the whole structure listing slightly to one side, as if exhausted, ready to give up entirely. The rubble at its base was dusted with ash that had never quite washed away, and a faint acrid smell lingered in the air—old smoke, ancient fire, the chemical tang of explosives long detonated.

Flashbacks hit him hard and fast, one after another like artillery fire: the blast near Ahvaz, the world exploding in white light and deafening noise; the shrapnel tearing through his flesh, the white-hot agony that had made him scream; Hossein's bloodied body crumpling, his brother's eyes wide with shock and then dimming; the trench's mud, cold and sucking at him as he tried to crawl toward Hossein; the smell of blood and sulphur and burned flesh that had clogged his nose and throat for days after.

His knees buckled, bones suddenly made of water, and he stumbled toward a low stone bench nearby—probably placed there for elderly shoppers needing to rest—its surface warm from the sun and worn smooth by years of use. His hands trembled violently as he gripped the bench's edge, his knuckles white, sweat beading on his forehead and upper lip despite the morning's coolness, his chest heaving as he tried to breathe, tried to remember he was *here*, in Isfahan, in 1988, not *there*, not in 1983, not dying.

"Zahra," he whispered, his baritone hoarse and cracking like he'd been shouting for hours. "I need... a moment." The words came out barely audible, his throat tight, his whole body shaking now with the adrenaline his mind insisted was necessary for a danger that no longer existed.

Zahra reacted immediately, setting her basket down on the cobblestones with barely a sound, the woven handle settling against the stone. She knelt beside him, her dress pooling around her, the fabric brushing the dusty ground. Her hand found his—warm, solid, real—and clasped it firmly, her fingers threading through his, her thumb rubbing gentle circles on his knuckles. The warmth of her touch was a steady anchor, pulling him back from the edge of the flashback's grip.

She had seen the war's toll on him in so many moments since his return—the garden tears when he'd broken down among the roses, the kitchen's bittersweet talk about rebuilding, the nightmares that woke him gasping. But air raids had been rare in Isfahan, limited to a few strikes that had sent them to shelters but never destroyed their immediate neighbourhood. She could only imagine the horrors he'd survived, the constant bombardment, the screams, the blood, the loss stacked upon loss.

She didn't speak, didn't press him with questions or platitudes. She simply sat quietly beside him, her presence a balm, her eyes soft with love that asked nothing and offered everything, her silence speaking volumes as he breathed deeply—in, out, in, out—grounding himself in her presence, in the sensation of her hand in his, in the familiar rosemary scent of her hair when she leaned closer.

The market's chaos faded slightly as he focused on her, on breathing, on the way a sparrow hopped nearby searching for dropped crumbs, on the warmth of the sun on his back, on anything but the bombed building and the memories it dragged up from the depths where he tried to keep them locked.

An elderly woman approached while they sat there, her frail figure wrapped in a faded black chador that had been washed so many times the fabric had gone thin in places, almost translucent where the sun hit it. Her face was deeply lined with wrinkles that mapped a lifetime of hardship—grooves around her mouth from years of worry, crow's feet at her eyes that somehow still held brightness despite everything.

Her eyes, though weary with the particular exhaustion of those who had survived too much, still held a spark of alertness, of determination. She moved slowly, carefully, one gnarled hand clutching a walking stick carved from olive wood, polished smooth by years of use, the other holding the edges of her chador together at her throat.

Zahra's breath caught, recognition dawning across her face like sunrise—her eyes widening, her mouth opening slightly in surprise. It was Mahin, the refugee woman she'd met three years ago during her wartime market visits. Zahra had first spotted her sitting alone just outside the bazaar's main entrance, looking utterly lost and out of place, her hands clutching a tattered shawl, her expression dazed with the particular look of someone who'd been violently uprooted. Zahra, drawn to her by some instinct she couldn't name, had approached, offering tea from the battered metal flask she always carried, learning Mahin's story in fragments as they'd shared that first cup.

Mahin had been a widow from a village near the frontlines—she'd never said exactly which one, the name swallowed by grief—separated from her children in the chaos of fleeing when the bombardment had started. She'd run with hundreds of others, the explosions behind them, smoke choking the sky, and somewhere in that panicked exodus, in the confusion of screaming people and burning buildings, she'd lost sight of her children and grandchildren. She'd ended up in Isfahan alone, surviving on charity and odd jobs—washing clothes for a baker's family, sweeping the steps of a mosque, accepting meals from kind strangers—always hoping, always searching for any news of her children.

Zahra had taken a quick liking to her, visiting often when she came to the market, sharing bread and stories, offering what comfort she could—a listening ear, sometimes a few rials pressed into her palm, once a warm shawl when winter came. But Mahin had vanished in 1986, disappearing without word or warning, leaving Zahra wondering if she'd died, if she'd moved on, if she'd found her children or given up hope. Her absence had been a another wound amid the war's larger losses, another person swallowed by the conflict's chaos.

Zahra rose from beside Reza, her heart leaping with joy and disbelief, and crossed the space between them in three quick strides. She embraced Mahin carefully, mindful of the older woman's frailty, feeling the chador's worn fabric soft under her arms, the scent of rosewater—probably from washing—and dust clinging to her. The embrace was fierce despite its gentleness, years of wondering released in that moment of contact.

"Mahin *khanoum*," Zahra said, her voice thick with emotion, tears pricking her eyes and then spilling over, hot on her cheeks. "You're here. You're alive."

Mahin's smile was frail but warm, genuine, the expression transforming her lined face into something almost young again for just a moment. Her hands, calloused from years of hard work, fingers bent slightly with arthritis, clasped Zahra's with surprising strength. "My dear Zahra," she replied, her voice raspy but kind, roughened by age and hardship. "I never forgot your kindness. You were a light in a very dark time."

Zahra pulled Reza to his feet, his composure gradually returning, the flashback's grip loosening as this new reality demanded his attention. She kept one hand in his, drawing him into this moment, and with the other gestured to Mahin. "This is Reza, my husband," she said, her smile radiant now, proud, her whole face glowing with the joy of introducing them.

Reza bowed slightly in respectful greeting, his military training showing through in the formal gesture, his eyes softening as he studied Mahin's face and saw there the same haunted look he recognized from his own reflection. The market's chaos receded further as he focused on her, sensing instinctively that her story mirrored the war's toll he knew too intimately—displacement, loss, survival against odds, the weight of memories that never quite lifted.

The Moonlit Rose of Isfahan

Mahin's eyes glistened with tears as she began to speak, her chador fluttering in the breeze that swept down the alley, carrying with it the scent of baking bread from a nearby oven. Her voice trembled with an emotion that was part gratitude, part lingering disbelief, as if even now she couldn't quite believe the words she was about to say.

"In 1986, I found my children," she said, the words rushing out as if she'd been waiting years to share them with Zahra specifically. "They'd been taken to Shiraz—a cousin I barely remembered had them, kept them safe all that time. I joined them there, rebuilt our life. We have a small house now, nothing grand, but it's ours. My youngest daughter is married, my son works as a carpenter." She paused, wiping her eyes with the edge of her chador, her fingers shaking slightly. "This is my first time back in Isfahan, to pay respects to the young men who never returned—like my grandnephew, lost near Ahvaz in 1983. He was only nineteen."

Her words struck Reza like physical blows, each one echoing Hossein's death, the shrapnel, the trench, the exact year and place where his brother had died. His throat tightened, emotion welling up so fast it nearly choked him. He squeezed Zahra's hand hard, needing her anchor, the market's noise fading entirely now as Mahin's story settled over them. "May their souls rest in peace," he managed to say, his baritone low and rough, the words a prayer for Hossein, for Mahin's grandnephew, for all the lost young men whose faces haunted him in nightmares, for Amir with his gap-toothed smile and photo of his daughter, for every soldier who hadn't made it home.

Zahra nodded, tears falling freely now, her heart full, almost bursting—Mahin's reunion with her children was a mirror of her own reunion with Reza, their newfound moments of tenderness in the garden and reignited intimacy, their shared breakfast and plans for the future. The parallel was almost too much to bear, the joy and pain of it intertwined like the threads of a tapestry.

They offered Mahin dates from their basket, the dried fruit sweet and sticky, and she accepted with a smile that trembled at its edges, her gratitude evident in every line of her face. "Come visit us if you can," Zahra said impulsively, pressing a scrap of paper with their address into Mahin's calloused palm, the paper crinkling between their hands.

"Please. We'd love to have you, to hear more about your children."

Mahin nodded, tucking the paper carefully into a pocket hidden in the folds of her chador, promising to write soon if she couldn't visit. Then she shuffled off, her figure gradually swallowed by the crowd—first her black chador blending with others, then disappearing entirely into the market's perpetual motion. Reza and Zahra stood hand in hand, the bombed building still behind them but somehow less looming now, the market alive with life continuing despite everything, their love a steady root amid the war's scars.

After Mahin's departure, her tale of reunion and loss lingering in the air like the market's dust, Zahra and Reza pressed on through the throng. The sun had climbed higher, casting shorter, sharper shadows, the heat building steadily though it wasn't yet noon. Sweat gathered at the nape of Zahra's neck beneath her scarf, and Reza's cotton tunic began to stick to his back between his shoulder blades.

Zahra paused at a vegetable stall presided over by a stout woman with a warm smile and flour still dusting her black sleeve—probably a baker's wife supplementing income by selling produce. The vegetables were arranged with obvious care: glossy purple eggplants like small, perfect sculptures; tomatoes still on the vine, their green tops contrasting with red flesh; cucumbers with tiny bumps still visible on their dark green skins; bundles of parsley and mint tied with twine, their leaves still beaded with water from morning washing.

Zahra's fingers brushed the eggplants, testing their firmness, their cool, smooth skins grounding her in this moment of simple domesticity. The vendor tossed in a bundle of fresh mint without being asked, its crisp, sharp scent cutting through the market's heavier smells—a gift, a kindness, perhaps recognition of something she saw in Zahra's face. "For your garden, *khanoum*, you can never have enough," the vendor said, and Zahra smiled, her natural shyness softening into genuine warmth, tucking the mint into her basket where its fragrance would perfume everything else. The scent triggered memories of her wartime garden rituals, tending roses through grief for her father and Hossein, the mint she'd planted along the border that had survived bombing and drought alike.

The Moonlit Rose of Isfahan

Reza stood close beside her, close enough that their shoulders brushed, his soulful brown eyes still darting occasionally, hyper-vigilant in a way he couldn't quite suppress. The crowd's clamour continued unabated: a woman's sharp voice bargaining over the price of chickpeas, her tone brooking no nonsense; a boy's shout advertising pistachios in a singsong chant he'd clearly perfected; the creak and groan of a wooden cart being pushed past, its wheels protesting against uneven cobblestones; somewhere nearby, the rhythmic thwack of a butcher's cleaver hitting wood.

The sounds were overwhelming, each one threatening to trigger memories. The return to civilian life felt more daunting than ever, despite the ceasefire's fragile relief and the joy of being back with Zahra. The market's vibrancy—the riot of colours, the assault of smells, the cacophony of voices—felt like a battlefield of normalcy where every moment demanded adjustment, where every sound was a potential trigger, where the weight of relearning life pressed down heavier than his rifle ever had.

"It's... too much," he murmured to Zahra, his baritone low and strained, barely audible over the market's noise. His grip on her hand tightened involuntarily, his boots scuffing the cobblestones as he shifted his weight, their uneven surface recalling muddy trenches where one wrong step could mean sliding into water contaminated with chemical weapons or worse.

Zahra sensed his unease immediately, attuned to every shift in his breathing, every tension in his muscles. Her touch remained steady, her fingers warm and firm around his. Her eyes, soft with love and understanding, met his. "You're here, Reza," she said, her voice melodic even in this chaos, squeezing his hand with gentle insistence, grounding him as she'd done by the bombed building earlier, as she'd done countless times since his return. "We'll go slow, my love. There's no rush."

She led him to a quieter stall tucked in a corner where the alley curved, away from the main flow of traffic. An old man with a weathered, sun-darkened face and white beard sat there on a low stool, selling saffron displayed in small glass jars that caught the light. The precious spice glowed within—crimson threads so delicate they looked almost unreal, their colour impossibly vivid. He had perhaps a dozen jars, each one carefully labeled with weight and price in neat script, his livelihood contained in these small vessels of concentrated value.

The saffron's delicate, floral aroma rose when the old man opened a jar to show Zahra the quality—a scent that was sweet but also slightly metallic, earthy, complex. Zahra selected a small jar, bargaining lightly in soft tones, her voice a soothing anchor for Reza as he stood beside her, breathing deeper now, forcing himself to focus on her—on the familiar cadence of her voice, on the memory of her reciting his letter buried in the garden, each word perfect because she'd memorized them all, on the way her green dress caught the light, on anything but the overwhelming press of too many people, too many sounds, too many memories threatening to surface.

They bought carrots and cucumbers for *mast-o-khiar* from another stall, the vendor wrapping them in coarse burlap cloth that scratched slightly, the texture rough against Reza's fingers—a sensation that triggered a faint, unwelcome echo of blood-soaked bandages, of the infirmary tent he'd been in multiple times where everything had smelled of antiseptic and suffering. He pushed the memory down, forced it away, concentrated on the present: the weight of vegetables, Zahra's presence, the simple act of shopping for dinner.

The crowd pressed close as they made their final purchases—a refugee woman with a tattered shawl and hollow eyes who looked right through them, her expression identical to ones Reza had seen on the frontlines, that particular thousand-yard stare of someone who'd witnessed horrors; a boy with a missing front tooth selling pistachios, his voice shrill and practiced, his small hands permanently stained brown from handling nuts all day; an old woman counting coins with arthritic fingers, her lips moving as she calculated prices with painful slowness.

Reza felt a pang of kinship with all of them, but especially the refugees—their shared scars invisible but palpable, written in the language of bodies that had survived too much, of eyes that had seen things that couldn't be unseen, of the particular way they moved through the world with a wariness that never quite faded. The market was a microcosm of the war's toll made visible, a place where survival and loss brushed shoulders with the mundane commerce of daily life.

They left as the sun neared its zenith, the heat building toward midday's peak, the basket heavy now with fresh lamb, chicken, rice, vegetables, dates, saffron and more—provisions that would feed them for days. The air was warm and thick with dust motes visible in shafts of sunlight, flavoured with lingering spices that clung to their clothes and hair. Their hands remained entwined, Zahra's fingers threaded through Reza's, both of them sweating now but neither wanting to let go.

The walk home was quieter, the route taking them away from the market's density into Isfahan's wider boulevards where buildings stood farther apart, where trees provided occasional shade, where the noise gradually faded to a more manageable hum. The bombed building's skeletal remains receded behind them, though Reza's earlier flashback still lingered at the edges of his mind—Hossein's blood warm and sticky, the shrapnel's bite, the way time had seemed to slow and speed up simultaneously in that moment of ultimate chaos.

Civilian life loomed before him like an uncharted battlefield where the rules kept changing, where the enemies were invisible—his own memories, his own reactions, the weight of normalcy itself. The market's chaos had underscored how much had changed since his soldier days, how different this life was from the one he'd known for eight years. Yet Zahra's warmth beside him was a miracle he still couldn't quite believe, her presence a tether to this new reality he was trying to learn how to inhabit.

She chattered softly as they walked, her voice a soothing melody telling him about the garden's jasmine bush that was about to bloom, about how she'd pruned it just days before, about a recipe she wanted to try with the eggplants. Her words washed over him like a gentle tide, pulling him away from the war's undertow. He thought of their reclaimed marital bed, of her poetic murmurs over his scars as she'd prayed healing into his wounded body, of the way she'd looked at him with such fierce love that it had nearly broken him open.

He forced a smile, managing to nod at appropriate moments in her narrative, his heart torn between relief at the war's end and the daunting task of rebuilding himself as husband, as man, as something other than soldier. The ceasefire was supposed to bring peace, but he was learning that peace was its own kind of battle.

Back home, the courtyard garden welcomed them with its serene beauty—a world away from the market's chaos. Crimson roses bloomed in careful rows, their petals soft as silk, their thorns a reminder that beauty required protection. White tulips stood tall on their stems, their cups open to the sun. Lavender buds clustered thick on their stalks, their grey-green leaves releasing fragrance when brushed. The scents mingled in the warm air with the faint ghost of rosewater from last night's bath, a reminder of their tender lovemaking that made Zahra's cheeks flush slightly at the memory.

The house interior was cool and dim, a welcome respite from the sun's intensity, its whitewashed walls holding the night's coolness like a blessing. The woven rugs under their feet were soft, their patterns familiar—colours that had long since faded, a continuity that mattered more than she'd realized. The kitchen still held the faint, rich aroma of yesterday's *kaleh pache*, the lamb's head soup that had been her father's favourite, that Reza had prepared for her as an act of love that had brought tears to her eyes.

Zahra set the basket on the scarred wooden table—its surface marked by years of chopping and cooking, burns from hot pots, the patina of daily life—her green dress catching the light from the small window that looked out on the garden. She began unpacking, her movements graceful and practiced, items appearing from the basket's woven depths: the sack of rice with its nutty smell, the glossy eggplants, the mint bundle still fresh, the sticky dates, the precious saffron in its small jar.

Reza helped, his scarred hands clumsy but eager, fumbling slightly with unfamiliar domesticity. The simple act of putting away groceries was both comforting and foreign—comforting in its normalcy, foreign because he'd spent eight years where routine meant checking weapons and digging trenches, not storing vegetables. Shirin and Simin wove figure-eights around their legs, the cats' fur brushing his ankles, their purrs a soft rumbling counterpoint to the market's remembered roar, their presence a grounding reminder that this was home, this was real,

The Moonlit Rose of Isfahan

this was his life now.

Once everything was put away, Zahra sat at the kitchen table, pulling out paper and a pen from a drawer that stuck slightly with humidity. The ink's faint, metallic smell rose as she unscrewed the pen's cap—an old fountain pen that had been her father's, one of the few things of his she'd kept. She touched the nib to paper, felt the slight scratch and drag of metal on fibre, and began to write.

First, a brief letter to Farhad, her half-brother in Tehran. Their relationship had always been complicated—he was from their father's first marriage, emotionally distant, already married with his own life by the time she was a toddler. But their shared grief for their father had softened some of that estrangement, created a fragile bridge between them. Her script was neat, practiced, the letters flowing: *Dear Farhad, Reza is home, safe, and doing well. The ceasefire holds, and we're rebuilding our life. Visit if you can—Isfahan misses you.*

The words were simple, but her heart was heavy with memories: Farhad's awkward presence at their father's bedside five years ago, standing stiff in the doorway as if he didn't quite belong; his letters from Tehran over the years, sparse but kind in their own distant way, checking on her welfare without quite knowing how to express care. She sealed the letter with a careful fold, no envelope needed for this.

Then she began a longer letter to her mother, now in Syria with her new family—a remarriage that had felt like abandonment at first, softened by time and understanding. Her hand moved with more emotion now, the pen's scratching louder as she wrote faster, words spilling out: *Mother, Reza is back, his heart strong despite the war's scars. The ceasefire brings hope, and our garden blooms with roses Father would have loved. Come visit, bring your family—let us be together again, as Father would have wanted. Isfahan holds memories of him in every stone, and I miss you more than I can say.*

She paused, tears pricking her eyes and then spilling over, hot tracks down her cheeks that she didn't bother to wipe away. The memories came unbidden: her father's passing five years ago, the cancer that had hollowed him out slowly until he was barely recognizable, his final words urging her to tend her heart, to keep growing like the gardens he'd taught her to love, the Persian mourning rituals.

And then, just weeks after losing her father, the devastating arrival of two letters: Hossein's, warm and alive, calling her "little sister," teasing about Reza's poetry, full of hope and plans for jasmine trees; and immediately after, Reza's letter bearing the news that Hossein was dead, killed near Ahvaz by the same blast that had nearly taken Reza too. The double blow had nearly destroyed her, left her terrified that Reza would be next, that she would lose everyone she loved to this endless war.

She finished the letter to her mother, folded it carefully, and set both letters aside to post tomorrow. Reza had been watching her from across the kitchen, seeing the tears, understanding without being told what memories had surfaced. He crossed to her, knelt beside her chair, and simply held her, his scarred arms solid and warm, his presence a reminder that he had survived, that they had both survived, that they were building something new from the ashes of what the war had taken.

That night, the bedroom was a quiet sanctuary—their refuge from the world's demands. The blue-and-gold quilts lay soft across the bed, the rose petals from last night's romantic gesture swept away, the air cool with jasmine drifting through the open window on a gentle breeze. Stars were visible through the window's frame, scattered across the dark sky like salt spilled on a black table.

Reza and Zahra lay entwined in their familiar configuration: her head resting on his scarred chest where she could hear his heartbeat, his arm wrapped around her fuller curves that he'd slowly grown accustomed to after eight years apart, their legs tangled together under the quilts. Their breaths gradually synced in the faint lamplight—in, out, in, out—a rhythm of shared peace. The lamp's flame flickered occasionally, casting dancing shadows on the walls, turning familiar objects mysterious.

Sleep came slowly for Reza, his mind still processing the day's overwhelming sensory assault, but it came eventually. And then it betrayed him.

The nightmare was more vivid than any before, with a clarity and

The Moonlit Rose of Isfahan

intensity that felt like reliving rather than remembering. He was back in the trench near Ahvaz in 1983, the air thick with sulphur's rotten-egg stench and blood's copper tang, the sky choked with smoke that turned day into perpetual twilight. Artillery screamed overhead in its distinctive whine-whistle-crash pattern, each impact shaking the ground, making his teeth rattle in his skull.

The blast erupted with no warning—one moment he was breathing, the next the world exploded. But in the nightmare's twisted logic, the shrapnel didn't tear his stomach, groin and thigh as it had in reality. Instead it found his chest, ripping through ribs and muscle, a white-hot agony searing directly through his heart. He felt it—actually felt the metal entering his body, the tearing, the burning, the wetness.

Blood gushed from the wound, warm and sticky, far too much blood, pooling in the mud beneath him, mixing with the trench's contaminated water. His hands clawed at his chest, trying to hold the wound closed, but blood kept coming, kept flowing between his fingers, impossible to stop. The metallic taste flooded his mouth—he was drowning in his own blood, choking on it, coughing it up in thick clots.

Hossein's face loomed over him, his brother's eyes wide with horror and helpless grief, his voice a desperate echo that seemed to come from very far away even though he was right there: "Live, Reza! Stay with me! Don't you dare leave me!" But in this nightmare version, Reza couldn't obey. His vision darkened at the edges, tunnelling down to a pinpoint of light. His breath stopped—not gradually, but suddenly, completely, his lungs unable to draw air through blood and torn tissue.

Zahra's face appeared as consciousness fled, a fading blur of beloved features—her almond eyes, her shy smile, the way her hair fell around her face. Her voice called his name from a distance he couldn't reach, couldn't cross, an impossible chasm opening between them. "Reza! Reza!" But he was already gone, already dead, leaving her alone, leaving her a widow, failing the most important promise he'd ever made.

The trench collapsed, mud falling in heavy clods, filling his mouth and nose and eyes. The screams of comrades blended into a cacophony of death: Amir's wet gurgle as blood filled his lungs, Hossein's gasping breaths as life left him too, the cries of soldiers whose names he didn't know but whose deaths he'd witnessed, all of it mixing together in a symphony of horror.

Reza woke in a cold sweat, his body trembling so violently the bed shook, the quilts damp with perspiration that had soaked through his nightclothes, his breath coming in ragged, shallow gasps that couldn't quite satisfy his lungs' demands. The nightmare's vividness lingered like a physical thing—he could still feel the phantom agony in his chest, still taste blood, still see the darkness closing in.

His heart pounded hard enough that he could see his chest moving, feel the pulse in his throat and temples. The room was dark—the lamp had guttered out while they slept—and for a moment he didn't know where he was, couldn't remember, panic rising. The jasmine scent from the window, which had been soothing earlier, now seemed cloying, too sweet, almost nauseating. The crickets chirped outside in their endless rhythm, a mocking calm that felt like an insult to the horror still vivid in his mind.

Zahra stirred beside him, pulled from sleep by his movements, by some instinct that sensed his distress. Her hand found his in the darkness, warm and real and alive, her fingers threading through his trembling ones. "Reza," she whispered, her voice soft but urgent, rough with sleep but focused entirely on him. "You're here. You're home. You're safe."

She repeated the words like a litany, a spell to pull him back from the nightmare's grip, her touch grounding him as it had in the market. Her warmth was a lifeline, solid and present, pulling him back from the trench that tried to claim him even in sleep. He nodded, unable to speak yet, his throat too tight, the nightmare's images still playing behind his eyes: Hossein gone, himself lost, the visceral terror of leaving Zahra alone resurfacing with brutal clarity.

She held him without speaking further, understanding that words weren't what he needed yet. Her fingers traced his scars gently over his clothes—the ones on his chest, his arms, his stomach—mapping the landscape of his survival with tender touches that said: You're alive. You made it. I'm here. Her presence was a steady anchor, pulling him gradually back to the present, to this room, to this bed, to this life they were building together.

By morning, Reza was calmer, though the nightmare's weight still clung to him like damp clothes, a heaviness he couldn't quite shake. He lay in the growing light watching dust motes dance in the beam of sunlight that had found its way through the window, listening to Zahra's steady breathing beside him, grateful beyond words that she was real, that this was real, that the nightmare had been just that—a nightmare, not reality.

His resolve to face civilian life's daunting path was strengthened paradoxically by the nightmare's horror—if he could survive eight years of war, certainly he could survive the market's overwhelming chaos, the bombed buildings' triggers, the gradual, difficult work of rebuilding himself. Zahra's letters to Farhad and her mother, sitting on the kitchen table waiting to be posted, represented a step toward rebuilding connections, toward creating a future that acknowledged the past without being imprisoned by it for them both.

Reza couldn't return to sleep after that. He carefully disentangled himself from Zahra's embrace, pressing a kiss to her forehead before padding quietly to the living room in his bare feet. The house was silent except for the soft tick of the clock, the distant chirp of crickets.

He found himself drawn to the bookshelf—Hafez, Saadi, Rumi, Zahra's favourite novels. And there, tucked between Saadi and a collection of modern verse, the Quran his father had given him for his graduation.

The green leather binding was dusty. How long had it sat untouched? Since before the war, certainly. Maybe even before his wedding, when faith had been more habit than need, more cultural rhythm than spiritual anchor. He pulled it from the shelf slowly, the weight familiar and foreign at once. He didn't open it. Couldn't yet. Just held it, feeling its heft, its presence.

In the trenches, he'd made desperate bargains with God—frantic prayers when shells screamed overhead, whispered pleas when Hossein fell. But all those prayers had felt hollow, unanswered. How did one pray to a God who let good men die? Who let brothers fall? Who seemed to favour survival by random chance rather than merit or devotion?

    Yet he couldn't quite let go either. Couldn't dismiss the years of his youth when prayer had been as natural as breathing, when his father's recitations had been the soundtrack to mornings, when faith had been a comfort rather than a question.

    He sat on the divan, the Quran in his lap, and simply existed in that liminal space between belief and doubt, between the faith he'd had and the faith he'd lost, between the man he'd been and the man he was becoming, one day at a time.

Chapter Sixteen

Southern Front, 1985

The night air on the southern Iran-Iraq front pressed down like a suffocating blanket, thick with the scent of dust, gun oil, and the faint, acrid tang of smoke from artillery exchanges that had torn through the darkness hours before. The war was grinding into its fifth year, and the landscape near Basra had become a scarred wasteland—craters pockmarked the earth like diseased flesh, rusted barbed wire coiled across the no-man's-land like metal thorns, and the skeletal remains of abandoned vehicles jutted from the dust like the bones of prehistoric beasts. The moon had abandoned the sky, leaving only starlight to illuminate the desolation.

Reza crouched in a shallow observation post carved into the hard-packed earth, his khaki uniform blending with the shadows. The silver star on his collar—his commander's insignia—caught faint glimmers of light from the shielded lantern beside him. His lean frame was tense but steady, coiled like a spring ready to release. Through binoculars, he scanned the enemy lines, the cool metal pressing against his skin, leaving indentations around his eyes. Every muscle in his body was alert, honed by years of survival and loss.

The promotion to commander had been both an honour and a curse—recognition of his bravery, his cunning, his ability to think like an engineer even in the chaos of war. But it was also a reminder of everything it had cost him. Hossein's death in Ahvaz still clawed at his

Jamila Mikhail

heart, the memory of his brother's bloodied body, his final gasping words—*Live, Reza... for Zahra... for Leyla*—echoing through every quiet moment. The shrapnel scars that crisscrossed Reza's flesh were a constant, dull ache, a physical testament to the inferno that had claimed his brother. Returning to the frontlines in 1983 had been the hardest decision of his life, but vengeance had burned in him—a fire to honour Hossein, to protect Iran, to earn the right to return to Zahra.

He had become a model soldier. In assaults, he was fearless, his engineering mind crafting meticulous infiltration routes that outwitted Iraqi defences. Twice before, he had slipped behind enemy lines like a ghost, stealing intelligence and sabotaging supply depots, impressing his superiors with his stealth and ruthless efficiency. Now, as commander of a small unit, he was leading his third raid, his voice low and controlled as he briefed his men.

Eight soldiers huddled close around him in the observation post, their faces streaked with camouflage grease that made them look like wraiths in the dim light. Their breaths misted in the chill night air, visible puffs that dissipated quickly into the darkness. The ground beneath their knees was damp, the mud cold and viscous, squelching softly with every small movement. Rifles were slung across their backs, knives sheathed at their sides. The tension was palpable—a living thing that coiled around them, tightening with each passing second.

"Remember, silent as shadows," Reza whispered, his baritone voice steady and commanding, echoing the guidance Hossein had once given him in another lifetime, another battle. The men nodded, their eyes fixed on him with trust that felt like a weight pressing on his chest. The enemy camp sprawled a hundred meters away—barbed wire glinting like silver threads in the starlight, guard towers silhouetted against the horizon like sentinels of death. The faint hum of generators and muffled Arabic voices carried on the wind, mixing with the distant howl of jackals.

Reza's plan was meticulous, crafted with the precision of an engineer: cut through the wire, infiltrate the supply depot, plant explosives, and retreat under the cover of darkness before the enemy could react. His heart hammered against his ribs, but his mind remained razor-sharp. In his thoughts, Zahra's face was a talisman—

The Moonlit Rose of Isfahan

her almond eyes, her poetic words from her latest letter tucked in his pocket, the worn paper creased from countless readings. "In the desert of my days, you are the oasis." Her love was a fire that burned against the cold, against the fear, against the ever-present shadow of death.

They moved.

Crawling through no-man's-land, the earth was rough and unforgiving under Reza's elbows. Thorns from dry scrub snagged his uniform, tearing small holes, scratching his skin. The scent of oil from nearby wells filled his lungs, mixing with the metallic tang of fear-sweat. Every sound was amplified in the silence—the rustle of fabric, the soft crunch of dirt, the distant mechanical groan of the generators. His unit reached the wire, and Reza's knife sliced through it with a faint twang that seemed to echo in his ears like a gunshot. The metal was cold in his grip, the blade gleaming faintly.

They slipped through the gap, shadows among shadows. The enemy camp was bathed in pools of yellow lantern light that created harsh contrasts—bright circles surrounded by deep darkness. Iraqi soldiers patrolled with lazy, confident steps, their cigarettes glowing like fireflies in the night. Reza signalled with precise hand gestures, and his men fanned out, each moving with practiced silence. They planted charges on ammunition crates, the explosives sticky with grease, the scent of gunpowder sharp and acrid in the air. Each man worked quickly, efficiently, their movements choreographed through countless drills.

Then, a shout shattered the silence.

A guard had spotted them, his voice piercing the night like a siren. Chaos erupted in an instant. Gunfire cracked through the air, the sound deafening, bullets whining past Reza's head with a high-pitched scream. The air came alive with the metallic tang of cordite, the smell of burnt powder thick in his nostrils. Reza's unit returned fire, the recoil of his rifle jolting his shoulder, the muzzle flash blinding in the darkness, leaving purple afterimages dancing in his vision.

An Iraqi soldier charged directly at him, knife drawn, his face twisted in fury and terror—a mirror of Reza's own fear. The man's eyes were desperate, not unlike his own, and in that split second, Reza saw him as a person, not just an enemy. But there was no time for mercy, no time for hesitation. They met in hand-to-hand combat, a frenzy of grunts and steel, bodies colliding with brutal force.

The Iraqi's knife slashed, the blade catching Reza's right arm in a searing arc. Pain exploded through him—white-hot, immediate, all-consuming. The burn of torn flesh was followed by the warm, sticky rush of blood soaking through his sleeve, the crimson stain spreading rapidly. The soldier's breath was hot on his face, reeking of cigarettes and fear. Reza's vision narrowed to a tunnel, his training taking over. He countered instinctively, his own knife thrusting forward with desperate strength.

The blade sank into the soldier's side with a sickening thud—the sound of steel parting flesh, the wet resistance before the knife slid deep. The man's gasp was hot and sharp against Reza's face, his eyes widening in shock and agony. For a heartbeat, they were frozen together, connected by the knife, by the moment of death passing between them. Then the soldier's body slumped heavy against Reza before crumpling into the dust. Reza pulled back, his hands trembling, slick with blood—the enemy's and his own, the red and the warmth indistinguishable.

The wound in his arm throbbed with his heartbeat, each pulse sending fresh waves of fire through his flesh. Blood dripped onto the dust, dark droplets disappearing into the thirsty earth. The scent of iron was overwhelming, mixing with the acrid smoke and his own sweat. He had killed before—at a distance, through a rifle scope, in the chaos of battle where faces blurred together. But this closeness, this intimacy of death—face to face, breath to breath, feeling the man's life leave his body—was different. The weight of it settled in his chest like a stone.

"Fall back!" Reza commanded, his voice steady despite the roar of battle, despite the pain, despite the horror clawing at the edges of his mind. His unit retreated, boots pounding against the hard earth. Behind them, the explosives detonated with a thunderous boom that shook the ground beneath their feet. Flames erupted into the sky, painting the darkness orange and red, the heat wave slamming against Reza's back with physical force. Debris rained down—chunks of wood, twisted metal, fragments of concrete—clattering against rocks and earth.

They ran through the hell they had created. Bullets pinged off rocks, whining ricochets that could have ended any of their lives in an instant. The ground shook with secondary explosions, ammunition cooking off in rapid staccato bursts. Reza's lungs ached from breathing in gas residue that lingered from earlier battles, each breath burning like fire. His arm was a constant stream of pain, but his mind remained sharp, focused on one thing: get his men out alive.

They made the trench. Comrades reached out, pulling them in, hands grabbing uniforms and arms, hauling them to safety. Reza collapsed against the muddy wall, the night still alive with sirens and shouts from the enemy camp. The mission was a success—the depot was in flames, visible as an orange glow on the horizon—but the cost was etched into his body and soul.

The trench was a narrow, claustrophobic ditch carved into the earth, its walls slick with mud that squelched under boots, oozing cold moisture. The air was damp and chill, carrying the faint sulphur of gas residue that made his throat burn. Reza's unit—his eight men, their faces still streaked with camouflage grease and grime—huddled nearby, their breaths ragged, rifles propped against the dirt walls. The faint clink of metal and low murmurs of relief mingled with the distant wail of Iraqi sirens.

The medic, a wiry young man named Behnam with steady hands and exhausted eyes, knelt beside Reza. His medical kit lay open on the ground, its contents—gauze, antiseptic, needle, and thread—scattered in the flickering light of a lantern. The trench smelled of wet earth, blood, and the sharp bite of iodine.

"Hold still, Commander," Behnam muttered, his voice gruff but kind. He poured iodine over the wound, and the sting was sharp enough to make Reza hiss through clenched teeth, a white-hot flare that momentarily drowned out the dull ache of his numerous other shrapnel scars. The pain was grounding, pulling him back from the haze of adrenaline and memory.

Behnam threaded a needle with practiced efficiency, the metal glinting in the lantern's glow. "This is going to hurt," he warned unnecessarily. Reza nodded, his jaw tight, forcing himself to breathe steadily. The needle pierced his skin with a sharp tug, and he felt each suture like a jolt of electricity. The thread pulled flesh together, closing the gash that wept blood and clear fluid. The trench's walls seemed to close in around him, the mud's chill seeping through his uniform, soaking into his bones.

The lantern cast grotesque shadows that danced on the walls like ghosts—Hossein's face, the Iraqi soldier's desperate eyes, Zahra's gentle smile. Reza's mind replayed the fight in vivid detail: the soldier's knife slashing through the air, the burn as it slashed his arm, the moment he drove his own blade into the man's side. The wet thud. The warmth of blood on his hands. The soldier's body crumpling into the dust, life draining from his eyes.

He had been trained to kill, and he'd done it numerous times before in this seemingly never-ending war, but never like this. Never close enough to feel the man's final breath, to see the shock and pain in his eyes, to know that this soldier—this enemy—had probably been someone's brother, someone's son, maybe even someone's beloved. The thought twisted in his gut like a knife of its own.

The emotional aftermath was a storm raging inside him. His heart ached for Zahra—her letters were his lifeline, tucked in his pocket even now, the paper creased and worn from countless readings. Her poetic words, "In the desert of my days, you are the oasis," were a prayer he clung to in the darkness. He fought for her, for Iran, for the memory of Hossein. But the killing, the blood, the nearness of death gnawed at him with relentless teeth.

What if the knife had struck deeper? What if he had died tonight, leaving Zahra alone, her letters unanswered, like Hossein's to Leyla? The thought was its own kind of wound, twisting deeper than the blade had gone. He was a commander now, responsible for his men—Behnam's steady hands, young Kamran's nervous glances, Armin's quiet prayers in the corner of the trench. The burden was crushing, the fear of failing them as he felt he had failed Hossein, not shielding him enough in that 1983 blast.

"You're doing well, Commander," Behnam said, tying off the stitches. The thread was dark with blood, and he wrapped gauze around the wound, the fabric rough but clean against Reza's skin. Reza forced a nod, his voice hoarse when he spoke. "Thanks, Behnam. Check Kamran next—he took a graze."

The Moonlit Rose of Isfahan

As Behnam moved off to tend to Kamran, Reza leaned against the trench wall, the mud cold and unyielding against his back. The lantern's light was dimming as its oil ran low, casting the trench into deeper shadows. He pulled out Zahra's latest letter, the paper soft and creased, the faint smell of ink a comfort amid the trench's reek of mud, blood, and gun oil. Her neat script spoke of the garden, her father's passing two years ago, her unwavering hope for his return. He traced her signature with trembling fingers, the pain in his arm pulsing with his heartbeat.

The victory tonight—explosives detonated, the depot in flames, intelligence secured—felt hollow against the cost. Another life taken. Another scar earned.

Another night survived, but not unscathed. He thought of Hossein, his brother's laughter, their shared tea in trenches like this one, and the vow to avenge him burned anew. But so did the longing for Zahra, the desperate need to return to her now more than ever, to hold her under the mulberry tree, to build a life beyond this endless war.

Relief flooded through him—a guilty, shameful relief. All eight of his men had made it back. They were alive. Wounded, exhausted, traumatized, but alive. Tonight, he had not failed them. Tonight, they would see another dawn. But the relief was poisoned by memory, by the faces that haunted him in the darkness.

Four months ago, another raid. Another night. Another plan that had seemed so meticulous on paper.

The memory rose unbidden, as it always did in moments of quiet, flooding his mind with images he could never escape. It had been his second mission as commander—an ambush of an Iraqi supply convoy moving through a narrow pass. Intelligence had been solid, the plan straightforward: position his men on the ridge, wait for the convoy, destroy the lead vehicle to block the pass, then rain fire down on the trapped enemies below.

But the intelligence had been wrong.

The convoy had been larger than reported, and it had been accompanied by a tank—a detail that reconnaissance had somehow missed. When they sprung the ambush, the tank's main gun had swivelled toward their position with terrifying speed. The first shell had struck the ridge with apocalyptic force, the explosion turning the world into fire and flying rock. Reza had been thrown backward, his ears ringing, his vision swimming. When he had scrambled back to the edge, three of his men were gone.

Navid. Habib. Mohammed.

The names were seared into his memory like brands. Navid, only twenty-one, who had talked endlessly about his mother's cooking and the girl he planned to marry when the war ended. Habib, thirty-two, a father of two young daughters whose drawings he kept folded in his pocket. Mohammed, twenty-four, who had saved Reza's life in an earlier skirmish, taking a bullet meant for him and laughing it off as "just a scratch" despite the blood.

They had been there one moment—solid, breathing, alive—and the next, they were simply gone. Vaporized. The shell had torn their bodies apart so completely that there had been nothing left to recover, nothing to send home to their families. Just blood and fragments scattered across the rocks, indistinguishable from the stone itself.

Reza had led the survivors in retreat, every step away from that ridge feeling like a betrayal. He had written letters to the families, his hand shaking so badly that the ink smeared. The official inquiry had cleared him of wrongdoing. The intelligence failure was not his fault, they said. He had made the best decision possible with the information available, they said. He should not blame himself, they said.

But their words meant nothing. In the darkness, in the quiet moments between heartbeats, the question always returned: What if?

What if he had questioned the intelligence more thoroughly? What if he had insisted on better reconnaissance? What if he had positioned his men differently? What if he had chosen a different location entirely? What if he had called off the mission when something in his gut had whispered that the timing felt wrong?

The questions had no answers. They never did. They simply circled endlessly in his mind, vultures feeding on guilt.

Now, sitting in this trench with the fresh wound on his arm still bleeding through the bandages, Reza felt the conflicting emotions tear at him with renewed savagery. Relief that his eight men had survived tonight. Gratitude that he would not have to write more letters, attend more memorial services, face more grieving families. But that relief felt like a betrayal of Navid, Habib, and Mohammed. How could he feel grateful when they were still dead? How could he celebrate survival when they had been denied that gift?

And the Iraqi soldier he had killed tonight—that desperate man with eyes so similar to his own—added another layer to his torment. That soldier had probably had a family too. A mother. Perhaps a wife. Perhaps children. Reza had extinguished a life that had been precious to someone, and that knowledge sat like lead in his stomach.

He understood the necessity of it. In that moment, it had been kill or be killed. If he had hesitated, if he had shown mercy, he would be the one lying in the dust, his blood soaking into foreign soil. His men would have lost their commander. Zahra would have received that terrible letter. Leyla would have lost another brother.

But understanding the necessity did not ease the weight. It did not make the man's final gasp any less haunting. It did not erase the feeling of the knife sinking into flesh, the warmth of blood, the terrible intimacy of taking a life with his own hands.

The faces swam before him in the dimming lantern light—Hossein, Amir, Navid, Habib, Mohammed, the Iraqi soldier. Ghosts, all of them. Some by his hand, some despite his efforts, all of them weighing on his soul like stones. In his nightmares—and he knew they would come tonight, as they always did after combat—they would speak to him. They would ask him questions he could not answer.

"Why didn't you save me, Commander?" Navid would ask, his young face still full of hope for a future that would never come.

"My daughters will grow up without a father," Habib would say, his voice flat, accusatory. "Was the mission worth it?"

"I took a bullet for you," Mohammed would remind him, his eyes disappointed. "And you couldn't save me from one shell."

And sometimes, in the worst nightmares, Hossein would join them, his blood-soaked uniform a stark reminder of Reza's inability to protect the people he loved. "You promised to have my back too, little brother," Hossein would whisper. "You failed."

Reza closed his eyes, pressing the heels of his palms against them until he saw stars. The trench had grown quieter, the sirens fading into the distance. His men were settling in for what remained of the night, their faces gaunt but alive. They looked to him with trust, with respect, with the belief that he would lead them through this hell and home again.

He could not fail them. He would not fail them again.

The commander's mantle settled heavier on his shoulders than any physical weight. Every decision he made could mean life or death. Every plan he crafted could lead to victory or catastrophe. Every order he gave could send men home or to their graves. The responsibility was crushing, but he straightened despite it, despite the pain in his arm, despite the exhaustion in his bones, despite the ghosts in his mind.

He fought for his men. For Iran. For Zahra. For the memory of Hossein and the three soldiers he had lost. But the emotional toll—the killing, the fear, the guilt, the ghosts—lingered like smoke on the horizon, an ever-present shadow that darkened even moments of triumph.

As dawn neared, the sky began to lighten to a bruised grey, streaked with red like wounds in the heavens. Reza clutched Zahra's letter in his uninjured hand, the paper soft and precious against his palm. His heart made a silent vow: he would survive this war. He would return to her. He would love her fiercely, completely, in defiance of all this death and darkness.

The new scar on his arm would be a testament to his will, a mark of survival etched in flesh. And his love for Zahra would remain a steady root in the war's chaos, an anchor in the storm, the one pure thing in a world drowned in blood.

He would live. He had to. Because the alternative—leaving Zahra alone, abandoning his men, joining the ghosts who already haunted his nights—was unthinkable.

So he clutched the letter, and he breathed, and he endured.

Chapter Seventeen

Isfahan, 1988

The afternoon sun bathed the Azad home in a warm, golden glow, its light filtering through the courtyard garden's jasmine vines, casting intricate shadows across the crimson roses, white tulips, and lavender buds that Zahra had tended through the war's long years. The air was soft with their mingled scents—jasmine's heady sweetness, lavender's calming musk, and a faint earthiness from the freshly watered soil—a stark contrast to the market's chaotic bustle from the previous day. Inside, the house was quiet, the morning's calm lingering like a blessing. The whitewashed walls and woven rugs absorbed the stillness, while the kitchen remained faintly fragrant with the memory of breakfast's *kaleh pache*.

Shirin and Simin lounged in a sunbeam by the window, their fur glinting as they stretched lazily after a nap. Zahra moved about the living room, her soft pink dress swaying with each step, her dark hair loose in soft waves, her eyes bright but reflective as she dusted a small wooden shelf. Her fingers lingered on a framed photo of her father, his smile frozen from before his passing, and her heart ached with the memory of his voice.

Reza sat nearby in a wooden chair, his cotton tunic and pants soft but still unfamiliar against his skin, his soulful brown eyes following her movements. His heart was still raw from last night's vivid nightmare of dying in the trench again, yet he found himself steadied by her presence, their shared love a root against the war's lingering shadows.

A knock at the door broke the quiet, and Zahra opened it to find her cousin, Kaveh, standing on the threshold. His lean frame was slightly stooped, his face weathered at thirty-five, his dark eyes carrying a quiet sorrow beneath a warm smile. His simple grey shirt and trousers were clean but worn, a sign of the war's toll on his life.

"Zahra, *salaam*," he said, his voice low, embracing her gently. The scent of dust and faint cologne clung to him. Reza rose from his chair, offering a handshake, his scarred hand firm but welcoming, his commander's poise softened by home's safety.

"Kaveh, good to see you," Reza said, his baritone warm, though his eyes flickered with the market's overwhelm from yesterday, the bombed building's echo of destruction seen in other cities still fresh in his mind.

Zahra invited Kaveh in, her smile shy but genuine, and they settled in the living room. The woven rug was soft underfoot, and a tray of tea and dates sat on the low table, the samovar's hum filling the air with earthy warmth. Kaveh's visit was brief, his presence a rare tether to family fractured by war.

Zahra's mind drifted to childhood memories of Kaveh's family—his parents' home in Shiraz, filled with laughter, his two brothers and sister playing in their orchard, the scent of orange blossoms heavy in spring. But the war had decimated them: his brothers killed in two different battles, his sister lost to illness in a refugee camp where she'd volunteered as a nurse, his parents frail and grieving. Kaveh, now a merchant in Isfahan, carried their loss in his quiet demeanour, his visits sparse but cherished.

"I heard you're back, Reza," Kaveh said, sipping tea, the glass warm in his hands. "The ceasefire... it's a blessing."

Reza nodded, his throat tight, thinking the war's toll, his comrades lost, the Iraqi soldiers he'd killed. "It is," he replied, his voice steady. Zahra's hand brushed his, grounding him in the present moment.

Kaveh shared news of Shiraz, his parents' health, and his small textile shop, his words measured but kind. Zahra listened, her heart aching for the family they once were, her father's doting voice—*"Girls*

The Moonlit Rose of Isfahan

deserve the stars"—echoing from her childhood. After a short visit, Kaveh rose, promising to return, his embrace with Zahra lingering, a silent acknowledgment of shared loss. As the door closed, the house settled back into quiet, the garden's scents wafting through, Shirin batting at a stray leaf, Simin meowing while following Zahra, wanting attention.

Zahra and Reza moved to the kitchen for a late lunch, the wooden table set with simple dishes—*ghormeh sabzi*, its herby aroma rich with lamb and kidney beans, a plate of fresh *noon-e barbari*, its crust golden, and a bowl of *mast-o-khiar*, the yogurt's coolness laced with cucumber and mint from the market. The air carried the faint scent of saffron from yesterday's purchases, and the table's scarred surface seemed like a map of their shared life.

They sat close, their knees touching under the table, the light from a small window painting their faces in soft hues. Reza tore a piece of *barbari*, dipping it into the stew, his movements deliberate, his eyes locked on Zahra's. The market's overwhelm and last night's nightmare still lingered but felt softened by her presence.

"Zahra," Reza began, his baritone steady but fervent, reaching for her hand, his scarred fingers warm against hers. "Yesterday, in the market, seeing all those people... the refugees, Mahin's story, it hit me hard. Our talk about rebuilding the country, using my engineering degree—it's stayed with me. I'm inspired, truly. I want to do it, to help repair what the war broke—roads, bridges, homes. For Hossein, for us, for Iran." His voice trembled slightly, the usual ghosts of war fuelling his resolve.

Zahra's eyes glistened, her smile radiant, her heart swelling with pride. "Reza, you'll do it beautifully," she said, her voice melodic, squeezing his hand. "You've always built things—our love, our home. Now the country."

Reza's gaze softened, his thumb brushing her knuckles, the gesture tender, recalling their garden moment, her recitation of his 1982 letter. "And you, my rose," he continued, his voice warm, "I meant what I said about university. Your beautiful mind deserves to be nourished— literature, horticulture, whatever calls you. You can still be a housewife after, if you want, but you're so much more. Let the world see your light, like your father said." His words echoed her father's encouragement, and Zahra's cheeks flushed, her shyness mingling with excitement. The idea of university was a spark ignited by Reza's brilliance, their shared dreams taking shape.

She nodded, tears pricking her eyes, the *ghormeh sabzi's* warmth a comfort, the mint's crispness a promise of growth. "I'll think about it, Reza," she said, her hand tightening on his, the table a haven of their shared future. They ate slowly, their laughter soft as Simin leaped onto the table, swiping at a stray cucumber, Zahra shooing her gently.

Reza paused, setting down his bread, and looked at her with such intensity that Zahra's breath caught. "I love you, Zahra," he said quietly, his voice thick with emotion. "We're so different, you and I—after everything, the last 8 years. But we have the same heart. The same love. That's what matters, isn't it?"

Zahra's eyes filled with tears, her smile trembling. "Yes," she whispered. "The same heart, the same love. I love you too, Reza. More than all the words in all the languages I could ever learn, but it's you that's the real poet between the two of us!"

He reached across the table and cupped her face in his scarred hands, his touch infinitely gentle. "Your love is my home," he whispered, his poetry a vow. Zahra smiled, her heart full, the war's scars fading in the afternoon's light, their dreams a steady root for tomorrow.

The early evening sun dipped low over the city. The air was thick with their mingled scents—jasmine's intoxicating sweetness, lavender's calming musk, and the earthy dampness of soil still wet from Zahra's afternoon watering. The garden hummed with the faint buzz of insects settling for the night, their wings a quiet counterpoint to the distant call of the *azan* from a nearby mosque, its mournful melody weaving through the streets.

Inside, the house was a haven of tranquility. The kitchen, still fragrant with the herby richness of the *ghormeh sabzi* from lunch, was quiet now, the scarred wooden table cleared except for a single white tulip in a small vase catching the last rays of sunlight. Shirin and Simin curled together in one of the remaining sunbeams by the window, their

The Moonlit Rose of Isfahan

fur glinting as they shifted in sleep.

Zahra moved to the living room, sitting on the divan, her dark hair loose, cascading in soft waves over her shoulders, catching the light from a brass oil lamp flickering on a low table. Her eyes, usually bright with quiet intelligence, were pensive, her fingers tracing the edges of a worn copy of Hafez's poetry, its leather cover soft from years of handling—a gift from her father before his passing. The book lay open in her lap, its pages yellowed, the Farsi script elegant, but her gaze drifted to the garden, her mind turning over Reza's words at lunch—his encouragement to attend university, to nourish her beautiful mind, to let the world see her light, echoing her father's final words to tend her heart.

The idea of university, sparked by Reza's belief in her and his words of encouragement, had taken root, blooming into a quiet aspiration that both excited and unnerved her. She'd never cared much for formal education, preferring her father's books—Hafez, Rumi, Saadi—and the garden's lessons, but the thought of deepening her love of literature, perhaps by learning a new language, stirred her soul.

She imagined studying Arabic or French, languages that could unlock new worlds of poetry and prose, letting her immerse herself further in the literature she'd always cherished. Arabic could connect her to the Quran's rhythms and the works of Al-Mutanabbi, whose verses her father had once read aloud; French could open Baudelaire or Hugo, their words a bridge to distant lands. The idea felt like a garden in bloom, vibrant and alive, yet daunting—she'd be older than most students, her shyness a hurdle, the war's lost years a reminder of time stolen.

She considered signing up a year or two from now, wanting to reclaim those lost years with Reza first, to savour their reconnection—the garden embraces, the bedroom's rose petals, the market's shared chaos—before devoting herself to study. Her heart ached for those years apart, the grief for her father and Hossein, the loneliness and terror during the air raids, and she longed to root herself in their love, to rebuild their life together before branching out.

She murmured a line from Hafez to herself, her voice soft: "Even after ages and ages, the sun never tells the earth, 'You owe me.'" The words were a prayer for patience, for balance, for love that gave without demanding. Her fingers lingered on the book's pages, the lamp's flicker casting shadows like her thoughts.

Reza sat across from her in a wooden chair, his cotton tunic and pants loose against his scarred frame, his eyes watching her with a mix of love and quiet turmoil. His hands, marked by warfare and chemical burns, rested on his knees, his posture still carrying the commander's resolve from his wartime days, though softened by home's safety.

The afternoon's visit from Kaveh and their lunch conversation about rebuilding Iran had solidified his determination to use his engineering degree to repair the country's war-torn infrastructure—roads cracked by tanks, bridges collapsed under airstrikes, homes reduced to rubble. The market yesterday, with its refugees and Mahin's story of loss and reunion, had fuelled his resolve even further—a way to honour Hossein's sacrifice, to build a future for Zahra, for Iran. Yet the prospect was daunting, a shadow as heavy as last night's nightmare, where he'd died in the trench, blood pooling, Zahra's face fading.

Leaving her again, so soon after returning, to travel to distant cities—Khorramshahr, Ahvaz, places scarred like his body—felt like tearing open a wound. The flashbacks of the carnage he'd faced, the rubble and ghosts of war, threatened to pull him back to raids he'd both participated in and commanded.

He shifted, the chair creaking, and spoke, his baritone low but resolute, breaking the room's quiet. "Zahra, my rose," he began, leaning forward, his scarred hand reaching for hers, the warmth of her skin grounding him. "I've been thinking about rebuilding—roads, bridges, homes. It's what I want, to make something lasting, like we talked about. For Hossein, for us." His voice trembled, the weight of leaving her surfacing. "But it means travel, seeing the war's scars again... I just got back to you. I'm not sure I can leave so soon, face that carnage again."

His eyes glistened, the memory of one of his raids—the Iraqi soldier's desperate eyes, the knife's slash, the blood on his hands—mixing with the nightmare's vivid terror, his imagined death.

Zahra set the book aside, her eyes meeting his, her hand tightening on his, her touch a balm as it had been in the market, by the bombed building. "Reza," she said, her voice melodic, steady, "you're strong enough for this. You've faced worse—mustard gas, the trenches, artillery blasts. Build for Iran, for Hossein, but come back to me. Always."

She paused, her cheeks flushing with her characteristic shyness, then shared her own thoughts, her voice soft but earnest. "I've been seriously thinking about university, too. Maybe in a year or two, after we've had time together. I want to learn a language—Arabic, maybe French—to dive deeper into literature, to read literature poetry in its own tongue and be able to recite it to you. It's scary, but exciting. I want those lost years with you first, though, to feel us again, to get to know each other again."

Reza's heart swelled, her ambition a mirror to his, her love a steady anchor. He pulled her close, their foreheads touching, the lamp's light casting their shadows as one, the jasmine scent wrapping them. "Your mind, Zahra," he whispered, "it's a garden of its own. Learn those languages, read those stories. We'll find a way—me rebuilding, you studying, us together."

They sat in silence, hands entwined, the garden's hum and the cats' purrs a backdrop. Their dreams were daunting but shared, and their love—the same heart beating in two bodies—was a root against the war's scars, strong enough to weather whatever came next.

Chapter Eighteen

Isfahan, 1980

The dawn broke over Isfahan with a heavy, foreboding stillness, the sky a bruised purple streaked with gold, as if reluctant to fully wake to the news that had gripped the entire country: Iraq had invaded Iran, the war's shadow descending like a storm. The air was crisp, carrying the faint scent of autumn leaves from the courtyard garden of Reza and Zahra's home, where crimson roses and jasmine vines, still blooming despite the season's turn, trembled in the early breeze.

The atmosphere was thick with worry, the city's usual hum—bazaar chatter, the *azan's* call, the clatter of carts—muted by whispered fears of airstrikes, rationing, and loss. News of Iraqi tanks crossing the border, of villages near Khorramshahr burning, had spread like wildfire, radios crackling with reports, neighbours gathering in hushed groups, their faces etched with dread. Inside the home, the whitewashed walls seemed to close in, the woven Persian rugs absorbing the tension, the air laced with the faint aroma of rosewater from Zahra's morning prayers and the earthy warmth of tea brewing in the kitchen, a futile attempt to anchor the family in normalcy.

Reza stood in the living room, his body tense in a newly issued khaki uniform, the fabric stiff and unfamiliar, its weight a reminder of the draft notice that had arrived days ago, pulling him from his teaching job and his new marriage to Zahra. His soulful brown eyes, usually bright with poetry and love, were shadowed with resolve and fear, his hands fidgeting with the strap of a small canvas bag packed with essentials—socks, a notebook, Zahra's first letter to him, written during their courtship.

Hossein stood beside him, his taller, broader frame filling the space, his own khaki uniform identical to Reza's, his hazel eyes steady but fierce, his jaw set beneath his neatly trimmed beard. Hossein had been Reza's guide and shield through every milestone—childhood scrapes, teenage dreams, their first meeting with Zahra, the wedding's joy last month—and now, true to his vow, he'd volunteered to join the army, refusing to let his little brother face the frontlines alone.

"I'm not letting you face this alone. You're not going without me, Reza," he'd said, his voice a mix of teasing and steel, clapping Reza's shoulder, the memory of their shared laughter over tea in their parents' garden now a distant echo in the face of what loomed ahead.

The family gathered in the courtyard, the garden's roses and jasmine a poignant backdrop, their petals catching the dawn's light, the air cool and heavy with dew. Zahra stood close to Reza, her simple blue dress clinging to her slender frame, her dark hair tied back under a scarf, her almond eyes red-rimmed from sleepless nights, her hands clasped tightly to hide their trembling. Her parents, Ahmad and Maryam, stood nearby, Ahmad's face lined with worry, his greying hair mussed from pacing, his hands clutching a small Quran. Maryam, her scarf tight, her eyes glistening, gripped Zahra's shoulder, her touch a silent strength, the memory of their family's unity—Zahra as their only daughter and her only child, doted on with extra care—now strained by war's intrusion.

Reza and Hossein's parents stood opposite, their faces a mirror of grief and pride: their father, Salar, his posture stooped but dignified, his eyes wet as he adjusted his cap; their mother, Fatemeh, clutching a handkerchief, her sobs muffled, the scent of her rosewater perfume mingling with the garden's fragrance. Qasem, Reza's former classmate, and Leyla, her face pale but resolute, completed the circle, their presence a fragile tether to the life before the draft.

The courtyard was quiet, the only sounds the rustle of leaves, the distant honk of a truck carrying recruits, and the soft clink of tea glasses

The Moonlit Rose of Isfahan

set on a low table, the tea cooling untouched, its saffron hue a faint nod to normalcy. Reza and Hossein stood at the centre, brothers side by side, their uniforms a stark contrast to the garden's softness, their bags slung over shoulders, rifles not yet issued but looming in their futures. The goodbye was imminent—basic training awaited in a camp near Tehran, then the battlefield, where Iraqi forces advanced with brutal speed. The weight of the moment pressed down, the war's reality a cold blade: Reza, drafted against his will, his dreams of a career and a family paused; Hossein, volunteering to protect his brother, his love for Leyla and their planned future sacrificed for duty.

Zahra stepped forward, her heart pounding, her hands reaching for Reza's, her fingers trembling as they entwined with his, the warmth of his skin a fleeting comfort. "Reza, my love," she whispered, her voice breaking, tears spilling down her cheeks, "come back to me. Write to me. I'll wait, always." Her words echoed their recent wedding vows, the memory of their first dance under lantern light, her wedding dress swirling, now a painful contrast to this farewell.

Reza pulled her close, his arms wrapping around her, the uniform's roughness against her softness, his lips brushing her forehead, the rosewater scent in her hair grounding him. "My moonlit rose," he murmured, his baritone thick with emotion, "I'll return. I promise. You're my heart." His eyes met hers, memorizing her face, the unspoken fear of never seeing her again a knot in his chest.

Hossein watched, his own heart heavy, then turned to Leyla, her dark eyes locked on his, her hands clutching a small locket he'd given her, its silver glinting. "Leyla," he said, his voice steady but soft, stepping close, his hand cupping her cheek, "I'll be back to plant that jasmine tree with you. We'll have a proper courtship, a proper engagement, a proper chance at falling in love like this poet and my new little sister."

She nodded, tears falling, her lips trembling as she smiled despite everything. He pressed his forehead gently against hers, their eyes closed, breathing together in a moment of profound intimacy that needed no words. When they pulled apart, his thumb brushed away her tears while doing his best to hold back his own. "Be safe, Hossein," her voice was a prayer, "and keep Reza safe." He nodded, his jaw tight, his vow to protect his brother a fire in his chest, the memory of introducing Reza to Zahra now a bittersweet anchor, a reminder that he needed to get his brother back to his bride.

Ahmad stepped forward, pressing the Quran into Reza's hands, his voice hoarse. "My sons, may God protect you both," he said, his eyes wet, the book's weight a symbol of more than faith—of family, of promise. Maryam embraced Hossein, her sobs breaking free, "You're our sons, both of you. Come home." Salar and Fatemeh joined, their hugs fierce, Fatemeh's handkerchief damp, Salar's voice cracking, "You're our pride, boys. Fight bravely, but live."

Reza accepted it with both hands, the leather warm from Ahmad's grip, his throat too tight to speak his gratitude. The weight of it felt like both blessing and burden—a father-in-law's prayer that he would return to his daughter.

Qasem clapped Reza's shoulder, his usual jokes absent, his eyes serious, "Don't forget us, poet." The group stood in a circle, hands linked, the garden's roses a silent witness, the dawn light fading as the truck's rumble grew closer, its engine a grim summons.

The brothers stepped back, their eyes meeting, a wordless vow passing between them—Hossein's promise to shield Reza, Reza's gratitude for his brother's loyalty. The truck pulled up, its horn sharp, soldiers calling for recruits. Reza and Hossein shouldered their bags, their boots heavy on the cobblestones, the garden's scent clinging to them.

Zahra clung to Reza one last time, her sobs muffled against his chest, his arms tight around her, the world narrowing to their embrace. Hossein pulled Leyla close, their foreheads touching once more in silent goodbye, then clapped Reza's back. "Together, little brother." They climbed into the truck, the engine roaring, the crowd waving, Zahra's scarf fluttering, her father's Quran in Reza's hand, the garden's roses blurring as the truck pulled away, the war's shadow swallowing them, their love and brotherhood a steady root in the uncertainty.

The dawn light faded into a grey morning over Isfahan, the air heavy with the weight of departure, the distant rumble of the army truck carrying Reza and Hossein to basic training now a faint echo swallowed

The Moonlit Rose of Isfahan

by the city's waking hum. The courtyard garden of Reza and Zahra's new home, where moments ago the family had stood in a tearful farewell, felt desolate, its crimson roses and jasmine vines drooping slightly in the cool September breeze, their petals trembling as if mirroring Zahra's grief. The scent of jasmine, once a comforting reminder of her budding romance with Reza, now carried a sting of absence, mingling with the faint rosewater from her morning prayers and the earthy dampness of the garden's soil, still wet from yesterday's tending.

The war's shadow, sparked by Iraq's invasion, loomed over everything, the atmosphere thick with worry—radios crackling with news of border clashes, neighbours whispering of rationing, the *azan's* mournful call from the mosque a reminder of lives now at risk. Zahra stood alone in the courtyard after everyone else left, her dress clinging to her frame, her dark hair now loose beneath her scarf, strands catching the breeze, her almond eyes red-rimmed and glistening with tears, her hands still warm from Reza's final embrace, his promise to return a fragile thread against the future's uncertainty.

She stepped into the house, the door creaking shut behind her, the sound sharp in the sudden silence. She hadn't even been married to Reza a full month, and now he was gone. Their wedding, a modest but joyful affair in Shiraz, felt like a dream she'd woken up from. Reza's poetry recited in his warm baritone, their first dance as husband and wife, her wedding dress swirling, Hossein's teasing laughter as he toasted them with *sharbat* and joked about them naming their future son after him. Now, the house was a hollow shell, the living room's low table still holding the tea glasses from the farewell, their saffron hue cold and untouched, the faint aroma of the tea mingling with the lingering rosewater from her scarf.

Shirin, one of their new kittens—a gift from Hossein to celebrate their marriage—padded softly across the rug, her purrs tentative, her green eyes searching for Reza, mirroring Zahra's own longing.

Zahra sank onto the cushioned divan, her hands trembling as she clutched Reza's last gift—a small notebook where he'd written a poem for her, its pages crisp, the ink's faint smell rising as she opened it. His words, *in the desert of my days, you are the oasis*, blurred through her tears, a reminder of their courtship, when he'd read Hafez to her under the stars, his voice weaving love into every verse. The notebook felt like a lifeline, but also a wound—Reza, drafted into the army, was gone, his dreams paused, his warmth replaced by the stiff khaki uniform she'd clung to in the courtyard.

Hossein's departure cut just as deep; in the year since meeting him, he'd become a true brother, his protective warmth and teasing filling the void left by Farhad, her half-brother, whose rare letters from Tehran and focus on his wife's family farm left little room for connection. Hossein had been there for every moment—introducing her to Reza, planning their wedding in Shiraz with its *sofreh aghd* spread with mirror and candles and Reza's own poetry volume, then promising to keep Reza safe on the frontlines. Now both were gone, the truck's dust trail a fading scar on her heart, the war's cruelty stealing her husband and her brother-in-law in one blow.

The house felt too large, its silence oppressive, the ticking of a small clock on the wall a relentless reminder of time stretching without Reza. The kitchen, where she and Reza had cooked their first meal as husband and wife—*fesenjan*, its pomegranate-walnut tang a shared joy—now smelled faintly of the morning's tea, the samovar silent, its brass dulled in the dim light.

Zahra moved to the bedroom, her steps heavy, the wooden floor creaking underfoot again, the air cool with the faint jasmine scent drifting through the open window. The bed, draped in a blue-and-gold quilt embroidered by her mother, was unmade, Reza's pillow still holding the indent of his head, the scent of his skin—sandalwood and sweat—lingering. She lay down, curling into his side, her tears soaking the fabric, her body shaking with sobs. "Reza," she whispered, her voice raw, "Hossein... come back to me. Both of you." The loss was visceral, her heart aching for Reza's touch, his poetry, his promise, and for Hossein's laughter, his vow to protect his little brother, a vow that now felt fragile against the war's brutality.

She thought of her parents' grief in the courtyard—her father Ahmad's Quran pressed into Reza's hands, her mother Maryam's muffled sobs—and Reza's parents, their pride and fear for both sons. Leyla's tearful goodbye to Hossein, their foreheads touching in that tender moment, Qasem's quiet farewell, all echoed in the empty house, amplifying Zahra's solitude.

She'd been married less than a month, their love barely rooted before the war tore Reza away, and Hossein's choice to volunteer, to stand by Reza as he always had, left her both grateful and bereft. Farhad's absence stung anew; his estrangement, his life in Tehran, made Hossein's brotherly warmth all the more precious, his loss now a double wound.

She clutched the notebook, her fingers tracing Reza's words, praying they'd survive, that the war wouldn't claim them as it threatened to claim everything—her father's dreams for her, their home, their promise of the future.

Zahra rose, her hands steadying as she moved to the kitchen, needing to anchor herself. She lit the samovar, its hum a small comfort, the steam rising with the earthy scent of tea leaves. She set out a single glass and sipped slowly, the warmth spreading through her, a faint echo of Reza's embrace. Shirin attempted to leap onto the table, wanting to nuzzle her hand, and Zahra stroked her fur, the softness grounding her. She resolved to write to Reza, to pour her love into letters, to tend the garden as her father had taught, to keep their home alive for his return. The war's shadow loomed, but her love for Reza, her bond with Hossein, were roots that would endure, her heart a garden of hope amid the emptiness.

Chapter Nineteen

Isfahan, 1988

Shirin and Simin lounged in a sunbeam on the rug as they always did, Shirin's fur glinting as she stretched lazily, Simin's purr a soft, rhythmic hum that filled the space with a gentle domesticity. The house, once empty during Reza's absence, now pulsed with the subtle presence of reunion. Reza sat at the low wooden table in the living room, his lean frame hunched slightly over a sheet of paper. His beard framed a face etched with quiet determination, his eyes focused but glistening with unshed tears as he dipped his pen into the inkwell, the faint scratch of nib on paper the only sound besides the cat's purrs.

The market outing had been overwhelming—the crowded streets, the bombed building triggering flashbacks to the trenches, the sensory chaos of scents and sounds after eight years on the frontlines—but it had also ignited a resolve in him, a desire to rebuild not just the country but his life with Zahra. Now, alone in the living room while Zahra tended the garden, he wrote a long, heartfelt letter to Leyla, Hossein's beloved, a woman he had only met once but felt connected to through his brother's stories and unfinished letter he'd finished and sent instead.

The act was a way to honour Hossein, to offer comfort to Leyla, and to process his own lingering emotions—the grief that surged like a wave, the guilt of survival, the ache of what could have been. Reza's hand trembled slightly as he began, the ink flowing in his neat, poetic script, each word a deliberate step through his heart's labyrinth, pausing to collect his thoughts as he wrote, the pen hovering, the ink beading at the tip.

Dear Leyla,

I am Reza, Hossein's brother. Though we have only met briefly I feel I know you through the light you brought to his life, the way his eyes would soften when he spoke of your letters, your jasmine tree, your shared dreams. He loved you deeply, Leyla, with a fire that burned brighter than any star in the trench nights. More than he was able to voice to you, I think. I write to honour him, to share the man he was, and to offer what comfort I can in this time of unbearable loss, even all of these years later.

He dipped the pen again, the scratch resuming, his mind flooding with memories of Hossein—their laughter when Zahra had chosen Reza over him, Hossein's teasing grin, his confession of true love for Leyla in the trench, his voice warm with hope. Reza's emotions poured onto the page, the ink smudging slightly where a tear fell, the paper absorbing it like the mud of the trenches. He described Hossein's final days—the 1983 assault near Ahvaz, the human wave order, the blast that took him, Reza's own shrapnel wounds, the infirmary's own kind of hell.

Hossein was my guide, my protector. From our childhood in Isfahan, where he taught me to ride a bike and defended me from bullies, to our courtship days when he stepped aside with grace, treating Zahra like the sister he never had. He was brave, Leyla, not just in battle, but in love. He carried your letters like talismans, reading them by lantern light, dreaming of a life with you. In 1982, he confided in me about you—your poetry, your strength. 'She's my oasis,' he said, his eyes alight. He planned to plant that jasmine tree with you, to build a home where love bloomed like our garden.

He shielded me, Leyla. His last words were of you and Zahra, urging me to live. He was brave to the end, his heart full of love for you. Know that he loved you as fiercely as a poet loves the stars. If you ever need anything, Leyla, write to me. You are family, his love making you so. May God grant you peace, as I pray for Hossein's soul.

Sincerely,

Reza

He included a poem Hossein had written to Leyla on crumpled paper, his hand lingering on it, the paper worn from trench handling, the scent of gunpowder faint but present. He sealed the letter, his heart lighter yet heavier, the process a catharsis, honouring Hossein's memory, offering comfort to Leyla, and processing his grief—the many brotherly nights despite the war, the scars that defined him, marks of survival offering hope for a future.

Meanwhile, in the garden, Zahra knelt among the roses, her dress brushing the soft grass, her fingers delving into the soil with a gentle touch, the earth cool and crumbly under her nails, the scent of lavender and mint rising as she pruned a wayward stem. The sun hung low, casting long shadows, the air cool with the approaching dusk, the distant *azan* calling from a mosque, its melody a soothing prayer.

Zahra paused, her eyes gazing at the mulberry tree, and she prayed silently, her lips moving, her heart full of gratitude. "God, thank you for ending the war, for bringing Reza home," she whispered, her voice soft, tears pricking her eyes. "He's not the same—his scars, his nightmares—but my gentle, sweet, poetic Reza is still there, underneath the weight. Help him heal, as I love him." She thought of their tender moments—the garden embraces, the bedroom's rose petals, the market's chaos—proud of their love, a root enduring like her roses.

Later, the early evening light faded into a soft twilight over Isfahan, the sky a tapestry of indigo and gold, the air cooling as the last warmth of the sun lingered in the courtyard garden's roses and jasmine vines. Inside the house, the living room was quiet, the brass oil lamp now lit, casting a warm, flickering glow across the rugs and the low table where Reza's letter to Leyla lay sealed, the faint scent of the ink mingling with the lavender wafting through the open window.

Shirin and Simin had both moved to the divan, their fur catching the lamplight as they nestled together the way they'd done their whole lives. Reza stood at the threshold between the living room and the courtyard, his eyes watching Zahra, his heart swelling with love and resolve after writing to Leyla—a cathartic act of honouring Hossein, offering comfort, and processing his own grief.

The transition to civilian life remained daunting, an alien landscape, but the letter to Leyla had left him lighter, braver, ready to take another small step forward. He wanted to act on his resolve, to seek information on how he could contribute to Iran's reconstruction, even if it meant venturing out alone, facing the city's bustle without Zahra's grounding hand. The thought of leaving her again, even briefly, to travel to devastated cities like Khorramshahr or Ahvaz, stirred a knot of fear—memories of these places during battles still haunted him in ways he couldn't entirely voice—but his love for his wife and his duty to Hossein pushed him onward.

Reza stepped into the bedroom to change, the air cool with jasmine from the garden, the quilt on the bed still rumpled from last night's sleep. He pulled on a fresh tunic, its beige fabric crisp, and a pair of sturdy trousers, lacing his boots with deliberate care, his scarred hands steady despite the tremor in his chest. He glanced at a small mirror, his beard speckled with premature grey and weathered face a reminder of the war's toll, but his eyes burned with purpose. He tucked Zahra's last letter into his pocket, a talisman, just as they had been during his entire military career.

"I'll be back soon, my rose," he murmured to her as he stepped out, kissing Zahra's forehead as she knelt by a tulip bed, her smile soft but knowing, her hand squeezing his briefly, the soil under her nails a grounding touch. "Be safe, Reza," she said, her voice melodic, and he nodded, his heart full, stepping onto the cobblestone street.

Isfahan's evening streets were quieter than the market's chaos, but still alive with the hum of post-war life—vendors closing stalls, children playing in alleys, refugees with tattered bags moving through the shadows, their faces etched with resilience. The air carried the scent of grilled kebabs from a nearby stall, the smoky char mingling with dust and the faint flowery aromas of roadside gardens, a contrast to the gunpowder and blood of Reza's wartime memories.

His boots scuffed the uneven cobblestones, each step a reminder of the market's overwhelm—the cumin, the shouts, the bombed building's echo of unspeakable things Reza had witnessed. Yet, he felt braver now. He headed toward a municipal office near the bazaar, rumoured to be coordinating reconstruction efforts, its location shared by Kaveh during his visit earlier. The office, a low brick building with cracked windows, stood at the edge of a square, its facade marked by a chipped corner. The door was open, a faint light spilling out just before

The Moonlit Rose of Isfahan

closing time, voices still murmuring inside.

Reza hesitated, his heart racing, the weight of everything pressing down on his shoulders. He breathed deeply, Zahra's letter crinkling in his pocket, and stepped inside, the air cooler, smelling of old paper, ink, and dust. The office was modest, its walls lined with maps and blueprints, tables cluttered with files, a few men in worn suits discussing plans, their voices low but urgent.

A clerk, a middle-aged man with a tired smile, looked up, his glasses reflecting the lantern light. "*Salaam*, how can I help?" he asked, and Reza, his baritone steady despite his nerves, explained his intent: "I'm an engineer, back from the front. I want to help rebuild—roads, bridges, anything needed." The clerk nodded, pulling out a form, the paper yellowed, the ink smudged, and handed Reza a pamphlet listing projects—roads in Khuzestan, schools in Tehran, water systems in Ahvaz.

Reza's eyes scanned the list, his engineering mind sparking, but his heart sank at the locations—war-torn cities, their names evoking shrapnel marks, knife wounds and bullet grazes, the blood on his hands. Leaving Zahra to work there felt like abandoning her again, the thought a weight heavier than his rifle. For a moment he was nauseous, but he took a series of deep breaths.

The clerk sensed his hesitation, offering, "We need men like you, trained, experienced. Start local if you want—Isfahan has a few projects too." Reza nodded, a bit of relief mingling with resolve, taking the pamphlet, its weight both a promise and a burden. He asked about local efforts—repairing a bridge over the Zayandeh River who had fallen into disrepair, assessing damaged buildings rattled by the rare airstrike—and the clerk shared details, his voice hopeful, describing engineers meeting weekly to plan.

Reza listened, his mind mapping possibilities, his fear of leaving Zahra tempered by the chance to work nearby, to rebuild while staying rooted in their love. He thanked the clerk, stepping back into the evening, the air now cooler, the stars emerging, the *azan's* call fading into the night's hum. He was still on edge, but he reminded himself to take everything one day at a time.

The walk home was even quieter, the streets emptying, the kebab stall's smoke dissipating, the jasmine scent stronger as he neared their home. Reza's heart was lighter, the pamphlet in his pocket a tangible step toward rebuilding, yet the fear lingered—facing war's carnage again, even in peace, felt like stepping back into the trench. He thought of Zahra, her prayers for him, her faith in his poetic soul beneath the scars, and his resolve strengthened. He entered the courtyard, finding Zahra sitting among the roses, her dress dusted with soil, her hands cupping a white tulip, her eyes glistening as she looked up, sensing his return.

"Reza," she said, her voice warm, rising to embrace him, her arms wrapping around his neck, the lavender scent on her skin grounding him. "Found something?" she asked, and he nodded, showing her the pamphlet, his voice soft but firm. "Local projects, maybe. I can't leave you again, not so soon." She smiled, her shyness fading, and took his hands in hers, her almond eyes meeting his with a tenderness that carried the weight of all they had endured.

"I'm proud of you, Reza," she said, her voice steady and full of emotion. "Proud of your sacrifices, proud of your strength. Proud of how you've carried the weight of war and still have room in your heart for kindness, for Leyla, for rebuilding our nation. And I'm proud of our love—it has endured through separation, through nightmares, through loss. You are my oasis, as I am yours. I love you."

Her words settled over him like a blessing, and he pulled her closer, his chin resting on her head as they stood together in the garden, the roses blooming around them, the twilight deepening into night. The garden's blooms were a promise of their shared future, roots planted deep in love and resilience as he whispered in her ear just how much he loved her too.

Chapter Twenty
Isfahan, 1985-1986

The bazaar in summertime pulsed with a subdued energy, the war's years casting a long shadow over the once-vibrant streets. The air was thick with the mingled scents of spices—cumin's earthy sharpness, saffron's floral sweetness, cinnamon's warm bite—and the tangy aroma of pickled olives and fresh bread from stalls lining the narrow alleys. Voices overlapped in a chaotic yet familiar symphony: vendors hawking their wares with hoarse shouts, women haggling in rapid Farsi, their scarves colourful against the muted tones of wartime rationing, children darting through the crowd, their laughter a fleeting spark of joy amid the worry.

The alleys were constantly overcrowded, Isfahan a refuge for those fleeing the frontlines—families with tattered bags, their faces etched with exhaustion, displaced from villages near the frontlines, now selling handmade crafts or begging for scraps. The cobblestones underfoot were uneven, worn from countless feet, the awnings overhead faded and patched, blocking the harsh sun but letting through dappled light that danced on the ground like uncertain hope. Stalls overflowed with what little was available—sacks of rice, piles of wilted vegetables, jars of honey—ration cards stamped with haste, the war's hunger a constant companion.

Zahra navigated the market with a woven basket on her arm, her simple purple dress swaying slightly, her dark hair tied back under a scarf, her almond eyes scanning the stalls with practiced care. The war had hardened her routine—rationed food, air raid drills, letters to Reza on the frontlines—but the garden at home offered solace, its flowers and herbs a symbol of endurance.

Today, her basket held a few dates and bread, her steps measured, her heart heavy with the absence of Reza, Hossein and her father. As she turned a corner near the market's edge, where the crowds thinned and the stalls gave way to quieter benches, she spotted an elderly woman sitting alone, her frail figure wrapped in a faded black chador, her hands clutching a shawl, her eyes distant, staring at the ground.

The woman's presence tugged at Zahra—out of place amid the market's bustle, her face lined with deep wrinkles, her skin weathered like old leather, her posture slumped with exhaustion. Zahra approached, her basket swinging lightly, her voice soft but kind.

"*Salaam, khanoum,*" she said, kneeling slightly to meet the woman's gaze. "Are you alright? You look like you could use some tea." The woman looked up, her eyes cloudy with age and sorrow, but a faint smile creased her lips. "*Salaam*, dear," she replied, her voice raspy, like dry leaves in the wind. "I'm Mahin. Just resting. The world moves too fast these days." Zahra smiled, her shyness easing, and sat beside her on the bench, the stone cool through her dress, the market's noise a distant hum. She offered a date from her basket, the fruit sticky and sweet, its flavour bursting on the tongue. Mahin accepted, her fingers trembling, and they shared the small treat, the act a bridge across their ages.

Over the next weeks, their encounters became a ritual, Zahra seeking out Mahin at the market's edge, the old woman's spot a constant amid the chaos. One afternoon in late 1985, the sun beat down, the market's scents intensified—roasted nuts mingling with sweat and dust. Zahra arrived with a thermos of tea, its earthy warmth a comfort, and a small parcel of bread and cheese, the bread crusty, the cheese tangy and soft.

They sat, the bench hard but familiar, the shade from a nearby awning offering relief. Mahin sipped the tea, the glass hot in her wrinkled hands, and reminisced about her youth in a village near the border, before the war. "We had a garden much like yours, dear," she

The Moonlit Rose of Isfahan

said, her voice cracking with memory, her eyes distant, as if seeing the past. "My mother taught me to weave rugs—patterns of vines and birds, each thread a story. Life was simple: milking goats at dawn, their milk warm and frothy, baking bread in a clay oven, the crust golden and crackling, the village square alive with laughter at weddings, the *setar's* strings singing under the stars." Her words painted a picture, the scent of fresh bread in Zahra's mind, the warmth of community a contrast to the war's isolation.

Zahra listened, her heart aching for that lost world, and shared her own stories, bragging about Reza with a shy smile. "My Reza is so handsome," she said, pulling a small photo from her scarf, the image faded but clear—Reza in his uniform, his frame straight, his soulful eyes gazing at the camera. "He's a commander now, brave and clever. He sneaks behind enemy lines, like a shadow, and comes back with victories. His poetry... he writes me verses that make my heart bloom."

Mahin squinted at the photo, her eyesight failing, the image a blur of colors, her fingers tracing the edges. "He sounds like a hero, dear," she said, her voice warm, though the details escaped her cloudy vision. "Tell me more—does he smiles as much as you do?" Zahra laughed softly, pocketing the photo, her cheeks flushing, the old woman's kindness a comfort amid the war's worry.

As the months passed into 1986, their meetings deepened, Mahin's gaze softening one spring day as her eyes drifted to a distant memory, the wrinkles around them deepening like the lines of a well-read book. "You remind me of my youth, dear Zahra," she said, her voice gaining strength, the words flowing like a river long dammed. "Before the war, before everything changed. I was married young, like you—seventeen, to my Ardalan. He was a farmer, strong as an ox, with hands rough from the soil but gentle as a summer breeze when he touched me."

She paused, her fingers tracing the edge of her shawl, the fabric worn and soft, its threads frayed from years of use. "Our wedding was in our village near the border, the air filled with the scent of blooming almond trees, their white petals falling like snow on our heads. The *daf* drum beat a rhythm that made our hearts dance, the women in colourful dresses swirling like leaves in the wind, the men clapping and singing old folk songs about love and mountains. Ardalan played the *tar* that night, its strings singing under his fingers, the music a melody that wrapped around us like a warm embrace. We had *halva* and *gaz*, the sweets melting on our tongues, sticky and nutty, the taste of pistachios and rosewater a promise of sweetness in life."

Zahra listened, her basket set aside, her hands folded in her lap, the market's sounds—a vendor's shout, a child's laugh—fading as Mahin's words painted a vivid picture. The old woman's voice trembled with nostalgia, her eyes glistening, the failing eyesight not dimming the clarity of memory.

"Life before the war was simple but full," Mahin continued, her gnarled hand reaching for Zahra's, the touch papery but warm. "Ardalan and I built a home—mud bricks baked in the sun, their earthy smell filling our days. We had a garden, much like yours, with roses climbing the walls, their petals soft as silk, the thorns a reminder that beauty comes with pain. He'd bring me jasmine from the fields, the scent clinging to his clothes when he came home at dusk, his hands calloused from plowing, but he'd hold me gently, like I was a delicate flower. We had three children—two daughters and a son—their laughter echoing through the house like birdsong, the patter of their feet on the dirt floor a joy that filled every corner. Before the war, the village was alive—festivals with dancing under the stars, the fire's crackle, the taste of fresh bread from the *tandoor*, crusty and hot, slathered with butter that melted instantly."

Mahin's voice softened, her eyes distant, the market's bustle a far cry from the peace she described. "Ardalan was my lifelong companion, Zahra. We shared everything—the hard harvests when the sun scorched the earth, the rain's blessing on our crops, the quiet nights by the fire, his head in my lap as I sang lullabies from my grandmother. He was kind, always—never raised his voice, even when money was tight, his laugh a rumble that made my heart flutter even after thirty years. He doted on our daughters, teaching them to read by lantern light, believing girls deserved the stars, just like your father did for you. Life wasn't easy—droughts that turned the soil to dust, winters where the cold seeped into our bones—but with Ardalan, it was beautiful. Until... until he widowed me a few years before the war broke out, his

The Moonlit Rose of Isfahan

heart giving out one harvest day, the sun beating down as he fell in the field, his hands still clutching the sickle, the scent of wheat heavy in the air. I still miss him so much."

Zahra's heart ached, her own losses echoing—her father's illness, Hossein's death in the same year, Reza's absence on the frontlines. She squeezed Mahin's hand, the old woman's skin fragile but resilient, like the garden vines.

"It sounds like a love from the poems," Zahra said softly, her voice melodic, sharing a piece of bread from her basket, the crust crackling, the inside soft and yeasty, a small comfort. Mahin nodded, her smile wistful, and turned the conversation to Zahra, her cloudy eyes squinting with kindness. "And you, dear, with your Reza—only three weeks married before the war took him. That's a cruel twist, like a flower cut before it blooms." Zahra nodded, her cheeks flushing with shyness, her fingers fiddling with her scarf. "It is," she admitted, her voice trembling, "but his letters keep me going. He's handsome, Mahin—tall, with eyes that see into your soul, a poet's heart."

Mahin chuckled softly, her laugh a raspy wheeze, patting Zahra's knee.

"Ah, young love. Let me give you some advice, dear, from an old woman who knew a lifelong companion. Marriage is like a garden—you plant the seeds of love, but you must tend it daily. Water it with kindness, pull the weeds of anger before they root, let the sun of laughter shine on it. Before the war, when times were good, Ardalan and I would talk every night by the fire, sharing dreams, even the small ones—like a new rug or a trip to the river. Don't let the war steal that. Write to Reza of your days, your garden, your love. And when he returns, hold him close, forgive the changes the war brings. Men like him, brave and gentle, need your light to find their way home."

Her words, wise and warm, hung in the air, the market's noise a distant hum, the scent of roasted nuts wafting over, a reminder of life persisting.

Zahra listened, her heart full, the advice a balm, and showed Mahin another photo of Reza, holding it close to the old woman's face. "See his smile?" she said, bragging softly, her voice proud. Mahin squinted, her failing eyesight turning the image into a blur of colours, but she nodded, her fingers tracing the photo's edge. "He's a prince, dear. Keep that smile in your heart." They shared tea from Zahra's flask, the hot liquid steaming in their glasses, its cardamom spice warming their hands, the market's bustle fading as they exchanged stories, the bond between the young wife and the widowed elder a quiet haven amid the war's storm.

Through the seasons, their encounters evolved, the bazaar's chaos a constant backdrop. On an unseasonably cold day, Zahra found Mahin shivering under an awning, her chador damp, and wrapped her in a spare shawl, the fabric soft and warm, sharing *halva*, the sesame treat crumbly and nutty, melting on the tongue. Mahin reminisced about her honeymoon, "Ardalan and I went to the mountains, the air fresh with pine, the snow capping the peaks like sugar on baklava. We stayed in a small hut, the fire crackling, his arms around me as we watched the stars, the world ours." Her voice cracked, the memory bittersweet, the pre-war peace a lost paradise.

Zahra spoke of her own wedding in 1980, her cheeks flushing, "Reza recited poetry, his voice like a song, our bed soft with quilts, his touch gentle as a breeze." Mahin smiled, her cloudy eyes soft, giving advice: "Cherish the small moments, dear. A shared glance, a hand held—those are the threads that weave a marriage strong."

When spring came, the market bloomed with colour, fresh fruits piling high—pomegranates red as rubies, their tangy seeds bursting on the tongue; apricots golden and juicy, their sweetness a burst of summer promise. The air was warmer, the rain's patter replaced by birdsong, the stalls alive with vendors shouting, "Ripe apricots, fresh from the orchard!" Zahra and Mahin sat, sharing *sabzi polo*, the herby rice fluffy, the fish flaky, the flavours a divine taste during wartime.

Mahin spoke of her children's births, "The pain like a storm, but the joy... like the sun breaking through clouds, their cries filling the room, Ardalan's eyes shining with tears." She advised Zahra on patience in marriage, "Men return from war changed, dear. Love them through it, like I loved Ardalan after he lost his father—gentle words, a warm meal, time to heal." Zahra nodded, her heart aching for Reza, showing a photo, Mahin squinting, "He's strong, like Ardalan. You'll have beautiful children one day."

Summer brought shimmering heat off the cobblestones, the air dry and dusty, the stalls shaded with awnings flapping in the breeze. Zahra brought cool *sharbat*, the pomegranate drink tart and refreshing, its ruby colour glinting in glass cups. Mahin reminisced about village festivals, "Dancing under the stars, the *daf*'s beat pounding like a heart, the fire's crackle, the taste of fresh bread and yogurt, life full before the bombs came." Her advice turned to endurance: "Marriage is like a vine—it twists through hard times, but grows stronger. Hold on to Reza's letters, dear—they're your root." Zahra bragged about Reza's bravery, "He's a decorated commander now, planning raids like a chess master," her voice proud, Mahin's failing eyes squinting at the photo, her smile kind. "He's your hero, dear. Keep him in your prayers."

One evening in mid-1986, the market winding down, the air cooling with dusk, the stalls' awnings sagging, Zahra found Mahin with a small gift—a handmade scarf, its threads soft and blue, woven during quiet nights. "For you, dear," Mahin said, her voice frail, her hands trembling as she handed it over. They shared dates and Mahin reminisced about her wedding, "The henna on my hands, red as roses, the music, the sweets—*gaz* and *halva* melting on the tongue." Zahra listened, her heart aching for her own wedding already six years ago now, Reza's vows, Hossein's toast. The encounters, over weeks and months, had built a tender friendship, Mahin's stories of youth a balm for Zahra's loneliness, Zahra's kindness a light for Mahin's isolation, their bond a quiet defiance against the war's cruelty.

Then, late one summer afternoon when the heat was oppressive, the air thick and humid, Zahra made her way to the market as usual, her grey dress clinging to her skin, her basket on her arm holding a few dates she had saved and a small parcel of bread. As she turned the corner near the market's edge, where the crowds thinned and the stalls gave way to quieter benches worn smooth by years of weary sitters, she scanned the familiar spot, her almond eyes narrowing against the glare, searching for Mahin.

The bench was empty, the stone seat bare under the awning's shade, a few scattered leaves from a nearby tree rustling in the breeze, the spot eerily vacant where Mahin had always sat, her faded black chador a constant in Zahra's visits. Zahra's breath caught, a pang of worry twisting in her chest, the market's noise—a vendor's shout, a child's cry, the clatter of a cart—fading as she looked around, her eyes darting to nearby stalls, the ground littered with date pits and crumpled paper from discarded ration slips.

"Mahin *khanoum*?" she called softly, her voice melodic but laced with concern, stepping closer, her basket bumping against her hip, the dates shifting inside. No response came, only the vendor's bell ringing nearby, the scent of roasted nuts wafting over, smoky and sweet, a reminder of their shared treats. Zahra's heart quickened, the worry blooming into fear—Mahin, the elderly refugee with her cloudy eyes and warm stories, had become a companion, a surrogate grandmother in the war's loneliness, their exchanges of tea, *halva*, and tales a lifeline. What if she was ill? What if she had passed away, another loss piling on like the war's relentless toll.

Zahra searched the market, her steps hurried, the cobblestones uneven under her shoes, slipping slightly on a spilled puddle from a vendor's water jug, the liquid cool and splashy against her ankles. She weaved through the throng, the crowd's press closing in—women in colourful scarves bargaining for wilted greens, their voices sharp and insistent; men with weathered faces hauling sacks of rice, their grunts mingling with the creak of wooden carts, children tugging at skirts, their small hands sticky from stolen bites of fruit.

The scents intensified in the heat—overripe apricots fermenting in a stall, the sour tang of yogurt from a dairy vendor, the smoky haze from a kebab grill where meat sizzled on skewers, fat dripping with a hiss. Voices swirled around her, men and women chattering, negotiating prices, talking about the war. Zahra scanned each bench, each shaded corner, her basket bumping against her hip, the dates shifting with a soft thump, her heart pounding with growing dread.

She asked a vendor she knew, a stout woman with a gap-toothed smile selling pickled vegetables, their jars glinting in the sun, the brine's tangy scent sharp. "Have you seen Mahin *khanoum*? The elderly woman

The Moonlit Rose of Isfahan

who sits near the edge?" The vendor shook her head, her scarf slipping slightly, "No, dear. Not for days. Maybe she's ill—God protect her." Zahra's stomach knotted, the fear deepening, the market's chaos amplifying her isolation—the war had already taken too much. Mahin's stories—of her marriage to Habib, her advice on patience and intimacy—had been a comfort, a way to feel less alone, and now she was gone, perhaps another casualty of the war's cruelty, her disappearance a void that piled on Zahra's losses.

Zahra searched further, her steps carrying her to the market's fringes, where the alleys widened and the stalls became sparse, the ground dustier, the air cooler under the shade of a few trees. She checked under awnings, behind carts, her voice calling "Mahin *khanoum*?" with increasing desperation, the words echoing faintly, swallowed by the market's din. A child bumped into her, his small body warm and hurried, apologizing with a grin, but Zahra barely noticed, her eyes scanning faces—old women with chadors, but none with Mahin's kind, wrinkled smile, her failing eyesight that squinted at Reza's photos, her voice raspy with stories of youth.

Sweat beaded on her forehead, trickling down her back, her dress clinging uncomfortably, the basket's weight pulling on her arm, the dates inside waiting to be shared with her friend. Fear turned to grief, the thought that Mahin may have passed away—alone, without her children, another soul claimed by the war's indirect cruelty—crushed her. "Not her too," Zahra whispered, her heart heavy, tears pricking her eyes, the market's bustle a mocking reminder of life moving on, vendors packing up as the day ended, the air cooling with dusk.

Zahra returned home, the walk a blur, the cobblestones uneven, her steps heavy, the basket swinging like a pendulum. The house felt even emptier, the courtyard garden a silent witness, the roses drooping as if in sympathy, their petals falling softly in the breeze. She sank onto the divan, her hands trembling as she set the basket down, the dates untouched, her heart heavy with the piling losses—her father in 1983, Hossein shortly thereafter, now Mahin, perhaps gone, the war stealing even this friendship.

She prayed softly, her lips moving, "God, protect her, protect Reza," her voice a whisper, the room's quiet a weight, the lamp's glow flickering as she lit it, the flame a small light in her darkness. The cats curled at her feet, their purrs a comfort, but the void lingered, Mahin's disappearance a mystery that haunted her, a reminder of the war's unrelenting toll on the living.

Autumn eventually turned to winter in Isfahan, the snow dusting the alleys, the ground slippery, the air crisp with the scent of roasted chestnuts from a vendor's cart, their smoky sweetness cutting the cold. She searched for Mahin every time she went to the market, her eyes scanning the benches, asking vendors, checking under awnings, but the old woman never returned.

Eventually, as the months passed and winter deepened, Zahra came to understand that she would have to stop looking, that Mahin—like so many others in this war—had simply vanished, leaving behind only memories of wisdom shared over dates and tea, stories of a life before the bombs, and the gentle reminder that even in darkness, human connection could bloom.

Chapter Twenty-One

Shiraz, 1988

The late autumn sun hung low over Shiraz, casting a golden glow across the city's ancient streets, the air crisp with the scent of cypress trees and the faint sweetness of oranges from nearby groves, their leaves rustling in a gentle breeze that carried a hint of impending rain. The weather was mild but changeable, the sky a vast canvas of blue streaked with wispy clouds, a coolness that seeped through clothing and into bones, the humidity low but the air fresh.

Shiraz, the city of poets and gardens, felt both familiar and distant to Zahra and Reza as they approached in the Heydaris' small car they'd borrowed, the engine humming softly, the tires crunching over gravel roads that wound through hills dotted with olive trees and wild poppies, their red petals a vivid contrast to the dry earth. The journey from Isfahan had been a reflective one, the landscape shifting from flat plains to rolling hills, the road lined with occasional checkpoints, remnants of the war's paranoia, though the ceasefire held, the soldiers waving them through checkpoints with weary smiles.

Zahra sat beside Reza, her dark green dress simple but elegant, its fabric soft against her skin, her dark hair tied back underneath her scarf, a few strands escaping to frame her face, catching the light like silk. Her almond eyes sparkled with excitement, her hand resting on Reza's knee, the touch a quiet reassurance as they neared the house where his parents now lived with relatives.

Jamila Mikhail

The trip was more than a visit—it was a return to the city where they had married in 1980, where they had explored each other's bodies with tender, clumsy passion in their first weeks as husband and wife, feeling as if the world held no worries beyond their shared laughter and whispered poetry, the memory of their honeymoon bed in a small inn, its quilts soft and the air scented with jasmine, stirring a warm flush in her cheeks.

Reza drove with a steady hand, his military uniform neatly pressed, the olive-green fabric hugging his lean frame, his white *chafiyeh* draped around his neck in the traditional style, its fringed edges hanging against his chest, the medals pinned above it glinting in the sunlight, a testament to his survival through raids and battles. His greying beard added a rugged maturity to his once-boyish face, his soulful brown eyes reflecting a mix of anticipation and nervousness, his scarred hands gripping the steering wheel, the leather worn under his fingers.

The uniform was a deliberate choice, the same one he had worn when he last saw his parents in 1980 before heading to the frontlines, a gesture to bridge the past with the present, to show them the son who had survived, though changed by the war's horrors etched into his soul. The road smoothed as they entered the outskirts of Shiraz, the city unfolding with its mix of ancient architecture and war's subtle scars—cracked walls from distant bombings, boarded windows, but also blooming gardens and the resilient hum of life rebuilding. The breeze through the open window carried the scent of pine from nearby hills, the temperature comfortable enough for light clothing, but with a hint of evening chill that promised a cozy reunion.

They pulled up to the house in a quiet neighbourhood, its stone walls weathered by time and wind, the surface rough and pitted, painted a faded white that peeled in places, revealing the grey beneath, like old skin shedding. The architecture was traditional Persian—thick walls designed to keep the summer heat at bay and retain warmth in winter, small windows with blue-painted wooden shutters that hung slightly askew on their hinges, the paint faded but cheerful. The roof was constructed of clay tiles in a mosaic of terracotta reds and browns, some cracked from years of sun and storm, sloping gently to shed rainwater into a small gutter system that emptied into the courtyard below. The single-story structure stretched in an L-shape around a small inner courtyard, creating a private oasis typical of Shirazi homes.

The wrought iron gate, adorned with scrolling designs of vines and flowers, was overgrown with jasmine vines, their white flowers releasing a heady, sweet scent that filled the air, the leaves rustling softly in the breeze, drops of recent rain clinging to the petals like tears. Beyond the gate, the courtyard revealed itself—small but well-kept, paved with uneven stones that glistened from a light drizzle earlier in the day, the air fresh with petrichor, the earthy smell of wet soil mingling with the jasmine.

A few potted geraniums bloomed pink and red in terracotta pots, their leaves green and glossy, arranged along the courtyard's edges. A small fountain, no longer functioning but charming in its decay, sat at the centre, its basin filled with rainwater where a sparrow bathed, shaking droplets from its feathers. The front door was wooden, its paint a deep green chipped at the edges, a brass knocker shaped like a lion's head gleaming despite the wear, its eyes fierce but welcoming.

The neighbourhood was serene, the streets narrow and lined with similar homes—whitewashed walls, clay-tiled roofs, gardens barely visible behind high walls that protected family privacy. Children played with a ball in the distance, their laughter echoing off the walls, a dog barked lazily, the overall atmosphere one of quiet resilience, the war's end bringing a tentative peace to these backstreets. Olive trees dotted the lane, their silvery leaves catching the late afternoon light, and the faint smell of bread baking in a nearby home drifted on the breeze, mixing with the jasmine's sweetness.

Zahra stepped out of the Heydaris' car first, her shoes crunching on the gravel path, the sound sharp in the still air, her woven basket slung over her shoulder, filled with gifts—dates sticky and sweet, their skins glossy and plump; pistachios with shells cracked open, their green nuts salty and nutty; and a small jar of rosewater from their garden, its glass cool and smooth, the liquid inside swirling with a faint pink tint. She adjusted her scarf, the fabric soft against her skin, her heart racing with a mix of excitement and nervousness, the memory of Shiraz's gardens and their honeymoon nights stirring a warm flush.

Reza followed, his boots firm on the gravel, the sound steady, his uniform's fabric rustling softly, the medals clinking faintly with each step, the *chafiyeh's* fringes swaying against his chest, his hands clenched slightly at his sides. He paused at the gate, taking in the house's appearance—the vines climbing the walls in tangled, green tendrils, the faint scent of cooking rice wafting from inside, a comforting reminder of home.

Reza lifted the lion-head knocker, its brass cool and heavy in his hand, and knocked, the sound echoing through the courtyard like a heartbeat, resonant and deep. The door creaked open slowly, revealing Fatemeh, Reza's mother. The eight years since he had last seen her—that morning in September 1980 when she had clutched her handkerchief, her sobs muffled—had aged her profoundly. Her small frame was now wrapped in a faded blue chador, the fabric soft and worn from years of use, its edges frayed slightly at the hem.

Her hair, which had shown only threads of silver that morning, was now fully grey, the colour of ash, peeking from beneath her scarf tied loosely around her face. The smooth skin of her younger days had given way to a map of wrinkles—deep lines around her eyes from squinting at letters in dim light, crow's feet from years of laughter now shadowed by sorrow, furrows across her forehead carved by worry and loss. Her skin was sallow and thin, spotted with age marks, her lips thin and pale but curving into a trembling smile.

Her eyes, once bright and sharp like Hossein's, were now clouded with cataracts, the iris barely visible through the milky film, but they widened with recognition, tears instantly spilling over her lashes, glistening on her cheeks. She wore a simple house dress beneath the chador, its floral pattern faded to ghosts of colour, her feet in worn slippers that shuffled slightly on the tiled entryway. Her hands—knotted with arthritis, the knuckles swollen and bent, the skin loose and veined—flew to her mouth, trembling as tears flowed freely. A silver necklace, a gift from Hossein before his deployment, hung at her throat, catching the light.

"Reza... my son," Fatemeh whispered, her voice raspy and breaking, and she stepped forward, throwing her arms around him, her embrace fierce despite her frailty, her body trembling with sobs, her height reaching only to his chest, her head pressing against the medals on his

The Moonlit Rose of Isfahan

uniform. Reza's composure crumbled, his strong frame bending as he wrapped his arms around her, his face buried in her shoulder, the familiar scent of her skin pulling him back to childhood—her cooking saffron rice in the kitchen, her lullabies by the fire, her hands combing his hair as a boy.

Tears streamed down his cheeks, hot and unstoppable, his voice choked as he murmured, "Madar... I'm here. I'm home." The words were a release, a piece of his shattered life falling back into place, his mother's warmth a balm for the war's wounds and the uncertainty of rebuilding a life with Zahra as a civilian. He kissed her cheek, the skin soft and papery under his lips, tasting the salt of her tears, the gesture a son's devotion, a bridge across eight years.

Zahra stood back, her own eyes misty, her hand clutching the woven basket, the sight of Reza and Fatemeh's reunion stirring memories of their wedding here in Shiraz—the courtyard filled with music, the *daf* drum's beat, the taste of *gaz* and *halva*, Reza's hand in hers as they danced under the stars, Fatemeh's warm embrace as she welcomed her as a daughter.

She stepped forward, her voice soft, "*Salaam, Madar* Fatemeh," using the affectionate term, her smile warm as she knelt slightly to embrace her mother-in-law. Fatemeh pulled her close, her tears dampening Zahra's scarf, her voice raspy with emotion, "Zahra, my daughter, you've kept him safe in your heart." The three clung to each other, the street quiet except for the distant hum of a neighbour's radio, the moment a fragile bridge across years of separation.

They stepped inside, crossing the threshold into a narrow entryway with tiled floors in geometric patterns of blue and white, the tiles cool underfoot, some chipped at the edges but still beautiful. The walls were whitewashed and bare except for a small framed verse of the Quran near the doorway, its calligraphy flowing in black ink. A wooden coat rack stood to one side, draped with a few worn shawls and a man's jacket. The house was cool and dim, the thick walls having kept out the day's heat, the air carrying the faint scent of cardamom from a simmering pot of tea in the kitchen.

The living room opened to the right, modest but welcoming, with high ceilings crossed by wooden beams darkened with age. Woven rugs in rich reds and blues covered the floor, their patterns intricate vines and flowers, the wool soft and slightly worn from years of footsteps. A low wooden table sat at the centre, its surface polished smooth, set with a tray of pistachios and dried figs, the nuts' shells cracked and salty, the figs chewy and sweet.

A small brass samovar bubbled softly on a side table near the wall, its steam curling upward, the sound a gentle hiss. The walls were adorned with family photos in mismatched frames—yellowed images of Reza and Hossein as boys, their grins wide in a garden; a wedding photo of Salar and Fatemeh, young and joyful, her dress white and flowing, his suit crisp; and a recent one of Reza in uniform, sent during the war, his face a reminder of hope amid loss. A small shelf held a leather-bound Quran and a volume of Hafez, their pages thumbed from years of reading, the edges soft and brown.

The furniture was worn but clean—a cushioned divan against the wall, its pillows plumped with faded embroidery in gold thread, patterns of peacocks and flowers barely visible; a carved wooden armchair with high arms, its seat cushioned with a flat pillow; and a smaller chair near the window. The window itself was small, its blue shutters half-closed to block the afternoon light, letting in slivers that striped the rug like bars of gold.

Beyond the living room, a doorway led to a modest kitchen, its tiled counters visible, pots hanging from hooks on the wall like silent bells, and another doorway suggested bedrooms deeper in the house. The overall feeling was one of cozy simplicity, the war's rationing evident in the lack of luxuries, but the space clean and cared for, the air warm with the scent of tea and the faint dust from the street outside.

Salar, Reza's father, sat in the carved wooden armchair, and the sight of him made Reza's throat tighten. Eight years before, on that morning in 1980, Salar had stood with his posture stooped but dignified, his eyes wet as he adjusted his cap, a man trying to hold himself together for his departing sons. Now, the years had carved him down to something more fragile.

His once-robust frame was now frail, his shoulders rounded forward as though bearing an invisible weight, his white beard long and sparse, trimmed unevenly with shaking hands, the hair thin and wispy.

The Moonlit Rose of Isfahan

His skin was sallow and wrinkled, spotted with age marks like rust on old paper, his hands gnarled with arthritis, the fingers bent at odd angles, resting on a cane of polished wood, its handle smoothed from constant use.

His eyes, which had once been sharp like Reza's, identical in their soulful brown depth, were now clouded with cataracts, the pupils barely visible through the milky haze, his gaze distant but alert, as though he saw the world through fog. He wore a simple white tunic and loose pants, the fabric hanging on his thinned body, his slippers worn and shuffling. When he saw Reza, he rose slowly, leaning heavily on the cane, his legs trembling with the effort, his breath laboured from old age and the war's stress—years of waiting, of opening letters with shaking hands, of burying one son while praying the other survived.

"Reza," he said, his voice deep but trembling, his hands reaching out, shaking as they grasped his son's shoulders, feeling the uniform's fabric, the medals hard under his palms, the *chafiyeh's* soft cotton brushing his wrists. Reza knelt before him, his uniform creasing, his head bowing as Salar's hands cupped his face, thumbs brushing away tears, the touch gentle despite the arthritis. "My boy, at last you've come back to us," Salar said, his voice cracking, the pride and pain of eight years—letters, photos, the loss of Hossein—etched in his words. Reza kissed his father's hand, the skin papery and veined, tasting the salt of sweat and tears, the gesture a son's respect, a bridge across the years.

"*Pedar*, I'm here," Reza whispered, his voice breaking, and Salar pulled him close, the cane clattering to the floor, forgotten, as he embraced his son, the room's lamplight casting their shadows as one against the whitewashed wall.

Zahra set the woven basket on the low wooden table, unpacking the gifts. Fatemeh insisted they sit, her hands bustling despite their tremor as she brought out a tray of tea, the glasses steaming with the scent of cardamom and mint, the liquid amber in the light, the samovar bubbling softly on the side table. They sat on cushions around the table, the rugs soft under them, the air warm with reunion.

Reza held his mother's hand, his fingers tracing her familiar knuckles, now swollen with arthritis, the uniform's sleeve and the *chafiyeh* brushing her wrist, a reminder of the soldier he became and the son he remained. Zahra sipped her tea, the warmth spreading through her, her heart full as she watched Reza with his parents, their voices overlapping in soft Farsi, catching up on years lost—Reza's survival, the battles, the garden Zahra tended in Isfahan, the letters that kept them tethered.

The conversation turned to Hossein, Fatemeh's voice soft but heavy as she spoke. "Your brother... he wrote to that girl, Leyla, you know. Three years of letters, his heart poured into them, but he never came home." Her eyes glistened, the pain of his loss forever raw, the memory of Hossein's love letters to a woman he barely knew a bittersweet thread, the envelopes arriving sporadically, their ink smudged from trench handling.

Salar nodded, his cane tapping softly on the rug as he retrieved it, his voice steady but laced with sorrow. "Leyla... she waited a while, but life moves on. She married someone else, a good man from her parents' village. She's happy now, pregnant with their third child." His words hung in the air, the room's lamp casting long shadows, the tea's steam curling like forgotten dreams. Reza's throat tightened, tears pricking his eyes, the news a mix of relief for Leyla and fresh grief for Hossein's unfinished life, the trench confession of his passionate love for her echoing in Reza's mind, Hossein's voice warm with hope, "She's my oasis."

Yet they were proud of Reza, not just for his military service—the medals on his uniform, the commander's rank earned in 1985, visible in the photograph on the wall—but for his recent work rebuilding the country. Reza shared, his voice soft but resolute, "I completed a local project in Isfahan—repairing a bridge over the Zayandeh. In a few weeks, I'll go to Tehran for another, rebuilding schools."

Fatemeh's eyes shone with tears of pride, her hand squeezing his, the skin papery but strong. "My son, you've always built things— dreams, now homes. We're proud, not just for the war, but for this." Salar nodded, his cane tapping softly, his voice deep, "Hossein would be too. You honour us all." The words warmed Reza, his uniform feeling less heavy, the *chafiyeh* around his neck a reminder of survival and purpose, the family's bond a light in the room's dim glow, the air rich with tea and memories.

The Moonlit Rose of Isfahan

As the evening settled over the city like a soft veil, the front door creaked open. The brass lion-head knocker clanked softly, announcing the arrival of Ramin, Reza's cousin, returning from a day at work. Ramin stepped into the room, his frame lean but sturdy, his face weathered by years of labor under the sun, his skin bronzed and lined around his dark eyes, which carried a mix of exhaustion and warmth. His short beard was neatly trimmed, also flecked with grey despite being only a few years older than Reza, his hair dark but thinning, swept back from a high forehead.

He wore a worn grey jacket over a simple tunic and pants, the cuffs frayed from use, his boots scuffed and dusted with the day's work at a local construction site, where he had also been helping rebuild Shiraz's infrastructure. Even if the city had been spared the worst, it still had its marks. The local infrastructure had been neglected while efforts were focused on the war. His hands, calloused and scarred, clutched a small cloth bag, likely holding his lunch's remnants, the faint scent of bread and dried herbs clinging to him.

"*Salaam*," he said, his voice deep and slightly hoarse, his eyes lighting up as they landed on Reza, a grin breaking across his face, revealing a missing tooth from a long-ago accident. "Reza, you old soldier! You made it!" He strode forward, dropping the bag on the rug, and pulled Reza into a bear hug, their embrace a collision of past and present, the scent of sweat and dust mingling with the room's warmth.

Reza returned the hug, his scarred hands gripping Ramin's shoulders, the uniform's fabric rustling, the *chafiyeh's* fringes caught between them, his heart swelling at the sight of his cousin, a link to a childhood fractured by war. "Ramin, it's been too long," he said, his baritone thick with emotion, his eyes misty as he stepped back to look at his cousin, noting the new lines on his face, the weariness in his posture, but also the familiar spark in his eyes, the same one from their teenage years.

Zahra rose, her dress swaying, and embraced Ramin warmly, her voice melodic, "*Salaam*, Ramin. It's good to see you." Ramin kissed her cheek, a familial gesture, his grin widening, "Zahra, you're still keeping this one in line, I see." The room filled with soft laughter, Fatemeh bustling to pour Ramin a glass of tea, the steam rising in delicate curls, the cardamom's spicy warmth blending with the room's cozy scents.

They settled around the low table, Ramin kicking off his boots to sit cross-legged on a cushion, the rug soft under his knees, his jacket draped over the divan. The lamp's glow highlighted the family photos on the wall, and Reza's gaze drifted to one from 1972—a faded image of him, Hossein, and Ramin as teenagers, standing under a mulberry tree in Isfahan, their arms slung around each other, grins wide and carefree. The memory washed over him, vivid and sharp, pulling him back to a summer when they were teenagers, spending lazy afternoons by the Zayandeh River.

They had skipped stones across the water, the flat pebbles skimming with a soft plink, the river's surface rippling under the sun, the air thick with the scent of wet earth and blooming oleanders. Ramin, always the boldest, would dive into the shallows, splashing Reza and Hossein, their laughter echoing as they wrestled in the grass, their clothes damp and clinging, the sun warm on their backs. Reza would pull out his notebook, reading poetry he had written, his voice steady and dreamy, while Hossein and Ramin teased him, calling him "our Hafez," though they secretly admired his words, the way they wove love and longing into the air.

Another memory surfaced, softer but heavier—a family vacation in 1974 to the Caspian Sea, the households piled into two cars, the journey long and dusty, the air filled with the scent of gasoline and packed lunches of *lavash* bread and feta. Reza and Ramin had shared a tent on the beach, the waves crashing rhythmically, the sand cool under their bare feet at night, the sky a blanket of stars.

They had stayed up late, whispering about girls and dreams—Ramin wanting to build houses, Reza dreaming of studying engineering, Hossein already in university and looking forward to the future. They had built a bonfire, the wood crackling, sparks flying into the night, the smell of smoke and salt clinging to their skin, their laughter mingling with Fatemeh's singing from the women's tent, her voice carrying a folk song about love enduring storms.

Those moments had felt eternal, the family whole—Reza's parents, Hossein, Ramin's parents and siblings. The war changed everything, scattering them like leaves. Ramin's mother died in a 1982 bombing in

The Moonlit Rose of Isfahan

Tehran, his younger sister lost to illness in 1984, Hossein killed in 1983, Zahra's father passing that same year, her mother now in Damascus with a new family, her half-brother Farhad distant in Tehran. The war's brutality left Reza and Zahra feeling like they had only each other, their cousins and relatives nearby but diminished, their bonds strained by loss.

Reza's throat tightened as he looked at Ramin, the cousin who once raced him across fields, now a man worn by labor and grief, yet still here, a survivor like him. "Remember the Caspian?" Reza said softly, his voice catching, the tea glass cool in his hand. Ramin nodded, his eyes glistening, "How could I forget? You reciting poetry by the fire, you Hossein to out-swim me." He chuckled, but it was tinged with sadness, the weight of their losses hanging between them.

Fatemeh, sitting nearby, wiped a tear, her chador slipping slightly, her grey hair catching the light. "You boys were trouble, but so full of life," she said, her voice raspy, her hands folding the edge of her chador. Salar, in his armchair, tapped his cane, his clouded eyes distant, "Hossein's letters to Leyla... he carried her in his heart, even in the trenches." Ramin added, "I saw her last year, in the bazaar. She's happy, Reza, with her husband and children. It's what Hossein would've wanted." The words were a comfort, but they stung, a reminder of Hossein's unfulfilled life, the letters Reza had found in his brother's belongings, their ink smudged with mud and blood.

The room grew quiet, the lamp's glow softening the edges of their grief, the tea's warmth a small anchor. Ramin shared his work, his voice steady but tired, "Iran is healing, but it's slow. We need men like you, Reza, for the bigger projects." Reza nodded, his heart torn between duty and staying with Zahra.

Zahra squeezed his hand, her touch grounding, her smile a reminder of their shared resilience, their garden in Isfahan a testament to love enduring war and separation. The evening deepened, the floral scents drifting through the open window, the family's reunion a fragile but precious thread, weaving past and present, loss and hope, into a tapestry of survival.

Chapter Twenty-Two

Isfahan, 1980

The kitchen in the Azad home was a quiet in the late autumn of 1980, the Iran-Iraq War a fresh wound, its chaos barely weeks old, seeping into the city's pulse. The air was cool, November's crispness carrying the scent of damp earth through the open window, where the courtyard garden's roses and lavender glistened with evening dew, their petals trembling in the faint breeze. The room was simple, its whitewashed walls glowing softly under the flicker of an oil lamp on the wooden table holding only a chipped ceramic teapot, its spout warm from an earlier brew, a bowl of untouched dried figs, their chewy sweetness neglected, and a small radio, its bent antenna crackling with a wartime broadcast.

The announcer's voice, tinny but urgent, cut through in Farsi: "Citizens of Isfahan, conserve resources. Air raid sirens may sound without warning. Stay vigilant." The words faded into static, followed by a burst of martial music, a patriotic hymn of sacrifice, its notes heavy with the war's weight. The kitchen smelled of cardamom from the tea, mingling with the earthy tang of herbs drying on a cloth near the sink, the faucet's soft plink against the metal basin a steady rhythm in the stillness.

Zahra sat at the table, her dark hair cascading over her shoulders, catching the lamp's golden light like a silken veil. Her eyes, usually warm with laughter, were shadowed with worry, her brow furrowed as

Jamila Mikhail

she gripped a fountain pen, its nib scratching against a sheet of paper, the indigo ink flowing in delicate, uneven strokes from her trembling hand. Before her lay an unfinished letter to Reza, called to the frontlines near Ahvaz just three weeks after their wedding, their honeymoon's tender moments—rose petals on the bed, whispered Hafez, their bodies entwining in shy, passionate discovery—shattered by war's sudden call. The paper held her heart, each word a thread to reach Reza across the miles, where bombs fell and trenches scarred the earth.

The radio crackled again, the announcer's voice grim: "Khorramshahr under heavy fire. Volunteers needed for medical aid." Zahra's heart clenched, her pen pausing, the ink pooling into a dark star, her breath catching at the thought of Reza's name among the fallen. She turned the radio's dial down, the sound fading to a low hum, a shield against the fear that gripped her.

My dearest Reza,

My heart, my radiant poet, the house is too quiet without you. The war has only just begun, but it feels like years since you left, since our nights in Shiraz, your hand in mine, your poetry filling the air like a song of stars. I sit in our kitchen now, the lamp flickering like a weary heart, the radio speaking of battles I can't bear to imagine you in. It's daunting to be here alone, the walls echoing with your absence, their silence a heavy shroud.

The garden helps—my roses, your lavender, their scents weaving memories of you—but even they can't fill the void you've left. I miss your laugh, a melody brighter than dawn, your touch, a warmth that rivals the sun, the way you'd tease me about burning the rice, your smile a lantern in my soul.

She paused, her eyes stinging, a tear hovering but unshed, her fingers brushing the paper, smudging the ink faintly, the texture rough under her touch. The radio hummed softly, now playing a mournful *santur* melody, its plucked strings resonating like a lover's sigh, blending with the faucet's drip and the distant coo of a pigeon in the courtyard. Then she continued, her words flowing like a river, carrying her heart to him.

Your parents came by yesterday. They're leaving for Shiraz to live with your cousin Ramin, saying the war's shadow is too dark here alone, both of their children off to battle. Fatemeh held my hands, her eyes so like yours,

The Moonlit Rose of Isfahan

shimmering with tears, pleading, 'Zahra, come, be safe with us.' Salar, steady as ever, offered a room in Ramin's house, a new start, his voice an anchor of kindness.

But I couldn't, Reza, my love. This house, our home, cradles you—the quilt we shared, its threads worn with our dreams, the garden we planted, its earth kissed by our hands, the kitchen where you kissed me before you left, your clothes still hanging in the wardrobe, their scent of you fading like a half-remembered poem. My parents urge me to join them too, their home warm but a relic of my childhood, not our future. I'll stay, my love, in this sanctuary of us, though the emptiness is a heavy cloak.

The radio shifted to a woman's voice, listing ration updates—"Rice and oil limited starting tomorrow"—and Zahra's pen hesitated, her heart heavy with the war's creeping austerity. She thought of their Shiraz wedding, the courtyard alive with the *daf* drum's pulse, the taste of *gaz* and *halva*, their first night a tapestry of shy touches and laughter, Reza's fingers tracing her skin under the lantern's glow, their love a flame untested by war.

Now, the kitchen was a shrine to that fleeting joy, the table where they had dreamed of a family now a desk for her longing. To lift his spirits, to weave their shared love of poetry into her words, she added a short verse inspired by Hafez, knowing it would make Reza smile, his heart warmed by the familiar rhythm they had recited in Shiraz's gardens.

O heart, in this storm of longing, seek the shore of love's embrace, for in the tavern of the soul, his light will guide your grace.

My Reza, these words inspired by Hafez are for you, a lantern in the dark of war. They remind me of our nights under Shiraz's stars, your voice reciting them, your hand in mine. I hold them close, as I hold you, praying they reach you in the trenches, a spark to warm your heart.

I tend the garden daily, Reza, as if it binds me to you. The lavender you loved blooms, its scent a balm against my fears, though the sirens test my courage, their wail a thief in the night. I pray for you, my heart, every evening, asking God to shield you from the bombs, to cradle you in His mercy. Your parents' offer to go to Shiraz tempts me some days—the thought of family, of comfort—but I belong here, in our home, waiting for you, my roots entwined with yours.

The *santur's* melody faded, the radio's hum a quiet companion as

Zahra paused in her writing, setting the pen down for a moment as a soft rustling caught her attention. The kittens, Shirin and Simin—now barely six months old—padded into the kitchen, their paws silent on the tiles, their small bodies still gangly with youth, all oversized ears and curious eyes.

Shirin, the bolder of the two, immediately pounced on a dried leaf that had blown in through the window, batting it across the floor with her tiny paws, her movements a blur of fur and enthusiasm. Simin, more cautious, crept along the edge of the room, her green eyes wide as she stalked an imaginary prey, her haunches wiggling before she sprang forward in a clumsy leap that sent her tumbling into her sister.

Zahra found herself smiling despite her heavy heart, watching them wrestle and play, their purrs and chirps filling the quiet kitchen with life. They were growing so fast—when Hossein had brought them, they had been tiny enough to fit in one hand, mewing piteously, only just weaned. Now they explored every corner of the house with fearless curiosity, climbing curtains, chasing dust motes in the lamplight, and curling up together in impossibly small spaces. Their antics were a daily gift of joy in the war's darkness, their innocence a reminder that life persisted even as bombs fell on distant cities.

Shirin scrambled up onto the table, sniffing at the dried figs with interest, her whiskers twitching, before Zahra gently scooped her up, the kitten's fur soft and warm against her hands. She held the small creature close for a moment, feeling the rapid thrum of her heartbeat, the purr that vibrated through her tiny body.

"You're both so silly," Zahra whispered, kissing the top of Shirin's head before setting her down. Simin immediately pounced on her sister, and they tumbled across the floor in a tangle of paws and tails, their play-fight both fierce and gentle, ending with them grooming each other, their pink tongues rasping over each other's fur. Zahra picked up her pen again, her heart lighter, and added to her letter.

The kittens bring me such joy, Reza. I wish you could see them—they've grown so much since you left, their personalities emerging like flowers. Shirin is bold and mischievous, always getting into trouble, knocking over teacups and stealing scraps from the counter. Simin is gentler, more thoughtful, watching the world with those knowing eyes before she acts.

The Moonlit Rose of Isfahan

They chase each other through the house, their tiny paws thundering on the tiles like a miniature storm, and at night they curl up with me on our bed, warm little bundles of comfort in your absence.

They are Hossein's gift to us, and in their play and purrs, I hear his laughter too, a reminder of the family we still have. Watching them explore and grow has been a blessing—their curiosity about every shadow, every sound, every flutter of fabric keeps me anchored to the present, to the beauty that persists even in wartime. They make me laugh, these little ones, when I didn't think I could. They are a light in this darkness.

She set the pen down again, watching as both kittens finally tired themselves out, settling at her feet in a heap of soft fur and rhythmic breathing, their purrs a gentle rumble that seemed to resonate with the lamp's flicker. The warmth of their small bodies against her ankles was a comfort she hadn't known she needed, their trust and affection a balm for the loneliness that threatened to overwhelm her. She thought of Reza receiving this letter in some muddy trench, reading about these silly kittens, and hoped it would make him smile, would remind him of the home waiting for him, full of life and love.

The radio crackled again, the announcer's voice returning with news of ration cards and curfews, and Zahra sighed, her fingers tightening around the pen as she added her final lines.

Write to me, my love, tell me you're safe, that you still dream of our garden, our life, that Hafez's words still dance in your soul. Tell me about the trenches, the stars above them, anything that connects us across this distance. I'll write to you every week, filling these pages with our home, our cats, our love—everything waiting here for your return.

She rose from the table, her dress rustling softly, and stepped to the window, the cool air brushing her face, carrying the scent of lavender and wet earth, grounding her. The garden was her vow to Reza, each plant a promise to endure. She thought of Fatemeh's tearful plea, Salar's steady offer, their love a mirror of her own for Reza, but her place was here, in their home, however daunting the solitude.

The kittens followed her, Shirin stretching with a tiny yawn, Simin kneading the air with her paws, and Zahra felt a surge of gratitude for their presence, these small companions who filled the empty spaces with their warmth. Returning to the table, Zahra picked up the pen one last time and added her closing words, her handwriting strong despite her trembling fingers.

I love you, Reza, my poet, my husband, my star in this endless night. Come home to me, to our garden, to these silly kittens who need their other parent, to the life we began in Shiraz. You are my heart, and I am yours, always.

Zahra

She folded the letter carefully, adding a dried flower between the pages, her fingers trembling, and sealed it with a kiss, the paper soft against her lips, a fragment of her soul sent to the frontlines. The lamp's flame flickered as if in blessing, and outside, the first stars appeared in the darkening sky, distant but steadfast, like her love for Reza—enduring, unchanging, waiting for dawn.

Chapter Twenty-Three

Isfahan, 1986

The summer cloaked the city in relentless heat, the air thick and shimmering, the temperature climbing quickly by midday, the dry breeze carrying the scent of dust from cracked streets, diesel from passing military trucks, and the faint sweetness of jasmine from courtyard gardens hidden behind whitewashed walls.

The Iran-Iraq War, now entering its sixth year, had etched its mark on the city, yet Isfahan's spirit endured, its turquoise-domed mosques and the arches of Si-o-se Pol bridge over the Zayandeh River standing defiant against the war's emotional scars. The streets hummed with a tense resilience, women in chadors clutching ration cards, children darting through alleys with makeshift toys, their laughter a fragile rebellion against fear. The sky was a hazy blue, tinged with smoke from distant battles, the horizon wavering with heat mirages, the air heavy with the weight of survival.

Zahra stepped out of the small home she shared with Reza, though he remained at the frontlines near Basra now, his letters arriving sporadically, their ink smudged with trench dirt, his words a lifeline she clung to. Her favourite green dress, faded from years of wear but neatly pressed, clung to her frame, damp with sweat, her dark hair tied back with a simple scarf, its edges frayed, a few strands sticking to her neck in the heat. Her eyes, once bright with innocence, now carried a quiet strength, tempered by six years of solitude, loss, and the purpose she'd

Jamila Mikhail

found in volunteering.

She carried a large woven basket, its handles worn smooth, filled with supplies for the relief centre near the Jameh Mosque—a ten-minute walk through Isfahan's winding alleys, where the scent of fresh naan from a bakery mingled with the acrid tang of smoke from a recent air raid's rubble. The basket held bandages, antiseptic, a notebook for registering names, a small jar of rosewater from their garden, and, today, a special addition: a tin of homemade *ghormeh sabzi*, the herb stew's aroma of dried limes and turmeric seeping through the lid, a labor of love from her kitchen.

Cooking had been Zahra's passion since childhood, her mother teaching her to knead dough at seven, her father praising her *kuku sabzi* at ten, the act of blending spices and simmering pots a way to weave love into sustenance. Now, with Reza at the frontlines, cooking for others had become her way to nurture hope, to fill the void of his absence. The garden, her sanctuary, bloomed despite the war, its lavender and roses tended daily, a vow to Reza to keep their home alive.

The relief centre, housed in a converted school, was a bustling haven for war-displaced families, wounded soldiers, and orphans. Its courtyard, shaded by tattered tarps, was alive with activity, the tiled walls chipped but vibrant with turquoise and gold patterns, dulled by dust. Tables lined the space, laden with sacks of rice, cans of oil, and stacks of blankets, while women volunteers moved with purpose, their voices a soft hum of Farsi, sorting supplies, comforting children, or bandaging wounds. The air smelled of antiseptic, sweat, and the faint sweetness of dates distributed to new arrivals—families from Dezful and Ahvaz, their clothes dusty, their eyes hollow from weeks of fleeing bombs.

Zahra set her basket on a table under a tarp, the canvas flapping in the hot breeze, and greeted Mahsa, a fellow volunteer, a stout woman in her forties with a warm smile and hands rough from work, her black chador practical but stained with flour and iodine.

"Zahra, you're here," Mahsa said, her voice kind but weary, passing her a list of names—new refugees needing registration. "We've got twenty more families today, and three wounded soldiers from the front. And you brought food again?" She nodded at the tin. "They'll be

The Moonlit Rose of Isfahan

grateful." Zahra smiled, her hands brushing the basket. "It's what I can do. Food brings us together." The memory of Reza's last letter, dated three weeks ago, steadied her as she moved through the courtyard, his words sparse but alive: *"My moonlit rose, the trenches are hell, but your letters are my sky. Keep the garden blooming."*

Zahra had been volunteering since 1982, her loneliness and grief channeled into action, her hands finding purpose in binding wounds, distributing food, and teaching children to read—a way to honour Reza's dreams that were on pause, especially after Hossein's death and her father's passing three years ago. She'd grown accustomed to the rhythm of this work—registering names, distributing rations, listening to stories of loss that echoed her own fears for Reza.

At a table, Zahra began registering a family—a mother, Laleh, her face lined with grief, and her two children, a boy of eight and a girl of five, their clothes patched, their eyes wide but silent. Laleh's husband had been killed during an Iraqi attack, her home destroyed, and Zahra listened as the woman spoke in a low, halting voice.

"We walked for days, bombs falling behind us. I carried them when they couldn't walk." Zahra wrote their names in her notebook, her pen scratching softly, her heart aching at the familiarity of loss. She handed Laleh a small sack of rice and a blanket, her voice gentle. "You're safe here. We'll help you."

The girl, clutching her mother's hand, stared at Zahra's rosewater jar, its glass glinting in the sun, and Zahra offered her a drop, rubbing it on the child's wrist, the scent calming her. "Like flowers," the girl whispered, a small smile breaking through, and Zahra's heart lifted, a fleeting victory against the war's despair.

Next, Zahra moved to the medical tent, its canvas walls stained with dust, the air inside sharp with antiseptic and the coppery tang of blood. A young soldier, no older than Reza had been when he left for war, lay on a cot after having been evacuated from the front, his leg bandaged, his face pale under a sheen of sweat. A nurse, Soraya, her hijab pinned tightly, instructed Zahra to clean the wound, a shrapnel gash on his thigh. Zahra knelt, her hands steady as she poured antiseptic, the soldier wincing, his breath hissing through gritted teeth.

"You're strong," she said softly, her voice a balm, her fingers deft as she rewrapped the bandage, the gauze soft but slightly frayed from overuse. She thought of Reza, his own wounds described in letters and her hands trembled slightly, the fear of his next letter—or its absence—ever-present. The soldier murmured, "Thank you, *khanoum*," and Zahra smiled, her eyes meeting his, seeing Reza in his youth, his courage, her resolve hardening to keep helping, to keep their love alive through action.

The day wore on, and Zahra made her way to the school's kitchen, a small room with cracked tiles and a single gas stove, its air thick with the scent of simmering lentils and the sharp tang of onions frying in a battered pan. This was her domain. Volunteers had scrounged ingredients—rice from rations, herbs from local gardens, a precious bit of lamb donated by a butcher moved by their work.

Zahra worked alongside two other women, Esther and Bahar, their hands swift as they chopped parsley and dill, the green scent rising like a promise. Zahra stirred the *ghormeh sabzi* she'd brought, its rich broth of kidney beans, herbs, and dried limes bubbling on the stove, the aroma filling the kitchen, a memory of her childhood in her mother's kitchen, rolling dough for *barbari* bread, laughing as flour dusted her nose.

"This stew will feed twenty today," she said, her voice soft but proud, her hands steady as she adjusted the flame, the heat warming her face. Esther, a young mother whose husband was missing, nodded. "Your cooking, Zahra—it's like a mother's hug." The words touched Zahra, her heart aching for Reza, for the family they'd dreamed of in 1980, their Shiraz honeymoon nights filled with rose petals and plans.

The cooking took hours, Zahra's hands moving with practiced grace, kneading dough for flatbread, the texture soft and elastic under her fingers, the act grounding her. She thought of her childhood, helping her mother prepare *fesenjan* for Nowruz, the walnut and pomegranate stew's sweetness a celebration, her father's smile as he tasted it, saying, "Zahra, you'll feed a village one day." Now, she did, her cooking a bridge across loss—her father gone, her mother in Damascus, Hossein's absence a wound, Reza's fate always uncertain.

The kitchen filled with the scent of baking bread, the dough rising golden in a makeshift oven, the crust crisp and warm. She prepared a tray of *kuku sabzi*, the egg and herb frittata vibrant with green, its edges slightly charred, a recipe she'd perfected for Reza, who'd loved its tangy bite during their courtship. Each dish was a prayer, a way to nurture others as she waited for him, her love poured into every pinch of saffron, every stir of the spoon.

By mid-afternoon, the food was ready, and Zahra joined the distribution in the courtyard, the heat pressing down, the tarp's shade a small relief. She set up a table with bowls of *ghormeh sabzi*, plates of flatbread, and slices of *kuku sabzi*, the aromas drawing a crowd— families with tired eyes, children clutching their mothers' hands, a few soldiers on crutches, their uniforms tattered.

Zahra served with care, her voice gentle as she handed a bowl to a woman, Roya, her face gaunt, her two sons clinging to her chador. "Eat, *khanoum*," Zahra said. "It's warm, it'll help." Roya's eyes welled up, her voice a whisper. "We haven't had a meal like this since leaving home." Her sons, seven and nine, took the bread, their fingers trembling, and Zahra knelt, offering them a slice of *kuku sabzi*, its green flecks bright.

"Like the garden," she said, smiling, and the younger boy nodded, his mouth full, a spark of joy in his eyes. The act mirrored her childhood, sharing sweets with neighbours, her mother's voice in her ear: "Food is love, Zahra." Now, it was her resistance against the war's hunger, her way to honour Reza's dream of building a better world.

As she served, Zahra listened to stories, each one a thread in the war's tapestry. A grandmother spoke of losing her home in a bombing the previous year, her voice breaking as she took a bowl of stew, the steam curling around her face. A teenage girl, orphaned, clutched a piece of bread, whispering of her brother lost in Khorramshahr. Zahra's heart ached, each tale echoing her own fears for Reza.

Yet serving food grounded her, the act of filling bowls a small victory, her hands steady as she poured stew, the broth rich and fragrant. She thought of Reza's parents, Fatemeh and Salar, in Shiraz with cousin Ramin, their letters urging her to join them, but her choice to stay in Isfahan, to tend their garden and volunteer, was her vow to Reza. The garden's lavender, the kitchen's warmth, this centre—they were her roots, her way to endure.

The afternoon wore on, the sun climbing higher, the courtyard a blur of movement—volunteers sorting clothes, children drawing in the dirt with sticks, a radio in the corner crackling with updates: "Abadan under siege. Civilians urged to evacuate." Zahra paused to sip water from a tin cup, the liquid warm but quenching, her scarf damp against her neck. She joined a group teaching children under a tarp, their ages ranging from five to twelve, their faces smudged with dust but eager.

She pulled out a worn copy of Hafez's poetry, its pages yellowed, a gift from Reza during their courtship, and read a short verse: *"When all is lost, then all is found."* The children listened, some mouthing the words, others shyly joining in, their voices a fragile chorus against the war's drone. Zahra taught them simple letters, guiding their hands to write "*salaam*" on scraps of paper, her patience a thread of hope, a way to honour Reza's dream of teaching, to keep their shared vision alive.

As the sun dipped lower, casting long shadows across the courtyard, the distribution continued into the evening, the sky deepening to indigo. Zahra's basket was nearly empty, the rosewater jar shared with children, its scent calming their fears. The work grounded her, each bandage applied, each name recorded, a small act of defiance against the war's chaos. A young girl, Mina, only six, approached, her dress patched, offering Zahra a pebble painted with a crude flower.

"For the food," she said, and Zahra's eyes stung, accepting the gift, her fingers brushing the smooth stone, tucking it beside the rosewater jar. She thought of her letter to Reza tonight, how she'd describe the stew's warmth, Mina's pebble, the Hafez verse she'd read to the children.

The day ended with a quiet moment in the courtyard, the jasmine's scent stronger now as dusk settled, mingling with the dust and antiseptic. Zahra sat with Mahsa under the tarp, their hands stained with iodine, their voices low as they shared a cup of tea, its cardamom warmth a small comfort. The *azan's* call from the Jameh Mosque echoed through the alleys, weaving through the courtyard. The courtyard quieted, families settling under tarps, volunteers sharing a final moment of rest.

Zahra walked home as twilight deepened, the pebble in her pocket, the night air cool against her skin, the scent of jasmine lingering. Her sandals were soft on the cobblestones, the weight of the day heavy but purposeful. In her kitchen, she would write to Reza tonight, telling him of the children, the wounded, Mina's flower pebble, pouring her love into ink with a Hafez verse to warm his heart. Her cooking, her volunteering—they were her bridge to him, her testament to their love's endurance, her way to survive until they could rebuild together.

Chapter Twenty-Four

Shiraz, 1988

The evening deepened the sky turned a velvet indigo, pinpricked with stars that glimmered faintly through the haze of a cooling autumn night. The air had cooled, carrying the sweet, lingering scent of jasmine from the vines curling around the iron gate of Ramin's house. The neighbourhood was quiet, the narrow streets lined with whitewashed homes, their clay-tiled roofs glowing softly under the moonlight, the distant hum of a neighbour's radio fading into the stillness, replaced by the soft chirp of crickets and the occasional rustle of leaves in the breeze.

Inside, the house was warm and intimate, the living room's lamp dimmed, its golden glow casting long shadows across the woven rugs. The air inside still carried the faint scent of cardamom from earlier tea, mingled with the earthy warmth of pistachio shells scattered on the table, where the family's reunion—Reza's tearful embrace with his parents, Ramin's arrival, stories of Hossein and Leyla—had left a tender weight in the atmosphere.

Reza and Zahra had retired to a small bedroom at the back of the house, its walls painted a soft cream, adorned with a single framed verse of Hafez in flowing calligraphy, the words a sweet reminder of their courtship and wedding in this very city. The room was modest, with a narrow bed covered in a quilt of deep burgundy, its threads worn but soft, a small wooden nightstand holding a flickering oil lamp, and a window cracked open, letting in the cool night air and the garden's perfume.

Reza lay on the bed, still in his olive-green military uniform, the fabric slightly wrinkled from the day's emotions, the medals pinned to his chest catching the lamplight, their glint a testament to his survival through the war's horrors. His beard framed a face etched with tiredness, his eyes heavy with the day's reunions, yet burning with a quiet fire as he looked at Zahra, his promise to her echoing in his mind: this trip to Shiraz would not just be a visit to his parents, but a partial reclaiming of their missed wedding anniversaries, stolen by eight years of war.

Zahra sat beside him, her dress replaced with a soft cotton nightgown, its pale blue fabric loose but clinging to her curves, her hair unbound, cascading over her shoulders like a silken waterfall, catching the lamplight in glossy waves. Her eyes shimmered with love and lingering emotion from the day—Fatemeh's tears, Salar's frail embrace, Ramin's stories of their childhood—yet they softened as she met Reza's gaze, her lips curving into a gentle smile. She leaned closer, her hand resting on his chest, her fingers brushing the uniform's rough fabric, feeling the steady beat of his heart beneath the medals.

"You're still wearing this," she murmured, her voice melodic, teasing, her fingers tracing the edge of a medal. Reza chuckled, his baritone warm but husky, his hand covering hers, his scarred fingers rough against her smooth skin. "I wanted to be the man they remembered," he said, his eyes locked on hers, "but with you, I'm just Reza, your poet, your love."

He shifted, sitting up to face her, his uniform rustling, and cupped her face in his hands, his thumbs brushing her cheeks, the skin soft and warm under his touch. His voice lowered, taking on the cadence of poetry, a habit born from their nights reciting Hafez under Shiraz's stars.

"Zahra, my moonlit rose, my dawn after the longest night, your love was my shield in the trenches, my light in the dark of war. Every bomb, every scar, every moment I thought I'd break—your letters, your heart, kept me whole. I love you, not just with my soul, but with every breath, every beat of this weary heart."

The Moonlit Rose of Isfahan

His words were a vow, each syllable heavy with the weight of their years apart, the beginning of their married life together cut short, the anniversaries marked only by ink and paper. Zahra's eyes glistened, her hand rising to touch his beard, her fingers threading through the premature grey strands, her heart swelling at his words, their poetry a bridge to their past.

She leaned closer, her lips brushing his ear, her voice playful yet tender. "I'm lucky, Reza, to have both a poet and a commander as my husband." Her tone carried a teasing lilt, hinting at his commanding presence—not just on the battlefield, but in their intimate moments, a spark of their fiery nights when his confidence, his gentle authority, made her feel cherished and desired. "My commander in the bedroom," she added, her smile mischievous, her fingers tugging lightly at his uniform's collar, a silent invitation.

Reza's laugh was soft, his tiredness fading, replaced by a warmth that spread through him, his eyes darkening with desire. "Then let me command your heart again tonight, my rose," he murmured, pulling her closer, their bodies aligning on the bed, the quilt soft beneath them.

They began with nuzzling, their touches affectionate, tentative, as if rediscovering each other after the day's emotional weight. Zahra pressed her face to his neck, inhaling the familiar scent of him—sweat, the faint musk of his uniform, the lavender from the garden that clung to his skin from earlier. Her lips grazed his jaw, the beard tickling, her hands sliding under his uniform jacket, feeling the warmth of his chest through his shirt, the steady rhythm of his breathing a comfort.

Reza's arms wrapped around her, his scarred hands gentle, tracing the curve of her spine through her nightgown, the fabric cool and soft. He kissed her forehead, her eyelids, her cheeks, each touch a reclamation of their love, the day's heaviness fading with each caress, replaced by the warmth of their shared past, their nights here in Shiraz eight years ago when they learned each other's bodies with shy, clumsy yet eager hands.

Zahra shifted, straddling his lap, her nightgown riding up, her thighs warm against his uniform's rough fabric. She kissed his lips, soft at first, then deeper, her tongue brushing his, tasting the faint bitterness of tea and the sweetness of his breath, a spark igniting between them. Reza's hands roamed her back, pulling her closer, his fingers tangling in her hair, the strands silky against his calloused skin. He broke the kiss, his lips trailing to her neck, finding the pulse point that made her sigh, her head tilting back, her hair spilling over her shoulders.

"My Zahra," he whispered, his voice a low rumble, "you're my home, my everything." His words stirred her, her hands moving to his uniform jacket, unbuttoning it slowly, her fingers brushing the medals, the fabric heavy with memory. She slid it off, revealing his white undershirt, the scars on his arms visible in the lamplight—jagged lines and puckered scars from eight years on the battlefield.

Zahra leaned down, her lips finding the scar on his forearm, kissing it gently, her breath warm against his skin, trailing her lips along the rough texture, a map of his survival. "These are beautiful," she murmured, her voice thick with emotion, "because they brought you back to me." She kissed the scar on his bicep, her lips lingering, her fingers tracing the shrapnel marks on his thigh through his trousers, each touch a vow of love, a healing of the war's wounds.

Reza's breath hitched, his hands tightening on her hips, the nightgown bunching under his fingers, his desire evident in his darkening eyes, the tension in his body. He lifted her nightgown, pulling it over her head, revealing her bare skin, the lamplight casting soft shadows across her curves, her breasts full, her waist soft, her skin glowing like moonlight. He paused, his gaze reverent. "You're more beautiful than ever, my rose," his voice a poet's prayer, his hands cupping her breasts, his thumbs brushing her nipples, drawing a soft gasp from her lips.

Reza laid her back on the quilt, the bed creaking softly, the jasmine's scent drifting through the window, mingling with their warmth. He kissed her collarbone, her breasts, his lips warm and deliberate, tasting the salt of her skin, the faint rosewater she'd dabbed earlier. Zahra arched into him, her hands roaming his chest, pushing his undershirt up, her fingers tracing the sparse hair, the scars on his abdomen, each touch a reclaiming of their intimacy.

She tugged at his trousers, unbuttoning them, her hands trembling with desire, helping him shed the uniform, leaving him bare, his body lean but marked by war, his arousal evident, a testament to their enduring passion. She pulled him down, their bodies pressed together, skin to skin, the heat of their connection a fire against the night's coolness.

Reza moved with care, his kisses trailing lower, across her stomach, her hips, his hands guiding her legs apart, his lips finding the sensitive skin of her inner thighs, drawing soft moans from her. He worshiped her, his touch both commanding and tender, his poet's heart guiding his hands, his lips, as he explored her, tasting her, her gasps filling the room, the quilt bunching under her fingers. Zahra's hands tangled in his hair, her body trembling, her voice a whisper. "Reza, my love, my commander…"

He rose, kissing her deeply, their tongues entwining, their breaths mingling, and positioned himself above her, entering her slowly, their bodies joining with a shared sigh, the connection another homecoming making up for years of longing. Their lovemaking began slowly, a sweet unfolding, their bodies remembering and continuing to relearn each other. Their rhythm was unhurried, each movement a dance, their bodies swaying together, the bed's creaks a soft counterpoint to their breaths, the lamplight flickering, casting their shadows on the wall like a poem in motion.

Zahra wrapped her legs around him, her hands gripping his shoulders, her nails leaving faint marks, her moans soft but growing, the pleasure building like a wave. Reza's movements deepened, his voice a low murmur against her ear. "My rose, my heart, you're my forever. I love you." His words, poetic and fervent, pushed her closer to the edge, her body responding, her hips meeting his, their love a flame that burned away the war's pain.

She kissed his neck, her lips finding the pulse there, her breath hot, her climax building, a sweet release that washed over her, her cry muffled against his shoulder, her body trembling. Reza followed, his own release a quiet groan, his body shuddering, their connection a moment of unity, a reclaiming of their love against the war's theft. They collapsed together, breathless, tangled in the quilt, the jasmine's scent wrapping around them, the night air cool against their flushed skin.

They lay there, holding each other, Reza's hand stroking her hair, Zahra's fingers tracing lazy circles on his chest, their breaths slowing, the room quiet but for the crickets outside. "I kept my promise," Reza whispered, his voice soft, "this night, in this city where we got married, for all our missed anniversaries. And there will be more my love, many more. I love you so much." Zahra smiled, her eyes heavy but warm. "And you're still my poet, my commander." They laughed softly, the sound a melody, their love a light in the darkness, the war's weight lifted, if only for tonight.

The morning sun rose over Shiraz, bathing the city in a golden glow, the air crisp, carrying the scent of blooming jasmine and the faint tang of woodsmoke from early fires lit in nearby homes. The Iran-Iraq War had ended, leaving Shiraz a city of resilience, its ancient beauty marred but enduring—cracked walls from distant bombings, boarded shopfronts, yet vibrant with life as markets reopened and laughter spilled from courtyards.

The sky was a clear blue, streaked with wispy clouds, the light catching the turquoise domes of mosques and the tiled arches of bridges, their colours softened by years of dust but gleaming with renewed hope. Reza and Zahra stepped out from Ramin's house, where they'd spent the previous night reclaiming their love, their bodies still humming with the intimacy of their reunion.

Reza wore a simple tunic and trousers, his military uniform left behind, beard framing a face less tired today, his eyes bright with anticipation. Zahra was radiant in a flowing crimson dress, its fabric catching the breeze, her dark hair loose under a light scarf, her almond eyes sparkling with joy, a woven basket slung over her shoulder with a small blanket and a jar of rosewater. Their hands entwined, fingers interlaced, as they set out to wander Shiraz's streets, fulfilling Reza's promise to make up for missed wedding anniversaries as much as possible on this trip, revisiting the haunts of their 1980 honeymoon, when they were young, newly married, and untouched by war's shadow.

Their first stop was the Vakil Bazaar, a labyrinth of vaulted ceilings and narrow alleys just a short walk from Ramin's house, its entrance framed by a tiled archway, the turquoise and gold mosaics chipped but vibrant, the air rich with the scents of saffron, dried limes, and freshly baked *sangak* bread. The bazaar hummed with post-war life—vendors

The Moonlit Rose of Isfahan

calling out in melodic Farsi, their stalls piled with bolts of silk, copper pots gleaming in the sunlight filtering through skylights, and trays of *gaz*, the nougat dusted with pistachio, its sweetness a memory of their wedding.

Zahra's fingers tightened around Reza's as they wove through the crowd, her dress brushing against sacks of spices, the colours vivid—crimson sumac, golden turmeric, green dried mint. She paused at a stall selling rosewater, the glass bottles glinting like jewels, and inhaled deeply, the scent pulling her back to 1980. "We came here after the wedding," she said, her voice soft, her eyes meeting his. "You bought me a bottle of this, teasing me that I'd smell like a garden forever."

Reza chuckled, his baritone warm, lifting her hand to kiss her knuckles, the gesture tender, his lips brushing her skin. "And you do, my beloved rose," he murmured, "then and now, you're my garden." He bought a small bottle, its glass cool in his hand, and tucked it into her basket, their fingers lingering, the touch a spark of their early days.

They wandered deeper into the bazaar, passing stalls of woven rugs, their patterns intricate vines and flowers, the wool soft under Zahra's fingers as she traced a design, remembering their visit when Reza playfully bargained for a small *kilim*, insisting it would grace their future home. "We spread it in our Isfahan kitchen," she said, her smile wistful, "and I stood on it writing to you during the war." Reza pulled her close, his arm around her waist, his lips brushing her temple, the scent of her hair—jasmine and rosewater—stirring his heart. "Your letters were my lifeline," he said, his voice low, poetic, "each word a thread pulling me back to you."

They bought a handful of *gaz*, the nougat sticky and sweet, and shared a piece, their fingers brushing, the taste a memory of their wedding night, when they fed each other sweets under a canopy of stars, their laughter mingling with the *daf* drum's beat. The bazaar's noise faded as they stood close, their eyes locked, the world narrowing to their shared breath, the crowd parting around them like a river around a stone.

Leaving the bazaar, they walked hand in hand toward the Eram Garden, a short distance away, the streets lined with sycamore trees, their leaves golden and falling, crunching underfoot, the air cooling as clouds drifted across the sun. The garden's entrance was a stone gate, its carvings weathered but elegant, leading to a paradise of cypress trees, rose beds, and bubbling fountains, the water sparkling in the sunlight, the scent of roses and citrus heavy in the air. The garden was quieter than in 1980, its paths less crowded, some flowerbeds trampled by war's neglect, but its beauty endured, the roses blooming in defiant reds and pinks, the cypresses tall and green, their shadows long across the gravel paths.

Zahra's eyes lit up, her hand squeezing Reza's, as they stepped onto a path lined with orange trees, their fruit bright against the leaves, the air alive with the hum of bees. "This was our place," she said, her voice a melody, "after our wedding, we walked here, you reciting Hafez, me laughing at your theatrics." Reza grinned, his hand trailing to her cheek, his thumb brushing her skin. "I was no Hafez, but for you, I tried," he said, his voice rich with love. "Let me try again." He paused, his eyes softening, and recited, "In the garden of my heart, your love is the rose that never fades."

Zahra laughed, her head tilting back, her hair catching the light, and pulled him toward a fountain, its stone basin carved with lotus flowers, the water cool as she dipped her fingers, flicking droplets at him playfully. Reza caught her wrist, pulling her close, their laughter mingling, their bodies pressed together, the fountain's spray misting their skin. They sat on a bench under a cypress, its shade cool, the quilt from Zahra's basket spread beneath them, the rosewater jar set beside it, its scent a quiet companion. Reza fed her a piece of *gaz*, his fingers brushing her lips, the sweetness lingering, and she kissed his fingertips, her eyes warm with memory.

"We sat here in 1980," she said, "planning our life—children, a bigger garden, your teaching." Reza nodded, his hand cupping her face. "And we'll have it, Zahra, all of it, now that I'm home." Their kisses deepened, soft but hungry, their hands entwined, the garden wrapping them in its embrace, the war's weight lifting with each touch.

Their next stop was the Tomb of Hafez, a sacred place for them, its marble pavilion gleaming under the midday sun, the surrounding

The Moonlit Rose of Isfahan

gardens lush with roses and oleanders, their petals vibrant against the green. The tomb was busier, pilgrims and lovers murmuring Hafez's verses, the air filled with the scent of incense and blooming flowers, the sound of a *santur* player strumming softly nearby, the notes floating like a prayer. Reza and Zahra approached the tomb, its marble cool under their hands, the poet's words carved in flowing Farsi, a testament to love's endurance. In 1980, they'd stood here, newlyweds, Reza reading aloud, his voice trembling with passion, Zahra's hand in his, their future bright.

Now, Reza knelt, touching the marble, his voice low. "Hafez kept us together, my rose. His words were in your letters, in my dreams." Zahra knelt beside him, her scarf slipping, her hair brushing his shoulder. "And in mine," she whispered, "when I wrote to you, his poetry was my courage." They left a rose from her basket at the tomb, its petals soft, a gift to the poet who wove their love.

They wandered the garden, hand in hand, the paths lined with poppies and lavender, the air warm now, the sun high, the temperature climbing, a breeze carrying the scent of roses and earth. Reza pulled Zahra into a secluded corner, a stone bench under a mulberry tree, its leaves rustling, the fruit long gone but the memory of 1980 vivid—they'd kissed here, hidden from view, their lips sticky with *gaz*, their laughter muffled by the leaves. He kissed her now, his lips warm, his hands framing her face, the taste of her a homecoming.

"My Zahra," he murmured, "you're my poem, my forever." She smiled, her fingers tracing his beard. "And you, my poet, my commander, my home." Their kisses deepened, their bodies close, the world fading, the garden a sanctuary for their love.

Their final stop was the Shah Cheragh Mosque, its mirrored interior a dazzling mosaic of light, the tiles reflecting the sun in a kaleidoscope of colours—turquoise, gold, crimson—despite cracks from wartime vibrations. The courtyard was serene, a fountain bubbling at its centre, the air cool and scented with myrrh from incense burners, the call of the *azan* echoing softly as evening neared. In 1980, they'd prayed here as newlyweds, their hands clasped, their vows fresh, the future a canvas of dreams.

Now, they entered, Zahra's scarf adjusted, Reza's head bowed, their steps reverent on the tiled floor, the mirrors sparkling like stars. They knelt, praying silently, their shoulders touching, the act a renewal of their bond. Afterward, they sat in the courtyard, huddled on the quilt, the fountain's spray misting their skin, the air cooling slightly, the sky deepening to twilight, the first stars appearing.

Reza pulled Zahra close, her head resting on his shoulder, her hair soft against his cheek, the rosewater jar open beside them, its scent mingling with the myrrh. He spoke, his voice low, poetic. "Zahra, my love, for the first time since I returned, I feel it—everything is going to be alright. The war took so much—Hossein, years, dreams—but you, this city, our love, it's all here, unbroken." His words were a vow, his hand squeezing hers, his scars a testament to their survival.

Zahra's eyes glistened, her voice soft but steady. "I pray for that every day, Reza. I pray for God to heal your soul, to give me the strength to support you the way you need." She paused, her fingers tightening around his. "Sometimes... sometimes I have moments of doubt. Doubts in myself—if I'm going to be able to be the support you need. What if I'm not enough?"

Reza turned to face her fully, his hands cupping her face, his brown eyes intense with love. "Zahra, listen to me. You are perfect just the way you are. Perfect. Do you understand? You've already been everything I needed—through eight years of letters, through keeping our home alive, through waiting for me when you had every reason to give up hope." His voice was firm but tender. "Thank you for standing by me so faithfully. Thank you for being you. You are enough, more than enough. You always have been."

He pressed his forehead to hers, his breath warm against her skin. "Please, my rose, don't worry. Don't try to be anything other than yourself. That's all I need—just you, just us, together. We're taking everything one day at a time. That's all we can do, and that's all we need to do." He kissed her softly, his lips lingering. "One day at a time, together."

Zahra smiled through her tears, nodding, her heart swelling with relief and love. "One day at a time," she whispered, echoing his words. They kissed, slow and deep, the quilt warm beneath them, the mosque's lights reflecting in their eyes, Shiraz wrapping them in its embrace, their love a light against the war's shadow.

Chapter Twenty-Five

Shiraz, 1988

The morning sun filtered through the thin curtains of the guest room in Ramin's house, bathing Reza and Zahra in a soft, golden light that seemed to bless their reunion. The house already hummed with gentle life—Fatemeh's soft footsteps on the tiled floor, Salar's cane tapping as he made his way to the living room, Ramin's voice murmuring a goodbye as he left for his construction site. In this cocoon of family warmth, Reza stirred first, his lean, scarred frame wrapped in quilts, his beard tickling Zahra's shoulder as he kissed her forehead.

"My rose, today is for us," he whispered, his baritone warm and poetic, his soulful brown eyes sparkling with anticipation. The memory of last night still glowed between them—their bodies reclaiming what the war had stolen, his poet's words and commander's touch weaving together like a prayer answered. Zahra opened her almond eyes, her dark hair splayed across the pillow like silk spun from midnight, her smile shy but radiant.

"Our anniversary trip," she murmured smiling, her voice melodic, her hand tracing his jaw where the premature grey testified to his survival. "Even if it's not our anniversary!" Today would be their pilgrimage to Persepolis, a journey to begin to reclaim eight stolen anniversaries.

They dressed slowly, savouring each moment like a precious jewel.

Reza chose a simple tunic and trousers, the light fabric kind to his skin, while Zahra slipped into a flowing blue dress—the colour a deliberate echo of their courtship when Reza first recited Hafez to her beneath Shiraz's stars. Her scarf draped loosely, ready for the day's adventure, and when she turned to him, the morning light caught in her eyes like promises kept.

In the kitchen, Fatemeh insisted on packing a basket, her arthritic hands moving with practiced care, filling it with fresh *barbari* bread whose golden crust crackled with possibility, soft tangy cheese, dates sticky and sweet, and a thermos of tea whose cardamom aroma spoke of home. "Enjoy, my children," Fatemeh said, her wrinkled face beaming, her grey hair peeking from her chador as she pressed a small bag of pistachios into Zahra's hands, the gesture carrying a mother's blessing.

Salar, settled in his armchair, nodded with the quiet pride of a father watching his son embrace life again. "The ruins are our heritage," he said, his clouded eyes glistening, his voice trembling with emotion. "Let them remind you of endurance." Reza kissed his mother's soft, papery cheek, tasting the salt of her joy, then took his father's hand—the veins prominent under thin skin—in a gesture of respect that needed no words.

The small car rumbled to life, tires crunching on gravel as they left the neighbourhood behind. The road to Persepolis wound through rolling hills like a ribbon of possibility, the landscape unfolding in layers—golden wheat fields swaying in the breeze like dancers, olive groves with silver-green leaves shimmering in the strengthening light, and distant mountains purple against the horizon like sentinels guarding ancient secrets. The temperature climbed as the sun rose higher, the air dry but fresh, carrying the scent of wild herbs and the faint tang of soil from recent rains—earth remembering how to live after war's drought.

Zahra rested her hand on Reza's knee, her fingers tracing gentle circles, her voice soft with memory. "Remember our first morning here, after the wedding? You were so nervous, reciting poetry to impress me." Reza laughed, the sound rich and warm, his hand covering hers. "And you, my rose, blushing like a tulip in spring. I

The Moonlit Rose of Isfahan

thought my heart would burst from loving you." He glanced at her, his grey-speckled beard framing a boyish grin that carried echoes of the young man she'd married. "You still blush for me," he teased, and Zahra's cheeks flushed pink, her laughter a melody that filled the car. "Only for you, my poet."

They reminisced as the landscape changed, the hills giving way to the vast Marvdasht Plain where Persepolis waited like a patient witness to history. As Persepolis emerged from the plain, Reza felt something shift in his chest—a loosening of the bands that had held his heart captive for eight years. The ruins rose before them like a prayer carved in stone, the ceremonial capital of the Achaemenid Empire standing defiant against time itself. Founded in 518 BC by Darius I as a symbol of imperial power, expanded by Xerxes and Artaxerxes, burned by Alexander the Great in 330 BC—the stones still bore history's scorch marks. Yet here they stood, 125,000 square meters of testimony to endurance, grand stairways and columns rising like guardians, the light-coloured limestone gleaming under the sun as if lit from within.

They parked in a dusty lot where gravel crunched under their tires, the ceasefire having allowed a trickle of visitors to return to this sacred ground. The entrance gate was a simple stone archway with a faded sign, the ticket booth a wooden shack where a guard in a worn uniform waved them through with a knowing nod—as if he recognized lovers on pilgrimage. Zahra's basket swung on her arm as they approached the grand double staircase, its 111 steps shallow and wide, designed for horses but perfect for two people walking together toward something greater than themselves.

Reza held Zahra's hand as they climbed, his scarred fingers gentle against hers, the limestone smooth but worn beneath their feet, each step a meditation. The air grew warmer, eighty degrees and climbing, a light sweat beading on their skin, but it felt cleansing, like the heat was burning away the war's residue. "My lady," Reza said, his voice playful, "the commander escorts you to the palace." Zahra laughed, her cheeks flushing in the way that made his heart quicken. "And the poet? Does he have verses for the queen?" He grinned, reciting from memory: "In the palace of love, your beauty outshines the stars." She squeezed his hand, her blush deepening, and for a moment they were twenty-two again, dancing in shadows, the world young and theirs.

They passed through the Gate of All Nations, its massive stone portal flanked by *lamassu*—winged bulls with human heads, their beards curled in ancient wisdom, eyes fierce but protective. Zahra traced her fingers along a carved wing, the stone cool despite the sun, and Reza felt the weight of history pressing gently against them. "Darius built this to welcome the world," he said, his voice taking on the cadence of teaching, something he'd dreamed of before the war interrupted everything. "Twenty-eight nations brought tribute here—gold, horses, ivory—all carved into these walls as testimony to unity built on strength."

Zahra leaned into him, her head on his shoulder. "Like our love," she whispered. "Strong enough to endure every storm."

They wandered through the Apadana Palace, where thirteen columns still stood from the original seventy-two, their fluted shafts towering sixty-five feet toward the sky, topped with double-headed bulls and lions whose stone eyes seemed to follow their movement. The reliefs on the stairways held Reza transfixed—Persian soldiers in flowing robes, Medes with rounded hats, Ethiopians with ivory tusks, Scythians with pointed hoods—all frozen in eternal procession, their expressions serene, the details so vivid he could almost hear their footsteps: braided hair, patterned tunics, weapons sheathed in peace. This was what they'd fought for, he realized. Not just territory or ideology, but this—the preservation of beauty, of memory, of the thread connecting past to future.

Zahra ran her fingers over a carving of a lion, its mane curling in stone waves, and laughed. "They look alive, like they're marching to celebrate us." Reza pulled her close, his arm around her waist. "They are, my queen. The empire bows to your beauty." She laughed, the sound echoing off ancient stone, and leaned into him.

"And to my commander's charm." Their flirting felt like reclaiming something essential—the lightness they'd shared before war taught them the weight of survival. Here, among ruins that had witnessed millennia, their love felt both insignificant and eternal, a single thread in history's vast tapestry yet somehow essential to its pattern.

The Moonlit Rose of Isfahan

They found shade beneath a tree whose branches spread like welcoming arms, and spread their quilt on ground that had witnessed the rise and fall of empires. Fatemeh's basket yielded its treasures— *barbari* bread whose crust crackled as they tore it, cheese tangy and soft on their tongues, dates sticky and sweet, tea steaming with cardamom that rose like incense.

They fed each other as they had on their wedding night, fingers lingering, laughter bubbling up from some deep well of joy that war hadn't managed to poison. The wind whispered through the ruins, carrying the scent of dry stone and wild thyme, and for the first time since his return, Reza felt the future opening before him like a door he dared to walk through.

"You still blush," Reza teased, his hand on her knee, feeling the warmth of her through the thin fabric. "Only for you," she replied, her voice husky with affection and memory, and when she kissed him, tasting of cardamom and sweetness, the tea was forgotten, the ruins were forgotten, everything was forgotten except the essential truth of them—together, alive, choosing each other again and again.

The wind moved through the columns like a blessing, and Zahra's hair caught the light like dark fire. *This*, Reza thought. *This is what I survived for. This moment, this woman, this impossible grace of being loved.*

They explored deeper into the ruins, hand in hand, discovering the Hall of a Hundred Columns where stone pillars stood like ancient witnesses, and the Palace of Xerxes with its reliefs of winged figures and intricate geometric patterns that seemed to shift in the changing light. The afternoon sun cast long shadows, turning the limestone gold and amber, and the temperature began its gradual descent. They climbed stone stairs worn smooth by countless feet, sat on ledges where kings once sat, traced carvings of chariots with spoked wheels and subjects in elaborate robes—the craftsmanship a marvel that made their hands reverent.

As they sat together on the steps of the Apadana, the stone cool beneath them, the wind ruffling their clothes, Reza pulled Zahra close, her head finding its natural place on his shoulder. The plain spread before them, a vast expanse of brown and green touched with gold by the lowering sun, and the mountains beyond held their ancient secrets.

His voice, when he spoke, carried the weight of eight years compressed into a single breath. "Zahra, my love, coming here with you again has made me feel alive after eight years of numbness and calculated focus." His hand squeezed hers, his eyes glistening with tears he no longer tried to hide. "It won't be easy going forward. The war left marks on my soul that won't heal quickly. But being here with you, walking where we walked as newlyweds, I can finally believe it will be alright."

Zahra's heart swelled, tears spilling down her cheeks as she turned to face him, her hands cupping his face where the grey in his beard spoke of suffering endured. "We're home, Reza, together, always." she whispered, her voice breaking with emotion and hope intertwined. "Look at how far you've come, not just how far you have to go. You're an engineer again, not a soldier. You prayed with me at the mosque. We're making up for lost time. It *will* be okay my love."

They kissed then, slow and deep, tasting salt and sweetness, the quilt forgotten, the ruins wrapping them in their ancient embrace. The day had been a melody of love, flirting, and memory—a reclaiming of their missed years, a promise that what the war had stolen, they would rebuild, stone by stone, kiss by kiss, day by day.

The late afternoon sun dipped toward the horizon as they made their way back to the car, hands entwined, steps reluctant to leave this sacred ground. The drive back to Shiraz unfolded in comfortable silence punctuated by soft observations and gentle laughter, the landscape shifting from the vast plain with its ancient stone guardians to the more intimate streets of the city.

Whitewashed homes lined the roads, their clay-tiled roofs glowing in the fading light, jasmine vines climbing gates in tangled cascades, releasing their heady perfume into the cooling air. The sky became a canvas of orange and purple, clouds brushed across it like poetry written in light, and Zahra leaned her head on Reza's shoulder, her hand resting on his thigh, her fingers tracing idle circles that spoke of contentment.

They arrived at Ramin's house as twilight deepened, the

neighbourhood settling into its evening rhythms, the streets bathed in purple haze. The iron gate creaked open, jasmine vines releasing their night-blooming secrets, and Fatemeh appeared at the door, her small frame wrapped in her blue chador, her face beaming with a mother's pride.

"You're back, my children," she said, her voice raspy but warm, her arthritic hands reaching first for Zahra in an embrace that smelled of rosewater and tea. Salar rose slowly from his armchair, his cane tapping the rug, his clouded eyes lighting up as Reza entered. "Tell us about Persepolis," he said, his voice trembling with eagerness, his shaking hand grasping Reza's arm—a father's anchor to his returned son.

They shared a light supper around the low table, *barbari* bread with its crisp, sesame-speckled crust, tangy yogurt, and sticky-sweet dates, while the samovar steamed and filled the air with cardamom's spice mingling with jasmine from the open window. Conversation flowed softly—Fatemeh's stories of Shiraz's resilience during the war, Salar's quiet pride in Reza's work rebuilding the city, Ramin's brief appearance with dust in his hair and a smile on his weathered face as he shared news of a new road project. Reza's hand found Zahra's beneath the table, their fingers intertwining, and she squeezed back, their love a quiet current beneath the family's warmth.

As night settled and the house grew quiet—Fatemeh and Salar retiring to their room, Ramin to his, the hallway dimming to the lamp's soft glow—Reza and Zahra slipped into the guest room. The door closed with a gentle creak, sealing them in their private world. The narrow bed waited, soft with quilts, the window open to the jasmine-scented darkness. Reza turned to Zahra, his eyes dark with desire tempered by tenderness, his voice low and intimate.

"My rose, tonight is ours to reclaim once again." Zahra smiled, her hands reaching for him, and in the room's quiet glow, their love unfolded like a prayer—gratitude for survival, celebration of return, promise of all the tomorrows war had tried to steal but couldn't, because love, like these ancient ruins, endures.

Chapter Twenty-Six

Isfahan, 1982

The summer evening cloaked Isfahan in a heavy veil of quiet, the war now in its second year, its relentless grip tightening on the city like a cold hand around her throat. The air outside was unseasonably crisp, carrying an autumn-like chill that felt wrong for August, where Zahra's roses and lavender had begun to droop under the strange cold snap, their petals curling at the edges as if in sympathy with her solitude.

The sky was a deep indigo, dotted with stars that seemed distant and indifferent, the moon a pale sliver casting weak silver light through the lattice shutters of the small home Zahra shared with Reza—or had shared, before the war dragged him away just three weeks after their wedding in Shiraz.

The streets were eerily silent, the usual hum of neighbours chatting over tea replaced by the occasional wail of an air raid siren in the distance, a grim reminder that bombs could fall at any moment, though Isfahan had been spared the worst of the frontlines' horrors. The city's ancient domes and minarets stood vigilant, their turquoise tiles gleaming faintly under the moonlight, but inside homes like Zahra's, the war felt intimately close, a thief that stole husbands, brothers, futures and peace.

Zahra sat at the living room table, hunched slightly over a sheet of paper, the oil lamp's flame flickering beside her, casting dancing shadows across the walls and floor. The rug's patterns seemed to twist like her thoughts. The room was modest, its furniture simple: the divan against the wall with its embroidered cushions, a small bookshelf holding her father's collection of Hafez and Rumi, their leather bindings cracked from repeated readings, and a framed photo of her and Reza on their wedding day, his clean-shaven face beaming beside her shy smile, the image now dusted with a thin layer of neglect.

The air inside was still, scented with the faint rosewater she'd dabbed on her wrists earlier, mingled with the earthy aroma of dried herbs hanging from the ceiling—mint and basil from the garden—and the subtle mustiness of the house settling into evening.

The radio in the kitchen crackled softly, tuned low to a state broadcast of patriotic songs, the singer's voice a somber melody about sacrifice and homeland, its notes echoing through the empty rooms like a ghost. Each word felt like an accusation, a reminder of what she'd given up—not just Reza's presence, but the future they'd planned, the children they'd dreamed of, the simple joy of waking beside him. Two years. Two years of marriage, and she'd spent most of it alone, writing letters to a man who existed now only in memory and ink-stained paper. The weight of it pressed against her chest, making each breath an effort.

Shirin and Simin—the "practice children" from Hossein to celebrate the wedding—curled at her feet, their fur soft and warm against her ankles, their fur sleek and shining in the lamp's light. Shirin purred intermittently, a low rumble that vibrated through the floor, while Simin stretched, her paws flexing, her green eyes watching Zahra with lazy curiosity.

The cats were her companions in this loneliness, their presence a small comfort, their soft bodies curling into her lap on cold nights, but they couldn't fill the void left by Reza—his laughter that once made these walls feel alive, his touch that had made her skin sing, his poetry that had filled the house like music now replaced by silence and the distant thunder of war.

Zahra's grey dress, simple and loose, draped over her knees as she sat cross-legged, her bare feet on the rug's soft weave, the fibres tickling her soles. Her almond eyes, usually bright with quiet intelligence, were shadowed with longing, her brow furrowed as she gripped the fountain pen, its nib hovering over the paper, the ink beading at the tip like a tear about to fall. How did one capture in words the ache of missing someone? How did she explain that the house felt too large without him, that the bed swallowed her whole each night, that even the cats' warmth couldn't chase away the cold that had settled in her bones?

The table held her writing supplies—a stack of thin paper, rationed and precious, an inkwell with its dark indigo liquid, and a small candle beside the lamp for extra light, its wax melting slowly, the flame steady but small. The radio in the kitchen continued its broadcast, the announcer's voice interrupting the song with updates: "Our brave forces hold the line near Ahvaz. Civilians are urged to report suspicious activity. Rationing will continue for oil and rice."

The words sent a chill through Zahra, her pen pausing, the scratch of nib on paper halting as fear gripped her—Reza and Hossein on the frontlines, their letters delayed, the war's hunger for young men insatiable.

Today marked their second wedding anniversary, a date circled on the calendar hanging on the kitchen wall, its paper yellowed, the red ink of the circle now faded, a mocking reminder of time stolen. Their first anniversary in 1981 had been hard, spent apart, but she'd understood his patriotic duty, been proud of his bravery, writing letters of support and encouragement. But now, missing the second, the grief and longing filled her like a rising tide threatening to drown her.

The house's emptiness was a constant ache, a wound that wouldn't heal, a reminder with every breath that he wasn't there to share it. She'd imagined, on their wedding day, that by their second anniversary they might be expecting their first child, or at least planning for one. Instead, she was alone with two cats and an ocean of loneliness.

She dipped the pen again, the inkwell's glass cool under her fingers, and began to write, her voice silent but her words pouring out like a river of emotion, each sentence a bridge to Reza across the war's chasm.

My dearest Reza,

My poet, my light in this endless night. Today marks our second anniversary, and my heart is so heavy with longing for you that I can barely

Jamila Mikhail

breathe. The house feels so empty without your voice reciting Hafez by the window, your laugh filling the air like sunlight, your arms around me as we dreamed of our future under the quilts. Sometimes I stand in the doorway of our bedroom and I can almost see you there, smell the scent of your skin, hear your breathing. Then I blink and you're gone, and the emptiness rushes back in like a flood.

The garden blooms, the roses red as the love we shared in Shiraz, but their thorns prick my fingers when I tend them, a reminder of the pain of your absence. I planted new lavender this spring, thinking of how you loved its scent, how you'd crush the buds between your fingers and hold them to my nose, making me laugh. But now when I smell it, it only makes me cry. The war has taken so much—our anniversaries, our nights, the simple joy of sitting beside you at dinner—but it hasn't taken my love for you, which grows like the jasmine vine, persistent and fragrant even in the storm.

The pen scratched softly, the sound a small companionship in the quiet room. Her hand trembled slightly as she paused, her eyes stinging with tears, a drop falling onto the paper, smudging the ink slightly, the spot spreading like her grief. Shirin leaped onto the table, her fur brushing Zahra's arm, her purr a vibration through the wood, and Zahra stroked her absently, the cat's body soft and warm, a fleeting comfort.

Simin joined, jealous of the attention, curling in her lap, her coat sleek against Zahra's dress. Their presence was a small balm, but not enough—nothing could be enough to fill the void of Reza's warmth, his body beside her in bed, his breath on her neck during their brief honeymoon, the way he'd held her as if she were something precious and fragile. She wiped her eyes and continued writing, her words turning to the small joys that sustained her.

My love, I must tell you about our so-called practice children. Shirin and Simin send their love to you and their uncle Hossein! They are two years old now, can you believe it? Two years since he gave them to us with that mischievous grin, saying we needed practice before the real babies came. Oh, Reza, how I long for those real babies, for the children we'll make when you come home. But until then, these two little souls are my companions, my comfort on the coldest nights.

Shirin has become quite the huntress—yesterday I found her stalking a moth with such fierce concentration I couldn't help but laugh. She

The Moonlit Rose of Isfahan

pounced and missed, landing in a most undignified heap, and looked at me as if to say, 'I meant to do that.' She still loves to sleep on your pillow, Reza. Every night she curls up there, and I pretend she's keeping it warm for you, guarding your place beside me. Sometimes when I'm very lonely, I bury my face in that pillow and imagine I can still smell you there.

And Simin! She's become such a princess, demanding attention whenever she feels neglected. This morning she knocked over my teacup because I was reading and not petting her. She has this way of sitting and staring at me with those green eyes until I give in and scratch behind her ears. She purrs so loudly you can hear her from the next room. When I cook, she sits at my feet, hopeful for scraps, and I talk to her as if she were you, telling her about my day, about the garden, about how much I miss you. I know it's silly, but she tilts her head and looks at me as if she understands.

Please tell Hossein that his 'nieces' are thriving—still playful, still getting into mischief, still filling my heart with their silly antics. Tell him Shirin tried to climb the bookshelf last week and nearly knocked over Father's Hafez collection. Tell him Simin has learned to open the cabinet where I keep the dried fish, and I caught her with her whole head in the jar, looking utterly guilty.

Their personalities continue to unfold like flowers, my love, and they bring me more joy than I can express. On the nights when the loneliness threatens to swallow me whole, when the silence becomes unbearable, they curl against me, one on each side, and their purring becomes a lullaby that carries me through until morning.

She smiled through her tears as she described them, the pen moving more easily now. Before long, Zahra's smile widened as she continued writing, genuine warmth spreading through her chest. She hadn't realized just how cathartic it was to pour her feelings out on paper until now, but her expression sobered as she returned to deeper feelings.

But oh, my Reza, they cannot replace you. Nothing can. They cannot hold me when I wake from nightmares of you wounded and bleeding. They cannot whisper poetry in my ear or make me laugh until my sides ache. They cannot give me the children I dream of, or make this house feel like a home instead of a tomb. I am grateful for them, truly, but they only highlight what I'm missing—you, always you.

My Reza, remember our first anniversary apart in last year? I understood your patriotic duty then, was proud of you and Hossein standing for Iran, defending our home. I wrote to you of my love, of the garden I tended in your name, and you wrote back of your resolve. But now, missing our second, the grief fills me like a river overflowing its banks, threatening to wash away everything I've built to keep myself strong.

She continued, her words turning poetic, weaving in Rumi's wisdom to warm his heart, knowing it would make him smile amid the trenches' horror. She wrote on, her emotions pouring onto the page like a confession she didn't know she needed to get off her chest.

I long for you, my love—your touch, your poetry, the way you made the world feel safe even when it wasn't. Let me share Rumi's words to ease your heart, as they ease mine: 'Sorrows are the rags of old clothes and jackets that serve to cover, and then are taken off. That undressing, and the beautiful naked body underneath, is the sweetness that comes after grief.' I cling to these words, my brave soldier, my poet. I tell myself that this sorrow is making room for the joy of your return, that every empty night is creating space for the fullness of our reunion. May these words be your shield, as your love is mine.

The radio crackled, the announcer's voice urgent: "Volunteer efforts needed for medical aid and ration distribution. Citizens, support our brave fighters." Zahra's pen hesitated, her heart heavy with the war's demands. She'd begun helping out neighbours and people she knew, a way to feel connected to Reza's fight, to do something useful instead of drowning in her loneliness, when she wasn't helping her mother take care of her father.

She thought of Reza's parents, Fatemeh and Salar, who had come by yesterday, their faces lined with worry, begging her to join them in Shiraz with cousin Ramin, their voices a chorus of concern. Fatemeh's tears, her hand clutching Zahra's, "Come, daughter, it's safer if we are together. The bombs could reach Isfahan any day." Salar's steady plea, "Ramin has room for you. We'll be family together." But Zahra had refused, her choice a vow to keep their home intact, the garden blooming, the bed waiting for Reza's return. To leave would feel like admitting he might never come back, and she couldn't—wouldn't—surrender to that fear.

Your parents begged me to go to Shiraz with them, to live with Ramin, saying being alone in the city's too dangerous now. Your mother held me, her tears wet on my shoulder, your father's voice kind but firm, both of them desperate to keep me safe as if I were their own daughter. But I couldn't,

The Moonlit Rose of Isfahan

Reza. I can't. This house is us—the doorway where you kissed me goodbye, your lips trembling against mine as you tried to be brave; the garden where we planted our dreams, talking about rose bushes and children's laughter; the bed where we whispered our future, your hands in my hair, your promises in my ear.

To leave would be to surrender to the war, to admit that Saddam's hatred could drive me from the home we made together. I won't give him that victory, my love. I'll stay, and I'll wait, though the emptiness is a heavy cloak that weighs on my shoulders, though the nights are cold without you, though every day feels like walking through water, each movement requiring effort I barely have. The cats curl at my feet, their purrs a faint echo of your voice, but they can't fill the void of your arms, your love that made me feel safe in a world now mad with war's cruelty.

The pen slowed, her tears falling freely now, the paper absorbing them like the garden's soil after rain, the ink blurring slightly, creating small pools of darkness that matched the darkness in her heart. The house's silence pressed against her, the ticking clock on the wall a relentless reminder of time without him, the faucet's drip in the sink a lonely echo that made the emptiness feel even more vast.

The lamp's flame sputtered as the wick burned low, shadows dancing across the walls like ghosts of all the moments they should have shared but couldn't. She thought of their wedding night, how nervous they'd both been, how gentle Reza had been with her, how he'd recited poetry until she stopped trembling after getting his draft notice. She thought of the three weeks they'd had before he left—three weeks to last a lifetime, if the worst happened.

I am yours, always and forever, waiting for the day when I can hold you again instead of just these words. Come home to me, my poet. Come home safe.

Your rose, your wife. I love you.

Zahra

She signed the letter with a trembling hand then sealed it with a kiss, her lips lingering on the paper, the taste of salt from her tears mixing with the ink's faint bitterness, and placed it in an envelope alongside dried rose petals, her handwriting addressing it to Reza at the front, her heart a piece of her sent into the unknown.

The radio played a soft melody, a *santur's* plucked strings resonating like a lover's sigh, and Zahra rose, her dress rustling, to place the letter by the door for the post. The cats followed, their tails swishing, Shirin rubbing against her legs, Simin meowing softly as if sensing her distress. She picked them both up, holding them close, burying her face in their soft fur, and allowed herself a moment of weakness—sobbing into their warmth, her body shaking with the force of two years of accumulated grief and longing.

When the tears finally subsided, she set the cats down gently, wiped her eyes with the back of her hand, and looked at their wedding photo on the shelf. Reza smiled back at her, frozen in a moment of pure joy, and she whispered to him, "I'll be here when you come home, my love. However long it takes, I'll be here."

The war's early years had already stolen so much, but her love for Reza, her resolve to stay, were roots that ran deep, unshakeable. Her letter was a bloom in the storm, a testament that even in the darkest night, love could still write its name in ink and hope and the stubborn refusal to give up. She would wait. She would endure. And when he came home—because he had to come home—she would be here, in this house, in this garden, ready to begin again.

Chapter Twenty-Seven

Shiraz, 1988

The guest bedroom in Ramin's house glowed with the soft, amber light of the oil lamp on the nightstand, its flame flickering gently, casting dancing shadows across the walls and the intricate patterns of the woven rug that covered the tiled floor. The room was a sanctuary of intimacy, the narrow bed with its wooden frame creaking faintly under the weight of the quilts, embroidered with vines and flowers that seemed to echo the jasmine climbing the courtyard walls outside. The air was warm and heavy inside the room, with the night's cool breeze coming through the open window a welcome relief as it rustled the leaves of the olive trees—silent witnesses to their reunion.

Reza lay on his back, relaxed against the pillows, his greying beard framing a face softened by the day's quiet joys—the reunion with his parents, the stories shared over tea, the simple act of being together without the war's shadow looming quite so darkly. His mind was already wandering to the promise he'd made to Zahra, to make this evening a celebration of their love, a reclaiming of the moments the war had stolen. The framed verse of Hafez on the wall seemed to bless them, its flowing calligraphy a quiet reminder of their courtship and wedding in this very city.

Zahra entered the room from the small adjoining bath, wrapped in a thin robe of pale silk, its fabric clinging slightly to her damp skin, the material translucent in places where the lamplight hit it, revealing gentle curves that made Reza's breath catch. Her hair hung loose, still wet and gleaming, cascading over her shoulders like a waterfall of midnight silk, releasing the scent of rosewater and lavender soap with every movement. Her almond eyes met Reza's, shimmering with a mix of shyness and anticipation, her cheeks flushed from the hot water, her lips curved in a soft smile that made his heart skip. After eight years of separation, every moment of intimacy still felt like a gift unwrapped, a treasure reclaimed.

She approached the bed, the rug soft under her bare feet, the cool tiles peeking through in spots, sending a slight shiver up her legs. "My poet," she murmured, her voice melodic and low, climbing onto the bed beside him, the mattress dipping under her weight, the quilts shifting with a whisper of fabric.

Reza reached for her immediately, his scarred hand gentle as he pulled her close, their bodies aligning, her head resting on his chest, the steady rhythm of his heartbeat a soothing drum beneath her ear. The warmth of his body seeped through his tunic, contrasting with the cool night air wafting through the window, creating a delicious tension that made Zahra sigh contentedly.

Reza's arm wrapped around her waist, his fingers tracing lazy circles on her hip through the robe, the touch light but electrifying, sending tingles through her skin. "My moonlit rose," he replied, his baritone deep and poetic, his other hand lifting to stroke her hair, the strands silky and damp against his palm, the scent of lavender filling his senses, stirring memories of their honeymoon here in Shiraz, when her hair had smelled of jasmine and their nights were filled with nervous discovery. Now, eight years later, they knew each other's bodies like sacred texts, yet the wonder remained.

They lay there for a moment, nuzzling affectionately, their noses brushing, his beard tickling her cheek, her lips grazing his jaw in a series of soft, playful kisses that made him chuckle low in his throat. The sound vibrated through his chest, a rumble that Zahra felt against her body, making her smile. "You're tired," she said, her voice tender, her fingers tracing the lines of his face, enjoying the warmth of his skin.

Reza shook his head, his eyes darkening with desire, his hand sliding

The Moonlit Rose of Isfahan

lower, the touch firm but loving, sending a warm flush through her. "Never too tired for you, my love," he teased, his lips finding her earlobe, nibbling gently, the sensation sparking a giggle from her, her body arching closer, pressing against his chest through the robe, the friction igniting a spark in both of them.

Zahra pulled back slightly, her eyes meeting his, her hand resting on his heart. "Days like these," she whispered, her voice thick with emotion, "they make up for the wedding anniversaries the war stole from us." Her words hung in the air, a poignant reminder of the years apart, the missed milestones, the letters that had bridged the gap but could never replace his touch.

Reza's eyes softened, his hand moving to cup her face, his thumb brushing her lip, the skin soft and warm. "They do, my rose," he agreed, his voice a poetic murmur. "But we'll make new ones, a lifetime of them." He leaned in, their lips meeting in a slow, deep kiss, tongues entwining with languid passion, the taste of him—faint tea and salt—filling her senses, her body responding with a warm, tingling wave that spread from her core.

As the kiss broke, Reza's tiredness faded, replaced by growing passion, his hands roaming her back, feeling the curve of her spine through the robe. He rolled her onto her back, the bed creaking softly, the quilts shifting with a whisper, and hovered above her, his weight on his elbows, his body aligning with hers, the heat of him pressing against her thigh.

"Let me love you, my Zahra," he said, his voice low and commanding, but laced with tenderness, his lips trailing kisses down her neck, the skin soft and sensitive, his beard tickling, sending shivers through her. She arched into him, her hands sliding under his tunic, feeling the warm, firm planes of his chest, the scars a map she knew by heart, her fingers tracing them with reverence. "Yes, Reza," she breathed, her voice breathy, her body already responding, warmth pooling between her legs.

Reza's hands moved to the tie of her robe, untying it slowly, the fabric parting like a curtain, revealing her bare skin, glowing in the lamplight, her curves that he liked so much, her softness, the body he'd dreamed of during eight years in trenches. He paused, his eyes drinking her in, his breath hitching. "You're a poem, my love, more beautiful than any verse."

He leaned down, his lips finding her collarbone, kissing a trail lower, his hands caressing her tenderly, the sensation sending waves of pleasure through her, her back arching, a soft moan escaping her lips. He touched her with affection and reverence, his movements slow and deliberate, building the heat between them, the warmth spreading through her entire body, her skin flushing with desire. "Commander Reza Azad," she whispered, her hands in his hair, the strands soft between her fingers, guiding him.

His mouth continued its worship, kissing and caressing, the sensations wet and warm, sparking electric tingles that made her thighs press together, her breath hitching, the pleasure a sweet ache building inside her. His beard brushed her skin, the prickly contrast adding to the sensation, her moans soft, her body responding beneath him. His touch was both tender and passionate, the dual nature of their connection building the heat in her core, her arousal growing with each caress. Reza's own desire pressed insistently against her thigh through his trousers, the fabric a barrier he longed to remove.

He looked up at her, his eyes dark with passion, and spoke words of love inspired by the poets they'd read together: "Let our love be the compass that guides us, the garden where joy takes root." The words washed over her, his breath hot, intensifying the pleasure, her body responding with a surge of warmth, her hips lifting slightly.

Zahra's hands moved to his tunic, unbuttoning it slowly, her fingers trembling with desire, the buttons popping free one by one, revealing his chest, the skin warm and firm under her touch, the scars—jagged line from shrapnel across his stomach, the puckered mark from the knife on his arm—a map she loved, each one a story of his survival. She traced them with her fingers, then her lips, kissing the scar on his shoulder, her breath warm, the taste of his skin salty, the texture rough but beloved, her touch a healing prayer.

"These are beautiful," she murmured, her voice thick with emotion, her lips lingering on the scar near his heart, the sensation sending a shiver through him, his body responding with a surge of heat. Reza's hand tangled in her hair, his fingers gentle, his voice a whisper. "You

The Moonlit Rose of Isfahan

make them beautiful, my rose. Your love heals what the war broke."

He shifted, his lips trailing lower, across her stomach, his hands guiding her thighs apart gently, the robe fully open, her body exposed to the cool air, goosebumps rising on her skin, the contrast heightening her sensitivity. His kisses continued, his beard tickling her inner thighs, the sensation a delicious tease, her breath hitching as he nuzzled closer to her centre, his touch sending tingles through her, her arousal growing.

He caressed her thighs, his hands firm but loving, the touch both relaxing and arousing, her body opening to him, her moans soft. "Reza, please," she whispered, her hands in his hair, guiding him, her shyness giving way to need. He obliged, his mouth finding her most sensitive places, the sensations sparking electric waves through her, her hips responding, the pleasure building like a storm gathering strength, her breath ragged.

He continued his intimate worship, his touch both gentle and passionate, the pleasure building steadily within her. He murmured words of love against her skin, speaking of beauty and connection in the language of Rumi they both cherished: "Where love dwells, the impossible becomes possible, and wounds transform into wisdom." The words heightened her sensation, her body responding with surges of heat, her climax building, a wave that crashed through her, her cry a soft moan of release, her body trembling, the pleasure leaving her breathless and undone.

Reza rose, his eyes dark with desire and love, and shed his trousers, his body ready. He entered her slowly, their bodies joining with a shared sigh, the connection a sweet completeness for her, the enveloping warmth a comfort for him, the friction sparking pleasure for both. Their rhythm was slow at first, each movement a dance they'd learned together, his hands caressing her tenderly, her moans mingling with his deeper sounds of pleasure.

He spoke poetry as they moved together, his voice rhythmic with their bodies: "In you, I find my home. In your arms, peace after war. Together, we are whole." The words washed over her, his movements deepening, the pleasure building, her body arching, her release crashing through her again, drawing his own, his groan a vow, their bodies shuddering together in shared ecstasy.

They collapsed together, breathless, tangled in quilts and each other, their skin slick with the sheen of passion, the room warm despite the cool breeze from the window. Laughter bubbled up between them, soft and intimate, their hands entwining, fingers interlaced. The lamp's flame flickered, casting their shadows on the wall like lovers in an ancient story, and the jasmine-scented air cooled their flushed skin gradually, bringing them back to themselves.

Reza pulled her close, his hand tracing lazy circles on her back, the motion soothing, sending gentle tingles through her. "My rose," he murmured, his baritone deep and content, his voice a rumble she felt in his chest, "that was... wonderful. Your body against mine, the way you melt into me—it always feels like coming home after the longest journey." His words were sincere, his eyes searching hers in the lamplight, the intimacy they'd shared leaving him sated but filled with tenderness.

Zahra smiled, her hand resting on his chest, feeling the steady beat of his heart, her fingers tracing a scar lightly, the texture rough but beloved. "It does, Reza," she replied, her voice melodic and breathy, her body still humming with aftershocks. "Being with you like this, feeling you—it's passion and peace, all at once. You make me feel so alive, so loved. I can't get enough of you."

They cuddled closer, their bodies entwining naturally, her leg draped over his, his hand sliding to her hip, squeezing gently, the touch affectionate. They laughed softly, the sound a melody in the quiet room, reminiscing about their early weeks of marriage in 1980, when their lovemaking had been awkward and clumsy due to inexperience.

"Remember our first night here in Shiraz?" Zahra said, her cheeks flushing with the memory, her fingers playing with his beard. "You were so nervous, fumbling with my dress, and I... I didn't know where to put my hands." Reza chuckled, his arm tightening around her, his lips brushing her forehead. "I do. Then, the second time I bumped my head on the bedframe after I pulled out, and you giggled, but it was the sweetest sound. We were like two poets trying to write with broken pens—clumsy, but full of heart."

Zahra laughed, her body shaking against his, the vibration a delightful friction. "And now, you know every spot, every touch that makes me melt," she teased, her voice playful, her hand sliding lower to trace his abdomen, the muscles firm under her fingers. Reza's eyes darkened with affection, his hand moving to caress her gently, his touch always tender.

"Ah, my rose, you've mapped me too," he replied, his voice teasing but warm. "But I'll never tire of exploring you." Zahra blushed, her endearing shyness surfacing even after their passion, and nestled closer, her arm draping over him, her head on his shoulder, the warmth of their bodies a cocoon against the night's coolness.

They lay in comfortable silence for a while, their breaths syncing, the lamp's flame flickering and casting dancing shadows, the jasmine breeze wafting in through the window. Zahra's fingers traced his scars delicately, her touch a prayer, murmuring Rumi's words that had carried him through dark moments in the trenches: "Sorrows are the rags of old clothes and jackets that serve to cover, and then are taken off. That undressing, and the beautiful naked body underneath, is the sweetness that comes after grief." Her voice was a whisper, her lips moving against his skin, the vibration soothing, her fingers lingering on the top of shrapnel scar, near his ribs, the texture rough, her heart aching for the pain he'd endured yet grateful for his survival.

Reza sighed contentedly, his tiredness returning, his eyes growing heavy, the day's emotions and their lovemaking pulling him toward sleep. "Zahra," he murmured, his voice fading, "your words, your touch... they heal me." She smiled, shifting to massage his back, her hands warm and firm, kneading the tense muscles along his spine, the skin warm but marked by more scars, each knot releasing under her fingers, the sensation a soothing wave for him, his body relaxing, his breaths deepening.

She continued, her murmurs of love and healing continuing softly: "From every wound flows the light of divine grace. Our love is the indestructible bridge between our souls. Rest now, my dear." Her voice was a lullaby, her touch a healing prayer.

Reza's breathing deepened, becoming slow and steady, and Zahra watched him for a while, her heart full, tracing his scars with delicate fingers, feeling their texture—each one a story of pain she wished she could erase, not because they marred him, but because of the suffering they represented.

She prayed silently, her lips moving, speaking quiet words of hope: "May peace find you in sleep, may your dreams be gentle, may the war's shadow fade." Her touch was a vow, her love a light for his darkness, and she curled against him, her arm over his chest, the quilts pulled up around them.

The lamp burned lower, its flame guttering slightly, casting softer shadows. The jasmine breeze continued its gentle whisper through the window, carrying the scent of night-blooming flowers and the distant sound of Shiraz settling into sleep. Zahra's own eyes grew heavy, her body relaxed and sated, and she let herself drift, secure in Reza's arms, believing that tonight—this perfect night of reunion and love—would bring him the peaceful rest he so desperately needed.

But peace did not hold.

In sleep, Reza's body began to twitch, his breathing quickening, his fingers clenching the quilts as his mind dragged him backward, away from Zahra's warmth, away from the garden-scented room, away from safety. The nightmares always began the same way—with hope.

The sky above him was clear for the first time in eight years, the smoke finally dissipated, the sun breaking through in shafts of golden light that felt like benediction. The ceasefire had been signed. It was over. He was walking through a field, headed back—back to where, he couldn't quite remember, but it didn't matter because he was going home, finally going home. His boots crunched on dry earth, and the sound echoed strangely, too loud in the unnatural silence. No artillery. No screaming. Just his footsteps and his breathing and the sun on his face.

Then the earth began to move.

Not a tremor, not a quake, but a shifting, a rising, as if the ground itself were breathing. Reza stumbled, catching himself, and looked down. The soil was cracking, fissures spreading like veins across the field, and from those cracks came hands—grey, dirt-covered hands clawing upward, fingers grasping at air, at light, at anything. His heart seized in his chest, his body frozen, as the hands multiplied, dozens of them, hundreds, pushing through the earth like plants growing in time-lapse, except these weren't plants, these were arms, shoulders, faces emerging from the ground.

The Moonlit Rose of Isfahan

And he recognized them.

Hossein burst from the earth first, his chest still torn open from the mortar blast, his eyes wide and accusing, dirt cascading from his hair. "Brother," he said, his voice wet and broken, "why didn't you save me?" His hand shot out, grabbing Reza's ankle, the grip impossibly strong, cold as the grave. "You promised to have my back too. You promised we'd be in this together."

Another hand seized Reza's other leg—a soldier from his unit, the boy who'd been eighteen and trembling, who'd died screaming for his mother when the gas came. "Commander," the boy wheezed, his face blistered and peeling, "you said we'd make it home."

More rose. An old woman from a village they'd tried to evacuate, her body crushed, her toothless mouth working: "My grandchildren burned. You were too late." A young girl, no more than seven, her skull caved in, reaching for him with small, dirt-caked hands: "Why didn't you stop the bombs?" They clawed at him, pulling at his clothes, his legs, their fingers digging into his skin, cold and relentless, and Reza tried to scream, tried to move, but his voice caught in his throat and his legs wouldn't obey.

"I tried," he finally choked out, yanking against their grip, but more hands emerged, more bodies, civilians and soldiers, Iranian and Iraqi, all of them dead, all of them grabbing at him. The smell hit him—earth and decay, copper blood and chemical rot, the stench of death he'd lived with for eight years, concentrated and overwhelming. "I tried to save you, I tried—"

But they didn't listen, didn't care, their voices rising in a chorus of accusation, each one asking the same question in different words: Why didn't you save us? Why are you alive when we're not? Why do you get to go home?

He fought them, kicking, twisting, trying to break free, but for every hand he pried loose, two more grabbed him. They were pulling him down now, dragging him toward the earth, and he could feel the soil giving way beneath his feet, soft and hungry, ready to swallow him.

"No!" he screamed, finally finding his voice, "No, please, I'm sorry, I'm sorry, I couldn't—" Hossein's face was inches from his now, so close Reza could see the insects crawling in the wound on his chest, could smell the wrongness of death on his breath. "Come with us, brother," Hossein said, almost gently. "You belong here, with us. You died too, you just haven't realized it yet."

The earth was swallowing him, up to his waist, his chest, the hands pulling him deeper, the soil closing over his head like water, filling his mouth, his nose, his lungs, suffocating him. He was underground, buried alive, the weight of all that earth pressing down, crushing, and all he could do was try to scream, scream, scream into the darkness—

"Reza! Reza, wake up!"

The voice broke through like a lifeline, and suddenly he was gasping, thrashing upward through layers of sleep and terror, his eyes flying open to the dimly lit room, his body drenched in cold sweat, his heart hammering so hard he thought it would break through his ribs. Zahra's face swam into focus above him, her hands on his shoulders, her eyes wide with concern and fear.

"You're here," she was saying, her voice urgent but controlled, practiced. "You're in Shiraz, you're with me, you're safe."

But he wasn't safe. He could still feel the hands, still smell the earth and death, still hear Hossein's voice echoing in his skull. The reality of the nightmare crashed over him like a wave, and something inside him broke—something that had been holding together through sheer force of will since the ceasefire. A sob tore from his throat, raw and animal, and then he was crying, really crying, his body shaking with the force of it, tears streaming down his face as eight years of suppressed grief and guilt and horror poured out of him in great, wrenching sobs.

"I couldn't save them," he gasped between sobs, his voice breaking. "Zahra, I couldn't—they died, so many died, and I—I'm still here, why am I still here when they—" His words dissolved into incoherent crying, and Zahra pulled him against her, wrapping her arms around him, cradling his head against her chest as his body shook. Her nightgown was quickly soaked with his tears and sweat, but she didn't care, just held him tighter, one hand stroking his hair, the other rubbing circles on his back.

"Shh, my love, I'm here," she murmured, her own voice thick with emotion, her heart breaking for his pain. "I'm here, you're safe, I'm here." She began to rock him gently, the way a mother rocks a child, and started to sing—softly at first, then louder, the Persian lullaby her mother had sung to her, the one she'd sung to him before during the worst nightmares. The melody was simple, ancient, the words a prayer for peace and protection, and she let the song wrap around them both like a blanket.

The Moonlit Rose of Isfahan

A sharp knock on the door made her look up. "Reza? Zahra?" Salar's voice came through, worried and uncertain. "We heard—is everything alright?" The door cracked open, and Fatemeh's face appeared, her grey hair loose, her eyes wide with maternal concern. Behind her, Ramin hovered, his expression anxious. They took in the scene—Reza sobbing in Zahra's arms, his bare, scarred chest heaving, his face buried against her—and Fatemeh's hand flew to her mouth.

"My son—" she started forward, but Zahra gently raised one hand, still holding Reza with the other, her fingers never stopping their soothing motion through his hair. Her eyes met Fatemeh's, and something passed between them, woman to woman, wife to mother—an understanding, a transfer of responsibility.

"I can handle this," Zahra said softly but firmly, her voice steady despite her own tears. "I've done this before. He needs... he needs privacy right now. Please." She saw Fatemeh's hesitation, saw Salar's worry as he joined his wife at the door, his cane in hand, his thin frame tense with the instinct to protect his son.

But she also saw them notice Reza's scars in the lamplight—the shrapnel wounds, the knife mark, all the evidence of suffering they hadn't fully understood until now—and she saw Reza's shoulders tense even through his sobs, his body trying to curl in on itself, hiding. He was self-conscious even in his breakdown, ashamed to be seen like this, vulnerable and marked.

"Please," Zahra repeated, more gently this time. "Trust me. I'll take care of him." Fatemeh's eyes filled with tears, but she nodded, reaching out to touch Salar's arm. Ramin, reading the room, had already stepped back. "We'll be right outside if you need us," Fatemeh whispered, and then they withdrew, the door closing softly, leaving Reza and Zahra alone again in the amber lamplight.

Zahra returned her full attention to Reza, resuming her lullaby, her voice a lifeline in the darkness. She sang verse after verse, the Persian words flowing over him like water, washing away the nightmare's residue bit by bit. His sobs gradually quieted, becoming shuddering breaths, then soft whimpers, then finally silence except for the occasional hitch in his breathing. She didn't stop singing, didn't stop holding him, didn't stop the gentle rocking motion. She felt him relax against her incrementally, his death grip on her nightgown loosening, his breathing deepening.

"I'm sorry," he mumbled finally, his voice hoarse and small, muffled against her chest. "I'm so sorry, Zahra. I thought—I thought I was getting better. I thought—" His voice caught, threatening to break again. She tilted his face up gently, her hands cupping his tear-stained cheeks, forcing him to meet her eyes.

"You are getting better," she said fiercely, her own tears spilling over. "One nightmare doesn't erase your progress. You survived a war, Reza. You survived. Your body, your mind—they need time to heal. We have time now. We have all the time in the world." She kissed his forehead, his closed eyelids, his wet cheeks, each kiss a promise. "Go back to sleep, my love. I'm here. I won't let go."

She eased him back down onto the pillows, lying beside him, keeping her arms around him, and began the lullaby again, softer now, barely more than a hum. His exhausted body, wrung out from emotion and terror, couldn't resist anymore. His breathing evened out, his muscles went slack, and within minutes he'd slipped back into sleep—hopefully a deeper, quieter one this time. Zahra held him, feeling his heartbeat against her, and only then did she allow herself to fully feel the fear that had gripped her when she'd woken to his screaming.

She stayed awake, unable to surrender to sleep herself, watching the shadows dance on the wall, listening to the breeze rustle the curtains. After a while, she began to pray, silently at first, then in whispered words directed at God the same way she'd turned to her faith so many times during the war, during the endless nights of waiting.

"Please," she whispered into the darkness, her lips moving against Reza's hair. "Please heal him. Take away his nightmares, his guilt, his pain. He's carried so much for so long. He deserves peace now. He deserves to sleep without terror, to live without this shadow following him." Her voice caught, and she paused, gathering herself. "He's still that sweet, gentle poet I fell in love with underneath all of this. I know he is. I can see him when he smiles at me, when he recites Hafez, when he holds me. He's still there, my Reza, my beautiful poet with the kind heart and the gentle hands."

She stroked his hair, her fingers trembling slightly. "Please don't let him get lost. He's made so much progress, come so far. Don't let the war win, not after he survived it. Not after we survived it." Her tears fell silently, landing in his hair and on the pillow. "And please... please let me be enough. Let my love and devotion be enough to help him heal. Give me the strength to hold him through the nightmares, the wisdom to know when to speak and when to just hold him, the patience for however long this takes. I don't want to fail him. I can't fail him. He's my everything."

She prayed until her words ran out, until there was nothing left but the silent communion of her heart reaching toward something greater, pleading for help she couldn't provide alone. The lamp finally guttered out, plunging the room into darkness broken only by the pale moonlight filtering through the window. Still she held him, still she kept watch, her body a shield between him and whatever demons might come for him in the night.

As the first faint light of dawn began to creep across the sky, Zahra finally felt her own eyes growing heavy. Reza slept on, his breathing steady, his face peaceful for now. She allowed herself to hope that the worst was over, that the nightmare had released its hold, that maybe—just maybe—he would wake with the sun and smile at her, and they could face another day together. One day at a time. One nightmare at a time. One healing moment at a time.

She pressed a final kiss to his forehead and let sleep claim her at last, her arms still wrapped protectively around the man she loved, the poet who'd survived a war but was still fighting its ghosts, the husband she would stand beside through every battle, seen and unseen, until healing came—however long that might take.

Chapter Twenty-Eight

Shiraz, 1988

Dawn broke gently over the city, the first rays of sun filtering through the window of the room in soft bands of gold and amber, painting the cream-coloured walls with light. Reza woke slowly, naturally, without the violent jerk of a nightmare dragging him from sleep. For a moment he lay still, disoriented by the peace of it—the absence of terror, the simple quiet of morning. His body felt heavy but not tense, exhausted but not broken. He'd slept. Really slept, after the nightmare, after the breakdown, after Zahra's lullaby had pulled him back from the edge.

He turned his head slowly, and his heart clenched at the sight beside him. Zahra lay curled against him, her arm still draped protectively across his chest where she'd held him through the night, her hair spilled across the pillow in silken waves, her face peaceful in sleep but showing the faint shadows of exhaustion beneath her eyes.

She'd stayed awake for him. He knew she had—could feel it in the bone-deep weariness of her body, could see it in the way she'd finally surrendered to sleep only when dawn began to creep across the sky. While he'd fought demons in his dreams, she'd fought to keep him anchored in reality. While he'd broken down sobbing, she'd held him together with her strength, her voice, her unwavering presence.

Gratitude washed over him, so powerful it made his throat tight. This woman—his moonlit rose, his poet's muse, his anchor in every storm—had given him eight years of letters that kept him alive in trenches, had tended their home and garden through scarcity and loneliness, had welcomed him back without judgment or expectation, and now watched over him through his darkest hours without complaint. The least he could do was let her rest. The least he could do was care for her the way she cared for him.

Moving with careful precision, he eased his body out from under her arm, holding his breath when she stirred slightly, her hand reaching for where he'd been. He stayed frozen until she settled again, her breathing evening out, and then he slipped from the bed, pulling the quilts up around her shoulders to keep her warm. The room was cool with morning air, the breeze from the courtyard below making the curtains flutter gently.

He found his tunic and trousers draped over a chair, pulled them on quietly, and paused at the door to look back at her one more time. She looked so young in sleep, the worry lines that had appeared during the war years smoothed away, her lips slightly parted. Beautiful. Always beautiful.

He stepped into the hallway, closing the door with a soft click, and made his way toward the kitchen. The house was quiet but not completely silent—the sounds of morning starting to wake around him, the distant call of birds in the courtyard, the creak of floorboards, the whisper of wind through the olive trees. As he approached the kitchen, he smelled it: fresh bread, cardamom tea, the earthy warmth of a house coming to life. And there, standing at the counter in her chador, her hair neatly covered, was Fatemeh, his mother, preparing the morning's first samovar.

She turned at the sound of his footsteps, and for a moment they simply looked at each other. Her eyes, clouded but still sharp, searched his face, taking in the shadows beneath his eyes, the evidence of last night's tears, the vulnerability he usually kept hidden. He saw her maternal instinct war with respect for his boundaries, saw her hands twitch as if wanting to reach for him, to pull him into her arms the way she had when he was a child with scraped knees and hurt feelings.

"Reza," she said softly, her voice rasping with age and emotion. "You're awake early." It wasn't a question, but it held one: *Are you alright?* He crossed to her, and though he'd grown taller than her decades ago, though his body bore scars she'd never seen until last night, though he'd become a man and a soldier and survivor of horrors she couldn't imagine—in this moment, he was simply her son again. He bent and kissed her cheek, the skin soft and papery, smelling of rosewater and age.

"I'm alright, *Maman*," he murmured against her hair. "Zahra... she took care of me. She always does." He pulled back, meeting her eyes. "Thank you for respecting our privacy last night. I know it wasn't easy."

Fatemeh's eyes filled with tears, but she blinked them back, her wrinkled hand coming up to cup his face, her thumb brushing his cheekbone. "Your wife is a blessing from God," she said, her voice thick. "And you are my son. I will always worry, but I trust her with you." She paused, then added more quietly, "The war took much from you, my boy. But you're home now. Healing takes time."

He nodded, not trusting his voice, and Fatemeh seemed to understand. She patted his cheek once more, then turned back to her samovar, giving him space. "What brings you to the kitchen so early?" she asked, her tone shifting to something lighter, more practical. Reza cleared his throat, grateful for the change in subject. "I want to make breakfast for Zahra. She stayed awake most of the night watching over me. I want to... to do something for her." A smile softened Fatemeh's features, crinkling the lines around her eyes. "A good husband," she said approvingly. "What do you need?"

Together they worked, mother and son in the quiet kitchen as morning light strengthened through the windows. Fatemeh showed him where things were kept—the good tray with painted flowers for special occasions, the small teacups for Persian tea, the jar of rock candy for sweetening.

"There's fresh *barbari* from yesterday," she said, pulling a cloth-wrapped bundle from a basket. "Ramin brought it from the bakery, and there's feta in the cooler, walnuts in the jar, honey in the cupboard." She moved slowly but with purpose, her arthritic hands steady enough, and Reza watched her with a mixture of love and sadness. She'd grown so much older while he was gone.

He worked methodically, arranging everything on the tray with care.

The *barbari* bread, its sesame-speckled crust still faintly warm, he tore into pieces and arranged on a small plate. The feta cheese, soft and tangy, he crumbled beside it. Walnuts, their shells already cracked, he placed in a small bowl. A dish of honey, golden and thick, caught the morning light. Fresh herbs—mint and basil from the courtyard garden—he washed and arranged on a separate plate. Sliced cucumbers and tomatoes, their colours bright and fresh. And tea, brewed strong and fragrant with cardamom, poured into two small glasses with rock candy dissolving slowly at the bottom.

Fatemeh watched him work, and when he finished, she reached out to adjust a napkin on the tray, making it perfect. "She'll love this," she said softly. "Go, before the tea gets cold." Reza lifted the tray carefully, testing its weight, and turned to her.

"Thank you, *Maman*. For everything." She waved him away, but he could see the moisture in her eyes, the pride and love and relief all mixed together. "Go tend to your wife," she said, her voice gruff with emotion. "That's what husbands do."

He made his way back down the hallway, the tray balanced carefully, and nudged the bedroom door open with his shoulder. Zahra was still asleep, curled on her side now, her hand stretched out to the empty space where he'd been. The sight made his chest ache with tenderness. He set the tray on the nightstand, then sat on the edge of the bed, his weight making the mattress dip slightly. She stirred but didn't wake, and he allowed himself a moment to simply watch her—the rise and fall of her breathing, the way her lashes lay dark against her cheeks, the small crease between her brows that appeared even in sleep.

Gently, he leaned down and pressed a kiss to her forehead, then her temple, then the corner of her mouth. "Zahra," he murmured against her skin, "my rose, wake up." She made a soft sound of protest, burrowing deeper into the pillow, and he smiled, continuing his gentle assault—kisses along her jaw, her cheek, the sensitive spot just below her ear that always made her shiver.

"Mmm, Reza," she mumbled, still half-asleep, her hand reaching blindly for him. "Is it morning already?"

"It is," he said, his lips against her hair. "And I have something for you."

The Moonlit Rose of Isfahan

That made her eyes flutter open, confused and sleepy, her almond eyes taking a moment to focus on his face. "Something for me?" she repeated, her voice muzzy with sleep. He gestured to the nightstand, and she turned her head, her eyes widening as she took in the breakfast spread.

"Reza," she breathed, pushing herself up to sitting, the quilts falling away to reveal her nightgown rumpled from sleep, her hair a glorious mess. "You made me breakfast?" The wonder in her voice, the way her face lit up like he'd given her jewels instead of bread and cheese, made his throat tight again.

"You stayed awake for me last night," he said simply, reaching for the tray and setting it carefully across her lap. "You held me through the nightmare, sang to me, watched over me until dawn. The least I can do is make sure you eat." Her eyes filled with tears, and she reached up to cup his face, her thumb tracing his cheekbone. "Oh, my love," she whispered. "You don't have to earn my care. I do it because I love you."

"I know," he said, turning his head to kiss her palm. "But let me love you back. Let me take care of you too."

She smiled through her tears and gestured for him to join her. He climbed onto the bed beside her, propping himself against the pillows, and they shared the breakfast between them. He tore off a piece of bread and spread it with feta and honey, the combination sweet and salty, and held it to her lips. She took a bite, her eyes closing in pleasure at the taste, and he watched her with satisfaction. They fed each other, their fingers brushing, laughter bubbling up between bites—her teasing him about his mother's obvious involvement in the meal's preparation, him defending his culinary skills with mock offence.

"She helped," he admitted finally, popping a walnut into his mouth. "But the arrangement, the care, the thought—that was all me."

Zahra leaned against his shoulder, chewing on a piece of cucumber, her body warm and soft against his. "It's perfect," she said quietly. "This moment, this breakfast, you. All of it is perfect." They sat in comfortable silence for a while, sipping tea, the rock candy slowly dissolving and sweetening each sip, the cardamom fragrance rising with the steam.

The morning light strengthened, filling the room with a golden glow, and Reza felt something settle in his chest—not peace exactly, not yet, but a glimpse of what peace might feel like someday.

"We should visit Mahin today," Zahra said after a while, setting down her tea glass. "I told her we would if we had the chance in my letter, and we're here in Shiraz, and—" She looked at him uncertainly. "Unless you're too tired? After last night, I understand if you need to rest, or if you just want to spend time with your family."

Reza shook his head, taking her hand in his. "No, I want to go. I want to properly meet this woman who kept you company when I couldn't. Who helped you survive." He squeezed her fingers. "Besides, getting out, seeing people, living—that's part of healing too. I can't hide from the world forever."

Relief and love washed across her face, and she kissed him softly, tasting of honey and tea. "Then we'll go," she said. "After we make ourselves presentable." She looked down at herself, at her rumpled nightgown and wild hair, and laughed. "I look like I've been dragged through a hedge backward."

"You look beautiful," he said honestly, but then grinned. "But yes, perhaps we should both bathe and dress before presenting ourselves to company."

They took turns in the small adjoining bath, Zahra going first while Reza cleared away the breakfast tray and thanked Fatemeh again in the kitchen. When he returned, she was dressed in a flowing green dress— her favourite colour—that made her eyes shine, her hair braided and pinned, a light scarf draped over her shoulders. She looked radiant, rested despite her vigil, and Reza told her so, making her blush. He washed quickly, shaved carefully, and dressed in a simple tunic and trousers, trying to look presentable, trying to look like a man worthy of his wife's pride.

They left the house mid-morning, Fatemeh pressing a small basket of sweets into Zahra's hands—"You can't visit empty-handed," she insisted—and Salar calling after them to give Mahin his regards. The streets of Shiraz were alive with morning activity, vendors setting up stalls, women with shopping baskets, children running to school, the city waking fully under a clear blue sky. The air was warming but still comfortable, carrying the scent of bread from bakeries and the faint sweetness of flowers from courtyard gardens.

They walked hand in hand, Zahra guiding them through neighbourhoods she'd memorized from Mahin's directions. "She lives with her son and his family, and her daughters visit often," Zahra explained as they walked. "She told me she has several more grandchildren now. After being separated from them during the war, finding them again was like... like a miracle."

Reza squeezed her hand, thinking of his own reunion with his parents, understanding the enormity of families torn apart and brought back together. "How long was she alone in Isfahan?" he asked.

"Years," Zahra said, her voice sad. "She was displaced, became a refugee, lost contact with her children. She didn't know if they were alive. We met at the market—both of us alone, both of us waiting for someone to come home." She looked at him, her eyes bright. "She understood what I was going through. We became friends. She was like... like a grandmother when I had no family nearby." Reza's heart clenched. "I'm grateful to her," he said quietly. "For being there when I couldn't be."

They turned down a narrower street, the houses closer together here, modest but well-kept, and Zahra pointed. "There," she said. "The one with the blue door and the olive tree in the courtyard, exactly as described in the letter." The house was small but welcoming, its whitewashed walls bright in the sun, clay tiles on the roof, and indeed a gnarled olive tree stood in the small courtyard, its branches providing shade. They could hear sounds from inside—voices, laughter, the high-pitched squeals of children playing.

Zahra knocked on the door, and within moments it swung open to reveal a woman in her forties, her dark hair streaked with grey, her face kind but tired in the way of mothers who've worked hard all their lives. Her eyes widened in recognition. "Zahra!" she exclaimed, breaking into a wide smile. "Mother said you might visit! Please, please come in!" She ushered them inside, calling over her shoulder, "*Maman! Maman,* they're here! Zahra and her husband!"

The interior was simple but alive with warmth—rugs on the floors, cushions against the walls, the smell of cooking coming from somewhere deeper in the house. Children's toys scattered in a corner, a samovar steaming on a low table. And there, in a cushioned chair near the window where the light was best, sat Mahin.

She was smaller than Reza had remembered from their one meeting in the market, shrunken with age, her body bent, her hands gnarled with arthritis resting in her lap. Her face was deeply lined, weathered by time and hardship, and her eyes—those eyes that had once watched the market stalls, that had guided her hands in choosing vegetables and bargaining with vendors—were clouded with cataracts, nearly completely sightless now.

But when she heard Zahra's voice, those clouded eyes turned toward the sound, and her face transformed with joy. "Zahra?" she said, her voice trembling, thin with age but strong with emotion. "Is it really you, my dear girl?" Zahra rushed forward, kneeling beside the chair, taking Mahin's gnarled hands in her own. "It's me, Mahin-jan," she said, her voice thick. "I've come to see you, just like I promised." Mahin's hands gripped hers, surprisingly strong, and the old woman's face crumpled with happiness, tears spilling from those clouded eyes.

"My dear girl, my dear, dear girl," Mahin murmured, one hand leaving Zahra's to pat her cheek, to touch her face, to see her the way the blind do—through touch. "You came all this way. And you brought him? You brought your poet?" Zahra laughed through her tears, turning to gesture Reza forward. "Yes, I brought him. Reza, come meet Mahin properly." Reza approached slowly, feeling suddenly shy, suddenly aware of his scars, his height, his presence in this small room with this tiny, blind old woman who had been such a lifeline to his wife.

He knelt beside Zahra, bringing himself to Mahin's level. "Salaam, Mahin-jan," he said softly. "It's an honour to finally meet you properly now, unlike that day in the market. Zahra has told me so much about your kindness to her." Mahin's head turned toward his voice, and her free hand reached out, searching the air. "Let me see you, these old eyes only keep letting me down," she said, her voice suddenly imperious despite its thinness. "Let me see this poet my Zahra bragged about for years." Reza felt his face heat—*bragged?*—but he leaned forward, letting the old woman's hands find his face.

Her fingers, gnarled and trembling but surprisingly gentle, traced his features—his forehead, his cheeks, his nose, his lips, his beard. She was thorough, methodical, her clouded eyes unfocused but her attention absolute. The room had gone quiet, everyone watching this intimate moment of discovery.

"A soldier," she murmured, her expression softening. "My Zahra's poet was also a soldier." Then her fingers completed their journey, and she pulled back, a slow smile spreading across her deeply lined face. "Well!" she announced to the room, her voice taking on a teasing lilt. "It seems my dear Zahra was not exaggerating after all. She spent years telling me how handsome her Reza was, how his eyes could melt stone, how his smile could light up a room. I thought perhaps love had made her as blind as I am now!"

She paused for dramatic effect, then cackled—a surprisingly youthful sound coming from such an ancient body. "But she was right! No wonder she waited so faithfully. With a face like this, who wouldn't wait?"

The room erupted in laughter—Zahra's daughters, their husbands who'd gathered in the doorway, children peeking around corners. Zahra herself was laughing and crying at once, her hand covering her mouth. Reza felt his face burning, his ears hot, completely mortified but also oddly touched. He'd commanded men in battle, had faced death countless times, had survived eight years of horror—but this tiny old woman who was almost completely blind had reduced him to a blushing boy with a single teasing comment.

"Mahin-jan," Zahra protested through her laughter, "you're embarrassing him!" "Good!" Mahin said, still chuckling, reaching out to pat Reza's burning cheek. "Men who blush are men with hearts. I like him already, my dear. You chose well."

Reza cleared his throat, trying to regain his composure, but he was smiling despite himself. "You honour me, Mahin-jan," he managed. "Though I think Zahra's descriptions were more poetry than truth."

"Nonsense," Mahin said firmly. "I can see with my hands what others see with their eyes. And I say she told the truth."

The laughter gradually subsided, and Mahin's daughter—the one who'd answered the door—came forward. "Please, sit, be comfortable. I'll bring tea." She gestured to cushions arranged around the low table.

"I'm Ava and this is my sister Farzaneh."

A second daughter appeared, younger, carrying a tray of glasses. "And our brother Bahram will be here shortly—he's just putting the younger children down for a nap." The daughters moved with practiced efficiency, settling the guests, arranging cushions, bringing out the tea service and a plate of sweets.

As they settled around the table—Reza and Zahra on cushions, Mahin in her chair brought closer so she could participate—more family members appeared. Bahram, the son, a man in his late forties with kind eyes and calloused hands that spoke of manual labor. His wife, round and smiling, with a baby on her hip. The daughters' husbands, respectful and curious. And grandchildren—several of them, ranging in age from teenagers down to toddlers, all gathering to see the visitors their grandmother had spoken of so fondly.

One of the grandchildren, a boy of perhaps seven or eight with enormous dark eyes and a serious expression, pushed forward through the crowd.

"Grandmother," he said loudly, as if speaking to someone hard of hearing rather than nearly blind, "you said Zahra's husband was a poet. But uncle Bahram said he was a soldier. Which is it?" The room went still, adults exchanging glances, and Reza saw worry flash across Zahra's face. But he found himself smiling, reaching out to ruffle the boy's hair gently.

"I'm both, little one," Reza said softly, his voice gentle. "Before the war, I loved poetry—reading it, writing it, reciting it. And when the war came, I became a soldier to protect the things I loved—my country, my family, the beauty that poetry describes." He paused, searching for words a child could understand. "Think of it like this: poets write about courage and sacrifice, about defending what's precious. Sometimes, we have to live those words, not just write them. But after the fighting, we can go back to being poets again. A person can be many things."

The boy's eyes widened, processing this, and then he nodded solemnly. "So you fought with guns and with words?"

"Something like that," Reza agreed, his throat tight. Mahin laughed softly from her chair. "Out of the mouths of children," she murmured. "Yes, little one, he fought with both. And now he's home, and he can be just a poet again, not a soldier." The boy seemed satisfied with this answer and ran off to play with his cousins, but the adults remained quiet for a moment, the weight of what had been said settling over them.

It was Bahram who broke the silence, leaning forward, his expression serious but warm. "Sir—Reza—I want to thank you." His voice was thick with emotion. "For your service. For what you gave to Iran during those terrible years. My mother told us about Zahra, about how you wrote letters from the front, about how you survived eight years..." He shook his head, seeming to struggle for words. "Too many didn't come home. My father, he died shortly before the war. I never served because I was caring for my mother and sisters. But I know what you sacrificed. We all do. Thank you."

The other men in the room murmured agreement, and Reza felt his face heat again, but differently this time—not with embarrassment but with the complicated emotions that always came when someone thanked him for surviving. "I just did what needed to be done," he said quietly. "Like so many others." Mahin's gnarled hand reached out across the table, searching, and Reza took it, feeling the fragile bones, the paper-thin skin, the strength that remained despite everything.

"Too many mothers lost sons," she said softly, her clouded eyes glistening. "Too many wives lost husbands. Too many children grew up without fathers. The war took so much from us all."

A heavy silence fell, heads bowing in respect for the lost, and Reza felt the familiar weight of survivor's guilt pressing on his chest. But then Mahin squeezed his hand and continued, her voice stronger. "But you came home. You survived. And now you can build the life the war tried to steal from you. That's not something to feel guilty about—it's something to honour. Live well, young man. Live for those who couldn't." Her words struck something deep in him, something that had been knotted tight since the ceasefire, and he felt it loosen slightly, just a little, just enough to breathe.

"Thank you," he managed, his voice rough. "Thank you, Mahin-jan." She patted his hand once more, then released it, and the mood lightened as the daughters began serving tea, pressing sweets on their guests, encouraging everyone to eat and drink.

Conversation flowed more easily now, stories being exchanged—Zahra recounting funny moments from the market, Mahin's daughters sharing tales of their mother's stubbornness. "She insisted on doing the cooking until last year, even when she could barely see the pots!"

At one point, Farzaneh, the younger daughter, leaned forward with a grateful smile. "Zahra-jan, I must thank you again for inviting Mother to your home in Isfahan. She talked about your kindness for months, about how you wanted her to visit, to see your garden, to properly meet your Reza when he came home." She glanced at her mother, then back at Zahra. "I'm sorry we couldn't make the journey. Mother's health, the difficulty of travel for someone her age, our young families. We wanted to, truly, but—" Zahra reached out to squeeze Farzaneh's hand, interrupting her gently.

"Please, don't apologize," Zahra said warmly. "I understand completely. The important thing is that we're together now, that we can visit here and see Mahin-jan surrounded by her beautiful family." She looked around the room, at the children playing, at the daughters and the son and their spouses, at the life that filled this home. "This is even better than if she'd come to Isfahan. Here, I can see how blessed she is, how much love surrounds her. This is what she survived for, what she searched for during those hard years. This." Her voice caught with emotion. "Thank you for welcoming us into your home, for sharing this with us."

Mahin's clouded eyes were streaming now, tears running freely down her weathered cheeks, and both daughters moved to her side, one pulling out a handkerchief to dab at her face, the other rubbing her bent shoulders.

"You see, *Maman?*" Farzaneh said softly. "You see why we love her? She understands." Mahin nodded, unable to speak for a moment, and when she did, her voice was barely a whisper. "Finding you at that market, Zahra, when I had nothing and no one—it was God's mercy. You gave me hope when I had none. You gave me friendship when I was alone. You reminded me that kindness still existed in the world."

Zahra was crying too now, and Reza found his own eyes burning, his hand finding hers and squeezing tight. This was what the war couldn't destroy—human connection, compassion between strangers who became friends, the invisible threads that bound people together across distance and hardship. Mahin lifted her trembling hands, and both Zahra and Reza leaned forward so she could touch their faces once more, her fingers tracing their features as if memorizing them.

"Be happy," she said, her voice taking on the authority of a matriarch delivering a blessing. "Build your life together. Have children—many children—and tell them about these hard years, but tell them also about love, about survival, about hope."

Her hands then moved to rest on their joined hands, her touch light as a bird's wing. "I'm old now, my time is short, but I'm content. I found my children again. I lived to see the war end. I met your poet, Zahra, and he's as good as you said he was." She smiled, that teasing glint returning. "Perhaps even more handsome in person." That broke the emotional tension, laughter rippling through the room again, and Reza found himself grinning despite the tears on his cheeks.

They stayed for another hour, drinking tea, eating sweets, playing with the younger grandchildren who warmed up to the visitors quickly. One little girl, no more than four, climbed into Zahra's lap and fell asleep there, her thumb in her mouth, completely trusting. Zahra held her gently, her face soft with longing, and Reza saw in that moment their future—Zahra holding their own child, rocking them to sleep, singing the same lullaby she'd sung to him through his nightmares. The vision made his chest ache with want, with hope, with the possibility of healing through creating new life.

Finally, as the afternoon began to wane, they rose to leave, conscious of not overstaying their welcome, not tiring Mahin too much. The goodbyes were long and warm, with promises to visit again. "If you're ever in Isfahan, please come!" Zahra told Farzaneh as she embraced her. "Take care of our Zahra—she's precious to us!" Bahram said, shaking Reza's hand firmly, with grandchildren hugging their legs and begging them to stay longer.

Mahin held Zahra's hands one last time, pulling her down for a kiss on both cheeks. "Thank you for coming, my dear girl," she whispered. "Thank you for not forgetting an old woman."

"I could never forget you," Zahra whispered back. "You saved me during the war, Mahin-jan. I'll never forget." Then Mahin turned her clouded eyes toward where Reza stood. "Poet," she called out, and he came immediately, kneeling before her chair. She placed both hands on his head like a benediction.

"May God heal your wounds, both those on your body and those in your heart. May you find peace. May you give this good woman the children she deserves. May your words flow again like water after drought. May you live long and die happy."

Reza couldn't speak, could only bow his head under her hands, feeling the weight and power of her blessing settling over him like a mantle. "Thank you," he finally managed. "Thank you, Mahin-jan." She patted his head once more, then released him, and they made their way to the door, the family crowding around to see them off, children waving from windows, voices calling out final farewells.

They walked back through Shiraz's streets hand in hand, the afternoon sun warm on their faces, neither speaking for a long while, both processing the visit, the emotions, the connections forged and reaffirmed. Finally, Zahra broke the silence. "That was..." She trailed off, searching for words. "Important," Reza supplied, and she nodded. "Yes. Important." He squeezed her hand. "Thank you for bringing me there. For introducing me to her family. For showing me another piece of your war years, another part of how you survived."

Zahra leaned into him as they walked. "She's right, you know. We should live well. For ourselves, for those who didn't make it home, for the future we almost lost." Reza nodded slowly, thinking of Mahin's blessing, her words about healing, about children, about peace. "One day at a time," he said quietly. "That's all we can do. One peaceful morning at a time, one breakfast in bed, one visit with friends, one moment of connection. Building a life out of small moments until they become something whole."

"Yes," Zahra agreed, her voice warm with love. "Exactly that."

They walked on through the ancient city, taking their time, simply enjoying each other's company. Somewhere ahead, Ramin's house waited with Reza's parents, with family, with the guest room that held both nightmares and healing in its narrow bed. Behind them, Mahin's house hummed with the life and love that made survival meaningful.

The Moonlit Rose of Isfahan

And between the two, walking through streets that had witnessed centuries of human joy and sorrow, were Reza and Zahra—two survivors, two poets of different kinds, building their life one small moment at a time, one day at a time, one act of love at a time.

The war was over. The healing had begun. And today, at least, had been a good day.

Chapter Twenty-Nine

Isfahan, 1988

The summer carried a fragile hope, the air thick with the scent of blooming jasmine and the faint, dusty tang of sun-baked earth, the temperature hot in the late afternoon, a dry heat that shimmered over the city's ancient domes and minarets. The Iran-Iraq War, now in its eighth gruelling year, had left its mark on the city—cracked walls from distant bombings, rationed supplies in markets, the absence of young men like Reza, Hossein, and countless others, their faces haunting the photographs on family mantels.

Yet, today, a new sound rippled through the air, not the wail of air raid sirens but the crackle of the radio in the Azad home, perched on the kitchen counter beside a vase of wilting lavender, their purple petals curling in the heat.

The radio, tuned to a state broadcast, hummed with static, the announcer's voice breaking through with a clarity that made Zahra's heart leap: "The United Nations has proposed Resolution 598, accepted by both Iran and Iraq. A ceasefire is imminent, to take effect in August. Our brave soldiers will soon return home."

The words hung in the air, a promise so long awaited it felt like a dream, the static fading as a patriotic song began, its *santur* notes soaring with hope, echoing through the quiet house. Zahra stood frozen in the kitchen, her eyes wide with a mix of disbelief and joy. Her hands, still dusted with flour from kneading dough for *noon-e barbari* after returning from helping out refugees like she did every morning, trembled as she gripped the counter, the wood smooth and warm under her palms, the scent of yeast and lavender mingling in the air.

The radio's announcement felt like a lifeline, a thread pulling Reza back to her, the man whose letters—scented with ink and longing—had been her anchor through years of separation, fear, and loss, especially the crushing blow of Hossein's death, a permanent wound that still ached in her heart.

But beneath the surge of relief, a quieter fear stirred in Zahra's chest, one she had pushed down through all the years of waiting. What if she wasn't enough? Eight years was a lifetime—she had been barely twenty when Reza left, a shy newlywed who blushed at his touch, and now she was twenty-eight, shaped by war and loss and loneliness. She had changed, hardened in ways she couldn't name, her hands no longer as soft as they were, her heart scarred by grief for Hossein, her father and many cousins, by the weight of empty nights and unanswered prayers.

What if Reza came home and found a stranger in his wife's skin? What if the girl he'd married—the one who giggled at his poetry, who melted under his kisses—was gone, replaced by someone too weary, too hardened, to be the woman he remembered? The thought made her stomach clench, a knot of anxiety tightening beneath the joy, and she gripped the counter harder, her nails digging into the wood.

Shirin and Simin wove around her ankles demanding attention and affection, their fur soft and warm, Shirin's tabby stripes glinting in the sunlight streaming through the window, Simin's grey coat sleek as she purred, her green eyes watching Zahra with quiet understanding. The cats had been her companions through lonely nights, their warmth a small comfort when Reza's absence left the bed cold, the house silent save for the drip of the faucet or the distant rumble of wartime planes.

Zahra knelt to stroke them, her fingers sinking into their fur, the purrs vibrating through her, grounding her as tears pricked her eyes—not just of grief, but of hope tangled with fear, a rare emotion after years of rationed food, air raid drills, and volunteering at the relief centre, where she cooked and distributed bread, her hands steady but her heart heavy with worry for Reza.

The Moonlit Rose of Isfahan

The sound of the postman's bicycle bell outside snapped her from her thoughts, the familiar clink of metal and crunch of gravel stirring her to her feet. She hurried to the door. The courtyard garden, visible through the open door, was a small oasis of resilience, its roses and lavender blooming despite the war's shadow, their petals vibrant but dusted with summer's heat, the scent heavy in the air.

The postman, a wiry man with a sun-weathered face, handed her a single envelope, its paper worn but intact, Reza's familiar handwriting scrawled across it, the ink slightly smudged, the sight sending a jolt through her heart.

"For you, *khanoum*," he said, his voice kind but tired, tipping his cap before pedalling away. Zahra clutched the letter, her fingers trembling, the paper warm from the sun, and returned to the kitchen, sinking onto a cushioned stool, the cats curling at her feet, their purrs a soft encouragement.

She opened the envelope carefully, the paper crinkling, revealing a single sheet folded tightly, the ink dark and bold, Reza's words leaping from the page like a melody. She read aloud, her voice soft but steady, the words filling the quiet kitchen: My dearest Zahra, my rose, my light in this endless night. The rumours of peace have reached us here on the front, whispers of a UN resolution that might end this madness. For the first time in years, I feel a spark of hope, a belief that this war will end, that I'll be back in your arms soon, holding you under our garden's jasmine, kissing you as we did in Shiraz, our love unbroken by these years apart.

Her voice caught, tears spilling down her cheeks, the salt warm on her lips, the paper trembling in her hands. Reza's optimism, so rare in his letters—usually heavy with the weight of battle, the loss of Hossein and other comrades, the fear of chemical attacks and longing for her— felt like a gift, a promise that the man she loved, the affectionate Reza beneath the soldier's scars, was still there. But as she read on, she detected something else threaded through his words, a hesitation that made her heart ache.

The letter continued, his handwriting slightly less steady: Yet, my rose, I confess a fear that haunts me in the quiet moments between battles. I am not the man who left you in 1980. This war has changed me in ways I cannot yet name—I have seen things, done things, that no amount of your rosewater letters can wash away. I carry scars, some visible, others buried deep where even I cannot reach them. What if I come home and you see a stranger in my eyes? What if the poet you married is gone, replaced by someone hollowed out by eight years of death and smoke? I fear I will disappoint you, that I won't know how to be a husband again, how to laugh or dream or love the way we once did. The trenches have taught me survival, not tenderness. What if I've forgotten how to be gentle with you?

Zahra's breath hitched, fresh tears streaming down her face, but these were different—not tears of joy alone, but of recognition, of shared fear. He was afraid too. He wondered if he would be enough for her, just as she wondered if she would be enough for him. The realization cracked something open inside her, a painful tenderness that made her chest ache. They were both broken in their own ways, both changed by the war's cruel hand, both terrified of disappointing the person they loved most.

She clutched the letter tighter, her vision blurring, and kept reading aloud the final lines through her tears: But even with this fear, my love, I cling to hope. I dream of you, my rose, tending our garden, your hands in the soil, your laughter like the *santur's* song. I carry your letters in my pocket, their flowery scent my shield against the smoke and blood. Perhaps we will both be strangers at first, fumbling to find each other again. But I believe—I have to believe—that our love can bridge even eight years of war. That we can rebuild, not just our home, but ourselves, together. That your touch can remind me how to be human again, and my arms can hold you through whatever fears you carry. Soon, we'll rebuild, not just our home, but our life—children, laughter, nights under the stars. I love you, Zahra, more than words, more than life. Please, wait for me a little longer. I am coming home.

Zahra's heart swelled, her fingers tracing his signature, the ink smudged as if his hand shook with emotion, the paper soft from being folded and unfolded, carried close to his heart through the trenches. She imagined him writing it, his hands gripping the pen, his beard that she'd only seen in photos catching the lamplight in a dusty tent, his soulful brown eyes filled with longing for her, the war's end a distant star now within reach. She saw his vulnerability laid bare on the page, and it made her love him even more fiercely. They were both afraid, but they would face that fear together.

She stepped into the garden, the tiles giving way to soft earth, the roses and lavender brushing her dress, their petals velvety under her fingers, their scent a balm to her racing heart. The sun was low now, painting the sky in hues of orange and pink, the air cooling with a breeze rustling the leaves, carrying the faint hum of a neighbour's radio echoing the ceasefire news.

She knelt beside the lavender, her hands sinking into the soil, the earth cool and crumbly, a ritual that had sustained her through the war—tending the garden as a symbol of their love, its blooms defying the bombs, its roots mirroring her resolve to stay in their home, despite Reza's parents' pleas to move to Shiraz with them and Ramin, and her mother pleading to join her in Damascus.

She prayed, her lips moving, thanking God for the ceasefire, for Reza's safety, for the hope of his return, her voice just a whisper: "O God, bring him home to me, whole in body and soul, let our love bloom again. Give us the strength to find each other through the changes, to be patient with the strangers we've become, to rebuild what the war tried to destroy. Let him see that I still love him, scars and all. Let me be brave enough to show him who I've become, and trust that he will love me still."

Zahra returned to the kitchen, pressed Reza's letter to her chest, and sat at the table, the radio now playing a soft melody. She imagined meeting Reza there, in that space beyond time and distance, their bodies entwined as they were in 1980, their honeymoon nights in Shiraz filled with shy touches, laughter, and the discovery of each other's bodies. The memory stirred a warmth in her core, a longing for his touch more than ever before, and his poetry, his love that had endured through letters, through loss, through the war's cruelty.

But now, that longing was threaded with something deeper—not just desire for the young man she'd married, but acceptance of the man he would be, and hope that he would accept the woman she'd become. She would not hide her scars from him. She would show him her her grief for Hossein and her fierce strength forged in his absence just as much as she would show him everything good that was gained. And she would ask him to show her his wounds too, the ones on his body and the ones in his soul. They would learn each other again, slowly, tenderly, two people remade by war trying to remember how to be two people in love.

The thought of him really returning to her after almost a decade was almost surreal, like she was in a dream that she would wake up from. Zahra fantasized about Reza's return for a few more moments and then took out her writing supplies wrote a reply, her pen scratching softly, the ink flowing like her emotions.

My Reza,

My poet, your letter is a light in this long darkness. The radio speaks of peace, and my heart sings with yours. But I hear your fear, and I must confess my own—I am not the girl you left behind either. Eight years have changed me, carved lines into my body and my heart that were not there when you kissed me goodbye. I am stronger now, but also more fragile, if that makes sense. I worry that you will come home expecting the shy bride from Shiraz and find instead a woman marked by war, by grief, by loneliness. I worry that I won't know how to be soft for you anymore, that my edges have grown too sharp.

But, my love, if you can accept a wife who has been remade by your absence, then I promise to accept the husband who returns to me, scars and all. We will be strangers at first, yes, fumbling in the dark to find each other's hands. But we will find them. We will learn each other's new shapes, trace the new lines war has drawn on our souls, and perhaps—God willing—we will fall in love all over again, not as the children we were, but as the people we've become. Come home, my love, to our garden, our bed, our life. I wait for you, always. I will wait for you forever if I must, but please, come home soon.

Your Zahra

She sealed it with a kiss, the paper absorbing the salt of her tears, added a dried flower and placed it by the door, ready for the post, her heart lighter than it had been in years. The fear was still there, coiled in her chest beside the hope, but somehow that felt right. Love, she was learning, was not the absence of fear, but the courage to move forward despite it.

Reza was coming home. They were both afraid. And perhaps that was exactly what they needed—to be afraid together, to be vulnerable together, to rebuild their love not on the foundation of who they used to be, but on the truth of who they had become.

Outside, the sun dipped below the horizon, and the first stars began to appear, bright and steady in the darkening sky. Zahra stood at the window, watching them emerge one by one, and thought of Reza somewhere far away, perhaps looking at the same stars. The war would end soon. He would come home. And together, they would learn to be husband and wife again, one careful step at a time, their love a bridge across eight years of sorrow and change, as fragile and as enduring as the jasmine blooming in their war-torn garden.

Chapter Thirty

Shiraz, 1988

The neighbourhood was alive with the gentle hum of daily life—children's laughter echoing from a nearby street, the clatter of a vendor's cart rolling over cobblestones, the faint call to prayer drifting from a distant mosque, its minaret piercing the sky like a needle threading the horizon. Inside, the house was quiet, Fatemeh and Salar resting in their room, their frail frames needing the reprieve after the emotional weight of Reza's return, while Ramin was at his construction site, his absence leaving a stillness broken only by the soft tick of a clock and the occasional chirp of sparrows outside.

Reza and Zahra lingered in the living room, the low wooden table still scattered with crumbs from lunch and the tea now cooling in their glasses. Reza sat on a cushioned stool, deep in thought. His face was softened by the days spent with Zahra, the Persepolis outing, visiting Mahin and her family, and the tender moments reclaiming missed anniversaries, yet his eyes perpetually carried a quiet weight, the war's scars ever-present beneath his rebuilding hope. Zahra sat beside him, her dress flowing over her knees, hair loosely draped under a scarf, eyes bright but thoughtful too, her hands folded in her lap, the fingers still dusted with flour from helping Fatemeh knead dough earlier.

A soft knock at the door startled them, the sound sharp in the afternoon's calm, like a pebble dropped in a still pond. Zahra rose, her dress rustling, and opened the door to find a woman standing there, her presence both unexpected and achingly familiar, like a figure stepping out of a half-remembered dream.

Leyla stood on the threshold, and for a moment, time seemed to collapse—the gentle teacher who'd stood in Reza and Zahra's home her eyes red from tears over Hossein's departure for the front, now transformed into this different woman before them, weathered by grief but radiating quiet strength.

Leyla was a vision of resilience, her kind face framed by a navy headscarf, her dark eyes warm but shadowed with a lingering grief that would never fully fade, her pregnant belly gently swelling under a loose floral dress. Beside her stood her husband, Abbas, a tall man with a neatly trimmed beard and gentle smile, and at their feet, two identical little girls—twin daughters with curious dark eyes and matching pink dresses, both just two years old, their tiny hands clasped together as they peeked shyly around their mother's legs. Leyla's hands, calloused from years of teaching, held a small bouquet of white tulips, their petals a nod to peace, their fragrance mingling with the jasmine air.

"*As-salamu alaikum,*" Leyla said, her voice soft but steady, her eyes meeting Reza's as he rose from his seat, recognition sparking between them like a shared secret. "Reza. Zahra." She paused, her smile tentative but warm. "I know we met so briefly at your home in 1980—it feels like another lifetime now, doesn't it? I heard you were in Shiraz, staying with Ramin. I had to come see you. After all these years of Hossein's letters telling me about you both, after carrying him in my heart for so long... I needed to finally truly know you, the people he loved so much."

Reza's throat tightened, his eyes glistening as he nodded, and the weight of Hossein's memory—a teacher turned soldier, his protector in the trenches, lost five years ago near Ahvaz—came crashing over him like a wave threatening to pull him under. His hands trembled slightly as he stepped forward, and for a moment he couldn't speak, couldn't breathe past the lump in his throat.

This was Hossein's Leyla. The woman whose photograph Hossein had kept wrapped in plastic in his breast pocket, whose letters he'd read by flashlight in the trenches, whose name he'd whispered like a prayer when the shelling grew too close.

The Moonlit Rose of Isfahan

"Leyla," he finally managed, his baritone thick with emotion as he clasped her hand gently, his scarred fingers warm against her skin. "I remember you from that day we left like it was yesterday. Hossein couldn't stop looking at you." His voice cracked. "He spoke of you constantly. Your letters—they kept him going, gave him hope when there was nothing else to hope for. He loved you so deeply."

Zahra's hand found his, squeezing gently, her own eyes soft with shared grief. She remembered that day too—watching her own young husband, her face pale with worry as Reza prepared to leave for basic training after getting his draft notice, the war stealing him away before their marriage could truly begin.

"Please, come in," Zahra said softly, gesturing them inside, her voice melodic but weighted with emotion. "We're honoured you came."

They settled in the living room—Leyla and Abbas on the divan, the twin girls playing quietly on the rug with a wooden toy Abbas pulled from a woven basket, their identical giggles a soft counterpoint to the adults' heavy silence.

The air grew warm with tea poured from the samovar, its cardamom scent filling the room, the glasses steaming as Fatemeh emerged, her wrinkled face lighting up at the sight of guests. Salar followed, his cane tapping, his white beard sparse, his clouded eyes bright with curiosity as introductions were made.

For a long moment, no one spoke. The weight of Hossein's absence filled the room like a physical presence, and Reza found himself staring at Leyla, trying to reconcile the grieving woman from 1980 with this woman before him—pregnant with her third child, her hand resting comfortably on Abbas's knee, her face marked by the years but radiant with hard-won peace.

The juxtaposition was almost unbearable. She had moved on. She had survived. She had built a new life. And Hossein was buried in a cemetery in Khuzestan, his dreams of children and laughter and growing old with this woman reduced to ash and memory.

"I came to pay my respects for Hossein," Leyla began, her voice gentle but steady, the strength of a teacher who had learned to speak through grief. "His loss—" She paused, her breath catching. "It took

Jamila Mikhail

me a long time to accept he wouldn't come back. Almost two years of waiting, of hoping, of denying what I knew in my heart. That we wouldn't have our happy ending. That the life we'd planned—children, a home, all those dreams we wrote about at length in our letters—that it was all gone."

She glanced at Abbas, her expression softening. "But then I found Abbas. He's a teacher too, at my school. He was patient with me, with my grief, with the fact that part of my heart would always belong to Hossein. And we've been building a family together. These are our daughters, Yasmin and Zaynab."

She gestured to the twins, who looked up at the sound of their names, their faces mirror images of innocent curiosity. "And I'm pregnant with our third now. Hossein would have wanted me to be happy. He told me so, in his last letter. He said—" Her voice wavered, tears pooling in her eyes. "He said if he didn't come home, I should find someone who would love me the way he did. That I shouldn't waste my life waiting for a ghost."

Reza felt something crack open inside his chest, a sharp pain that radiated through his ribs. Guilt flooded him—hot, acidic, overwhelming. Why had he survived when Hossein hadn't? Why was he sitting here with Zahra, planning their future, their children, while Hossein's bones lay in a cold grave? What right did he have to happiness when his big brother, his protector, the man who had given his life so he could live, had been robbed of everything?

"He loved you so deeply," Reza said, his voice barely above a whisper, his hand tightening around Zahra's until his knuckles went white. "Your letters truly were his light in the trenches. He carried them everywhere, read them until the paper fell apart, then read them again. He told me—" Reza's voice broke, tears spilling down his cheeks into his beard. "He told me you were the reason he fought so hard. That he was going to come home to you, build a life with you, become a father. He had names picked out for your children. Did you know that?"

Leyla shook her head, fresh tears streaming down her face. "No. He never told me."

"For a boy, Omid. For a girl, Setareh." Reza's chest heaved with sobs he'd been holding back for five years. "Hope and Star. He said those were the two things you gave him—hope that the war would end, and you were his star guiding him home."

The room fell silent except for quiet weeping. Even Abbas had tears in his eyes, his arm wrapped protectively around Leyla as she wept openly, her shoulders shaking. Zahra was crying too, her hand pressed to her mouth, her heart breaking for Hossein, for Leyla, for the future that had been stolen from them both.

"I'm so glad you found happiness, Leyla," Reza continued, forcing the words out past his grief. "Truly. Hossein would be happy for you. He was the most selfless person I've ever known. He died saving me, you know. Pushed me out of the way of shrapnel. His last words were about you. He said—" Reza closed his eyes, the memory searing. "He told me to live for Zahra, and to live for you."

Leyla stood abruptly, crossed to where Reza sat, and pulled him into an embrace. He stiffened at first, then melted into it, sobbing against her shoulder like a child, five years of survivor's guilt pouring out in great, wracking waves. Zahra moved beside them, her arms encircling them both, and they stood there—three people bound by love for a man who would never come home, mourning together in a way that felt both devastating and healing.

When they finally pulled apart, Leyla cupped Reza's face in her hands, her teacher's authority softening into something maternal and kind. "Hossein saved you for a reason, Reza. You have to believe that. He wanted you to live, to come home to Zahra, to build the life he couldn't have. Don't dishonour his sacrifice by drowning in guilt. Live. Love. Have children. Be happy. That's what he died for—so you could have all of that."

Reza nodded, unable to speak, and Leyla turned to Zahra, taking her hands. "Hossein told me so much about you in his letters. How brave you were, staying in Isfahan during the the war. How your letters to Reza smelled like the dried flowers you often included in them and kept him sane. How much he admired your strength. I feel like I already know you, even though we'd only met once in some of the worst circumstances."

Zahra squeezed Leyla's hands, her voice thick with emotion. "Hossein was family to me too. Reza spoke of him constantly, with

Jamila Mikhail

such love. I grieved him as a brother. We're honoured to know you, to see that you've found peace. Thank you for coming. Thank you for sharing him with us one more time."

Abbas spoke then, his voice calm and measured, his hand resting on one twin's head as she leaned against his leg. "Hossein's stories about you, Reza—your poetry, your courage in the trenches, the way you looked after the younger soldiers—they've become part of our family's history. We tell them to the girls sometimes, age-appropriate versions, so they know about him like an uncle they'll never meet but who gave their mother the gift of moving forward. We brought these pomegranates from our garden, a small gift." He gestured to the basket on the table, the fruit's ruby skins gleaming like jewels, a symbol of life persisting.

The visit stretched on, no longer brief but lingering, necessary, cathartic. They talked about Hossein—his terrible jokes, his love of teaching, the way he'd sing off-key in the trenches to make everyone laugh, his fierce protectiveness of those he loved. Leyla shared stories from his letters, moments Reza hadn't known, and Reza shared stories from the front, moments Leyla had never heard. The girls played, oblivious to the weight of the conversation, their laughter a reminder that life continued, that joy could coexist with grief.

As the sun began to dip lower, casting long shadows across the courtyard, Leyla finally stood, the twins tugging at her dress, their small voices asking when they could go home. Abbas gathered the children, and Leyla pressed the white tulips into Zahra's hands, her touch warm, her eyes glistening with fresh tears. "Keep his memory alive," she said, her voice fierce despite the tears. "Tell your children about him someday. Tell them about the man who loved books and teaching and life, who died so others could live. Don't let him be forgotten."

"Never," Reza promised, his throat too tight for more words. The door closed softly behind them, the jasmine air swallowing their footsteps, and the house felt heavier, the weight of Hossein's absence palpable and permanent. Yet the visit had woven a thread of connection, a bridge between past and present, between grief and healing.

The Moonlit Rose of Isfahan

Reza and Zahra stepped outside to the courtyard, needing the open air, needing to breathe after so much emotion. The sun hung low on the horizon now, the breeze carrying the tree's leaves in a gentle dance. They sat on a stone bench under the tree, its shade deepening as evening approached, the leaves casting flickering patterns on their faces, the jasmine vines nearby releasing their fragrance, a soothing contrast to the emotional storm within. The courtyard was small but vibrant, the flowers blooming, their petals soft, the soil dark and fertile, a testament to Ramin's care.

Reza's arm wrapped around Zahra's waist, her head resting on his shoulder, her scarf slipping slightly, revealing her dark hair, gleaming in the fading sunlight. The silence between them was heavy but tender, their hands entwined, his scarred fingers tracing her knuckles, the touch grounding them both. For a long time, neither spoke. They simply sat, processing the afternoon's emotional deluge, the grief that had been reopened and, in some strange way, finally allowed to breathe.

"Leyla's happiness—it's what Hossein would have wanted," Reza said finally, his voice low, rough with emotion, his eyes distant, fixed on the roses. "But seeing her, seeing those beautiful children, her life moving forward—" His voice cracked. "It brings him back so vividly. The trenches, his laughter, the way he'd recite poetry to the younger soldiers to calm them during bombardments. His letters to her, how carefully he wrote them, how he'd ask me to check his spelling because he wanted them to be perfect, even if he was the teacher! God, Zahra, I miss him. I miss him so much it still hurts to breathe sometimes."

His shoulders shook with silent sobs, and Zahra tightened her grip on his hand, her own tears falling freely now. "He's with us, Reza," she said softly but firmly. "In our love, in this garden, in every choice we make to keep living despite the pain. Leyla's strength reminds me of ours—we've endured too. We've survived. And we owe it to Hossein, to everyone we lost, to build something beautiful with the life we've been given."

Reza nodded slowly, his face buried in her shoulder, and they sat that way for a long time, holding each other as the light faded and the first stars began to appear. When he finally lifted his head, his eyes were red but clearer, as if Leyla's visit had lanced some infected wound in his soul, letting the poison drain even as it hurt.

"Seeing Leyla's children," Zahra said gently, her voice careful, "seeing her pregnant again—it made me think about what we talked about before. About our own children. Our own future."

Reza was quiet for a moment, his thumb tracing circles on her hand. "When we married," he said finally, his voice wistful, "we promised each other at least two children, remember? Laughter in our home, little feet running through the garden." He paused, his brow furrowing, shadows crossing his face. "I want that, Zahra. More than anything, I want to see you pregnant, to hold our child, to build a family with you. But—"

He stopped, struggling with words, and Zahra waited, patient, her hand steady in his. "But the war took so much from me," he continued, his voice breaking. "Hossein, my strength, my certainty about the world. I used to think I knew what kind of man I was, what kind of father I'd be. Now I don't know anything. I have nightmares, Zahra. I wake up screaming, thinking I'm back in the trenches, thinking I'm dying. Sometimes I can't go to the market because the crowds feel like enemy soldiers closing in. What kind of father would I be, traumatized like this? What if I scare our children? What if I fail them the way that I—"

He couldn't finish, but Zahra understood. *What if I fail them the way I failed Hossein by being unable to save him?* The guilt was still there, raw and festering, survivor's guilt that no amount of Leyla's forgiveness could fully heal.

"Reza, my darling," Zahra said, shifting to face him, her hands cupping his face, her thumbs brushing his beard, the grey strands coarse but beloved. Her voice was steady, bright with an optimism he desperately needed. "I have fears too. I'm afraid of childbirth, afraid of losing myself in motherhood, afraid that I won't be a good enough mother because I've spent years alone after my own mother left. But look around—the country is rebuilding. Iran is healing. Children are playing in the streets again. The economy will grow, shops will open, life will return to normal. We'll make a home for our children, filled with love, protected by us. That optimism we had after the revolution, we'll have it again."

Her eyes searched his, fierce and determined. "You're not broken, Reza. You're healing. Yes, you have nightmares. Yes, the crowds overwhelm you sometimes. But you're here. You came home. You're trying. That's what our children will see—not a traumatized soldier, but a father who fought for their future, who loved their mother enough to survive hell and come home. They'll be so proud of you."

Reza's eyes glistened with fresh tears, but these were different—tinged with hope instead of just grief. "You really believe that?" he whispered.

"I know it," Zahra said firmly. "And we'll do this together, Reza. We won't rush. Once your engineering work is steady—those roads, those bridges you'll help rebuild—and once I've graduated from university, we'll fill our home with laughter, with our children's voices. We'll take our time. We'll heal first, then we'll grow our family."

He pulled her closer, his lips pressing against her forehead, lingering there as he breathed her in—rosewater and jasmine and uniquely Zahra. "I mean it about university, Zahra," he said, his voice earnest, pulling back to look into her eyes. "Your mind—your words, your strength, your brilliant, beautiful mind—it's too precious to leave untended. Even if you choose to focus on our home and children after, give yourself that chance to grow, to learn, to become everything you're capable of being. You deserve it. You deserve the world."

Zahra's cheeks flushed, her heart swelling with love for this man who believed in her even when she sometimes struggled to believe in herself. "I will, Reza," she promised, her voice warm, leaning in to kiss him. Their lips met, soft and lingering, the taste of salt and tea and shared tears, a promise sealed under the stars. "We'll build that future together—children, learning, love, everything. We'll honour Hossein by living fully, by loving fiercely, by not wasting a single moment of this second chance we've been given."

They sat huddled under the tree for a long time, their love a root in the healing earth, the future a bloom waiting to unfold. Above them, stars pierced the deepening blue, one by one, like prayers being answered. Somewhere, Hossein was at peace. Leyla had found happiness. And they—Reza and Zahra—were finally beginning to believe that happiness was possible for them too, that the war hadn't stolen everything, that love could rebuild what violence had destroyed.

In the quiet of the courtyard, with Zahra in his arms and the promise of tomorrow stretching before them, Reza allowed himself to hope. Not the desperate, clinging hope of a soldier in the trenches, but something softer, gentler—the hope of a man who had survived and was learning, slowly, painfully, to live again.

Chapter Thirty-One

Shiraz, 1988

The stars had fully emerged by the time Reza and Zahra returned from the courtyard, their hands still entwined, their hearts still heavy with the afternoon's emotions. The house wrapped itself in the hush of evening, Fatemeh and Salar having retired to their room after supper, their voices a low murmur of contentment at having their son home. Ramin had excused himself to his own quarters, his weary body needing rest after a long day at the construction site. The hallway was quiet, lit only by a single lamp in the living room, its golden light fading into shadows.

The weight of Hossein's memory, of Leyla's visit, of the future they'd discussed—it all pressed down on them like a physical thing, leaving them drained but also strangely cleansed, as if the tears they'd shed had washed away some layer of accumulated grief. They moved through the house in silence, their footsteps soft on the tiled floor, until they reached the small bathroom at the back—a modest space with pale blue tiles and a deep porcelain tub, already filled with warm water that Fatemeh had thoughtfully prepared earlier.

"Let me tend to you," Zahra whispered, her voice soft in the quiet space. Reza nodded, too tired and too raw to protest, and let her help him undress, her fingers gentle as she unbuttoned his shirt, peeling away the layers that had absorbed the day's emotions, the heavy ones and those that had left him feeling both hopeful and terrified.

She guided him into the tub first, the warm water enveloping him like an embrace, and he sank down with a sigh that seemed to come from his very soul. Zahra slipped in after him, settling behind him so his back rested against her chest, her arms wrapping around him from behind. For a long moment they simply sat that way, the water lapping gently at their skin, the warmth seeping into tired muscles and aching hearts.

"You carry so much," Zahra murmured against his shoulder blade, pressing a kiss there, her lips soft against his skin. She reached for the olive oil soap, working it into a lather between her hands before beginning to wash him—slow, tender strokes across his shoulders, down his arms, tracing the familiar topography of scars and muscle. Her touch was reverent, loving, each pass of her hands a prayer of gratitude that he was here, alive, home.

Reza's eyes drifted closed, his head falling back against her shoulder. "I don't know how you do it," he whispered. "How you hold me together when I feel like I'm falling apart."

"Because you did the same for me," she replied softly, her hands moving to his chest, washing away the day's dust and sweat and tears. "For eight years, your letters held me together. Your words. Your love. Even if you didn't realize it back then. Now it's my turn to hold you."

She washed his hair next, her fingers massaging his scalp, working the soap through the greying strands of his beard and hair, rinsing it away with a small bowl, the water running in rivulets down his face. He turned in the tub then, careful in the confined space, until he faced her. Their eyes met in the lamplight, and something shifted—the grief was still there, would always be there, but beneath it burned something else. Love. Desire. The fierce need to reclaim what the war had tried to steal.

"My turn," Reza said, his voice rough with emotion. He took the soap from her, lathering it between his palms before beginning to wash her with the same tender care she'd shown him. His hands moved across her shoulders, down her arms, cupping water to rinse away the soap, revealing skin that glowed in the lamplight. He washed her hair, his fingers gentle as they worked through the dark strands, massaging her scalp until she hummed with contentment, her eyes closing, her face softening into an expression of pure trust.

The Moonlit Rose of Isfahan

"You're so beautiful," he murmured, his lips brushing her temple. "Eight years I dreamed of this. Of having you in my arms again. Of being allowed to touch you, to care for you."

Zahra opened her eyes, reaching up to cup his face, her thumb tracing the line of his beard. "I'm here," she whispered. "We're here. Together. Finally. I've waited a long time for those hands of yours to wander my body!"

They stayed in the bath until the water began to cool, washing away the day's heaviness, the salt of tears, the weight of grief. When they finally emerged, Reza dried her first, wrapping her in a soft towel, patting the moisture from her skin with gentle reverence. She did the same for him, her touches lingering on the scars she knew so well, each one a story of survival, a testament to his return.

"Wait here," Reza said softly, disappearing into the guest room at the back of the house where they would sleep. Zahra heard him moving about, and when he emerged a few minutes later, she couldn't help but smile.

He wore his military uniform—the olive-green jacket with its medals gleaming even in the dim lamplight, the trousers pressed, his posture somehow straighter, more commanding. It had become a game they played, one Reza knew Zahra loved. The uniform had once been a symbol of everything miserable in Reza's life, but now it was different—a playful reclamation of intimacy, a way to merge the commander and the poet, the soldier and the husband.

"My commander," Zahra breathed, her eyes traveling over him with open appreciation. She'd put on a thin silk robe of pale rose, her damp hair falling loose over her shoulders, and she felt the familiar flutter of anticipation in her belly, the same feeling she'd had on their wedding night, when everything was new and clumsy and beautiful.

Reza's eyes darkened with desire, but there was tenderness there too, love threading through passion. He extended his hand. "Come with me my rose, Commander's orders."

The guest bedroom felt like a sanctuary for them both. The window was cracked open, letting in the cool night breeze, carrying the heady fragrance of jasmine from the courtyard vines, mingling with the lingering scent of rosewater from Zahra's hair. Reza closed the door behind them, the soft click a promise of privacy, of intimacy reclaimed once more. A soothing melody playing on a neighbour's radio drifted through the open window, weaving through the air like a thread of faith, a reminder that they had endured, that they had been brought back together against all odds.

He led her to the bed, and she sat on the edge, looking up at him with eyes that shimmered with love and desire and something deeper—gratitude that after everything, after eight years of separation and war and grief, they were here. Together. Alive.

"My poet," she murmured as he knelt before her, his hands gently parting the robe to reveal her skin, warm and glowing in the lamplight. His touch was reverent, his scarred fingers tracing the curve of her knee, her thigh, mapping her body with the care of a man who had dreamed of this moment in trenches and foxholes, who had held onto the memory of her like a lifeline.

"Live the love that kindles your soul's flame," he whispered, his lips brushing her collarbone, and she recognized the words of Rumi, the ancient poet whose verses had threaded through their love from the beginning. His kisses traveled lower, tender and unhurried, each one a vow, a reminder that they were rebuilding what the war had tried to destroy.

Zahra's fingers found the buttons of his uniform jacket, working them open one by one, revealing the thin undershirt beneath, the body she knew by heart—scarred but strong, marked by survival. She pushed the jacket from his shoulders, the medals clinking softly as it fell, and pulled him up onto the bed beside her. They lay facing each other, the quilts soft beneath them, their bodies aligned, and for a moment they simply gazed at one another, drinking in the reality of this—of being together, of being home.

"I love you," Zahra breathed. "I love you so much it frightens me sometimes. The thought of losing you again—"

"Shh," Reza silenced her with a kiss, deep and slow, tasting of salt and tea and promise. "I'm here. I'm home. And I'm never leaving you like that again."

Their lovemaking was slow, deliberate, each touch infused with years to make up for. Reza worshipped her body with his hands and

The Moonlit Rose of Isfahan

lips, relearning every curve, every response, murmuring poetry against her skin—fragments of Rumi and Hafez mixed with his own words, turning her into verse, into song. Zahra responded with equal tenderness, her hands exploring the familiar landscape of his body, tracing the scars she'd come to love like they were sacred texts, each one a story she wanted to honour.

"In your beauty is how I make verses," he whispered against her throat, his voice rough with desire, and she arched into him, her breath hitching as pleasure built like a tide. The lamplight flickered across their bodies, casting shadows that danced across the cream walls, and outside the scented breeze carried the sound of night birds, of distant music, of a world slowly healing.

When they finally joined, it was with a shared sigh that seemed to echo through the small room, through their very souls. The rhythm they found was ancient and new all at once, a dance of bodies that remembered each other despite the years, moving together with an intimacy that transcended the physical. Zahra's hands gripped his shoulders, feeling the strength there, the solid reality of him, and tears slipped from the corners of her eyes—not from pain but from the overwhelming rightness of this moment, of being whole again.

"My moonlit rose," Reza breathed, his forehead pressed to hers, their breath mingling. "My sanctuary. My home."

"My commander," she whispered back, her voice breaking. "My poet. My heart."

The pleasure built slowly, wave upon wave, until it crested and broke over them both, leaving them breathless and trembling, clutching each other as if afraid to let go. Reza collapsed beside her, gathering her into his arms, and they lay tangled together, their hearts gradually slowing, their breathing evening out. The room settled into a peaceful quiet. Somewhere in the distance, a dog barked, and farther still, the faint sound of a *santur* drifted from a neighbour's radio, its plucked strings like a heartbeat, like a lullaby.

Zahra nestled closer, her head on Reza's chest, listening to the steady thrum of his heart beneath her ear. His hand stroked her hair absently, his fingers gentle, and she could feel the tension of the day finally beginning to drain from his body, replaced by a deep, bone-weary contentment.

"Nights like this," she murmured, her voice drowsy, "they make up for the stolen moments. For the years apart. For all the nights I slept alone in our bed in Isfahan, wondering if you were alive, if you were thinking of me."

Reza pressed a kiss to the top of her head, his lips lingering in her hair. "They do, my rose. And we'll have many more. Our love is a garden that blooms eternal, remember? Through war and peace, through grief and joy, through everything. It endures. May neither one of us ever forget that, especially in moments of doubt."

She tilted her face up to look at him, her almond eyes luminous in the lamplight. "Do you really believe that? After everything we've been through, everything the war took from us—from you—do you really believe our love can survive it all? That it will be enough?"

He cupped her face in his hands, his thumbs brushing away the fresh tears that had gathered at the corners of her eyes. "I have to believe it, Zahra. Because without that belief, without this—" he gestured at the space between them, at the tangle of their bodies, at the room that held them like a prayer, "—without this love, I don't know who I am anymore. You are the thread that holds me together. You always have been."

She kissed him then, soft and slow, tasting the truth of his words on his lips. When they pulled apart, she settled back against his chest, her arm draped across his waist, her leg tangled with his. The uniform jacket lay discarded on the floor beside the bed, the medals catching the lamplight, and Zahra found herself staring at them—symbols of his service, of his survival, of the eight years that had carved them both into different people.

"Reza?" she said quietly.

"Mm?"

"What Leyla said today—about Hossein wanting you to live, to be happy, to have the life he couldn't have—she was right, you know. You honour him by being here, by loving me, by building our future. Not by drowning in guilt."

Reza was quiet for a long moment, his hand stilling in her hair. When he spoke, his voice was thick with emotion. "I know that in my

The Moonlit Rose of Isfahan

head. But my heart—it's harder to convince. The guilt, it's like a weight I can't put down. Every time I'm happy, every time I laugh or feel joy, there's this voice that says I don't deserve it. That Hossein should be here instead of me. That I'm alive because he died."

Zahra pushed herself up on one elbow, looking down at him with fierce intensity. "Then I'll say it every day if I have to. You deserve this. You deserve happiness, and love, and a future filled with children and laughter and peace. Hossein died so you could have that. Don't make his sacrifice meaningless by not allowing yourself to live."

He pulled her back down to him, holding her tightly, his face buried in her hair. "Say it again," he whispered, his voice breaking. "Please. I need to hear it."

"You deserve this," she repeated, her lips against his ear. "You deserve love. You deserve happiness. You deserve to live, Reza. You deserve every beautiful thing this life has to offer. And I will spend the rest of my days making sure you never forget it."

They held each other as the night deepened around them. The war was over. They had survived. And here, in this small room in Shiraz, wrapped in each other's arms, they began the slow, painful, beautiful work of learning to live again.

Eventually, exhaustion claimed them both. Zahra's breathing evened out first, her body going soft and pliant against his, and Reza listened to the rhythm of it, matching his own breath to hers, finding a kind of peace in the synchronicity. His eyes grew heavy, the lamplight blurring at the edges of his vision, and for the first time in longer than he could remember, he wasn't afraid of sleep. Wasn't afraid of the nightmares that usually waited in the darkness.

Because Zahra was here. Because her arms were around him. Because her love was a shield against the demons that haunted him, and her presence was proof that he had made it home, that he had survived not just the war but everything that came after—the grief, the guilt, the fear that he would never be whole again.

As sleep finally took him, his last conscious thought was of Hossein—not the dying soldier in the trench, but the laughing teacher before the war, quoting from books and making terrible jokes, his arm slung around Reza's shoulders like the big brother he was. And Reza sent a silent prayer into the darkness: *Thank you for saving me. For giving me this chance. I promise I won't waste it. I promise I'll live for both of us.*

The lamp burned low, its flame flickering one last time before Reza reached out and extinguished it, plunging the room into darkness softened only by starlight filtering through the window. In that darkness, held safe in Zahra's arms, Reza finally let go of the day's emotions, the afternoon's tears, the weight of survivor's guilt that would take years to fully release. For now, it was enough to be here. To be loved. To be home.

Outside, Shiraz slept, its ancient stones holding the memories of a thousand wars, a thousand loves, a thousand stories of loss and survival. And in a small room in the back of a modest house, two people who had been torn apart by violence found each other again in tenderness, their love a quiet rebellion against everything that had tried to destroy them, a testament to the enduring power of hope in even the darkest times.

Chapter Thirty-Two

Isfahan, 1988

The late afternoon sun bathed Isfahan in a golden glow as Reza and Zahra returned from their weeklong trip to Shiraz, the small borrowed car rumbling along the dusty roads, its engine humming softly, the scent of sun-warmed leather and the faint jasmine from Shiraz's gardens lingering inside. The city unfolded before them, its turquoise domes and minarets gleaming against the clear autumn sky, a gentle breeze carrying the earthy tang of fallen leaves and the distant aroma of baking bread from a nearby *tannur*. The war, officially ended by the UN ceasefire in August, had left scars—cracked walls from distant bombings, quieter streets missing familiar faces—but the air felt lighter, the hope of peace settling like dust after a storm.

Reza pulled up to the Heydari house first, parking the car carefully in their small yard beside the geraniums that bloomed bright red against the stone wall. This time, his face had been softened by the Shiraz trip—the tearful reunion with his parents, reconnecting with Mahin, the unexpected visit from Leyla, the romantic day at Persepolis, and the tender nights in Ramin's guest bedroom. His soulful brown eyes carried a new lightness, the weight of the war—Hossein's death, his own wounds, the years of survival—still present but less crushing as he returned to the life he had before, his heart buoyed by Zahra's love and the promise of rebuilding.

Zahra stepped out beside him, her dress flowing, her hair loose under a scarf, her almond eyes bright with joy at being home as she carried a woven basket of gifts from Shiraz—pomegranates, their ruby skins gleaming, and a jar of rosewater syrup. The week in Shiraz had woven them closer, their love a steady root, their talk of children and her university plans a bloom of hope.

Mrs. Heydari emerged before they could knock, her stout frame wrapped in a floral scarf, her face creasing into a warm smile. "Zahra, Reza, welcome home!" she exclaimed, her voice rich with genuine pleasure. Her husband appeared behind her, a wiry man with kind eyes, wiping his hands on a cloth.

"The car served us perfectly," Reza said, handing Mr. Heydari the keys, his voice warm with gratitude. "We cannot thank you enough—for the car, for watching over our home, for caring for our cats. You've been more than neighbours. You've been family."

Zahra pressed the basket into Mrs. Heydari's hands, the bread still warm, wrapped carefully in cloth. "This is nothing compared to your kindness, but please—fresh *noon-e barbari* from Shiraz, and *fesenjan* made by Reza's mother. She sends her regards and thanks as well."

Mrs. Heydari's eyes glistened as she accepted the gifts, pulling Zahra into a tight embrace. "Your cats were angels, truly. Well, Shirin was an angel. Simin tried to dig up half your lavender and brought me two dead mice as gifts, if they can be called such a thing!" She laughed, the sound full of affection. "But your garden is thriving. We watered it every evening, just as you asked."

Mr. Heydari clapped Reza on the shoulder, his grip firm. "It was our honour, Reza. You've given enough for this country. The least we can do is watch over your home while you reconnect with your family."

They lingered a few more minutes, exchanging stories and making plans for tea later in the week, before Reza and Zahra finally walked the short distance to their own home, their fingers intertwined, their hearts full. The familiar sight of their whitewashed walls and the jasmine vines climbing the gate made Zahra's breath catch—after a week away, even this short absence had felt too long.

The moment they opened the gate to their courtyard, two furry missiles launched themselves at Zahra's legs. Shirin and Simin wove around her ankles in figure eights, their purring so loud it sounded like small motors, their bodies vibrating with joy. Their fur caught the afternoon light, gleaming as if they'd both been grooming themselves in preparation for their return.

"Oh, my sweet ones!" Zahra laughed, setting down her bag to kneel on the courtyard tiles, which were still warm from the sun. "Did you miss us? Were you good for Mrs. Heydari?"

Simin immediately wanted to climb into her lap, head-butting her with such force that Zahra was taken aback, while Shirin wove around Reza's legs, meowing insistently until he bent down to scoop her up. The cat immediately began kneading his chest, her claws catching slightly in his tunic, her purr rumbling against his heart.

"I think Shirin missed you more," Zahra teased, watching as the normally reserved tabby melted into a puddle of affection in Reza's arms.

Reza pressed his face into Shirin's fur, breathing in the familiar scent—dust and sunshine and something indefinably cat-like. "I missed them too," he admitted, his voice muffled. "It's strange, isn't it? How much comfort these little creatures bring. During the war, I used to dream about coming home to them too. To you and them. This exact moment."

Zahra looked up at him, Simin still purring in her arms, and her eyes shimmered with emotion. "Hossein knew," she said softly. "When he gave them to us, he knew we'd need them. That they'd be our comfort when he couldn't be here himself."

The moment hung between them, bittersweet and tender, before Simin broke it by launching herself out of Zahra's arms to chase a leaf skittering across the courtyard. They both laughed, the heaviness lifting, and spent the next several minutes simply playing with the cats—dangling strands of jasmine vine for them to bat at, watching them stalk invisible prey through the roses, marvelling at how something so simple could feel so healing.

Eventually they made their way inside, the cats following like furry shadows. The house welcomed them with familiar silence—everything was exactly as they'd left it, yet somehow it felt different. Lighter. More like a beginning than a continuation.

Jamila Mikhail

That first evening back passed in quiet domesticity. Reza lit the samovar, the hiss of steam and cardamom filling the air, while Zahra unpacked their bags, hanging up clothes and tucking away the small treasures they'd brought from Shiraz—a pressed flower from Persepolis, a smooth stone from Ramin's courtyard, a recipe card written in Fatemeh's shaky handwriting. They ate a simple dinner of leftover *barbari* bread and cheese, sitting cross-legged on cushions in the living room while the cats curled between them, and talked about nothing and everything—the trip, the neighbours, the way the light hit the courtyard differently now that autumn had truly arrived.

As darkness fell, they retreated to their bedroom, and Reza recited Hafez to her in the lamplight while she ran her fingers through his hair, and their lovemaking was slow and tender, unhurried, the kind that spoke of having all the time in the world instead of only three short weeks in 1980. Afterward, Zahra fell asleep first, her body curved into his, and Reza lay awake listening to her breathe, feeling the solid weight of Simin at his feet, and thought: *This is what I survived for. This exact peace.*

The next morning dawned clear and cool, autumn settling more firmly over Isfahan. Zahra woke first, slipping from bed carefully so as not to disturb Reza, and padded barefoot to the kitchen to make tea. She found him a half hour later in the courtyard, already tending to the garden, his hands in the soil, examining the roses that had bloomed in their absence.

"The Heydaris did well," he said without looking up, his fingers gentle as he deadheaded a spent bloom. "But the lavender needs trimming, and I think we should move this rose—it's getting too much shade here."

Zahra set down the tea tray on the wooden bench and knelt beside him, her dress pooling in the dirt. "Then let's move it together. Where were you thinking?"

They spent the morning working side by side, their hands in the earth, transplanting the rose to a sunnier spot near the jasmine vines, trimming back the lavender, pulling weeds that had sprung up despite the neighbours' care. It was mundane, ordinary work—the kind of thing Zahra had done alone for eight years—but doing it together

The Moonlit Rose of Isfahan

transformed it into something sacred. Reza's presence beside her, his quiet commentary about root systems and soil drainage, the brush of his shoulder against hers as they worked—it made her heart ache with gratitude.

Halfway through, they abandoned the gardening entirely to lie on their backs in the grass, staring up at the sky through the jasmine leaves, their hands loosely intertwined. A cloud shaped like a bird drifted past, and Reza pointed it out, which led to a game of finding shapes, which dissolved into laughter when Zahra insisted she saw a teapot and Reza argued it was clearly a boot.

"Read to me," Zahra said eventually, rolling onto her side to face him, propping her head on her hand.

Reza didn't need to ask what she wanted. He closed his eyes, and his voice took on that particular cadence that meant he was reciting from memory, pulling up verses that had sustained him through the war:

"When I sought the world's secret from the Wise One, the answer came softly," he whispered, quoting Rumi, "some mysteries cannot be spoken, but rest in silence."

Zahra's eyes filled with tears—not sad ones, but the kind that came from beauty, from recognition. "That's what we're doing, isn't it? Discovering it. The secret of the world, here in our garden."

"Yes," Reza said simply, reaching up to brush a tear from her cheek. "I think we are."

They stayed there until the sun climbed high and the air grew warm, forcing them to retreat to the shade of the mulberry tree. Shirin appeared from wherever she'd been hunting, depositing a dead mouse at Zahra's feet with obvious pride before settling in for a grooming session, while Simin stalked the lavender as if it might suddenly sprout legs and run.

The days that followed settled into a gentle rhythm. In the mornings, they worked in the garden—sometimes actually working, sometimes simply existing in that space together, reading poetry or talking or sitting in comfortable silence like they'd done during their courtship and early marriage. Reza repaired the courtyard gate, which had started to sag, and rebuilt a section of the stone border around the roses.

Zahra spent hours with her hands in the soil, replanting bulbs for spring, pruning back the jasmine that had grown wild in their absence, all while Reza watched and recited Hafez, or sometimes simply watched lovingly and encouragingly, his eyes soft with an affection that made her blush like a new bride.

One afternoon, Zahra looked up from where she was kneeling by the roses to find him staring at her with such intensity that she laughed. "What?" she asked, self-consciously tucking a strand of hair behind her ear, aware that she was probably smudged with dirt.

"You," he said, his voice rough with emotion. "Just you. I spent eight years trying to hold onto the memory of you, and now you're here, real, solid, with dirt on your nose and your dress hiked up around your knees, and you're so much more than memory. You're everything."

Zahra set down her gardening shears and crossed to where he sat on the bench, settling into his lap despite her dirty hands, uncaring that she was probably getting soil all over his clean tunic. She kissed him thoroughly, tasting tea and sunshine and home, and whispered against his lips, "Then look your fill, my poet. I'm not going anywhere."

That evening, after a simple dinner of rice and stew, they sprawled on cushions in the living room, the lamp burning low, a book of Hafez open between them. Reza read aloud while Zahra listened, her head pillowed on his thigh, Simin purring on her stomach, Shirin curled against Reza's hip. The words washed over them, beautiful and timeless:

"His eye is the mirror-holder which reflects His expression."

Zahra turned her face up to look at him. "You do," she said softly. "Every day, you show me. Your love is a mirror that reflects me back to myself, and to God, whole and worthy."

Reza set aside the book, his hand coming to rest on her hair, stroking through the dark strands. "And yours does the same for me. I was so lost, Zahra. So broken. But your love—it's teaching me how to be human again. How to be more than just a survivor."

They made love that night with a tenderness that bordered on

The Moonlit Rose of Isfahan

worship, their bodies speaking what words couldn't fully capture—gratitude, wonder, the fierce joy of being alive and together and home. Afterward, as they lay tangled in the sheets, the lamp extinguished, the room dark save for starlight filtering through the window, Zahra thought about how much had changed and how much had stayed the same. The war had carved them both into different shapes, had left scars that would never fully fade, but this—their love, their connection, the sanctuary they'd built together—this had not only survived but deepened.

As the days went on, their little bubble of domestic bliss felt both fragile and unshakeable, like something that could be destroyed by the outside world but that would also somehow endure no matter what came. They sat in the garden as the sun began to set, the air cooling, the jasmine releasing its evening perfume. Reza had his arm around Zahra's waist, her head on his shoulder, and they watched as Shirin stalked something in the roses while Simin rolled in a patch of fading sunlight, her belly exposed in absolute trust.

"Reza," Zahra said quietly, breaking the comfortable silence. "Your engineering job in Tehran—it starts next month, doesn't it?"

She felt him tense slightly, his arm tightening around her. "Yes. Two months of bridge and road work. It's important—necessary for rebuilding. But the thought of leaving you so soon after coming home—" His voice caught. "Eight years apart wasn't enough? Now I have to leave again? I don't think I'll ever get used to that, no matter how well I'm doing."

Zahra turned in his arms to face him, her hands framing his face. "Then I'll come to you," she said firmly. "Not every day, but I could visit. Stay for a few weeks maybe I could even see Farhad while I'm in Tehran—my half-brother is so busy with his farm and his job, but it's been too long since we've properly connected. We'll make it work, Reza. We've survived eight years of war. We can survive two months of occasional separation."

Relief and love flooded his face in equal measure. "You'd do that? Come to Tehran?"

"Of course I would," she said, as if it were the most obvious thing in the world. "You're my husband. My heart. Where you go, I go—maybe not every step, but enough. Always enough."

He kissed her then, deep and grateful, and when they pulled apart his eyes were bright with unshed tears. "I love you," he said, his voice fierce. "God, Zahra, I love you so much. You make everything bearable. You make everything possible."

"Good," she said with a small smile, settling back against his chest. "Because you're stuck with me, Commander. For better or worse, for war and peace, for every mundane domestic moment and every grand adventure. You're mine, and I'm yours, and that's how it's going to stay."

Reza's response was lost in her hair as he buried his face in it, breathing in the scent of rosewater and lavender and home. His arms wrapped around her more tightly, and they sat that way as the stars emerged one by one, as the temperature dropped and the jasmine's perfume intensified, as the cats eventually tired of their games and came to curl at their feet.

"Tell me about the bridges," Zahra said eventually, her voice soft in the gathering darkness. "The ones you'll be working on. I want to be able to picture you there, to know what you're building."

So Reza described them—the damaged overpasses that needed reinforcement, the roadways that required new foundations, the technical challenges of rebuilding infrastructure in a country still recovering from war. His voice grew animated as he talked about load-bearing calculations and steel reinforcements, about how each bridge represented a connection restored, a pathway rebuilt, a promise that Iran would recover.

Zahra listened with her eyes closed, seeing it all in her mind—her husband with his engineering plans spread out before him, his hands steady as he measured and calculated, his mind sharp despite the trauma he carried, building something concrete and useful and hopeful. Pride swelled in her chest, fierce and warm.

"You're going to rebuild this country," she said when he finished, her voice thick with emotion. "You and people like you. You're going to take all this destruction and turn it into something beautiful. Something lasting."

"We'll rebuild it you and I," he corrected gently. "You with your university education, your literature, your strength. Me with my bridges. Our future children with their hope and energy. All of us together, making something new from the ashes."

The mention of children made Zahra's breath catch, a warmth blooming low in her belly—not desire exactly, but something deeper. Possibility. The future they'd talked about in Shiraz suddenly felt more real, more tangible. Children running through this courtyard, learning to tend these roses, playing with the descendants of Shirin and Simin. A family built in the shadow of war but rooted in peace.

"Not yet," she said softly, more to herself than to him. "But soon. Once you're settled in your work, once I've graduated university. Then we'll fill this house with laughter."

"Soon," Reza agreed, his hand coming to rest on her belly through the fabric of her dress, warm and possessive and tender all at once. "I can't wait to see you pregnant, Zahra. To watch our child grow inside you. To become a father and watch you become a mother. It's going to be beautiful."

They fell silent again, but it was a comfortable silence now, filled with the promise of tomorrow and the day after and all the days stretching out before them. The war was over. They had survived. And this—this ordinary, extraordinary life they were building together in their small house in Isfahan—this was victory. This was peace. This was everything they'd fought for, everything they'd endured for, made real and solid and finally, finally theirs.

As the night deepened and the air grew cool enough to drive them inside, they gathered the cats and retreated to the living room. Reza rekindled the lamp while Zahra made fresh tea, and they settled on the cushions with their poetry book between them, taking turns reading verses aloud, their voices weaving together in the golden lamplight.

Later, much later, after they'd made love again with a playful intensity that had them both laughing and breathless, after they'd cleaned up and climbed into bed with the cats claiming their usual spots, Zahra lay awake listening to Reza's breathing even out into sleep. His arm was heavy across her waist, his face buried in her hair, and she could feel the steady rise and fall of his chest against her back.

She thought about the girl she'd been eight years ago—twenty years old, three weeks married, watching her husband leave for a war that had already stolen too much. She'd been so young, so terrified, clinging to Reza in their doorway and making him promise to come back, to survive, to love her through the distance. She'd had no idea what the next eight years would bring—the air raids, the grief, the loneliness, the way she'd have to hollow herself out and rebuild from scratch just to survive each day.

But she'd done it. They'd both done it. And now here they were—changed, scarred, not the people they'd been but something new, something forged in fire and tempered by endurance. The love between them had been tested in ways most couples never faced, and it had held. More than held—it had deepened, become something unbreakable. That made Zahra happier than anything else ever had in the world. She thanked God for it, because it was a divine miracle.

Zahra reached down to where Reza's hand rested on her hip, lacing her fingers through his even in sleep. Tomorrow they would wake and tend the large garden again, would read more poetry, would probably laugh about something silly that one of the cats did. It was ordinary. It was mundane. It was everything they'd ever wanted.

And as sleep finally claimed her, Zahra's last conscious thought was a prayer of gratitude—for this man beside her, for this home they'd built, for the cats purring at their feet, for the garden blooming despite everything, for the simple, profound gift of being alive and together and home.

Chapter Thirty-Three

Tehran, 1988

The late autumn in Tehran carried a crisp edge, a gentle breeze whispering through the city's bustling streets, bringing the scent of roasted chestnuts from vendors' carts and the faint tang of exhaust from old cars rumbling along the avenues. The sky was a pale blue, streaked with wispy clouds, the sun a warm orb that cast long shadows over the urban landscape—a mix of ancient minarets piercing the skyline, modern buildings pockmarked by war's scars, and leafy boulevards lined with sycamore trees, their leaves turning golden and crunching underfoot.

Iran's sprawling capital, pulsed with post-war energy, the ceasefire still holding like a fragile truce, the streets crowded with people rebuilding their lives—shopkeepers reopening shuttered stores, construction workers hammering at rubble, refugees from the frontlines blending into the throng, their faces etched with resilience.

Zahra stepped off the bus at Tehran's central station, her woven basket slung over her shoulder, containing gifts from Isfahan—dates sticky and sweet, a jar of rosewater from her garden, and a small volume of Hafez for Farhad's family. Her favourite green dress swayed slightly in the breeze, her dark hair tied back under a black scarf, a few strands escaping to frame her face, her eyes scanning the crowd with a mix of anticipation and nervousness.

The station was a hub of activity, the air thick with the scent of diesel and street food—kebabs sizzling on grills, their smoky aroma mingling with the tang of pickled cucumbers from a nearby vendor. The war's end had brought a surge of movement, families reuniting, but the scars remained—crutches on a veteran, empty sleeves on a former soldier, the hollow eyes of those who had lost loved ones.

Farhad, her half-brother, waited near the entrance, his tall frame leaning against a lamppost. At forty-six, he looked weathered, his skin tanned and lined from years on his wife's family farm just outside Tehran and his job as a mechanic in the city. His dark hair was greying at the temples, his beard neatly trimmed but speckled with white, his eyes—similar to their father's—warm but distant, reflecting the age gap that had kept them relative strangers throughout Zahra's life. He wore a simple grey jacket over a tunic, its sleeves rolled up, revealing calloused hands stained with oil, his trousers dusty from the day's work.

"Zahra, sister," he said, his voice deep but reserved, stepping forward to embrace her lightly. The hug was awkward but genuine, the scent of grease and earth clinging to him. "It's good to see you. The car's this way."

Zahra smiled, her shyness easing as she hugged him back, her basket bumping his side. "Farhad, thank you for having me. How's the family?"

He nodded, leading her to his old Peugeot, its body dented but reliable, the engine rumbling to life with a cough. "Good—my wife, Amira, is excited to welcome you. Our daughter Sara just had her second child, a boy. You'll see him."

The drive to Farhad's home took half an hour, the roads crowded with traffic—buses packed with commuters, motorcycles weaving through, the honk of horns a constant chorus. Tehran sprawled around them, its skyline a mix of modern towers and ancient mosques, the Alborz Mountains looming in the north, snow-capped peaks glinting against the blue sky. Farhad's home was a two-story stone house with a small yard, its walls painted a fresh white, the iron gate decorated with scrollwork, the yard filled with potted herbs—their scents strong in the afternoon sun, a chicken clucking in a wooden coop near the back wall.

Amira, Farhad's wife, greeted them at the door. She was a woman of about forty with a round, kind face, her cheeks still holding a youthful flush despite the lines around her eyes. Her dark hair was covered with a cheerful floral scarf in shades of blue and yellow, and her dress was simple but colourful—a deep burgundy with small embroidered flowers at the collar. Her hands were dusted with flour from baking, and when she embraced Zahra, she smelled of warm bread and rose water. "Welcome, Zahra," she said, her voice warm and maternal. "Come in, come in. You must be tired from the journey."

The house opened into a narrow hallway with worn but clean tile floors in a geometric pattern of brown and white, the walls painted a soft cream colour and adorned with a few framed verses of Quran in elegant calligraphy. To the right, a staircase with a simple wooden banister led to the second floor. Amira guided Zahra through to the living room, which was cozy and lived-in, filled with the warmth of family life.

The living room was modest but comfortable, with woven rugs in earthy tones of rust and olive covering most of the floor, their patterns traditional and slightly faded from years of use. Low cushions in rich jewel tones—deep reds, golds, and teals—were arranged around the perimeter of the room against the walls, inviting people to sit and lean back.

A low wooden table sat in the centre, its surface scratched and worn smooth by countless family meals, already set with small glass cups for tea and a plate of dates. In one corner stood a samovar, its brass surface polished to a warm shine, steam rising gently from its spout, filling the air with the comforting scent of cardamom-infused tea.

Against the far wall was a small fireplace with a simple wooden mantel, currently cold but clearly well-used during colder months, its hearth swept clean. Above it hung a large framed photograph of Farhad and Amira on their wedding day, much younger, their faces bright with hope. On either side of the fireplace were built-in shelves holding a small collection of books, a few decorative pieces—a small brass vase, a carved wooden box—and more family photographs. The windows were dressed in simple curtains in a cream fabric, pulled back to let in the afternoon light, which cast warm rectangles across the rugs.

Sara, Farhad's daughter, sat on the divan near the window, cradling her newborn son. She was twenty-two, with her father's height and her mother's round face, her features soft and pretty. Her dark hair was pulled back in a loose braid, a few wisps escaping to frame her face, and she wore a simple dress of pale blue that made her look young and fresh despite the tiredness in her eyes—the exhaustion of new motherhood. The baby was swaddled in a soft cream blanket embroidered with tiny blue flowers, his tiny face peaceful in sleep, his small fists clenched near his chin.

Nearby, Sara's first child—a little girl of two—toddled about on chubby legs, her dark curls bouncing with each step, her round cheeks flushed with the exertion of play. She wore a little dress covered in a pattern of flowers, and she clutched a wooden toy horse that clattered against the floor as she moved. When she saw Zahra, she stopped, her dark eyes curious and shy, one finger finding its way to her mouth.

Zahra's heart swelled at the sight of them. She set her basket down carefully and moved toward Sara, her hands already reaching out. "May I?" she asked softly, and Sara smiled, tired but happy, shifting the baby carefully into Zahra's waiting arms.

The infant's weight was warm and light, his body so small and perfect it made Zahra's breath catch. His skin was impossibly soft, his breath carrying that sweet, milky scent unique to newborns. She rocked him gently, instinctively, her body knowing the motion even though she'd never held a baby of her own. "He's beautiful," she whispered, unable to look away from his tiny, perfect face. "What's his name?"

"Hassan," Sara said, her voice soft with exhaustion and love. "After my grandfather."

Zahra felt tears prick her eyes. This was what she and Reza talked about in their garden, in their quiet moments alone. This weight in her arms, this tiny perfect being, this possibility. The longing was physical, an ache that settled in her chest and wouldn't leave.

The toddler tugged at Zahra's dress, emboldened by curiosity. "Baby," she announced, pointing at her brother with her wooden horse.

"Yes, that's your baby brother," Zahra said, smiling down at her. "And what's your name, little one?"

"Samira," Sara supplied, reaching out to stroke her daughter's curls. "Say hello to Aunt Zahra, Samira."

The Moonlit Rose of Isfahan

But Samira had already lost interest, toddling off to explore the fascinating world of the living room, her horse clattering behind her.

Over tea and dates, they talked—Amira asking about Isfahan, about Zahra's garden, about the journey. Farhad spoke briefly of the farm, his wife's family's land that had become his responsibility when she'd had no brothers left to take care of it, the fields of wheat and small orchard demanding his time alongside his mechanic work in the city. There was weariness in his voice but also pride—he was providing for his family, keeping the land alive, honouring the memory of those who hadn't come home.

"And your husband?" Amira asked gently, refilling Zahra's tea. "He's working today?"

"Yes," Zahra said, her voice warming at the mention of Reza. "He's at a bridge repair site. Engineering work. Rebuilding."

"Good work," Farhad said, nodding approvingly. "Important work. The country needs men like him."

Zahra stayed that afternoon and into the evening, helping Amira in the kitchen—a small but efficient space with tiled walls and open shelves holding spices in neat jars. They prepared *sabzi polo*, the herbs fresh and fragrant, the rice perfectly fluffy, fish frying in a pan with a satisfying sizzle. Zahra held baby Hassan whenever he fussed, rocking him against her chest, breathing in his sweet scent, while little Samira tried to help by bringing her toy horse to show everyone repeatedly.

"You're natural with him," Sara observed, watching Zahra soothe the baby back to sleep with gentle shushing and swaying.

Zahra felt her cheeks warm. "Reza and I... we want this someday. Children. A family."

"You will," Amira said firmly, squeezing Zahra's shoulder as she passed with a platter. "You're young still. You have time. And after everything you've both been through, you deserve that happiness."

When Reza arrived that evening, dusty from the construction site, Zahra's face lit up in a way that made Amira smile knowingly. He embraced her carefully, mindful of his dirty clothes, but Zahra didn't care, pressing her face into his chest briefly before pulling back.

"The bridge is coming together," he said, his voice carrying a quiet pride. "Slowly, but it's coming together."

Jamila Mikhail

They sat together for dinner, the living room warm with family and food, and Reza held baby Hassan for a long moment, his hands so gentle with the tiny bundle, his face softening in a way that made Zahra's throat tight with emotion. He would be a good father. She knew it with absolute certainty, watching him smile as Hassan's tiny hand wrapped around his finger.

Two days later, the dynamic shifted entirely when a taxi pulled up outside Farhad's house and Zahra's mother stepped out.

Maryam looked much as Zahra remembered but older—her face more lined, her hair now streaked with more grey than black, though still thick and pulled back in her characteristic neat bun. She wore a dark blue dress that was slightly more European in cut than what most Iranian women wore, a concession perhaps to her years in Damascus with her Lebanese husband, and a lighter scarf than she used to favour, its fabric a soft lavender. But her eyes were the same—dark and warm and full of emotion—and when they landed on Zahra standing in the doorway, they immediately filled with tears.

"Maman," Zahra breathed, and then she was running, flying down the path and into her mother's arms, both of them crying, holding each other as if they could make up for three and a half years of separation with the strength of their embrace.

"My girl, my Zahra," Maryam kept saying, her hands cupping Zahra's face, examining her as if she were a precious artifact that might have been damaged in her absence. "Let me look at you. Oh, you look so different! Are you—"

"I'm fine, *Maman*," Zahra laughed through her tears. "I'm more than fine. I'm so glad you're here."

Behind Maryam, a man emerged from the taxi, and Zahra's attention shifted to him with curiosity and a slight nervousness. This was Wissam—the man her mother had left Iran for, the reason Maryam now lived in Syria, the person who had given her mother a second chance at love after her Ahmed's death from cancer five years ago.

Wissam was in his late fifties, with a kind, weathered face that spoke of a life lived largely outdoors. He was stockier than Reza or Farhad, with a bit of a belly that suggested a man who enjoyed good food and didn't worry overly about it. His hair was mostly grey, receding slightly at the temples, and he wore it combed back from his forehead. His eyes were a warm brown, crinkled at the corners from years of smiling, and he had a neatly trimmed moustache that was completely grey. He dressed slightly more Western than the Iranian men—pressed slacks and a button-down shirt rather than a tunic, though he'd clearly tried to dress respectfully, his shirt buttoned all the way up, his manner a bit formal.

"Zahra," he said, his accent immediately apparent, his Farsi heavily accented and careful, "is... pleasure. Much pleasure." He smiled warmly, extending his hand for a handshake, which Zahra accepted, charmed despite herself by his obvious effort.

"The pleasure is mine," Zahra said in Farsi, speaking slowly so he might understand better. "Welcome to Tehran. Thank you for taking care of my mother."

Wissam beamed, clearly understanding at least the general sentiment, and replied in Arabic to Maryam, who laughed and translated: "He says your mother takes care of him, not the other way around."

Inside, introductions were made all around. Farhad greeted Maryam with warmth—she had been, after all, a good stepmother to him after his own mother had died, and they'd maintained a friendly if distant relationship over the years. Amira fussed over them both, immediately putting the kettle on for more tea, while Sara emerged with baby Hassan and Wissam's face transformed into pure delight.

"Baby!" he exclaimed in Farsi, one of the words he clearly knew, reaching out his hands. "May... I?" He looked at Sara hopefully, his hands making a cradling gesture.

Sara smiled and carefully transferred the baby to him, and Wissam held Hassan with the confidence of someone who'd held many babies before, cooing at him in a mix of Arabic and fractured Farsi that made everyone smile. "Beautiful boy," he said in Farsi, then added something in Arabic that made Maryam laugh.

"He says Hassan looks like a little prince," Maryam translated.

It was later that afternoon when Reza returned from the work site that the truly significant moment came. Zahra heard his footsteps first, the familiar tread on the path outside, and she moved to the door to greet him. But as she opened it, she saw her mother standing by the window, frozen, her hand at her throat, her face suddenly pale.

Because the man walking through the door was not the Reza that Maryam remembered.

The last time Maryam had seen her son-in-law, he had been a clean-shaven young man of twenty-four, fresh-faced and nervous, his eyes bright with love for Zahra but shadowed with the knowledge that he was about to leave for war. That had been 1980, eight years ago, just three weeks after their wedding in Shiraz. She'd hugged him goodbye, this boy who was taking her daughter's heart to the front lines, and told him to come back safe.

The man who stood before her now was unrecognizable despite that Zahra had sent her numerous photos over the years. His face was bearded, the dark hair streaked through with grey, making him look older than his thirty-two years. His frame was leaner, harder, the softness of youth completely gone.

But it was his eyes that struck her most—they still held love when they looked at Zahra, but they also held shadows, depths of experience that hadn't been there before. There was a scar visible on his arm, disappearing under his sleeve. His hands, reaching out to embrace Zahra, were also marked with both scars and burns from mustard gas attacks.

"Maryam," Reza said, noticing her, his face breaking into a smile. "*Maman* Maryam. I didn't realize it was today you were coming." He moved toward her, arms opening for an embrace, but she just stood there, staring, her hand still at her throat, tears streaming down her face.

"Reza?" she whispered, as if she needed confirmation that this weathered, bearded, scarred man was really the boy she remembered.

"It's me," he said gently, lowering his arms, understanding her shock. "I know I look different. The war—" He shrugged, a gesture that encompassed everything: the beard grown in trenches, the scars earned in combat, the youth lost to survival.

Maryam moved then, closing the distance between them and

throwing her arms around him, sobbing into his shoulder. "You came back," she kept saying. "You came back to her. Thank God, you came back."

Reza held her, his own eyes bright with emotion, one hand patting her back awkwardly but gently. "I promised I would," he said quietly. "I promised Zahra."

Zahra watched them, her own tears flowing freely, and when her mother finally pulled back to look at Reza properly, Maryam reached up to touch his beard, wonderingly, as if trying to reconcile this man with her memory.

"You've been taking care of my daughter," Maryam said, her voice fierce now, her hands gripping his arms. "Haven't you? All these years, even apart, you've been taking care of her."

"She took care of herself," Reza replied, glancing at Zahra with such love that it made Maryam's heart ache. "She's stronger than anyone gives her credit for. But yes. I tried. With letters. With love. With coming home."

Wissam, who had been watching this exchange with obvious confusion, leaned toward Maryam and asked something in Arabic. She replied quickly, and his face softened with understanding. He approached Reza, hand extended, and said in heavily accented Farsi, "I am... Wissam. Maryam... *khosrem*." He clearly meant *husband* but had gotten the word slightly wrong, saying something closer to *son-in-law*, which made Farhad cough to cover a laugh.

Reza, gracious, shook his hand warmly. "Welcome to the family, Wissam. I'm Reza, Zahra's husband."

Wissam nodded enthusiastically, clearly pleased to be understood even partially, and replied with a string of Farsi that was so mangled that everyone blinked in confusion before Maryam translated, laughing: "He's trying to say he's happy to meet you and he's heard good things about you from Zahra."

"What did I say?" Wissam asked in Arabic, looking confused by everyone's barely suppressed smiles.

"You said you had good ears from him," Maryam explained in Arabic, and Wissam burst out laughing, shaking his head.

Jamila Mikhail

That evening, they all gathered for dinner—a larger affair now with Maryam and Wissam added to the group. The living room felt fuller, warmer, the cushions all occupied, the low table laden with food Amira and Maryam had prepared together—*sabzi polo*, *khoresh*, fresh bread, and a salad of cucumber and tomato. Little Samira was overexcited by all the company, running between guests showing off her toy horse until Sara finally scooped her up and settled her down for sleep. Baby Hassan nursed contentedly in the corner, and the air was filled with the comfortable sounds of family: conversation, laughter, the clink of glasses.

Wissam's attempts at Farsi provided ongoing entertainment throughout the meal. At one point, trying to compliment Amira's cooking, he said something that came out roughly as "Your food makes my stomach celebrate!" which wasn't quite right but was close enough to be endearing. Everyone chuckled, and Amira beamed, understanding the sentiment if not the exact words.

Later, when Wissam tried to ask Farhad about his work and somehow confused the word for 'farm' with the word for 'pharmacy,' creating a very confusing minute where Farhad thought he was being asked if he grew medicine in his fields, the gentle teasing began in earnest.

"Maybe we should plant antibiotics next to the wheat," Farhad joked, and everyone laughed, including Wissam once Maryam translated.

"My Farsi is terrible," Wissam admitted cheerfully in Arabic for Maryam to translate. "I try, but—" He made a helpless gesture, and everyone warmed to him further for his self-deprecating honesty.

It was then that Reza, sitting beside Zahra, nudged her gently with his elbow and leaned in to say quietly but loud enough for others to hear, "This is why you should go to university and learn Arabic or French. So you don't sound like Wissam at the dinner table when we visit go your family."

The room erupted in laughter, and Wissam, catching the gist even without full translation, pointed at Reza and said something in Arabic that Maryam translated as, "He's right! Learn from my mistakes!"

Maryam seized the moment, her face lighting up as she turned to

The Moonlit Rose of Isfahan

Zahra. "He's absolutely right, *azizam*. You should pursue your education. I've been learning French in Damascus—Wissam's been teaching me, and I've been taking classes. It's opened up so many opportunities. And my Arabic is fluent now. It's like..." She paused, searching for words. "It's like having new eyes. You see the world differently when you can speak to more of it."

"You're learning French?" Zahra asked, impressed. "*Maman*, that's wonderful."

"It's hard," Maryam admitted, laughing. "I sound like Wissam sounds in Farsi, I'm sure. But it's worth it. It'll be helpful if we ever get the chance to go back to Beirut, if Lebanon's own war can ever end. And you're so much younger than I was when I started, Zahra. You could become truly fluent in Arabic, maybe even French, if you studied properly at university."

"We've been talking about it," Reza said, his arm finding its way around Zahra's shoulders. "After I finish this work in Tehran, we'll look into universities in Isfahan. Or maybe even here in Tehran, if that's what Zahra wants."

Zahra felt a warmth spread through her chest—not just at the encouragement, but at the image of it. Her mother speaking Arabic and French fluently, living a whole new life in Syria. Herself, perhaps, studying at university, learning languages, expanding her world beyond the garden walls she'd hidden behind during the war. It felt possible in a way it hadn't before.

Later that night, after the dishes were cleared and the men had moved to drink tea and talk while baby Hassan slept, Zahra found herself alone with her mother in the small kitchen. Amira had gone upstairs to put Samira to bed, and Sara was resting, and suddenly it was just the two of them, mother and daughter, with three and a half years of separation between them.

Maryam was washing dishes at the sink, her hands moving in the soapy water, and Zahra picked up a towel to dry. For a few minutes they worked in comfortable silence, the domestic rhythm familiar despite the years apart. But then Maryam's hands stilled in the water, and when Zahra looked at her, her mother's face was crumpling, tears streaming down her cheeks.

"*Maman?*" Zahra set down the towel, alarmed. "What's wrong?"

"I left you," Maryam whispered, her voice breaking. "I left you alone during a war. What kind of mother does that?"

Zahra felt her chest constrict. She'd known this was coming, had felt it in every too-tight hug, every searching look her mother had given her since arriving. The guilt had been there, hovering between them, waiting for a private moment to emerge.

"*Maman—*" she began, but Maryam turned from the sink, gripping the counter, her knuckles white.

"Do you know what it was like?" Maryam asked, her voice raw. "Sitting in Damascus, safe, comfortable, while my daughter was in Isfahan during air raids? Wissam would hold me while I cried, reading your letters, terrified every time there was news about bombing in Iran. I kept thinking—what if something happened to you? What if you died and the last thing I'd done was leave you? How could I live with myself?"

"But I didn't die," Zahra said gently, moving closer. "I'm here. I'm fine."

"You shouldn't have been alone," Maryam insisted, her voice fierce now, angry at herself. "You were so young—barely twenty-three when I left. Your father had been dead for just a few months, and I abandoned you to grieve alone. I chose Wissam over you. I chose my happiness over my daughter's safety."

"You chose love," Zahra corrected softly. "Just like I did."

Maryam blinked at her, confused, and Zahra took her mother's hands, soapy and wet, in her own.

"*Maman*, listen to me. Father died in 1983. You'd already lost your husband, you'd already grieved, you'd already spent years being strong for me since Reza was drafted. When Wissam came into your life, when he offered you love and a new beginning in Damascus—you deserved that. You deserved happiness. And I wanted you to have it."

"But I left you—"

"You asked me to come with you," Zahra reminded her gently. "Multiple times. You begged me to come to Syria. But I said no. Because I wanted to stay in Isfahan. Because our home was there.

Because—" Her voice caught. "Because Reza was coming back to Isfahan, and I needed to be there when he did. I needed to tend our garden. I needed to wait for him."

Fresh tears spilled down Maryam's cheeks. "You stayed for Reza. You chose him over your own safety."

"Just like you chose Wissam," Zahra said firmly. "We both chose love, *Maman*. You went to Syria to be with the man you loved. I stayed in Isfahan to wait for mine. We made the same choice, just in different directions."

Maryam pulled Zahra into a fierce embrace, both of them crying now, holding each other over the sink full of cooling dishwater. "You're not angry with me?" Maryam whispered into her daughter's hair.

"No," Zahra said firmly. "Never. You taught me something important, *Maman*. You taught me that it's okay to choose love, even when it's hard. Even when people don't understand. Even when it means leaving behind other things you care about. You chose Wissam, and look at you now—you're happy. You're learning languages. You're building a new life. You deserve all of that."

"And you deserved to have your mother with you during a war," Maryam said, pulling back to cup Zahra's face, her thumbs wiping away tears.

"I had Reza's letters," Zahra said. "I had our garden. I had Reza's parents, our neighbours the Heydaris and the relief centre and purpose. I was okay, *Maman*. I survived. We both did. And now look at us— you're here, I'm here, Reza came home, Wissam is in your life. Everything worked out the way it was supposed to."

"You're too forgiving," Maryam said, but she was smiling through her tears now.

"I'm not forgiving anything," Zahra corrected. "Because there's nothing to forgive. You didn't abandon me, *Maman*. You went to be with the man you love. And you taught me, by example, that love is worth fighting for. Worth staying for. Worth building your life around. I learned that from you."

They held each other for a long time, the kitchen growing dark around them, until Wissam's voice called out in Arabic from the other room, asking where Maryam had gone. They both laughed, a bit watery, and Maryam called back that she was coming.

As they finished the dishes together, working side by side in comfortable silence, Zahra felt something shift and settle inside her. The guilt her mother had carried, the fear that Zahra resented her—it was gone now, washed away like soap bubbles down the drain. They had both chosen love. They had both survived. And they had found their way back to each other, here in this kitchen in Tehran, three and a half years and an entire war later.

The rest of the visit passed in a warm blur. Maryam and Wissam stayed for four more days, and the house felt full in the best way—multiple generations under one roof, babies being passed from lap to lap, Wissam's enthusiastic but terrible Farsi providing constant entertainment, and long evenings of tea and conversation that flowed between Farsi and Arabic depending on who was speaking.

One afternoon, Reza took Wissam to see the bridge reconstruction site, and they returned hours later, both dusty and animated despite the language barrier, Wissam gesturing enthusiastically about engineering and Reza nodding along, somehow understanding through the universal language of construction and building. Wissam had apparently helped the workers lift some materials, insisting despite Reza's protests, and both men seemed to have bonded over the simple act of physical work toward a common goal.

Maryam spent hours with baby Hassan, her grandmother's heart clearly aching for grandchildren of her own. "When you and Reza have babies," she told Zahra, "you'll visit me in Syria, yes? Or I'll come here. I won't miss them growing up. I already missed too much of your marriage."

"We'll visit," Zahra promised. "Once things are more settled. Once Reza's work is stable and I've graduated university. We'll bring our children to meet their grandmother in Damascus."

The promise felt real, tangible, a bridge being built between their current life and the future they were imagining.

On the last evening before Maryam and Wissam's departure, they all

The Moonlit Rose of Isfahan

gathered once more in the living room, the low table cleared except for tea and sweets. Little Samira was asleep upstairs, and baby Hassan dozed in Zahra's arms, his tiny perfect face peaceful in the lamplight. The adults sat in comfortable silence, the kind that comes when people have talked themselves out but don't want the evening to end.

Wissam said something in Arabic, and Maryam smiled, translating: "He says this reminds him of his family gatherings in Lebanon, before the war. Different language, same feeling. Family is family."

"Family is family," Farhad agreed, raising his tea glass in a small toast, and everyone followed suit, the gesture simple but meaningful.

Later, as they prepared for bed in the small guest room Farhad had given them, Reza pulled Zahra into his arms and held her close. "Your mother loves you very much," he said quietly. "It's written all over her face every time she looks at you."

"I know," Zahra whispered back. "And she's happy with Wissam. Really happy. I can see it."

"He's a good man," Reza said. "Even if his Farsi is terrible." They both laughed softly, careful not to wake anyone. "And your mother's right about university. About languages. You should do it, Zahra. You're so smart, and you've spent so many years just surviving. It's time to grow again. To learn again."

Zahra tilted her face up to look at him in the darkness. "You really want me to?"

"I really want you to," he confirmed. "I want you to have everything, Zahra. Education, travel, children, purpose—all of it. You deserve all of it."

She kissed him then, soft and grateful, and when they finally fell asleep, it was with the future spreading out before them like an unwritten page, full of possibility and promise and hope.

The week in Tehran had done something neither of them had fully anticipated. It had reminded them that they weren't alone—that they had family, scattered and complicated as it was, and that family would support them as they built their future together. Farhad with his quiet steadiness, Amira with her maternal warmth, Sara with her young family showing them what was possible, Maryam with her fierce love and hard-won wisdom, and even Wissam with his terrible Farsi and generous heart.

Chapter Thirty-Four

Tehran, 1988

The morning sun filtered through the thin curtains of the guest room in Farhad's house. The air was cool, carrying the faint scent of fresh bread baking in the kitchen below and the earthy tang of dew from the small yard outside, where potted herbs—mint and basil—released their crisp fragrance through the open window.

The room was intimate and lovely, with a narrow bed pushed against the wall, its wooden frame polished but creaking under movement, the mattress firm but yielding under the quilts. A small wooden nightstand held a brass oil lamp, now extinguished, and a vase of wildflowers Zahra had picked the day before, their petals—pink poppies and white daisies—still dewy. The walls were a soft cream, adorned with a framed verse of the Quran about love in elegant calligraphy, the words a quiet blessing that resonated with their love.

Zahra stirred first, wrapped in the quilts, her dark hair splayed across the pillow like a silken fan, catching the sunlight in glossy waves. Her eyes fluttered open, her skin glowing with the restful sleep from the previous night. She turned to Reza, who lay beside her, his lean frame relaxed in sleep, his grey-speckled beard framing a face serene, unmarred by the nightmares that often plagued him.

The week in Tehran had been a balm—Reza's engineering job repairing bridges and roads a healing purpose, Zahra's visit a joy, their time with her mother and stepfather, with Farhad's family, especially the children, reassuring their dreams of parenthood. Today was Reza's day off, a rare gift in the post-war chaos, and they had planned a romantic day out in the city, exploring its post-war beauty, their love radiant with possibility, a light against the shadows of the battlefield's losses.

Zahra leaned over, her lips brushing Reza's forehead, the skin warm under her touch, waking him with a gentle kiss. His eyes opened, meeting hers with a smile that crinkled the corners, his hand rising to cup her cheek, his scarred fingers rough but tender against her smooth skin.

"My rose," he murmured, his baritone husky with sleep, pulling her closer, their bodies aligning under the quilts, the warmth of her curves pressing against him, sparking a faint tingle of desire.

"Good morning, my poet," she replied, her voice melodic, her fingers tracing his beard, the strands coarse but beloved, her heart swelling with gratitude for his peaceful rest. They nuzzled for a moment, their noses brushing, his facial hair tickling her cheek, her laughter soft as she kissed him, the taste of sleep on their lips, the intimacy a sweet start to the day.

They rose, the bed creaking softly, the quilts falling away, and dressed for the outing—Zahra in a flowing dark green dress, its fabric light and swaying, a scarf draped loosely over her hair, Reza in a simple tunic and trousers, his scarred arms exposed, the uniform left behind for a day of freedom.

Downstairs, Farhad's home was alive with family—Farhad, his face weathered from farm work and mechanic jobs, sipping tea at the kitchen table, his greying hair swept back, his calloused hands wrapping around the glass. Amira bustled about, her floral scarf tied neatly, her round face beaming as she packed a basket for them—*barbari* bread, its crust golden and sesame-speckled, cheese tangy and soft, dates sticky and sweet, and a thermos of tea, its cardamom aroma wafting.

Sara held her newborn son, the baby swaddled in a soft blanket, his tiny face peaceful, his small fists clenched, while her two-year-old daughter toddled around, her curls bouncing, her laughter bright. The kitchen was cozy, its tiled counters cluttered with pots, the air warm with the scent of fresh bread and tea, the samovar humming softly.

"Take this, Zahra," Amira said, handing her the basket, her voice warm, her hands floured from baking. Zahra smiled, hugging her, the embrace soft, the scent of Amira's rosewater mingling with the tea. "Thank you, Amira *khanoum*. We'll be back by evening."

Reza knelt to play with the toddler, his hands gentle as he lifted her, her giggles filling the room, the sensation of her small weight a joy that stirred his longing for children with Zahra. The baby gurgled in Sara's arms, and Zahra took him briefly, his milky scent sweet, his tiny fingers wrapping around hers, the touch reassuring their future as parents.

Farhad clapped Reza's shoulder, his grip firm. "Enjoy the city, brother. Tehran's healing—bridges like the ones you're repairing are the foundation of it all."

Reza nodded, his heart steady, the work a salve for his war scars. "I'd like to show Zahra the bridge I'm working on. It's on our way."

Farhad's eyes lit up. "She should see it. You're building the future, Reza. Literally."

They set out in Farhad's car, the engine rumbling to life, the streets of Tehran unfolding around them—a city of contrasts in post-war 1988, the Alborz Mountains looming in the north, snow-capped peaks glinting against the blue sky, the morning temperature mild and climbing as the sun rose higher.

Tehran sprawled before them with a mix of ancient grandeur and modern scars—wide boulevards lined with sycamore trees, their leaves turning golden and crunching underfoot when the wind scattered them across the pavement; towering minarets piercing the skyline, their calls to prayer echoing over the honk of taxis and the chatter of crowds; construction sites buzzing with workers in hard hats, the clatter of hammers and the whine of saws mingling with the scent of fresh cement and dust.

The war's marks were everywhere but healing was visible too—cratered roads patched with fresh asphalt, their surfaces smooth and dark; buildings with pockmarked walls from shrapnel slowly being repaired, scaffolding rising like metal skeletons against their facades; boarded windows being replaced with glass that caught the morning

Jamila Mikhail

light. But more than the physical repairs, the city pulsed with revival—markets reopening with colourful stalls of fruits and spices, pyramids of pomegranates ruby-red, sacks of saffron threads like captured sunlight, the vendors calling out prices in cheerful Farsi; children playing in parks, their laughter a melody of hope, kicking soccer balls across patchy grass that was struggling to grow back; families walking together, mothers with strollers, fathers with sons on their shoulders, the simple normalcy of peacetime a miracle after eight years of war.

The streets were crowded, refugees from towns that had been on the frontlines blending with locals, their faces a mosaic of resilience—some bearing the visible scars of conflict, an empty sleeve here, a crutch there, but all moving forward, rebuilding, living. The air was alive with Farsi conversations, snippets of laughter, the occasional argument over prices at a street vendor's cart. The scent of street food wafted through the car's open windows—kebabs sizzling on grills, their smoky aroma rich with cumin and sumac, making Zahra's stomach rumble; falafel frying with a hiss in bubbling oil, the tang of chickpeas and herbs; fresh *sangak* bread being pulled from traditional ovens, its surface dimpled and seeded, still steaming.

"Look," Zahra said, pointing to a newly painted mural on a building wall—a depiction of doves flying over the Iranian flag, the colours bright and hopeful. Reza followed her gaze, a slight smile touching his lips. "Peace is more than just the absence of fighting. It's... this. Doves instead of missiles. Children instead of soldiers."

They drove north through the city, weaving through traffic, the honks and shouts a symphony of urban life that felt almost festive compared to the silence of trenches. After twenty minutes, Reza turned onto a smaller road that led toward the river, the buildings giving way to a more industrial area with warehouses and construction yards. Then, ahead of them, spanning the wide, brown-grey ribbon of the river, rose the bridge—Reza's bridge.

It was a magnificent structure, even half-completed. Massive concrete pillars rose from the riverbed like sentinels, their surfaces still raw and textured, the reinforcing steel visible at the tops where construction continued. Steel girders stretched between the pillars, creating the skeleton of the roadway, workers moving like ants across

The Moonlit Rose of Isfahan

the framework, their orange hard hats bright against the grey sky.

Cranes towered over the site, their arms swinging slowly as they lifted materials, the mechanical groan of hydraulics audible even from the car. The bridge was designed with graceful arches that would, when complete, give it an elegant profile—function meeting beauty, infrastructure as art.

Reza parked the car at the construction site's edge, near a temporary fence with signs warning of hard hat areas. He grabbed two yellow hard hats from the back seat—he'd planned this, Zahra realized, wanting to share this with her. He handed her one, and she placed it on her head, feeling suddenly like she was entering his world, the world of rebuilding.

"Come," he said, taking her hand, his eyes bright with something she hadn't seen in him often—pride. Not the pride of a soldier, but the pride of an engineer, a creator. "Let me show you what we're making."

They walked onto the site, their shoes crunching on gravel, the air thick with the scent of wet concrete and diesel from the machinery. Workers nodded to Reza as they passed, calling out greetings—and he returned them warmly, introducing Zahra as his wife, the men's faces breaking into grins, offering congratulations, their camaraderie genuine. The noise was tremendous—hammering, drilling, the clang of metal on metal, the rumble of cement mixers turning—but it felt alive, purposeful, so different from the destructive sounds of war.

Reza led her to a point near the middle pillar, where they could see both the completed sections and the work in progress. He pointed to the foundation, his voice rising to be heard over the construction noise.

"The foundation goes down fifteen meters," he explained, his hands gesturing, his engineer's mind clearly at work. "The river here is deep and the soil is unstable from years of erosion and war damage—bombs shook the ground for eight years, Zahra. So we had to dig deep, pour massive amounts of concrete reinforced with steel, make it strong enough to last centuries. This bridge will carry thousands of people every day. Families. Children. It has to be perfect."

Zahra watched his face as he spoke, seeing the animation there, the engagement. This was healing for him, she realized—not just having purpose, but creating something permanent, something good. Every piece of infrastructure he built was the opposite of what he'd done in the war. Instead of destroying, he was connecting. Instead of dividing, he was joining.

"It's beautiful," she said, and she meant it. The raw concrete, the steel girders, the purposeful chaos of construction—it was beautiful because it represented hope, because it was the physical manifestation of Iran healing, Tehran recovering, people building their future instead of just surviving.

Reza turned to her, his expression softening. "Do you know what I think about when I'm working here?"

She shook her head, her heart full.

"I think about us. About our future children." He gestured toward the bridge, his voice thick with emotion. "Maybe one day, fifty years from now, our grandson or granddaughter will drive across this bridge on their way to university. Or cross it to visit their grandparents. They'll never know it was built by their grandfather's hands, by men who survived a war and chose to build instead of letting bitterness consume them. But they'll benefit from it. That's what matters. That's what all this suffering was supposed to be for—so the next generation doesn't have to endure what we did."

Tears filled Zahra's eyes, her heart overflowing. She squeezed his hand, unable to speak for a moment. This was why she loved him—not just for his poetry or his gentleness in every aspect of life, but for this, this vision of the future, this stubborn insistence on hope despite everything he'd seen and suffered, despite his doubts and insecurities.

"They'll know," she finally said, her voice fierce. "Because I'll tell them. I'll tell them Reza Azad was a poet who became an engineer who became a soldier. That he survived eight years of hell and came home and built bridges. Literally built bridges. That's the story they'll know."

He pulled her into his arms then, right there among the noise and dust, holding her close, their foreheads pressed together. This moment—standing on ground that would become a bridge, surrounded by the sounds of creation instead of destruction—felt sacred somehow, a benediction on their future.

When they finally pulled apart, Reza led her across the partially completed span, their steps careful on the wooden planks laid temporarily across the steel framework. From the middle of the bridge, they could see Tehran spreading out in both directions—the city they were helping to rebuild, scarred but resilient, broken but mending.

"Look at it," Reza said, his arm around her shoulders, both of them gazing out at the urban landscape. "Six months ago, this was just damaged piers and collapsed roadway. Now it's becoming something new. Tehran is like this everywhere—rising from the rubble. Iran is healing, Zahra. Slowly, painfully, but healing."

"We're healing too," she said softly, leaning into him. "Both of us. Together."

He kissed the top of her head, his heart full. "Yes. We are."

After leaving the bridge site, they drove to Golestan Palace, a short journey through Tehran's northern districts, the car weaving through traffic that felt almost festive compared to wartime restrictions. The palace, a UNESCO treasure from the Qajar era, stood as a testament to Persian elegance and endurance—its gardens lush with cypress trees and rose beds despite the years of neglect during the war, the scent of roses heavy in the air, the fountains bubbling with cool water that misted the stone paths, creating tiny rainbows in the sunlight.

The buildings, with their mirrored halls and tiled facades, gleamed in the morning light, the tiles a mosaic of turquoise, gold, and cobalt blue, intricate patterns of flowers and birds and calligraphic verses that made Zahra gasp with delight.

They wandered around, the gravel paths crunching under their shoes, the air warm with a gentle breeze rustling the leaves of ancient trees. Other couples strolled through the gardens—young lovers stealing kisses behind hedges, elderly pairs walking slowly arm in arm, families with children who ran laughing between the flower beds. It was a scene of normalcy so profound it almost hurt, the simple joy of people enjoying beauty without fear of air raids, without sirens, without the shadow of death.

"Remember our wedding night?" Zahra said, her voice melodic, her fingers interlacing with his as they paused beside a fountain, its water clear and cold, lotus blossoms floating on its surface. "You recited poetry in our room, making me blush with your words."

Reza laughed, a genuine sound of joy, pulling her close, his arm around her waist, his lips brushing her ear. "And you, my rose, were shy but eager, your hands trembling as you reached for me. You were so beautiful that night. You're even more beautiful now."

He whispered Rumi then, his voice low and intimate, the Persian words flowing like honey. "Beyond the veil of good and evil lies a garden where lovers meet." His breath was warm against her ear, sending a shiver through her, her body pressing against his despite the public setting.

The palace's beauty became a mirror to their love—the intricate tile work like the complex layers of their relationship, the fountains like the flow of their affection, the roses like the sweetness they'd cultivated despite the thorns of war. They explored the Throne Hall, its marble throne carved with lions and dragons, the room's mirrors reflecting infinite images of them, the light bouncing in a kaleidoscope of colours that dazzled the eye.

Zahra stood before the mirrored wall, her reflection multiplied endlessly, and Reza joined her, his hand on her shoulder, both of them gazing at their infinite selves.

"Like our love—endless," he said, his fingers tracing her arm, sparking goosebumps on her skin despite the warmth of the day.

She blushed, leaning into him. "And you, my commander, conquering my heart anew with every word, every touch."

They laughed, their kisses soft in the hall's quiet, the mirrors capturing their intimacy, a private world amid the public space, the other visitors smiling indulgently at the young couple so clearly in love.

As midday approached, the temperature rising to a comfortable warmth, they drove to the Grand Bazaar, Tehran's beating heart, a maze of covered alleys spanning ten kilometres, its vaulted ceilings echoing with the calls of vendors, the air thick with spices—turmeric's golden dust making Zahra sneeze delicately, sumac's tart red powder colouring the light, cinnamon's sweet warmth mixing with the sharp bite of black pepper. The scent was intense, overwhelming, mingling with the rich smell of leather from bag stalls where craftsmen worked their tools, and the sweet, heady perfume of attar oils in tiny glass bottles, concentrated rose and jasmine and amber.

The Moonlit Rose of Isfahan

The bazaar pulsed with post-war energy—vendors who had hidden or fled during the worst years were reopening their shops, their shelves stocked with carpets rolled in colourful stacks, their patterns telling stories of Persian heritage; copper pots and trays gleaming in the filtered light, their surfaces hammered and etched with intricate designs; jewelry glinting in glass cases, turquoise and gold catching the eye.

The crowd was dense but cheerful, Farsi chatter filling the air in a constant hum, women in chadors of black and navy bargaining with vendors over prices, their voices rising in mock outrage at first offers before settling on fair trades; men hauling goods on wooden carts, the clatter of wheels on ancient stone echoing through the vaulted passages.

Zahra navigated with ease, her basket filling with treasures—threads of saffron red as blood, each one precious, the vendor wrapping them in paper with careful hands; dates sticky and sweet, their flesh dark and yielding, bought from an old man who blessed their marriage with a grandfather's wisdom; pistachios roasted and salted, their shells split to reveal green meat; dried mulberries like tiny, wrinkled jewels.

Reza felt the civilian world becoming less alien with each step. The bazaar's bustle was healing in its own way—chaotic but purposeful, loud but joyful, crowded but communal. It was so different from the trenches, from the eerie quiet before battle, from the screams and explosions. Here, life asserted itself in every haggled price, every laughing child, every bag of spices changing hands.

Yet sometimes the memories surfaced—the crowd's press reminding him of human wave assaults, the spice vendors' calls triggering echoes of shouted commands, the dim lighting under the vaulted ceilings feeling momentarily like bunkers.

But Zahra's presence grounded him, her laughter as she haggled for pistachios a melody that cut through the noise and anchored him to the present, to peace, to the life they were building together. She caught him staring and smiled, reaching up to touch his cheek.

"You're here with me," she said softly, understanding without him having to explain. "Not there. Here. In Tehran. On a beautiful day.

Buying spices for my brother's home. For the kitchen where we cook with love and laughter and then eat too much."

He nodded, breathing deeply, the scent of cardamom and cinnamon filling his lungs, replacing the phantom smell of gunpowder. "Here with you," he repeated, the words a vow, a grounding, a return to the present.

They ate lunch at a traditional tea house tucked into a corner of the bazaar, the space cozy with low tables and cushions, the air warm with steam from the samovar, the scent of mint tea and kebabs sizzling on grills. They shared *sabzi polo*, the herby rice fluffy and fragrant with dill and cilantro and parsley, the fish flaky and delicate, dressed with sumac and lemon. They fed each other bites, their fingers lingering, the taste a burst of flavour after years of wartime rations. The intimacy of sharing food, of caring for each other in this small way, felt precious—a luxury they'd been denied during the war years.

"My poet," Zahra teased, her eyes sparkling, "recite something for me. Something hopeful."

Reza grinned, setting down his tea glass, his hand finding hers across the table. He spoke Rumi softly, his voice intimate despite the tea house's hum around them: "Do not grieve your losses—they return to you transformed, wearing new faces. The places where we break are the very places where light finds its way in."

His words hung between them, weighted with meaning—all they'd lost, all they'd survived, all the light that had entered through their wounds. Zahra's eyes filled with tears, but she was smiling, her hand squeezing his under the table.

"Yes," she whispered. "The light is finding its way in. Can you feel it?"

He could. Here in this tea house, in this bazaar, in this healing city, surrounded by people rebuilding their lives, with Zahra's hand in his and the taste of herbs on his tongue and the future spreading out before them like an unwritten poem—yes, he could feel the light entering, bright and warm and full of promise.

The afternoon found them driving to Darband, the mountain trail in the north, a forty-five-minute journey through Tehran's suburbs that gradually gave way to greener, more elevated terrain. The Alborz

The Moonlit Rose of Isfahan

Mountains rose majestic before them, their peaks snow-capped even in autumn, the road winding through valleys with streams gurgling over rocks, their water crystal clear and cold from mountain snowmelt, the air growing cooler and fresher with each kilometre gained in elevation, scented with pine and water and the earthy smell of mountain soil.

Darband was a romantic escape beloved by Tehranis, its trail lined with tea houses and small restaurants built into the mountainside, the path made of uneven stone worn smooth by generations of feet, the sound of waterfalls cascading down the slopes providing a constant, soothing music, the mist from the falls cool on their skin as they climbed. Other couples walked the trail too, young and old, some with children, all seeking the same thing—beauty, peace, a moment away from the city's density, a taste of the natural world that war couldn't touch.

They walked hand in hand, the trail ascending gently, the air alive with birdsong and the laughter of other visitors, the war's scars fading in the natural beauty that surrounded them. Trees overhung the path, their leaves golden and red, dappling the sunlight, and wildflowers grew in crevices between rocks, hardy blooms that had survived the seasons and the war alike.

They stopped at a tea house built into the rock face, its wooden balcony overlooking a stream that tumbled over smooth stones, the water bubbling and frothing white, the air moist and fresh, carrying the scent of wet stone and green growing things. They found a table on the balcony, the wood worn but sturdy, and ordered tea and sweets—the tea arrived hot and cardamom-spiced in delicate glass cups, and the baklava came on a painted plate, its layers flaky and dripping with honey, studded with pistachios and walnuts.

They fed each other pieces of the sweet pastry, their fingers sticky with honey, their kisses tasting of nuts and sugar and spices, their laughter soft and intimate.

The call to prayer drifted up from the city below, faint but clear, carried on the mountain breeze. The ancient words echoed off the peaks and Reza found himself setting down his tea glass, listening with something he hadn't felt in years. Not the bitterness that had coloured such moments during the war, not the angry silence that had followed him home, but something softer. Something like recognition.

"I've been praying again from time to time," he said quietly, almost surprised to hear himself speak the words aloud. "It's still awkward—I stumble over words I used to know by heart, my prostrations aren't as smooth as they once were. But I'm trying."

Zahra turned to him, her eyes bright with emotion, but she didn't speak. She simply took his hand, understanding that this was his moment, his confession, his step forward.

"In the trenches," Reza continued, his voice low, "I used to think God had abandoned us. That He'd turned His face away from all that suffering, all those young men dying in the mud. I was so angry. So lost." He paused, watching the water tumble over stones below them, endless and patient. "But lately, I've been thinking—maybe it wasn't God who abandoned us. Maybe it was war that tried to make us forget Him. And maybe finding my way back isn't about God forgiving me, but about me forgiving myself enough to approach Him again."

A tear slipped down Zahra's cheek, and she squeezed his hand. "I know my love, I've watched you a few times. God never left you, my poet," she whispered. "But I'm so glad you're finding your way back to Him. To peace. To yourself."

The call to prayer faded, absorbed by the mountains, and Reza breathed in the cold, clean air. It wasn't a sudden restoration of perfect faith. But it was something. A crack in the wall he'd built, where light could enter. And for now, that was enough.

Below them, the stream sang its endless song, and above them, the mountains stood eternal, and between these two ancient forces, Reza and Zahra sat in perfect, peaceful joy.

"You're sweeter than baklava," Reza flirted, his hand on her knee under the table, his eyes dark with affection and desire.

Zahra laughed, her cheeks flushing, her heart full to bursting. "And you, my commander, conquer with words as much as with actions."

They reminisced about their early days—1980 in Shiraz, their walks through gardens, their shy kisses behind the walls of her father's house, their love a flame that had somehow remained untainted through eight years of war, growing stronger rather than being extinguished.

"I knew literally the moment I saw you that I would marry you,"

The Moonlit Rose of Isfahan

Zahra said, her voice soft, her eyes on the stream below. "Even when you left for the front, even when the letters stopped coming for weeks at a time, even when I thought I might die from missing you—I knew we'd have this. Days like this. A lifetime like this."

Reza's throat tightened with emotion. "There were nights in the trenches when I'd close my eyes and imagine exactly this—you and me, in a beautiful place, at peace, with our whole lives ahead of us. It was the only thing that kept me sane sometimes, that vision of the future. And now we're living it."

"We're living it," she agreed, her hand finding his, their fingers interlacing. "And we're going to keep living it. For decades. With children and grandchildren and a house full of roses. We're going to grow old together, Reza. We've survived the worst. Now we get to live the best."

The sun began its slow descent toward evening as they made their way back down the mountain trail, the light turning golden and soft, painting everything in warm hues. By the time they reached the car, the temperature had dropped to a comfortable coolness, the air carrying the first hint of night, and they drove back through Tehran's northern districts as twilight settled over the city, the sky a canvas of purple and orange and deepening blue.

The neighbourhoods they passed through were bathed in the gentle light of dusk, the streets quieter now, families returning to their homes, shops closing for the evening, the air growing cool and carrying the scent of woodsmoke from cooking fires and early heating as autumn deepened. Tehran looked beautiful in this light—softened, healing, hopeful. The construction sites they'd seen in the morning were now silent, the workers gone home, but the evidence of their labor remained, tangible proof of a nation rebuilding, a people refusing to be broken.

When they arrived back at Farhad's house, the windows were lit warmly from within, and they could hear the sounds of family life— children's voices, the clatter of dishes, Amira's laughter. The day had been radiant, their joy a light against the darkness of the war years, Reza's heart fuller than it had been in eight years.

Inside, they shared their adventures with the family over dinner—Farhad asking technical questions about the bridge construction, Amira cooing over the spices Zahra had bought, Sara's daughter begging to hear about the mountains before going to bed. It was warm and loud and chaotic in the best way, the kind of evening that war had stolen from them for too long.

Later, in the quiet of their guest room, they prepared for bed in comfortable silence, the day's joy still glowing between them. Zahra changed into her nightgown and Reza shed his tunic and trousers for loose sleeping clothes.

They slipped under the quilts, the bed creaking softly, the room cool enough that they naturally gravitated toward each other's warmth. Zahra's head found its place on Reza's chest, her hair splaying across his skin, and his arms wrapped around her, holding her close. Their hands entwined, their breathing synchronized, the quilts soft around them, the scent of jasmine from the garden below drifting through the window on the night breeze.

"Everything is going to be alright," Reza whispered into the darkness, his voice a vow, a promise, a prayer. "The war is over. Tehran is healing. Iran is healing. We're healing. Everything is going to be alright."

Zahra smiled against his chest, her heart steady and sure. She thought of the bridge rising from the river, of the gardens blooming again, of the bazaar full of life, of the mountains eternal and strong. She thought of their future children who would perhaps cross Reza's bridge on their way to university one day, who would play in parks that had once been battlegrounds, who would know peace as their birthright rather than war as their inheritance.

"Yes," she whispered back, her love for him overwhelming in its depth, as steady and strong as the mountains they'd climbed that afternoon. "Everything is going to be alright. We made it, my poet. We made it through to the other side. And now we get to live."

Outside, Tehran slept under its blanket of stars, a city wounded but recovering, scarred but determined to heal. And in a small guest room in the outskirts, two survivors held each other close, their love a steady root that had weathered the storm and would grow stronger in the peace to come.

Chapter Thirty-Five

Isfahan, 1990

The summer afternoon in Isfahan wove a tapestry of golden hues and gentle warmth, the temperature hovering comfortably without being overwhelming, a soft breeze carrying the scent of various herbs and the sweet perfume of jasmine from the courtyard garden of the Azad home.

The city, two years into post-war recovery following the Iran-Iraq War's ceasefire in 1988, pulsed with quiet resilience—turquoise domes of mosques gleamed under the sun, the Zayandeh River flowed gently under the Si-o-se Pol Bridge, its ancient arches reflecting in the water like a prayer made stone, and the bazaars hummed with vendors selling saffron, pistachios, and handwoven carpets, their colours vibrant against the war's fading scars.

The streets, once marked by bomb craters and boarded windows, now showed signs of renewal—freshly paved roads still smelling of asphalt, rebuilt storefronts with new glass catching the afternoon light, and children's laughter echoing from parks, a melody of hope that would have been unimaginable just two years earlier.

Yet the war's shadow lingered in the faces of veterans who walked with canes or empty sleeves, in the empty chairs at family tables, and in the memorials rising throughout the city to honour the fallen. Hossein's name was among them, and his absence remained a quiet ache in Reza and Zahra's hearts—a wound that had scarred over but never fully healed, a brother and friend whose memory blessed their every day.

Their home stood sturdy behind its whitewashed walls that glowed in the sunlight, the iron gate draped with jasmine vines, their white petals unfurling in the breeze and releasing a fragrance that mingled with the earthy scent of the garden's roses and lavender. The courtyard was a small oasis that Zahra had tended through eight years of separation and two years of reunion—every flower a defiance of war and drought, every bloom a testament to survival. The garden had become something of a neighbourhood legend, visitors often pausing at the gate to admire the explosion of colour and life that seemed almost defiant in its beauty.

The tiled path was lined with potted herbs—mint, basil, and dill—their scents mingling with the faint tang of woodsmoke from a neighbour's fire. Shirin and Simin, the cats gifted by Hossein ten years ago, lounged on the stone bench beneath the jasmine vine, their fur glinting in the dappled sunlight. At ten years old, they moved more slowly now, their muzzles touched with white, but their purrs remained a soft hum of contentment, their green eyes half-closed as they basked in the warmth. They had outlived their giver, and somehow that made them even more precious—living links to Hossein, to the beginning of Reza and Zahra's love story, to a time before war had touched their lives.

Inside, Zahra moved through the kitchen with practiced grace, her curves draped in a flowing blue dress, its fabric swaying with each graceful step, her hair loose and cascading over her shoulders, gleaming like polished ebony in the sunlight streaming through the window. Her almond eyes were bright with purpose and joy, her hands—still nimble from years of gardening and wartime volunteering—kneading dough for *noon-e barbari*, the scent of yeast and sesame rising as she shaped the bread with movements that were almost meditative, a ritual rooted in her childhood love of cooking.

In just a few weeks, Zahra would start university, having enrolled to study literature and French. Her brilliant mind was eager to explore the worlds of Molière and Hugo, to expand beyond the garden walls

The Moonlit Rose of Isfahan

that had been her sanctuary during the war. The decision had been a fulfillment of Reza's encouragement during their visits to Shiraz and Tehran, and also her mother's example—Maryam, who now in her fifties was learning French in Damascus with Wissam, proving that growth had no age limit.

She'd also been attending Arabic classes at the local mosque for the past year, and had become quite proficient—enough that when Maryam and Wissam had visited just two weeks ago, bringing Wissam's two children from his first marriage, Zahra had been able to converse with them in their native tongue, watching her mother's face light up with pride. The visit had been sweet and chaotic, the house full of laughter and multiple languages, the children fascinated by Shirin and Simin, Wissam still mangling Farsi in endearing ways while Zahra responded in increasingly confident Arabic. It had felt like family—complicated, blended, but undeniably family.

Yet even as she prepared to step into this new chapter, Zahra cherished her role as a housewife, her garden and kitchen her canvas, her home the foundation from which she would grow rather than something she was leaving behind. She wanted both—the domestic peace she'd fought to preserve during the war, and the intellectual expansion that peace now made possible. She wanted it all, and for the first time in her life, it was within reach.

Reza entered the kitchen, and Zahra's heart did what it always did when she saw him—it lifted, it swelled, it sang a quiet song of gratitude. His frame had put on a healthy amount of weight and was clad in a simple tunic and trousers, his beard—with even more grey now—framing a face lined with both weariness and joy, his soulful brown eyes softened by the peace of home. He looked older than his years—the war had stolen some of his youth, carved lines into his face that shouldn't have been there yet—but he was alive, he was happy, he was here, and he was hers.

His engineering job, part of the government's ambitious rebuilding plan, took him across Iran—repairing bridges in Mashhad, roads in Tabriz, water systems near Ahvaz. The work was a lifeline for the country's infrastructure and his own healing, each beam placed a mending of his war-torn heart, each bridge rebuilt a connection restored. The physical and emotional scars remained, etched into his skin and soul, but his poet's heart shone through more and more with each passing month. His love for Zahra was a light that kept the war's ghosts at bay, though nightmares of Hossein's death still haunted him on quiet nights, his brother's final words echoing in the dark.

Today marked their tenth wedding anniversary. Ten years. A decade. They had been married for ten years, but they'd only lived together for about two of those years when you added it all up—not even one whole month in 1980 before he left for the front, and these past two years of peace. The math was brutal and beautiful at once. They'd lost so much time, but they'd kept their love alive across distance and danger and despair. That had to count for something. That had to count for everything.

Zahra turned from the counter, her hands dusted with flour, and smiled at Reza with a radiance that made his breath catch even after all these years.

"My poet," she said playfully, her voice melodic, wiping her hands on a cloth, the scent of yeast clinging to her fingers. "You're home early—did the bridge in Qom surrender to your command?"

Reza chuckled, his baritone warm and rich, stepping closer to wrap his arms around her waist from behind, his hands settling on her hips through the soft fabric of her dress, the touch sparking a familiar tingle of desire and comfort intertwined.

"The bridge stood no chance, my moonlit rose," he replied, his lips brushing her temple, then her ear, the scent of her hair—rosewater and lavender—filling his senses and grounding him in the present, in peace, in home. "But I hurried back for our anniversary. Ten years, Zahra. A decade of being yours."

His voice carried a weight of emotion that made her eyes sting with tears. Ten years. They had survived. Against odds that had seemed insurmountable, against a war that had tried to tear them apart, against eight years of separation and uncertainty and fear—they had survived. They had kept their love alive. They had made it to ten years.

Zahra turned in his arms, her flour-dusted hands coming up to cup his bearded face, her thumbs stroking his cheekbones, tracing the lines that war and time had carved there.

The Moonlit Rose of Isfahan

"Ten years," she echoed softly. "Do you remember our first anniversary? You were at the front, and I was here, and I sat in this garden and cried because I missed you so much. I thought I might die from missing you."

Reza's throat tightened. "I remember. I wrote you a poem that day, in the trench. About how loving you was worth every moment of suffering, how I'd choose you again and again, even knowing what the war would cost us."

"I still have that letter," Zahra whispered. "I've kept every single one, there on the shelf. Sometimes, when you're traveling for work and I miss you, I read them. And I remember that if we survived eight years of war, we can survive anything."

He kissed her then, deep and slow and reverent, tasting of tea and salt and home, and she melted into him, her body remembering his after all these years of relearning each other, of healing together. When they finally pulled apart, both were breathing harder, their eyes dark with emotion and desire.

"I have something for you," Reza said, reaching into his pocket with the slight nervousness of a young man on a first date, though they'd been married a decade. He pulled out a small velvet box, its blue fabric worn soft with age.

Zahra's eyes widened, her hands flying to her mouth. "Reza..."

He opened the box to reveal a delicate silver necklace, the pendant shaped like a jasmine flower, its petals intricately crafted, a tiny emerald at its centre catching the light.

"For ten years of love," he said, his voice thick with emotion, his poet's soul pouring into every word, "and a lifetime more. Jasmine, because it's what was blooming in your father's garden the first time I kissed you. Remember that clumsy kiss when the chaperone wasn't looking? Because it's what you planted here, in our garden, and tended through the war. Because its fragrance reminds me of many of the letters you wrote, every prayer you prayed, every moment you waited for me."

Tears spilled down Zahra's cheeks as he moved behind her to clasp the necklace around her throat, his scarred fingers gentle against her skin, the silver chain cool and delicate, the pendant settling just above her heart. She touched it with trembling fingers, feeling the smooth metal, the tiny emerald that matched her dress.

"It's perfect," she whispered, turning to kiss him again, tasting salt from her own tears. "You're perfect. This—us—it's perfect."

They decided to celebrate their anniversary with a simple meal in the garden, the place where so much of their love story had unfolded. Zahra finished the bread while Reza set up the stone bench beneath the jasmine vine, arranging cushions and laying out a cloth. The cats followed him, weaving between his legs, their purrs a contented soundtrack.

When everything was ready, they sat together in the golden afternoon light, the table before them laden with *sabzi polo*—its herby rice fragrant with dill and cilantro and parsley, the fish flaky and dressed with sumac and lemon—fresh *barbari* bread still warm from the oven, *mast-o-khiar* with cucumber and mint, and a bowl of *gaz*, its rosewater sweetness a deliberate nod to Shiraz, to where their love had begun.

They ate slowly, feeding each other bites, their fingers lingering, their laughter soft and intimate. The roses bloomed around them in shades of pink and red and white, their petals occasionally falling like soft blessings. The jasmine vine above their heads was heavy with white flowers, their perfume almost dizzying in its sweetness. This garden—this small patch of earth—had been Zahra's act of resistance during the war, her way of fighting back against the destruction. And now it was their sanctuary, proof that beauty could survive anything.

They sat in comfortable silence for a moment, simply looking at each other. Ten years of love and survival was written in every glance, every touch. The weight of the anniversary—not just the number, but everything it represented—settled over them like a blessing.

"Zahra," Reza said softly, his voice taking on that particular quality it had when he was about to say something important, something from his poet's heart. "I need to tell you something. Ten years is a milestone, and I want you to know..." He paused, gathering his thoughts, his scarred hand holding hers. "What I admire most about you—what has sustained me through everything—is your devotion. Your unwavering faithfulness. It's a testament to your strength."

Zahra's eyes widened slightly, surprised by the sudden seriousness, but she remained quiet, letting him continue.

"In eight years of war, through every nightmare and every doubt I had, you never wavered. Not once," Reza continued, his voice thick with emotion. "You could have left Isfahan when my parents begged you to go to Shiraz or your mother repeatedly asked you to join her in Damascus. You could have given up when the letters stopped coming for weeks. You could have doubted me, doubted us, when I came home different than when I left. But you never did. Not even once. Despite your own fears and insecurities—and I know you had them, my rose, I read them in your letters—you never let me down. You were my constant. My north star. The one thing I could count on when everything else in the world had gone mad."

Tears spilled down Zahra's cheeks, and she reached up to touch his face, but he gently caught her hand, bringing it to his lips.

"I need you to know that I see that devotion, Zahra. I treasure it. It's the foundation of everything we've built and everything we'll build together. Your faithfulness is a gift I'll never take for granted, not for a single day of whatever life we have left together."

Zahra was crying freely now, her heart so full it felt like it might burst. When she could finally speak, her voice was soft but steady, her melodic tone carrying the weight of her own truth.

"And you, my poet-commander," she said, her thumb brushing across his bearded cheek, "what I love most—what I've always loved most—is your gentleness. Do you know that in ten years of marriage, you have never once raised your voice at me? Not once. Not when I burned the rice in our first week together. Not when you came home from the war carrying so much pain and trauma. Not when you've had nightmares and woken up disoriented and frightened. Not even during our disagreements or when I've been difficult or when my own insecurities have made me push you away."

Reza's eyes glistened, and he looked down at their joined hands, almost embarrassed by the praise.

"You're so gentle, Reza," Zahra continued, her voice fierce now with the need to make him understand. "With me, with the cats, with children, with everyone you meet. The war tried to make you hard, tried to turn you into something brutal, but it couldn't touch your core.

You're still the gentle poet who recited Hafez under my father's jasmine vines. You're still the man whose hands, even scarred from battle, touch me like I'm something precious. That gentleness is your strength, not your weakness. It's what makes you extraordinary."

She leaned forward, pressing her forehead against his, their breath mingling, their tears mixing on their cheeks.

"I love you," she whispered. "I love you with everything I am, everything I've been, everything I'll ever be. You are my heart, Reza. My poet. My husband. My home."

"I love you too," he whispered back, his voice breaking. "God, Zahra, I love you so much. You are the reason I survived. The reason I came home. The reason I can still believe in goodness and beauty despite everything I've seen. You are my everything."

They kissed then, soft and deep and reverent, tasting salt and sweetness, ten years of love poured into that single moment. When they finally pulled apart, both were smiling through their tears, their hands still clasped, their hearts still beating as one.

"Do you remember," Zahra said after a long moment of silence, her voice soft and nostalgic, "when Hossein gave us Shirin and Simin after our wedding? He said they were practice children, and that we would definitely have children with all of that poetry you recited."

Reza's eyes grew misty. "He was always thinking ahead even if he never could have imagined these little balls of fur would bring you so much comfort during the war. He was always trying to take care of everyone, especially me."

"And do you remember," Zahra continued, a small smile playing at her lips despite the tears in her eyes, "his joke during the reception? When he teased us about having children, and said if we ever had a son, we should name him Hossein?"

"How could I forget that?" Reza said, wiping his eyes. They sat in comfortable silence for a moment, remembering Hossein—his jokes, his kind heart, his generous spirit, his laughter that could light up a room.

Then Zahra took a deep breath, her hand finding Reza's, her fingers interlacing with his.

"Reza," she said softly, her voice steady despite the emotion in her

The Moonlit Rose of Isfahan

eyes, "if we have a son—when we have a son—I want to name him Hossein. Not as a joke this time. As a way to honour him. To keep his memory alive. To give his name to a child who will grow up in peace, who will never have to fight in a war, who will live the life Hossein should have had."

Tears welled in Reza's eyes, spilling over, running into his beard. The name was a wound and a gift, a weight and an honour. He thought of Hossein's last moments—his blood on Reza's hands, his final words about Zahra and Leyla, his insistence that Reza live. He thought of all the moments they'd shared—the jokes in the trenches, the poetry recitations, the plans for the future they'd never have.

"Yes," he managed, his voice breaking. "Yes. Hossein. It's perfect. It's exactly right." He pulled Zahra into his arms, holding her close as they both wept—for Hossein, for all they'd lost, for all they'd survived, for the future they were building from the ashes of war.

"He would have made terrible jokes about it," Zahra said, laughing through her tears. "He would have said something about how we should have named him 'Hossein the Actually Good Poet' to distinguish him from 'Hossein the Clumsy Teacher.'"

"He would have loved our son," Reza said. "He would have taught him terrible jokes and made him laugh and probably would have let him get away with everything."

"Yes," Zahra agreed softly. "He would have been the best uncle."

They sat together as the afternoon light began to soften toward evening, holding each other, surrounded by flowers and cats and the promise of the future. Above them, the jasmine bloomed eternal, its fragrance a benediction.

As dusk approached, they prepared to attend a memorial service for the war's martyrs at the local mosque, its turquoise dome already glowing in the lowering sun. Zahra dressed in her blue dress, the jasmine necklace gleaming at her throat, her scarf arranged carefully over her hair. Reza changed into his uniform—the same one that had become a playful symbol between him and Zahra in their private moments, a reclaimed intimacy.

But wearing it for this purpose felt different—heavier, more

Jamila Mikhail

somber. The olive-green fabric carried the weight of memory differently here, at a memorial for the fallen. It wasn't a costume exactly, but a bridge between who he'd been and who he was becoming. The medals gleamed with both pride and grief, each one a story he'd survived to tell, each one a reminder of brothers who hadn't.

They walked to the mosque hand in hand, the evening air cooling, the streets of Isfahan painted in shades of gold and purple by the setting sun. Other families moved in the same direction—veterans in uniform, widows in black, children who had lost fathers, parents who had lost sons. A community of survivors, all bearing the weight of memory, all choosing to remember together.

The mosque's courtyard was filled with people, the air heavy with grief and honour intertwined. The tiled walls shimmered with intricate patterns of blue and gold, the mihrab's calligraphy a prayer for peace made permanent in ceramic and gold leaf. The scent of frankincense rose from burning braziers, mixing with the faint rosewater from mourners' perfumes, creating an atmosphere both somber and sacred.

A large board displayed photographs of the fallen—hundreds of faces, each one a story cut short, a future stolen. Reza and Zahra moved through the crowd until they found what they were looking for: Hossein's face among the martyrs, his kind eyes and teacher's smile frozen in time, a stark reminder of his death in 1983 near Ahvaz. The photograph was from before the war, when he'd been young and unmarked by conflict, when he was preoccupied with silly things.

Reza's heart tightened, his chest constricting as the memories flooded back with visceral intensity—the blast that had torn through their position, the shrapnel that had shredded Hossein's body, the blood that had poured hot and red over Reza's hands as he'd tried desperately to stop it. Hossein's last words echoed in his mind as they did periodically: *Live Reza.*

His eyes glistened with tears, his grip on Zahra's hand tightening until his knuckles went white. She squeezed back, her thumb stroking his hand, her presence a lifeline keeping him tethered to the present, to peace, to the life Hossein had begged him to live.

The ceremony began with a recitation of the Quran, the imam's voice resonant and soothing, rising and falling in the ancient rhythms that Reza had known since childhood. The Arabic words washed over the crowd, and Reza found himself not just hearing them but *listening*—letting them reach past the walls he'd built during the war, past the anger and grief and guilt that had hardened around his heart.

"Indeed, with hardship comes ease," the imam recited, the verse flowing like water over stones, smoothing edges Reza had forgotten were there. *Indeed, with hardship comes ease.*

Reza's lips moved silently, forming words he'd memorized as a boy, verses the war had never quite erased even when he'd stopped believing in their truth. And as he recited along—quietly, haltingly, his voice joining the murmur of hundreds of others—something shifted inside him. Not a miracle. Not a sudden restoration of the faith he'd lost in the trenches. But something smaller and more profound: an opening. A softening. A recognition that he could approach the Divine again, even with all his scars, even carrying all his grief.

When the prayer ended and the crowd began to prostrate, Reza hesitated only a moment before following, his body remembering what his mind had tried to forget. His forehead touched the ground—the cool courtyard tiles solid beneath him, Zahra's presence warm beside him—and for the first time in years, the prostration didn't feel empty. It felt like coming home.

Live, Reza. Hossein's last words echoed in his mind, but this time they didn't carry only grief. They carried permission. Permission to heal. Permission to pray. Permission to find his way back to God despite everything he'd seen and done and survived.

He rose with the others, his eyes bright with unshed tears, and Zahra's hand found his, squeezing gently. She knew. She understood. This moment—this act of prayer in a courtyard full of mourners, this reconnection with the faith that had sustained him before the war tried to destroy it—this was its own kind of victory.

Then came speeches honouring the martyrs, their sacrifice woven into Iran's healing narrative—young men who had given everything for their country, for their families, for the future that people like Reza and Zahra were now building.

Reza's poet heart stirred, but the commander within trembled. The ghosts were so close tonight—Hossein's laughter echoing from the trenches, the mud that had tried to swallow them whole, the sting of shrapnel, the screams of the dying, the weight of all those young lives cut short. His breathing grew shallow, his vision tunnelling, the mosque courtyard threatening to transform back into a battlefield.

Zahra sensed his turmoil immediately. She leaned close, her lips near his ear, her voice soft but firm.

"He's here, Reza," she whispered. "Not in the past. Here, now, in our love. In our home. In the son we'll name after him. In every bridge you build, every student I'll perhaps teach in the future, following in his footsteps too, every rose that blooms in our garden. He's here because we carry him forward. That's how we honour him—by living."

Reza nodded, unable to speak, but her words grounded him, pulling him back from the edge of memory into the reality of now— her warmth beside him, the scent of jasmine from her necklace mixing with the frankincense, the mosque's beauty surrounding them, the peace they had fought for and survived to see.

When the ceremony ended, they approached Hossein's photograph together. Zahra had brought a white tulip from their garden, its petals pristine and perfect, and they laid it at the base of his image, their hands brushing as they did so, their love a steady root that had weathered every storm.

"We'll tell our children about you," Reza whispered to the photograph, his voice hoarse with emotion. "Your terrible jokes, your kind heart, your generous spirit. How you gave us cats and companionship and laughter. How you died saving me. How you made us promise to live. We're keeping that promise, brother. Every single day."

The crowd began to disperse as evening deepened into night, the air cooling further, stars emerging one by one in the darkening sky. The mosque's turquoise dome became a silhouette against the indigo heavens, evening prayers having ended, leaving only the soft murmur of conversations and farewells. Reza and Zahra prayed together daily again, just as he'd promised her. He'd found peace in prostration again, even if he still preferred to pray alone at home than in a group setting.

The Azads walked home hand in hand through Isfahan's quiet

The Moonlit Rose of Isfahan

streets, the city settling into its evening rhythm—lights flickering on in windows, families gathering for dinner, the normal peaceful activities of a city at peace. The jasmine-scented air wrapped around them like a blessing, carrying the promise of the garden waiting for them at home.

"Reza," she said softly, breaking the comfortable silence, "I've been thinking. We honour Hossein here, at the mosque, with flowers and prayers. But he's buried in Khuzestan, isn't he? Near where he fell?"

Reza nodded, his throat suddenly tight. "Yes. Near Ahvaz. There's a martyrs' cemetery there. I... I've never been back. I couldn't. Not even when I worked on infrastructure in the city. The thought of seeing that exact place again, of standing where he died..." He trailed off, unable to finish.

Zahra squeezed his hand, understanding flooding through her. "I know. I know it's too soon, still too raw. Khuzestan still bears so many scars from the war—bombed buildings, minefields, the earth itself wounded. And you're not ready."

"I'm not. Engineering work is one thing, but facing my brother's headstone, that's something else entirely. And I'm not ready for that." Reza admitted, relief in his voice at not having to pretend otherwise. "The nightmares are better, but Khuzestan... that's where so much of the worst happened. That's where Hossein died right in front of me. That's where I lost so many other comrades. I can't face that cemetery yet. I don't know when I'll be able to."

They walked a few more steps in silence before Zahra spoke again. "But one day," she said, her voice gentle but certain, "when you're ready. Perhaps when Khuzestan has healed more, when the land itself has had time to recover from the war's wounds. When your heart is strong enough to face it. One day, we'll go together. You and I. We'll visit Hossein's grave. We'll bring flowers from our garden—roses and jasmine, the flowers he knew, the flowers that represent our love that he helped nurture. We'll give him a proper memorial, tell him about our children, about the son we'll name after him. We'll thank him properly for the sacrifice he made."

Reza stopped walking, turning to face her in the dimming light, his eyes bright with unshed tears. "You'd do that? You'd come with me to that place?"

"Of course I would," Zahra said fiercely, both of her hands coming up to cup his face. "Hossein was my brother in everything but blood too. I loved him. I still grieve for him. And when you're ready—not now, not next year, but someday when your soul can bear it—we'll make that journey together. I won't let you face that alone."

Reza pulled her into his arms, holding her so tightly she could barely breathe, his face buried in her hair sticking out of her scarf. "Thank you," he whispered, his voice muffled and thick with emotion. "Thank you for understanding. Thank you for being patient with me. Thank you for..." He couldn't finish, overcome.

"I promise you, Zahra," he finally managed, pulling back to look into her eyes, his hands framing her face. "One day, when I'm stronger, when I can face those ghosts without falling apart, we'll go. We'll honour him properly. We'll tell him about our son Hossein, about the life we've built that he made possible. We'll thank him for loving us enough to save me, to give me the chance to come home to you."

"One day," Zahra echoed softly, rising on her toes to kiss him gently. "There's no rush, my love. Hossein understands. He would want you to heal first, to be whole. He wanted you to live, not just survive."

They resumed walking, their arms around each other now, the promise made but not demanded, the future stretching out with room for healing, for growth, for the journey they would one day take together to honour the brother they had both loved and lost.

When they reached their gate, Reza paused, turning to look at Zahra in the dim light of the streetlamp. She was so beautiful it made his heart ache—her dark hair loose now, her scarf slipped back, the jasmine necklace gleaming at her throat, her eyes luminous with love and hope and the weight of all they'd survived together.

"Ten years," he said softly. "And I love you more now than I did on our wedding day. I didn't think that was possible, but it is. Every day, I love you more."

Zahra smiled, her hand coming up to touch his bearded face, her fingers gentle against the scars that marked his jaw.

"Ten years," she echoed. "And ten more, and ten after that, and as

The Moonlit Rose of Isfahan

many as God grants us. We survived the war, my poet. Now we get to live. Really live. With children and studies and bridges and gardens and growing old together. We get to live the life Hossein wanted for us. That's our gift to him—living well."

They entered their home to find Shirin and Simin waiting by the door, meowing softly, wanting their evening meal. The normalcy of it—the domestic peace of feeding cats, of preparing for bed, of tomorrow stretching out with its ordinary joys and challenges—felt like a miracle.

Later, as they lay in bed with the quilts pulled up against the cooling night, the window open to let in the jasmine breeze, Zahra's head on Reza's chest, his arms wrapped around her, their hands entwined, he whispered into the darkness: "Live out the beauty you love. The divine welcomes worship in a thousand forms—through hands building, through hearts healing, through lives lived with purpose."

Rumi's words hung in the air, a blessing and a vow. Zahra smiled against his chest, feeling the steady beat of his heart beneath her ear—that heart that had survived trenches and shrapnel and eight years of separation, that heart that loved her with a depth that still took her breath away.

"Yes," she whispered back. "This is how we live with purpose. By loving. By building our future. By naming our son after a brother who died so we could have this peace."

Outside, Isfahan slept under its canopy of stars, a city wounded but recovering, scarred but healing, building its future stone by stone and bridge by bridge. The war was over. The martyrs were honoured. The survivors were living. And in a modest home behind jasmine-covered gates, two people who had loved each other through eight years of hell held each other close, their bodies warm under embroidered quilts, their hearts full of hope.

The garden waited outside their window, roses and jasmine blooming in the darkness, tended by love, watered by tears, proof that beauty could survive anything. Tomorrow, Zahra would wake early and walk among the flowers, touching their petals, breathing their perfume, preparing to step into her new life as a university student. Tomorrow,

Reza would return to his work repairing the country's infrastructure somewhere, connecting what war had divided, creating infrastructure for a future he'd once thought he'd never live to see.

But tonight, they simply held each other, enjoying the beginning of a romantic night together, two survivors who had kept their love alive across distance and death and despair. They had made it to ten years. They would make it to twenty, to thirty, to growing old together with children and grandchildren and stories to tell about the war they'd survived and the brother they'd lost and the love that had endured through everything.

Their love was a garden that bloomed eternal, roots deep enough to weather any storm, blossoms bright enough to light even the darkest night. And as sleep finally claimed them, wrapped in each other's arms, their last thoughts were of the future spreading out before them like an unwritten poem, full of promise and hope and life.

The war was over. The healing had begun. And love—stubborn, resilient, beautiful love—had won.

Afterword

When I set out to write *The Moonlit Rose of Isfahan*, I knew I was taking on the responsibility of depicting one of the modern Middle East's most tragic conflicts—the Iran-Iraq War of 1980-1988. This war, ignited by Saddam Hussein's invasion of Iran, resulted in over a million casualties and left deep scars on both nations that persist to this day.

While this novel is set in Iran and follows Iranian characters, I want to acknowledge clearly that suffering knows no borders. Iraqi families also lost sons, fathers, and brothers. Iraqi cities were also bombed. Iraqi civilians also lived in fear. War makes victims of everyone it touches, and this story's Iranian perspective should not be read as diminishing the very real trauma experienced on the other side of that border.

Iran during this period was also grappling with the aftermath of its 1979 Revolution—a time of tremendous political, social, and cultural upheaval. Readers familiar with this era may notice that I have largely kept these political complexities in the background of this narrative. This was a deliberate artistic choice. My goal was not to write a political novel or to make commentary on governance, ideology, or revolution. Instead, I wanted to explore something more intimate and universal: how ordinary people survive extraordinary circumstances, how love endures through separation and trauma, and how healing becomes possible even after unspeakable loss.

Reza and Zahra are fictional characters, but their experiences—of forced separation, of waiting in uncertainty, of learning to rebuild after trauma—echo the real experiences of countless couples who lived through this war. My hope is that their story honors the resilience of all those who endured, on both sides of the conflict.

At its core, this is a novel about love—not as escapism from tragedy, but as the stubborn, defiant force that allows us to keep living, keep hoping, and keep building even when everything around us crumbles.

Thank you for reading.

Reader's Guide: Discussion Questions

1. **The Nonlinear Structure**: The novel moves back and forth between 1980, the war years, and 1988-1990. How did this structure affect your reading experience? What might have been lost if the story had been told chronologically?
2. **Gardens as Resistance**: Zahra tends her garden throughout the war years as an act of defiance against destruction. What does the garden symbolize in the novel? How does cultivating beauty during wartime become its own form of resistance?
3. **Poetry as Survival**: Reza recites and translates Persian poetry throughout the novel, especially Rumi and Hafez. What role does poetry play in his survival and healing? Why might poetry be particularly important during wartime?
4. **Hossein's Legacy**: What kind of person was Hossein? Why does his death affect Reza so profoundly, beyond the trauma of witnessing it? What does it mean that his gift of the cats becomes so important?
5. **Women's War**: While Reza fights at the front, Zahra survives in Isfahan—managing air raids, working at relief centres, maintaining their home. How does the novel portray women's wartime experiences? Is Zahra's war less "real" than Reza's, or simply different?
6. **Maryam's Choice**: Zahra's mother chooses to leave Iran for Syria with Wissam during the war, leaving Zahra behind. Was this decision selfish, or was it an act of self-preservation and choosing love? How did you feel about Zahra's forgiveness of her mother?
7. **Rebuilding Infrastructure, Rebuilding Lives**: Reza's post-war work involves literally rebuilding bridges and roads. How does this physical work parallel his emotional healing? What does it mean to rebuild a country while also rebuilding yourself?
8. **Survivor's Guilt**: Reza struggles deeply with guilt over surviving when Hossein died. How does the novel portray

survivor's guilt, and what does it suggest about the path to healing? Do you think Reza's guilt is resolved by the end, or will it always be part of him?

9. **The Cost of War**: By the end, Reza has survived but carries physical and psychological scars. Hossein is dead. Families are scattered. What does the novel ultimately say about the cost of war? Are there really any "winners" in wars?

10. **Personal Reflection**: If you were in Zahra's position—would you have stayed in Isfahan waiting for your spouse, or would you have sought safety elsewhere? If you were in Reza's position, how do you think you would have coped with eight years of war?

Glossary of Terms

Allahu Akbar – Arabic phrase meaning "God is greatest." Used in Islamic prayer and as an expression of faith.

Alborz Mountains – Major mountain range in northern Iran, running along the southern coast of the Caspian Sea. Visible from Tehran.

As-salamu alaikum – Full Arabic/Islamic greeting meaning "peace be upon you." Often shortened to "salaam." The traditional response is "wa alaikum as-salaam" (and upon you be peace).

Attar – Concentrated essential oil, typically derived from flowers (especially roses). Used in perfumes and traditional medicine.

Aush – Traditional Persian soup or thick stew, often made with noodles, beans, herbs, and sometimes yogurt or kashk (whey).

Aza – The mourning period observed in Islam after someone's death, during which specific customs and prayers are followed.

Azan – The Islamic call to prayer, recited from mosques five times daily to summon Muslims to prayer.

Azizam – Persian term of endearment meaning "my dear one" or "my beloved." Used for family members and loved ones.

Baba – Persian word for "father" or "dad."

Baklava – A sweet pastry made of layers of filo dough filled with chopped nuts (usually pistachios or walnuts) and sweetened with honey or syrup.

Baradar – Persian word meaning "brother."

Barbari / Noon-e barbari – A thick, oval-shaped Persian flatbread with a golden crust, often topped with sesame or nigella seeds. One of the most popular breakfast breads in Iran.

Basra – Major city in southern Iraq, near the Persian Gulf. Saw heavy fighting during the Iran-Iraq War.

Chador – A large piece of cloth worn by some Iranian women as a full-body covering, typically black, that wraps around the body and is held closed at the front.

Chafiyeh – Traditional head covering or scarf (regional variant spelling of keffiyeh).

Jamila Mikhail

Chehelom – The 40th-day memorial ceremony held after someone's death in Islamic tradition, marking the end of the primary mourning period.

Daf – A large Persian frame drum with metal rings inside the frame that jingle when played, used in traditional and classical Persian music.

Damascus – Capital of Syria, one of the oldest continuously inhabited cities in the world.

Darband – A popular mountain hiking trail and recreation area in northern Tehran, featuring tea houses and restaurants built into the mountainside.

Divan – A long, low cushioned seat or couch, often placed against a wall. In Persian homes, used for seating in living rooms where guests sit on cushions around the perimeter.

Du'a – Personal supplication or prayer in Islam, as opposed to the formal ritual prayers (salat).

Falafel – Deep-fried balls or patties made from ground chickpeas or fava beans, mixed with herbs and spices. Common street food.

Fesenjan / Fesenjān – A rich Persian stew made with ground walnuts and pomegranate molasses, traditionally served with chicken or duck over rice.

Gaz – A traditional Persian nougat candy from Isfahan, made with rosewater, pistachios, and egg whites. Often given as gifts.

Ghormeh sabzi – One of Iran's most popular stews, made with herbs (parsley, cilantro, fenugreek), kidney beans, dried limes, and meat, served over rice.

Golestan Palace – A historic royal palace in Tehran dating to the Qajar dynasty, known for its mirrored halls and intricate tile work. A UNESCO World Heritage Site.

Grand Bazaar (Tehran) – One of the world's largest and oldest covered markets, spanning approximately 10 kilometers with thousands of shops and stalls.

Hafez (Hafiz) – (c. 1315-1390) Beloved Persian poet from Shiraz, known for his lyrical ghazals exploring themes of love, wine, and mysticism. His tomb in Shiraz is a pilgrimage site.

Haft roozé – The seven-day mourning period observed after someone's death in Persian/Islamic tradition.

Halva – A sweet, dense confection often made from sesame paste or flour, sugar, and oil. Commonly prepared and distributed at funerals and memorial services.

Hijab – General term for modest dress in Islam; often specifically refers to a headscarf worn by Muslim women to cover the hair and neck.

Imam – An Islamic religious leader, particularly one who leads prayers at a mosque.

Iran-Iraq War (1980-1988) – Eight-year conflict between Iran and Iraq, sparked by Iraqi President Saddam Hussein's invasion of Iran. One of the longest conventional wars of the 20th century, resulting in over a million casualties.

Iranian Revolution (1979) – Islamic revolution that overthrew the Pahlavi monarchy and established the Islamic Republic of Iran.

Isfahan – Major city in central Iran, known for its stunning Islamic architecture, bridges, and historical significance. Often called "half the world" for its beauty.

Janazah – The Islamic funeral prayer performed for the deceased before burial.

Kafan – The white burial shroud used in Islamic funerals to wrap the body of the deceased.

Kaleh pache – A traditional Persian breakfast dish made from sheep's head and feet, slow-cooked until tender. Considered a delicacy.

Kebab / Kabab – Grilled meat (often lamb, chicken, or beef) on skewers, seasoned with spices. A staple of Persian cuisine.

Khanom / Khanoum – Respectful title for women, equivalent to "Mrs." or "Madam." Often used with names.

Khoresh – General term for Persian stews, which are typically served over rice. Many varieties exist.

Khoresht-e bademjan – Persian eggplant stew made with tomatoes, eggplant, meat, and often dried limes.

Khosrem – Attempted Farsi word meaning "my husband" (correctly: "shawhar-am"). In the novel, Wissam mangles this word.

Khuzestan – Province in southwestern Iran along the Iraqi border. Site of heavy fighting during the Iran-Iraq War due to its oil resources.

Khorramshahr – City in Khuzestan province that saw some of the heaviest fighting in the Iran-Iraq War, changing hands multiple times.

Kilim – A flat-woven rug or tapestry with geometric patterns, traditional to Iran, Turkey, and Central Asia. Unlike pile carpets, kilims have no knots.

Kofte tabrizi – Large Persian meatballs from Tabriz, often stuffed with dried fruits and nuts, served in tomato sauce.

Kuku sabzi – Persian herb frittata made with eggs and a large amount of fresh herbs (parsley, cilantro, dill), sometimes with walnuts. Served hot or cold.

Lamassu – Assyrian and ancient Persian mythological creature with a human head, bull's body, and wings. Large stone sculptures guard the gates at Persepolis.

Lavash – Thin, soft unleavened flatbread common throughout Iran and the Caucasus, often used to wrap kebabs or eaten with cheese and herbs.

Maman – Persian word for "mother" or "mom."

Mashhad – Iran's second-largest city, located in northeastern Iran. A major pilgrimage site.

Mast-o-khiar – A cold yogurt and cucumber dish seasoned with herbs (usually mint or dill), similar to Greek tzatziki. Served as a side dish.

Mihrab – A semicircular niche in the wall of a mosque that indicates the direction of Mecca (qibla), toward which Muslims pray.

Mosque / Masjid – An Islamic place of worship.

Mullah – An Islamic cleric or religious teacher, often one who has studied Islamic theology and law.

Noon-e berenji – Persian rice flour cookies or bread, often sweetened and flavored with rosewater or cardamom.

Noon-e sangak / Sangak – A traditional Persian flatbread baked on hot stones (sang means "stone"), giving it a distinctive dimpled texture.

Pedar – Persian word for "father."

Persepolis – Ancient ceremonial capital of the Persian Empire, located near Shiraz. A UNESCO World Heritage Site with impressive ruins.

Qiblah / Qibla – The direction of Mecca, toward which Muslims face during prayer. Indicated in mosques by the mihrab.

Qom – Holy city in Iran, important center of Shia Islamic scholarship.

Quran / Qur'an – The holy book of Islam, believed to be the word of God as revealed to the Prophet Muhammad.

Rosewater – Fragrant water made by steeping rose petals, used in Persian cooking, cosmetics, and religious ceremonies.

Rumi (Jalal ad-Din Muhammad Rumi) – (1207-1273) Persian poet, Islamic scholar, and Sufi mystic. His spiritual poetry exploring divine love is beloved worldwide.

Saadi (Sa'di) – (c. 1210-1291/1292) Persian poet from Shiraz, known for his works *Gulistan* (The Rose Garden) and *Bustan* (The Orchard). His tomb is in Shiraz.

Sabzi polo – Herbed rice dish made with rice mixed with fresh herbs (typically parsley, cilantro, dill, and sometimes fenugreek). Often served with fish.

Salaam – Arabic/Persian greeting meaning "peace." Short for "Assalamu alaikum" (peace be upon you).

Samovar – A traditional heated metal container used to boil water for tea. The teapot sits on top while water stays hot below. Central to Persian tea culture.

Santur – A Persian hammered dulcimer with 72 strings, played with light wooden mallets. Produces a distinctive tinkling, cascading sound.

Sé roozé – The three-day mourning period observed immediately after someone's death in Persian tradition.

Setar – A Persian long-necked lute with four strings (the name means "three strings," though a fourth was added later), used in classical Persian music.

Sharbat – A traditional Persian sweet drink, often made with fruit, herbs, or flower essences mixed with water and sugar. Many varieties exist.

Sharbat-e sekke – A traditional Persian drink made from vinegar and herbs, often consumed for its refreshing and digestive properties.

Shiraz – Major city in southwestern Iran, known for its poetry, gardens, and wine-making history. Birthplace of the poets Hafez and Saadi.

Shirini – General term for sweets, pastries, or desserts in Persian. Often brought as gifts or served to guests.

Si-o-se Pol Bridge – Famous 33-arched bridge over the Zayandeh River in Isfahan, built in the 17th century. An iconic landmark.

Sofreh – A cloth spread on the floor on which food is placed for traditional Persian meals, with diners sitting around it on cushions.

Sofreh aghd – The ceremonial wedding spread in Persian weddings, beautifully decorated with symbolic items including mirrors, candles, sweets, and religious texts.

Tabriz – Major city in northwestern Iran, capital of East Azerbaijan province.

Tahdig – The crispy, golden rice crust that forms at the bottom of the pot when making Persian rice. Highly prized and often fought over at meals.

Tandoor / Tannur – A traditional cylindrical clay oven used for baking bread, common throughout the Middle East and Central Asia.

Tar – A Persian long-necked lute with six strings, one of the most important instruments in classical Persian music. Larger than the setar.

Tehran – Capital and largest city of Iran, located at the foot of the Alborz Mountains.

UN Ceasefire (August 1988) – UN Security Council Resolution 598 that ended active hostilities in the Iran-Iraq War, though a formal peace treaty wasn't signed until years later.

Ya Allah – Arabic exclamation meaning "O God!" Used to express surprise, distress, or to invoke God's help.

Zayandeh River – River flowing through Isfahan, spanned by several historic bridges including Si-o-se Pol.

Zuhr – The midday Islamic prayer, one of the five daily prayers required in Islam.

Zulbia – A sweet, crispy fried pastry shaped in pretzel-like loops, soaked in saffron or rosewater syrup. Often eaten during Ramadan.

About the Author

Jamila Mikhail, better known simply as Mila, is an award-winning author from Ottawa, Canada. In 2018 she was one of the people who received the title of *Top Writer* on Quora and over the years she has also received several awards for her poetry and short stories ever since she started writing on a serious basis in 2011. Mila graduated *magna cum laude* from the University of Ottawa in 2025 with an Honours B.A. in Indigenous Studies and Environmental Studies.

Mila lives surrounded by books, video games and good food with her three cats Squeaker, Carling and Radwan. When not writing or attending university lectures, she likes to visit museums, attend protests and spend time on Ottawa's numerous bodies of water. She thinks that writing about herself in the third person is strange.

Visit **www.jamilamikhail.com** for news, updates, free downloads, book reviews and more!

www.ingramcontent.com/pod-product-compliance
Lightning Source LLC
LaVergne TN
LVHW041617060526
838200LV00040B/1321